Select praise for internationally bestselling author Rachel Reid

"Reid's fifth Game Changers romance takes on heavy themes . . . without ever losing the heat and heart between her two leads."

—*Library Journal*, starred review

"Reid keeps on scoring in her fifth hockey-themed Game Changers romance."

—*Publishers Weekly*

"My new favorite book in a series that I absolutely adore! Rachel Reid crafted a story of true heart, beauty, heat, and glorious, hard-won redemption! I loved both heroes and their journey to love was a gorgeous one to watch!"

—Lauren Blakely, #1 *New York Times* bestselling author of *Scoring with Him*

"Steamy and sweet and also hilarious . . . A journey about learning that growth is hard and love is worth working for."

—Cat Sebastian, author of *The Queer Principles of Kit Webb* and *The Soldier's Scoundrel*

"Rachel Reid continues to blow me away with this thoughtful, deeply romantic and scorchingly sexy series. *Role Model* proves that you can take on sensitive topics and still deliver a heartfelt and sexy sports romance. Grumpy/sunshine at its best."

—Adriana Herrera, *USA TODAY* bestselling author

Also available from Rachel Reid

Time to Shine
The Shots You Take

The Game Changers Series

Game Changer
Heated Rivalry
Tough Guy
Common Goal
Role Model
The Long Game
Unrivaled

ROLE MODEL

RACHEL REID

HARLEQUIN

HARLEQUIN®

Recycling programs for this product may not exist in your area.

ISBN-13: 978-1-335-00412-3

Role Model

First published in 2021. This edition published in 2026.

All Illustrations by Monika Roe (Apple).

Stock Image: © warmworld/stock.adobe.com (Speech bubble).

Harlequin Enterprises ULC
22 Adelaide St. West, 41st Floor
Toronto, Ontario M5H 4E3, Canada
www.Harlequin.com

HarperCollins Publishers
Macken House, 39/40 Mayor Street Upper,
Dublin 1, D01 C9W8, Ireland
www.HarperCollins.com

Printed in the United Kingdom

26 27 28 29 CPI 10 9 8 7 6 5 4 3

Role Model contains mentions of sexual assault and rape culture. There are no graphic descriptions or on-page depictions of assault, but the story does include depictions of victims not being believed.

For Matt.

success of the Game Changers series was largely driven simply by readers recommending the books to their friends and online followers. It was driven by booksellers and librarians, by reviewers and bloggers, and by BookTokers and Bookstagrammers. I will always remember and appreciate that support.

Thank you for the love, and I hope you enjoy having these beautiful special editions on your shelves.

Love,
Rachel

ROLE MODEL

CHAPTER ONE

"Maybe try without smiling."

Troy Barrett nodded at the photographer—a young woman with short silver hair and a French-Canadian accent—and packed away his awkward attempt at a smile. He replaced it with his usual cold, blank stare.

"Better," she said.

Troy had never been traded before, and posing for the camera in a black-and-red and, frankly, ugly Ottawa fucking Centaurs jersey felt weird. Until yesterday, Troy had been a top forward on the division-leading Toronto Guardians. Until this week, he'd had friends, a shot at the Stanley Cup, and a sweet condo with a view of the CN Tower. Now Troy was living in a hotel room outside Ottawa with a view of a Costco parking lot. Definitely not the cool part of town.

Did Ottawa even have a cool part? Toronto had Raptors games and big concerts and awesome parties. Ottawa had government buildings and rivers.

And the worst hockey team in the NHL.

"That's probably enough," the photographer said, stepping

out from behind the camera. "And, hey. Good for you, calling out Dallas Kent."

The name made Troy flinch. Maybe it always would. "It's complicated," he mumbled. It was a word he'd been using a lot lately.

"Sounded pretty clear to me." Her smile was warm and a little teasing. Troy didn't return it, but she was right. There'd been nothing unclear about what Troy had yelled in Kent's face during practice. Everyone on the ice had heard it, and everyone who watched the leaked video afterward had heard it.

You're a piece of shit rapist, Dallas.

Not much to deconstruct there.

Troy wished the league gave a shit that one of their biggest stars was a monster. He wished he'd never met the guy. He wished he'd never been his roommate on the road, his linemate on the ice. His best friend.

He wished he'd been paying closer attention to what Dallas had been doing all those years. To what kind of person he was.

Learning the truth about his friend had been the first blow. Learning that the team he'd worked so hard to be a part of—that he was so *proud* to be a part of—was determined to protect Dallas had been the knockout punch.

He thanked the photographer, then, in a clumsy attempt to be friendly, said, "Sorry, what did you say your name was?"

"Gen."

"Nice to meet you, Gen." He searched for a polite question he could ask her. "Do you do most of the team photography?"

She began detaching her camera from the tripod. "I do the off-ice stuff, mostly. Portraits and promo shots. I work with Harris. Have you met him yet?"

Troy had been introduced to equipment managers, coaches, trainers and the team doctor, but he assumed Harris wasn't any of those people. "I don't think so, but I'm not great at remembering people."

"He runs the team's social media. And trust me, you won't forget him."

Troy couldn't imagine what that meant. Was Harris an asshole? A weirdo? Hot? Also, Gen was vastly underestimating his ability to not remember people.

And, if he had his way, he would be interacting as little as possible with the team's social media manager. Troy had no interest in that shit.

He left Gen to pack up her gear and made his way to the locker room. The room had been mostly empty when he'd arrived very early for practice, but he knew it must have been getting full by now.

The first person he noticed when he entered the room was Wyatt Hayes, the one guy on the team who had played with Troy in Toronto. Wyatt had been the Guardians' backup goalie until two seasons ago. Now he was Ottawa's starting goalie, and a damn good one. He was a nice guy, but he probably hated Troy, and not because Troy had yelled at Dallas Kent. Because Troy had been friends with Dallas in the first place. And also because Troy had devoted his entire career to being a fucking prick. He hadn't been friendly to Wyatt when he'd been a backup goalie, so he didn't deserve to be friends with him now that Wyatt was an NHL All-Star.

Wyatt glanced up at him from where he'd been tying his skate. "So it's true then?"

"I'm afraid so," Troy said, trying for a joke. The room, which had been buzzing with chatter when he'd walked in, had gone silent.

Wyatt stood. "Is this the new and improved Troy Barrett?"

Troy forced himself to meet Wyatt's gaze. There was nothing

stern or intimidating about Wyatt, but Troy had always found his unwavering goodness to be unsettling. Troy tended to gravitate toward men on the opposite end of that spectrum. Men who sneered at and made fun of nice guys like Wyatt.

Troy answered him as honestly as he could. "I'm trying."

Wyatt offered him a smile that seemed cautious, but certainly warmer than Troy's earlier attempts for the camera. "The enemy of my enemy is my . . . well, I'm not gonna say friend yet, but I'll give you a chance."

Troy's gaze fell to the floor. "Thanks."

Relieved *that* was out of the way, he found his stall and began getting undressed. The room once again filled with chatter, and he no longer felt his new teammates' eyes on him. He was hauling on his new black-and-red socks when he heard a familiar Russian-accented voice cut through the commotion of the room.

"Is Harris here yet?" The team captain, Ilya Rozanov, was scanning the room as if this Harris guy everybody seemed to be obsessed with was hiding among the players somewhere.

"I don't think so," said Evan Dykstra, a defenseman Troy had played against but never actually met before. "But the new guy's here. Barrett." He nodded, and the brim of his camo trucker hat pointed in Troy's direction.

Rozanov glanced briefly at Troy, then quickly turned his attention to Wyatt. "Harris said he was bringing a puppy today."

The back of Troy's neck heated with embarrassment. This was how it was going to be if he wanted to keep playing hockey: teammates who either hated him for ever being associated with Dallas Kent, or who hated him for being a traitor. Friends weren't going to be an option.

Probably for the best. Friends sometimes turned out to be monsters.

"I'm sure he'll be here soon," Wyatt said. "And you have to greet your new teammate, Roz. It's part of the whole team captain deal."

"Fine." Rozanov strode over to where Troy was sitting. He loomed over him for a moment, frowning. Rozanov was much larger than Troy's five-nine frame, and Troy had difficulty not squirming under his hard stare. "Am I supposed to like you now? Think you are a good guy because you finally noticed that your best friend is a fucking scumbag?"

Troy managed to hold his gaze. "I'm just here to play hockey." It was a weak reply, but it was also the truth. He couldn't promise more than that.

Rozanov studied him another moment, then finally extended his hand. "Welcome to Ottawa. I hope you like boring museums."

The handshake was more of a hand slap, and as soon as it was over, Rozanov turned and walked away. It wasn't a warm welcome, but it wasn't as bad as it could have been. Troy's former teammates in Toronto had been furious with him, calling him everything from a traitor to . . . worse.

You actually believe those attention whores?

They're obviously lying, Barrett. Women are fucking liars.

I thought you had my back.

A commotion broke out near the entrance of the locker room as Troy was tugging on his practice jersey. He heard a loud voice he didn't recognize, followed by Rozanov exclaiming, "Fuck yes! Finally."

There was a small black puppy in the middle of the room. It was adorable in every way, from its too-big feet, to its soft floppy ears, to its excitedly wagging tail. The puppy had instantly reduced a room full of macho hockey players into cooing heart-eye emojis.

But while Troy's new teammates were captivated by the

puppy, Troy's attention quickly shifted to the man who was accompanying it. He was nice to look at. Stocky and rugged, with neatly combed dark-blond hair and a trim beard. He was wearing a denim jacket over a plaid shirt, and, Troy noticed immediately, he wore at least three Pride-related pins on his jacket.

Troy felt like ice water had just been injected into his veins. Mandatory official Pride Nights aside, he had never seen anyone blatantly displaying rainbow symbols in a locker room before.

Troy knew he wasn't the only gay NHL player—Scott Hunter, for example, never shut up about it—but he was terrified of coming out. Of doing anything that would suggest to anyone that he might be gay. That he had a boyfriend.

Except he didn't have a boyfriend anymore. Not after Adrian had dumped him over FaceTime last week. Two years of dating in secret, of exploring each other's bodies and figuring out the whole gay sex thing. Two years of protecting each other, trusting each other, and being comfortable with each other. Two years of being in love. Finished. Ripped away so unexpectedly that Troy hadn't had a chance to fully process it, leaving him without anyone who he could fully be himself with.

And now this man—he must be Harris, the social media guy—was boldly hanging out in an NHL dressing room, covered in rainbows like it was no big deal. He seemed to be well-liked, the way the guys were gathered around and laughing with him. Troy felt a flash of jealousy at his ability to be himself and have people like him for it.

The puppy, for whatever reason, bounded over to Troy. It immediately snatched one of Troy's gloves off the bench and began chewing on the thick, padded thumb. It seemed to smile up at him as it did it, and Troy stared warily back at the one member of this team who seemed happy he was here.

"Oh shit. Chiron, you goof! Don't eat the equipment." The man who was probably Harris came to a stop in front of Troy. "Sorry about him. He's going to be a therapy dog, but he hasn't started school yet." He gently removed the glove from the dog's mouth. "Those gloves cost like a jillion dollars each, buddy."

Troy leaned forward and gave the puppy a tentative pat on the head. He'd never owned a pet in his life, not even as a child, so he was awkward around animals. "What did you say his name is?"

"Chiron. Y'know. Like the centaur."

Troy did not know. "He's cute."

"You'll be seeing a lot of him. He's the new official team dog. Oh, and I'm Harris. You'll be seeing a lot of me, too." Harris offered Troy his hand. His handshake was a little too firm and a little too hearty, but it was the friendliest touch Troy had experienced in a while. He almost hated for it to end.

"I'm Troy."

"Yep. I worked that out for myself." Harris put his hands on his hips and smiled down at him. Troy wasn't particularly tall, but if he stood now he'd probably have a couple of inches on the guy. "Part of the whole social media manager thing. It helps if you know the names of the players." He laughed so loudly that Troy almost winced.

Troy's eyes kept landing on the pins on Harris's jacket. "You been with the team long?"

"Longer than you," Harris joked. Troy got the impression that Harris was rarely serious. "It's my third season." He picked up Chiron, who immediately began licking Harris's face. Harris laughed—again, too loudly—and said, "This is the most I've been licked by a member of this team."

It was a ridiculous joke, but it still seemed shockingly bold to Troy. Harris probably hadn't meant to put an image in Troy's mind of . . . licking him, but that's where his imagination went.

He had never had such a vivid sexual thought in a locker room before because he always kept careful control over that sort of thing. But he'd never been confronted in a locker room by someone who comfortably advertised themself as queer before. And it didn't help that the man was attractive.

He was also, Troy realized, talking to him. And Troy wasn't listening.

"Sorry?" Troy said.

"Just sayin' that you don't seem to have a social media account."

Not one that anyone knows about. "Uh, no. I don't."

"Management wants all of the players to have at least an Instagram account. Doesn't have to be fancy or personal. You can just repost official team stuff if you're not comfortable doing more. I can help you set one up, if you want."

"It's mandatory?" Troy *hated* publicity stuff. All he wanted was to play hockey and be left alone. The celebrity part of it sucked.

"Basically. But if it's a problem I can probably—"

Nope. Troy wasn't going to start out with his new team by reinforcing the notion that he was difficult. "I can set one up. It's fine."

Harris smiled like Troy had just told him he'd give him a million dollars. "Awesome! Also, I want to do a Q and A with you. Just a little video to introduce you to the fans. Maybe later this week."

Ugh. "Uh, I guess. If you want."

"I'll go easy on you," Harris promised with another flash of his warm, earnest smile. "Softball questions only."

His eyes were a comforting mossy green and they shone with playfulness that wasn't even a tiny bit mean. If Troy had to describe his own eyes, he would use words like *cold* and *dead.* And his smile wasn't worth mentioning.

"We can wait until Sunday at least. Let you get a game under your belt."

"Whenever." Troy's gaze found Harris's pin collection again. What would it be like to be that comfortable—that open—about yourself?

When he realized he was staring, Troy snapped his attention back to Harris's face. Harris had stopped smiling. He was looking at Troy strangely—suspiciously—as if he'd spotted contempt in Troy's expression when he'd been examining the pins. Troy wanted to correct him. Explain himself. But years of being rigorously careful made him unable to find the words now.

"Hey, Harris! Stop hogging the puppy!" That was Rozanov, interrupting Troy before he could make a fool of himself. But also before he could convince Harris that he wasn't a homophobe.

One more disappointed glance from Harris, then the smile returned to his face as he walked off toward Ilya with the dog cradled in his arms. "I keep telling you to just adopt one of your own, Roz."

"Who will take care of it when I am on the road? You?"

There was laughter on the other side of the room, and Troy was left alone and forgotten.

After all these years, Troy still got a thrill from stepping onto a pristine, freshly resurfaced sheet of ice. A couple of quick laps later, he began to feel settled. His life might be a mess, but hockey still made sense.

He knocked a couple of pucks that were sitting on the boards in front of the bench onto the ice and headed for the net with one. He fired a quick wrist shot that sailed into the top corner. Always satisfying.

When he turned back to the bench to grab another puck, he

was surprised to find one already headed his way. He took the pass, then did a double take when he saw who'd fed it to him.

"Coach."

"Barrett. First one on the ice. I like that."

Ottawa's head coach, Brandon Wiebe, was only in his early forties, barely older than some of his players. He'd had a long—though not exactly distinguished—NHL career himself as a forward, and this was his first season as a head coach.

Troy passed the puck back. "Just needed to clear my head a bit."

"Best way to do it. You probably have a lot of shit to clear."

That was the fucking truth. "I won't be distracted."

"Didn't say you would be, though I wouldn't blame you if you were." Coach smiled wryly. "I think you'll like it here, though. I'm a bit different from Bruce Cooper."

Troy's throat tightened at the mention of his former coach. Cooper was a hard-ass, but he had liked Troy a lot.

Not as much as he'd liked Dallas Kent, apparently, because he'd insisted on having a final meeting with Troy, minutes after Troy had learned he'd been traded. Cooper had spent several devastating minutes tearing a strip off Troy before he finally let him go home to pack. Troy had left the office with his eyes burning and his stomach twisting with shame. He'd always had a hard time withstanding the furious disappointment of men like Coach Cooper. Men like Troy's father.

"I'm ready to work hard," Troy promised. "I want to get us to the playoffs."

Coach Wiebe smiled in a way that Coach Cooper and Troy's father never did—warm and patient. "That's good. I'm going to try you up front with Rozanov and Boodram."

"Really?" Troy was used to being a starting forward, but it was still a surprise to hear his coach wanted to put him on the top line right away. "I mean, thank you."

"Thank me on the ice, Barrett. Let's show Toronto they backed the wrong horse, okay?"

Delight bubbled up inside Troy. He even came close to smiling. "You got it, Coach."

Coach squinted at the bench, where several players were gathered and laughing animatedly. "Oh Jesus. They've got a puppy."

Rozanov stepped onto the ice with Chiron bundled snugly in his arms. "He wants to try out."

"Ten minutes with the puppy." Coach's voice was stern, but his eyes twinkled with amusement. "Then we've got work to do."

"Twenty," Rozanov countered.

Troy couldn't believe his audacity. Was he about to witness Ilya Rozanov getting yelled at by his coach?

But Coach Wiebe only chuckled fondly and said, "Fifteen."

Definitely a different coaching style than Cooper.

For fifteen minutes, the rest of the members of the Ottawa Centaurs frolicked on the ice with an excited puppy while Troy stood near the bench, watching and waiting for the real practice to start. What the fuck was the deal with this team? Was there going to be cake and lemonade at the end of practice?

"Are you allergic to dogs?"

Troy turned to find Harris standing in front of the bench, leaning casually on the boards. His golden hair was now hidden under a red-and-black Ottawa Centaurs pom-pom toque. In the bright arena lights, his green eyes looked more like sparkling emeralds than moss.

"No."

"Phew. I should have asked before I brought a dog into the dressing room. I'd checked with everyone else already, but—aw jeez, look at that." He lifted his phone and snapped a few pictures of the puppy standing with his front paws pressed against one of Wyatt's goalie pads. "That's going on Instagram for sure."

"He's a popular guy."

"Who? Wyatt?"

"The puppy."

Harris beamed. "Of course he is! He's new and adorable."

And Troy was new and . . . not.

It actually made a ton of sense that he would show up at his first practice with a new team and only be the second most interesting thing there. If that.

His grumpy thoughts were broken by an air-horn-level burst of laughter from Harris. "Get him, Chiron! Atta boy!"

Chiron was trying to steal a puck from Zane Boodram. Everyone was laughing and having a great time, and Troy wasn't sure what to do. He felt like he'd walked into a party he hadn't been invited to.

"Do dogs like the ice?" Troy asked. Chiron seemed to be sure-footed and happy as he chased pucks, but he asked anyway.

"Not every dog, but Chiron is part Labrador, part mountain dog. He's built for the cold."

"And he's going to be a . . . therapy dog? Like a Seeing Eye dog?"

"He's going to be trained to assist people with anxiety or PTSD. If he gets in the program."

"Does he have to write an exam or something?"

That weak joke earned Troy another horrifyingly loud laugh. "He just needs to be physically able to be a therapy dog. We'll know in a few months."

Harris kept talking about dogs, probably, while Troy's gaze, once again, went to the rainbow pins on Harris's jacket. The stab of longing and intense jealousy that he always felt when he saw Pride symbols must have shown on his face as apparent contempt again, because when he glanced at Harris's face, he found another disappointed frown.

Okay. Enough was enough. Troy needed to say something now to clear up any misunderstanding. He swallowed. "I, um—"

A whistle blew, and then Coach Wiebe called out, "All right, time to work. Harris, thank you for the special guest."

Rozanov scooped up the puppy and brought him over to the bench. He booped the dog's nose with his gloved fingertip, then very reluctantly handed him to Harris. "Where does he go when he is not here?"

"He stays at a training facility. They take good care of him, I promise."

Ilya frowned. "Is it fun for him?"

"Definitely. He doesn't have to start doing the hard work until he's older. If he qualifies."

"He will qualify. This is a good dog. Will he get big?"

Chiron licked Harris's face. He licked his *mouth* and Harris didn't seem to mind *at all*. Troy tried not to wrinkle his nose, but he probably did.

"He'll be a pretty big boy," Harris said. "Won't be able to cuddle him like this for long."

Coach blew his whistle again. "Roz, Barrett. Let's go."

Troy's face heated. Why had he even been standing by the benches still? He wasn't a dog person and he wasn't friends with Rozanov or Harris.

"You are in trouble already," Ilya said. His tone was flat, but his eyes were playful. "Bad start."

Troy didn't answer him. He just put his head down and got to work.

CHAPTER TWO

Damn. Troy Barrett was a looker all right.

Harris was in his office, staring at a headshot Gen had just taken of the newest Ottawa player. He had always thought Troy was one of the hottest players in the NHL, and meeting him in person today had only reinforced that belief. Troy's intense blue eyes, glossy dark hair, and pouting lips made him look more like a pop star than a hockey player. His narrow face had a razor-sharp jaw, shaded with dark stubble, and his cheekbones were frankly astonishing.

But it was his eyes that Harris couldn't look away from. Glinting like blue flames from under dark, heavy brows and long, full lashes.

Harris remembered the bare contempt that had been in those eyes when he'd been staring at Harris's pin collection. Harris knew the look. He got it in grocery stores, on the bus, and sometimes, yes, at work. None of it would stop him from wearing his queerness proudly on his chest, or on his wrist, or on one of several pro-queer T-shirts he owned. He always felt disappointed, mostly, when he received looks like the one Barrett had given his rainbow flair.

Extra disappointed in this case, because Harris had been hoping that Troy Barrett was a better man than rumors had described him to be.

Still, though. He was pretty.

Harris had never hooked up with an NHL player because he was determined to keep things *professional*. Also because the opportunity had never *presented itself*.

NHL players were basically gods, with spectacular bodies and loaded bank accounts. And Harris was . . . Harris. Short, a little pudgy, unathletic, and definitely not rich. He earned less in a year than some of the players did in a *day*. So Harris's personal pledge to never sleep with a member of the team he worked for showed about as much resolve as pledging not to take too many trips to the moon.

But *if* Harris ever went to town on an NHL player, he wouldn't mind if that man looked something like Troy Barrett.

Gen's email had mentioned that she'd included one photo of Troy smiling, but she'd also suggested not using it. As soon as Harris opened that one, he barked out a laugh. Gen hadn't been kidding; Troy's smile looked like it had been trampled on. Not only did it not meet his eyes, it barely met his *mouth*.

Harris imagined if he'd been able to play in the NHL—if he'd been able to play hockey at *all*—he'd never stop smiling. Hell, he barely stopped smiling as it was.

Harris picked one of the stern-faced photos of Troy—they all looked more or less the same—and dropped it into the frame he'd created for posts that introduced new players.

"There you go, buddy," he said as he posted it to the team's Instagram account. "You're officially a Centaur."

Next he opened up the document that was a running list of questions he'd thought of for player Q and A videos. He began cutting and pasting a few into a new list that he titled *Questions for Troy Barrett*. In a few minutes, he had a decent list, but it contained none of the questions that Harris *really* wanted to ask. Questions about Dallas Kent that would definitely not be appropriate for a friendly promo video. But damn, Harris had so many questions.

When the first post about Kent had shown up on Reddit, Harris had been horrified, but not especially surprised. The woman, posting anonymously, described being raped by Kent at a party at his house. The post was long, and detailed, and very hard to read, but Harris had read every word. He'd also read every word of the infuriating replies that mocked, dismissed, or threatened the original poster. He'd read the equally dismissive conversations between hockey fans on social media. He'd watched and read the mainstream hockey media's response, which was largely to defend Kent. And Harris had noted the way the league and its players were determined to either ignore the whole thing, or to loudly complain about how easy it was for people to make shit up on the internet.

More posts appeared online. More women with horrific stories of their own about Kent. Harris read them all, wishing there could be formal accusations that could lead to an arrest. He understood why the women were choosing to remain anonymous, though. He didn't need to look any further than those awful replies to see why Kent's victims weren't pressing charges.

While there were plenty of guys in the Ottawa locker room who were disgusted by Kent, and wanted to see him in jail, none of them said anything publicly. Overall, the hockey world stayed silent about the Dallas Kent situation. The accusations made hockey players uncomfortable, and most were happy to ignore it.

Troy Barrett hadn't ignored it. He'd been the only one who had stood up to Kent. Actually got in his face during team practice and called him a *rapist*. Clear as a fucking bell. Had

Troy been a witness, or did he just know, after years of being Kent's teammate and friend, what he was capable of? What had made him snap like that?

Arguments and even fights happened between teammates, and many had been caught on camera over the years. But hockey players had a tendency to stand behind their teammates when accusations of abuse or assault emerged. If Troy believed Kent's victims, that was a pretty big deal. This sport, as much as Harris loved it, had a horrible track record when it came to punishing players for, well, anything, really. Troy couldn't be all bad.

Though, Harris considered, you could be horrified by the actions of a sexual predator and still find time to be grossed out by gay men. So maybe he still sucked.

For reasons he couldn't quite explain, Harris opened the photo of Troy trying to smile again. Instead of laughing this time, Harris contemplated Troy's eyes. They were so striking that Harris hadn't noticed the anxiety they held. He noticed it now, and couldn't help wondering what Troy would look like if he smiled for real. Would his eyes crinkle? Would there be dimples? Maybe Harris could make him laugh . . .

Except, right. Probably a homophobe.

He shook his head and closed the image. Enough of Troy Barrett for now. He had puppy photos to post.

When Troy got back to his hotel room, he logged into his secret Instagram account. He'd barely posted anything on it; he just used it to follow Adrian, mostly. And maybe Troy shouldn't be doing that anymore, but he still couldn't quite believe that things were over between them.

When they'd first been introduced at a party in Vancouver two years ago, Troy hadn't been able to stop looking at him. And Troy was *good* at not looking at attractive men. Adrian

Dela Cruz, the star of a popular superhero television show, was firmly in the closet himself, and had been just as taken with Troy. Through some miracle combination of pheromones, silent communication, and luck, both men had clued into the fact that they'd wanted the same thing. Later that same night, they'd given it to each other.

A recent post by Adrian showed the reason he had ended things with Troy. The *real* reason, not the bullshit ones he'd given him about how they weren't really in love, or that they'd only been together because it was easy.

Troy hadn't understood that argument at all because there was *nothing* easy about their relationship. Living in constant fear that someone would find out about them wasn't easy. Living three time zones away from your boyfriend wasn't easy. Not being able to talk about your favorite person in the world with your friends, family, and teammates wasn't easy. Going fucking *months* without sex wasn't easy.

No. The real reason was Justin fucking Green, the director of a Netflix movie Adrian had filmed *ten months* ago. Which was, Adrian had admitted, when he'd started to fall in love with Justin. And now, as of four days ago, Adrian was out and proud and *engaged*.

And Troy had no idea how he was supposed to continue existing. He had no one to talk to about this. No one *knew* about Adrian. No one even knew that Troy was gay.

And of course Troy's first road game with his new team was in Vancouver. As if everything wasn't terrible enough, he'd soon be in the city that had always been his refuge. This time he would be completely alone.

He stared at the photo of Adrian and his fiancé, hoping if he looked for long enough the surreal wrongness of seeing Adrian in someone else's arms would fade.

God, he was beautiful. Obviously he was attractive; he

played a superhero on television. But Troy had gotten to see him when he wasn't made-up for the camera—rumpled and sleepy in the morning, or crashed out on the couch after a long day of filming—and he'd been even more taken with him then. Troy had loved every precious moment they'd had together.

And now they were over. Now Justin Green was enjoying those sleepy smiles and unhurried morning sex while Troy was staring at a fucking photo. Alone. In Ottawa.

Troy's life had imploded so quickly he hadn't had a chance to fully absorb it yet. He was going through the motions of being an NHL player on autopilot, knowing that if he paused to examine his shattered heart he may never move again. Two days—*two days*—after being dumped, Troy had seen the first of the accusations against Dallas Kent online. The words on his laptop screen had blurred through his damp eyes, and his throat had burned with the need to scream or cry or maybe throw up. Every detail of the woman's account was so *familiar.* Troy hadn't been a witness, but her description of the things Dallas had said . . .

It had been easy to believe. By the time Troy had read the fourth account, two days later, his blood had boiled with rage.

The comments beneath each of the posts were full of people defending Kent, and saying vile things about his accusers. When Troy had gone to his next practice, he'd heard his teammates saying similar things about them. During the practice, he'd watched Kent laughing and having fun, completely unbothered, and Troy had just snapped. He'd gotten in his best friend's face and unloaded all the rage that had been churning inside him. All of the disgust that Kent should have been getting from everyone on the ice. From everyone on *earth.*

Not that it had done any good. Hockey media was rallying behind Dallas, seemingly only concerned about the mental strain this unfortunate business would cause the young hockey star.

Mental strain. Jesus fuck. If anything, Dallas was probably more angry at Troy than bothered by the accusations. He certainly wasn't burdened by guilt or shame. He probably wasn't even a little bit afraid of repercussions. Because why would he be?

Troy was suddenly very tired, and thought about going to bed early even though he knew he wouldn't sleep. Except, shit. He was supposed to set up an Instagram account. A real one that wasn't just a burner account for looking at hot men.

So, maybe a *less* real one.

He deleted the burner account. Maybe he'd set up another one so he could follow hot men again, but he'd start fresh. When he was ready. For now, he would do his homework and start a professional account.

He was in the process of deciding on a password when he got a text message from his mother.

MOM:

Look at where you are!

A photo quickly followed that showed a Funko Pop! figure of Troy—in his Toronto uniform—balanced on a balcony railing. Behind it were beautiful misty mountains blanketed in thick blue-green forest.

TROY:

Wow. Where are you?

MOM:

Hakone. That's the view from my hotel room! I took it this afternoon.

Troy's heart lifted a bit. There was no one he wished were here with him now more than his mom. Unfortunately, she was on the other side of the world.

TROY:
Isn't it the middle of the night in Japan?

MOM:
Can't sleep. Ready for your big debut tomorrow night?

TROY:
I want to get it over with.

MOM:
Has it been bad?

Troy chewed his lip. Mom only knew a fraction of why his life had been hell lately. Hers had been the first supportive voice he'd heard after the video of him yelling at Dallas had hit the internet, and it had been hard not to break down crying as she'd assured him that he'd done the right thing. That he was a good person.

She didn't know about Adrian. Not only that Troy had just had his heart broken, but that he'd been dating someone at all. He'd never introduced Adrian even as a friend. He'd been so scared that his parents would see them together and *know*.

Especially his dad. Troy could almost imagine coming out to his mother, but not his dad. Never.

Finally, Troy wrote, Not too bad. Just different.

MOM:
Sometimes bad things happen so better things can happen.

Mom would know that more than most people. After Troy's father had left her for a much younger woman three years ago,

Mom had been devastated. She'd told Troy, one night over a shared bottle of wine, that the worst part was the embarrassment.

"It's not just that he replaced me with an *upgrade*," she'd told him. "It's that I'm ashamed of having ever been with him in the first place. Do you know how many people have told me that they always thought he was an asshole?" Then she'd apologized for talking about Troy's father that way in front of him. Troy had waved her apology away. Curtis Barrett *was* an asshole.

And now, because of Dallas Kent, Troy knew the shame of standing beside someone for years who was, well. A villain.

TROY:

You should get some sleep.

MOM:

I'll try. Charlie says hi.

TROY:

Charlie's awake too?

MOM:

No, but if he were awake he'd say hi.

Troy chuckled quietly and typed, Good night, Mom. Love you.

MOM:

Love you too. Good luck tomorrow.

He fell back on the mattress, letting out a long sigh of exhaustion and frustration. He should probably finish setting up his new Instagram account and maybe post something, but he didn't feel like it. His last team had barely involved players in their social media outreach, and Troy had been extremely fine with that, but this was a new team with a new vibe, and he should make an effort to fit in.

He opened Instagram again, created a password, and then hit a roadblock when it asked for a profile picture. All he had saved on his phone were promo shots of himself in a Toronto uniform.

He wondered if the team had posted one of the photos Gen had taken today yet. He went to the team's official account and found his own too-cool-to-smile face staring back at him.

Well, it would have to do.

He was about to take a screenshot, but then he made the mistake of scrolling down to read the comments.

Barrett's a fucking disgrace.

Always thought he was overrated. Now I think he's a fucking scumbag.

Barrett believes lying whores over his own teammates. Trash.

Ottawa deserves him. Shit team. Shit player.

I can't believe we signed this loser.

Troy put the phone down, screen pressed against the mattress. He was used to being hated by opposing players and their fans. But that had been because of his skill and, yes, because of his mouth. He'd always been good at getting under people's skin, if he wanted to. But this time he was hated for using that mouth to say something that was actually, maybe, *right*. Something he should be proud of.

The Instagram account could wait. Maybe if he stalled long enough, Harris would drop it. It's not like Troy would be posting anything interesting anyway. Troy didn't want to be interesting; he just wanted to play hockey.

CHAPTER THREE

"Harris! I've got something for ya!"

Harris glanced up from his phone. He was in the hallway outside the Ottawa locker room, posting some pregame tweets to the team's account. Wyatt Hayes was jogging toward him with a thick, colorful book in his hand.

"This is that *Thor* comic I was telling you about, all collected into one book. I think you'll like it. It's fun."

"Oh, awesome!" Harris had mentioned to Wyatt once that he used to read comic books a lot, and Wyatt had been eagerly lending him books ever since. So far he'd enjoyed everything Wyatt had given him, even if he always felt pressured to read the books quickly because Wyatt was keen to discuss them with him. "Thanks. Hey, we should do another edition of *Hazy's Heroes*! It's been a while since the last one."

"For sure. I've got an endless list of books to recommend."

It had been Harris's idea, last season, to film little segments where Wyatt would talk about some of his favorite comic books. The videos were so popular that Harris created similar video series for some of the other players: *Riding with Roz*, where Harris—bravely—sat in the passenger seat of a luxury sports car that Ilya Rozanov drove, and *BBQing with Bood*, where Zane Boodram would show off his grill mastery, even in the dead of winter in Ottawa.

"I was thinking," Wyatt said, "that I might buy a bunch of all-ages comics when we visit the children's hospital and give them out. Nothing against signed hockey pucks, but they aren't a great read, y'know?"

"They'd love that," Harris said with certainty. He knew exactly how much hospital visits from NHL players meant to the kids there, and he also knew how exciting it was to be gifted with *anything* that might pass the time when you were confined to a hospital bed.

"Don't tell Roz because he'll try to one-up me. He'd probably give them all Ferraris or something," Wyatt joked.

Harris laughed. He could totally see that, as ridiculous as it was. The last time the team had visited the children's hospital, Ilya had stayed long after the team bus had left. Harris had heard that he'd taken a cab home after an epic *Mario Kart* tournament he'd challenged a bunch of the kids to.

"Maybe if I tell him, he'll show up in a Batman costume," Harris said. "That would be worth it."

At that moment, Troy Barrett walked by. He had just arrived at the arena, earlier, Harris noted, than most of his teammates. He was wearing a suit that looked like it had been pulled from a suitcase, and a black toque that was pulled down to meet his equally black eyebrows. He was also clutching an enormous Starbucks cup.

He nodded at Harris and Wyatt, no warmth in his expression. It wasn't chilly either. It was . . . nervous, Harris decided. Timid.

"You found the Starbucks," Harris said cheerfully.

"Huh?" Troy reached under his toque and pulled an earbud out.

Harris pointed to the cup. "You found the Starbucks," he repeated.

"Yeah." Troy didn't smile. His eyes were wide and uncertain, as if he was unsure if the conversation was over. The hand holding the earbud hovered near his temple.

Harris almost said something like *good luck tonight*, but he didn't want to add to Troy's nerves. So instead he asked, "Whatcha listening to?"

For a long second, honest to god, Harris thought Troy was going to say *you*. His eyes had narrowed and then he blinked, as if trying to force the snark back down inside him. "Uh, just, y'know. EDM."

"Cool." In Harris's experience, if you asked any NHL player what music he was listening to, the answer was always either EDM, country, hip-hop, or Mumford & Sons.

With another nod, Troy popped his earbud back in and walked away.

"He still shows up early," Wyatt said, once Troy was out of sight.

"Did he used to in Toronto, too?"

"Oh yeah. It was one of the things that made him different from Kent." Wyatt put his hands on his hips. "He's a fucking dick, but he takes his job seriously."

"You think he'll still be a dick here?"

"Well, I don't think he got a personality transplant during the trip from Toronto to Ottawa, but he might be a little quieter here without his buddy."

"I don't think he and Kent are buddies anymore," Harris reminded him.

"I'm still surprised about that. Even guys who hate Kent's guts are taking his word over his victims'."

"So you believe the women?"

"A thousand percent. I played with Kent for years. He's

fucked up when it comes to women. I can't believe anyone who's spent a minute with him believes he's innocent. But even so, Barrett being the one to call him out was a shock."

"Do you think he witnessed something?" Harris knew he was being a horrible gossip, but he couldn't help it.

"I don't know. Honestly, I would have assumed Barrett was participating in whatever shitty things Kent was doing at clubs and parties. Thought he was, like, his wingman, y'know? Maybe I was wrong."

"I hope so. It's my job to make him look like a role model."

Wyatt huffed out a laugh. "Yeah. Good luck with that." He held out a fist. "I gotta get back in the room."

Harris bumped his fist. "Have a good game."

Wyatt grinned. "Any game I get to start is a good game."

He left, and Harris smiled after him. Wyatt had been a backup goalie for years in Toronto, but had not only earned the top goalie spot in Ottawa, he had also become an NHL All-Star. Harris was pretty sure a lot of his success could be owed to the fact that he had more fun than probably anyone else on the ice. He was truly happy just to be there, every game.

Harris knew the feeling.

He went back to work. He had promotional tweets from the official team store and from sponsors scheduled throughout the night; he'd posted tonight's official rosters on Twitter and Instagram. He'd also done a post promoting Troy Barrett's debut in Ottawa. He checked the comments on that post on Twitter now, and yikes. Barrett was not exactly getting a friendly welcome.

The comments came from a mix of Toronto and Dallas Kent fans who wanted him dead, and Ottawa fans who were disgusted that their team had traded for him. When Harris checked the same post on Instagram, he saw that the comments were similar.

The thing was, even though Ottawa had gotten Barrett for far less than he was worth, they'd given up some sweet draft picks to Toronto. Not to mention having to take on the burden of Barrett's significant salary. The only way Barrett was going to win the hearts of Ottawa fans was if he played the best hockey of his life.

There were a lot of empty seats. That was the first thing that Troy noticed. There were a lot of filled seats, but . . . there were a lot of empty seats.

He was standing on the blue line, waiting for his name to be announced as tonight's starting right wing player. In Toronto, game tickets were hard to get, sold out well in advance of every game. Here in Ottawa it looked like you could walk up to the box office on game day and buy a ticket.

Troy knew Ottawa had been a pretty terrible team for years, and that a lot of fans had lost interest. He would have thought the addition of Ilya Rozanov and even the unexpected rise of Wyatt Hayes as one of the best goalies in the league would have brought some fans back. And maybe there *were* more fans than usual, but damn. The energy that Troy was used to in Toronto wasn't in this building tonight.

"Number seventeen, Troy Barrett!" The announcer boomed out his name and the crowd went . . . tepid. There was applause. Some cheers. But also the low buzz that was, likely, the sound of about eleven thousand people murmuring uncomfortably.

He hadn't expected to be welcomed with open arms in Ottawa. Some hockey fans would never forgive him for not blindly supporting his scumbag teammate. And even besides that, until this week Troy had been a Toronto Guardian, a fierce Ottawa rival. Well, fierce in the way that a great white shark and a starfish were rivals.

Troy shouldn't be thinking that way about his new team.

Rozanov's name was announced and the uncomfortable murmuring turned into a full-blown roar of approval. Ottawa loved their captain. Zane Boodram, the alternate captain who had been playing for Ottawa since his very first NHL game, got a huge cheer as well.

Would they ever cheer for Troy like that? Did he even care? He'd do his best on the ice, and the fans could do whatever they wanted.

The game did not go well. Not for Troy, at least. He hadn't been able to connect with his new linemates, and he'd missed passes and had managed to be offside an embarrassing number of times, stopping play when he could have had a good scoring chance.

He'd had zero scoring chances. His only shot at the net had gone wide. He'd lost the two face-offs he'd taken. He'd accidentally shot the puck over the glass and earned his new team a delay of game penalty. It was a complete shit show from start to finish.

Somehow, Ottawa had still managed to defeat the superior Pittsburgh team. Mostly due to Wyatt's outstanding goaltending, and also because of Rozanov's two goals. Not only had Troy not contributed to the win, his sloppy play hadn't prevented it. He didn't matter at all.

After the game, the dressing room filled with reporters. Of course, they all wanted to talk to Troy after his first game as a Centaur.

He answered them all as blandly as possible. Yes, Ottawa had a different style of play than Toronto and he would need to adjust. No, he wasn't distracted.

His answers were all variations on the same thing: he was focused on hockey and excited to contribute to his new team. Both statements were lies, but he would like them to be true.

Then some dickbag asked if he regretted what he'd said to Dallas Kent. As if it was a simple question, and not one that would send Troy spiraling. As if he wasn't asking if Troy wished he hadn't lost everything that mattered to him within a week.

Was anyone asking Dallas if he regretted what *he* did? Definitely not.

Troy swallowed down his anger and tried to form words. He glanced up and spotted Harris, obviously standing on a chair or something, snapping photos from behind the media scrum. They locked gazes, and Troy thought he saw sympathy in Harris's eyes.

"I'm not talking about that anymore," Troy finally said. He was proud of how flat his tone was, not giving away any of the storm of emotions that were raging inside him. But he also was hit by a fresh pang of guilt and shame. Because he knew in his heart that he *should* be talking about it. Everyone should be.

The reporters took the hint, and the scrum broke apart as they went to talk to Wyatt instead. Harris lingered behind. He'd lowered himself from the chair he'd been balanced on, and offered Troy a friendly smile.

"Not sure what that guy was expecting you to say."

Troy could only grunt in response, but Harris kept smiling, and Troy kept looking at him. He had a nice smile, easy and genuine.

"Well, I should—" Harris gestured toward the reporters that were gathered around Wyatt.

"Yep."

"I'll see you tomorrow. For the Q and A. If you're still available?"

Right. That thing. Troy had forgotten, and he really didn't want to do it. "Look, um. I know your job is to, like, make us seem like fun guys or heroes or whatever, but I'd rather just focus on hockey. The other stuff isn't for me."

The light in Harris's eyes dimmed. "Got it."

Troy nodded, ready to be done with the conversation. "Okay. I'm gonna . . ."

"Sure." Harris gave a forced smile that looked all wrong on his face. "I've got other hockey players to bother anyway."

Troy almost replied. He almost assured Harris that he wasn't bothering him, even if it wasn't exactly true.

But he didn't, because this was as gently as he could possibly let Harris down. In the past he probably would have just sneered at Harris, or let Dallas Kent do it for him. This was growth.

But he still felt like a fucking asshole as he watched Harris walk away.

CHAPTER FOUR

"What do you think of Barrett?" Harris asked. It was the morning after Troy's first game with Ottawa, and for both professional and personal reasons, Harris couldn't stop thinking about him.

Gen glanced up from her computer. Their desks faced each other in their small office. "According to pretty much everyone in the world of hockey, he's a dick. And he hasn't proved otherwise yet."

"Everyone said Rozanov was a dick," Harris pointed out. "That turned out to be wrong."

Gen laughed. "Rozanov *is* a dick. He's just a fun one. Troy is the not-fun kind."

Harris frowned as he scrolled through the replies to his latest Instagram post, not really reading them. "I was thinking that maybe . . ."

Gen squinted at her screen, then clicked her mouse a few times. "What?"

"I don't know. That he could use a friend right now? He seems . . . sad."

That got Gen's full attention. She leaned back in her chair, eyebrows raised. "You want to be Barrett's friend? Wait. Never mind. You want to be *everybody's* friend."

"It's my job!"

"Sort of." She went back to clicking and squinting. "He's pretty," she said casually.

Harris folded his arms protectively across his chest. "He's not ugly," he agreed.

Gen's lips curved up, though she didn't look away from her computer screen. "Didn't you tell me last season that you thought he was the hottest player in the league?"

Harris had definitely said that. "I don't remember."

"We were playing Marry, Fuck, Kill and you said 'fuck Troy Barrett' three times."

Oh. Right. "I may have had a few beers in me."

"Mm."

"His looks have nothing to do with anything, though. I don't know if he's just a jerk, or if he's *being* a jerk as, like, a defense mechanism or something. Maybe he just needs people to be nice to him."

Gen snorted. "NHL stars have it so rough. If only someone would adore them."

"Have you seen any of the replies on our posts? The fans are vicious to him."

"No. Looking at replies is *your* job. All I care about is that you use my good photos and not your shitty iPhone ones."

"The photo of him on the ice during the anthem before his first game here," Harris continued, ignoring her. "On both Twitter and Instagram there are about a billion nasty replies."

"Pro or anti–Dallas Kent?"

"Both. But definitely anti–Troy Barrett. This one says 'Barrett is jealous that Kent won't fuck him.' And then they use some slurs that I won't repeat."

"Hockey fans are idiots. What else is new?"

Harris didn't bother defending hockey fans, and instead asked, "I don't know why Barrett isn't a hero right now."

"Yes you do."

"But he did the right—"

"Men never believe women. *Women* don't believe women. Come on, Harris. You *know* this. What were you expecting to happen? The whole league rallies behind Barrett, and Kent gets kicked out of hockey?"

"That's what should have happened."

"No fucking shit. But instead, Barrett probably regrets saying anything. I'll bet he didn't even mean to say it! He didn't have much to say when I mentioned it to him."

Harris nearly dropped his phone. "You mentioned it to him? When?"

"When I was taking his official photo. I told him it was good, calling Kent out."

"What did he say?"

"He said that it was complicated, which doesn't actually mean anything." She sighed. "I hate that word. It's not complicated; Kent is a rapist and Barrett called him a rapist."

A heavy silence filled the room. Gen was always blunt, but she was also usually right.

"Do you think," Harris asked, "that Troy, like, knew for sure?" It was the question that had been on his mind for days.

"You mean do I think he witnessed his best friend assaulting women and didn't say anything until now?" Gen shrugged. "I don't know. Maybe. I hope not."

"I hope not too."

She turned her attention back to her computer. "It's not my job to like them; it's my job to make them look good. And Barrett's pretty face makes my job easy. Hopefully he's not an accomplice to sexual assault, but if he is, well, he's not the only player in this league who is, I'm sure."

Harris chewed his lip. Probably not. For whatever reason, though, he didn't think Troy was an accomplice. He'd barely met the man, but he wanted to believe Troy was a good person, even if only for professional reasons. Harris liked every member of the Ottawa team, and he didn't want that to change.

"Okay," Gen said, pushing back from her desk with a loud rumble of chair wheels against the hard floor. "I have to go take photos of Haas modeling some of the new fan gear."

"That sounds easy," Harris said. "Haas is adorable." Luca Haas was a twenty-year-old rookie from Switzerland with blond hair and a baby face that flushed easily. He'd been the number two overall draft pick a couple of years ago, and Ottawa fans were excited to have him on the team this season.

"I'll bet I can get him to do some really ridiculous poses. Do you think he'd let me dump a bucket of water on him if I told him we needed a wet look?"

Harris laughed, imagining it. Luca was extremely polite and very eager to please. "Be nice to him. He gets enough shit from his teammates."

"It's his fault for being so fun to tease."

Harris was alone in the office for about five minutes before he heard a knock on the door. "Come in."

The door, which had already been ajar, slowly pushed open, and Harris could not have been more surprised when Troy Barrett walked into the room.

Troy watched as Harris's smile was replaced by a confused frown when he entered his office.

"Oh," Harris said. "Hi."

"Hi."

Harris stood from where he'd been sitting behind his computer. "This is a surprise."

"Yeah, um." Troy rubbed his own neck. He may as well get

this over with. "I'm sorry. I was rude last night. You were being nice and I was a dick, as usual."

Harris raised his eyebrows. "You came all the way here to apologize to me?"

Troy had done exactly that, but now that he was being asked, point-blank, he felt a little silly. "I'm just at the hotel down the road." Damn. He should have said he needed to be here anyway for something else. That would have been cooler.

Harris's smile returned. "Apology accepted."

"Good. Thanks." Now Troy wasn't sure what to do. Leave, he supposed.

"Actually," Harris said before Troy could escape, "I was thinking this morning, about you and social media. I don't blame you for hating it. I've seen how people have been talking about you online. It's . . . not nice."

"I try not to pay attention to any of that."

"Good plan. But if you wanted to put a different image of yourself out there, I'm very good at my job."

Troy wasn't sure what being good at posting shit on Twitter meant, but he was determined to be more open-minded. "I'll think about it."

This time he really was going to leave, but Harris stopped him again with another question. "How do you like Ottawa so far?"

Troy's knee-jerk reaction was to say something bitchy about the dull city he was being forced to call home, or to remind Harris that he lived in a hotel room that was practically attached to the rink, but he managed to be civil. "It's okay. Haven't seen much of it."

"I've lived here my whole life, so I can answer any questions."

Troy had no doubt, even though he barely knew the guy, that if he asked Harris to recommend a restaurant, he would enthusiastically rattle off a hundred options, along with detailed reasons why each were great.

"Have you looked for a place to live yet?" Harris asked.

"No. I'll do that when we get back from our road trip."

"Are you thinking downtown, or closer to the rink?"

"Not sure." To be honest, Troy didn't care. He was planning on renting something furnished and simple because he had no intention of staying in Ottawa past this season. He would use this year to prove that he was still a valuable asset, then move on to a better team. "Where do you live?"

"The Glebe. Nice little apartment. Nothing fancy."

Troy had no idea what the fuck the Glebe was. "Cool."

Harris seemed to take Troy's one-word response as an invitation to keep talking. "I've only lived there for a year and it's still weird living alone. I grew up in a full house. Forty acres of land and we still had to share a bathroom."

That sounded awful. "Big family?"

"Two older sisters, Mom, Dad, Grandma before she died, three dogs, a cat, and a ghost."

Troy decided to ignore that last thing. "Jesus. That's crowded." God dammit. No, he couldn't ignore that last thing. "Ghost?"

"Yep. Grandma used to tell me it's my great-great-uncle Elroy. He was a quiet guy, and a mostly quiet ghost. Knocks stuff over sometimes."

That struck Troy as being extremely impossible. For lots of reasons. "You must be glad to be out of there."

"Oh no, I loved it. The family, I mean. Uncle Elroy I could do without sometimes, but I suppose he's family too. I still love going home. I help out a lot when I'm not working here. Oh jeez, I didn't even tell you. My family owns an apple orchard. Fourth generation." He pointed proudly to a button on his jacket that said *Drover Family U-Pick*. "So, you know, let me know if you need any apples."

Harris's cheeks looked a little like apples, rosy and plump above the line of his trim beard. His near-constant smile molded them into round little balls that Troy had a fleeting, confusing desire to bite. He wouldn't be surprised if Harris *tasted* like apples, sweet and wholesome. "I'll let you know."

Harris kept smiling at him, as if there was nothing that would make him happier than being asked to gift Troy with apples. He was, Troy considered, almost the complete opposite of Adrian. Where Adrian had been tall, with golden skin, dark hair and eyes, and a physique that was more muscular and defined than even Troy's pro-athlete body, Harris was compact, pale, and soft. Adrian smiled easily, but at least some of it was performance. He could put on a friendly face no matter his actual mood, if he needed to. Harris's good humor seemed completely natural and genuine.

Adrian was also a bit of a snob, and would never wear a pom-pom toque, or a denim jacket covered in pins. Or a Wonder Woman T-shirt, which Harris was definitely wearing right now. In fact, Adrian probably would have had something bitchy to say about Harris's entire vibe, which Troy hated to think about.

Troy wondered if Harris had a boyfriend. He seemed like a good guy. He was probably very affectionate. The kind of boyfriend who bought thoughtful gifts. Or who *made* thoughtful gifts.

"Hypothetically," Troy said, "if I did the Q and A video, how long would it take?"

"Not long. Maybe fifteen minutes? It gets edited down to about ninety seconds."

"Is it something you could do . . . now?"

Harris beamed. "I could totally do it now."

"Just easy questions, right? Crunchy or smooth peanut butter? That kind of thing?"

Harris's eyes went wide in mock horror. "No way. You don't

want the crunchy peanut butter fandom coming for you online. Best to avoid controversial subjects like that one."

"Maybe I like crunchy."

"The smooth fans are even worse."

Troy didn't laugh, but he felt lighter than he had in days. "Let's do it."

"Have a seat. I just need to finish setting this stuff up."

Harris watched as Troy took one step toward the chair, then stopped. He frowned at the floor and chewed his lip, as if trying to make a decision.

"Something wrong?" Harris asked.

Troy fixed his intense, cobalt gaze on Harris. "No." He resumed moving to the chair, then stopped again. "I'm not a homophobe."

For a rare second, Harris was speechless. Then he said, "Good to hear."

"You're, um, gay? Right?"

Harris wanted to make a joke about the pin he was wearing that said *Big Gay Libra* being a subtle clue, but he held his tongue. "I am."

"That's cool. I know when we met, I probably looked like I was judging you for your . . ." Troy gestured to his own chest. "Pins. And stuff."

"It'd crossed my mind," Harris admitted.

"I wasn't. I swear. It just surprised me. I really don't have a problem with . . . y'know."

"Pins?" Harris bit the inside of his cheek. He was enjoying teasing this guy more than he should, probably.

Troy's cheeks pinked, just slightly. "Right."

For a moment, Harris was mesmerized by the way Troy's lips had formed into something close to a bashful smile. His eyes softened, and Harris was reminded that Troy was only twenty-five. The same age as him. "Let's start over, then." He stuck out his hand. "I'm Harris."

Troy's smile grew another millimeter. "Troy."

His hand was as solid and warm as Harris remembered it being from their first handshake, his grip firm and his skin a bit dry. "Nice to meet you, Troy. Get comfortable there and I'll make sure this is quick and painless."

Troy sat in the chair, legs spread and hands folded in his lap. He was wearing loose shorts that draped over his bulging thigh muscles. Harris had seen more than his fair share of perfectly sculpted thighs and asses during his time working for the Ottawa Centaurs, but he still allowed himself a moment to admire Troy's legs before checking the light levels on his face.

"You know it's cold outside, right?" Harris teased.

Troy glanced at his own bare legs. "I kind of half jogged over here."

To apologize to Harris. Which was distractingly sweet and didn't at all align with everything people said about Troy.

"You're not down south in Toronto anymore. Winters are brutal here."

"South," Troy scoffed. "Toronto has the same winters."

"You might sing a different tune in January. If you haven't frozen to death by then."

"I promise I'll wear pants in January."

Harris laughed, then stole one more glance at Troy's muscular thighs before moving the conversation away from his impressive lower half. "If you decide to set up an Instagram account, I can help you with some content for the first posts."

"Okay."

Despite his reputation for being mouthy during games, Troy was definitely not a talker off the ice. Fortunately, Harris had no trouble filling a silence. "You can keep it totally professional, and just post official team stuff. Some of the guys barely use their accounts, and some are super into it. Wyatt posts a lot of comic book stuff. Bood basically does my job for me, with all the videos he posts. Ilya didn't used to use it, but now he's super into taking photos of random stuff in different cities." Harris laughed. "I wish he'd turn the camera around sometimes. The fans would probably rather see their hero than a weird fire hydrant, right?"

"I guess."

"Sorry. I'm chatty."

Troy pinned him with that gaze for a moment, his blue eyes sharp but not cold. He almost seemed amused. "I noticed."

"I'd say just tell me to shut up, but it probably wouldn't work."

"It's fine." Troy returned his gaze to the floor, his shoulders slumped. He looked tired. Harris decided to move things along.

"I just need to get this mic on you and then we're all set." He grabbed a little clip-on mic out of his equipment bag and walked over to Troy. He crouched down between Troy's wide-spread legs and carefully clipped the mic to the collar of his Centaurs T-shirt.

When he glanced up at Troy's face, he found those deep ocean eyes studying him. An unwelcome burst of heat shot through Harris, as his dick noticed that he was wedged between the muscular thighs of a very handsome man.

He stood quickly and walked back behind the camera so he could observe Troy on the little screen, instead of from between his legs. "Ready when you are."

"Okay." Troy rolled his shoulders back and sat up straight. He kept his hands folded in his lap, all business and probably not at all distracted by sexual thoughts.

Harris started off with hockey questions, because he found hockey players were the most comfortable talking about their sport. He asked about Troy's favorite players as a kid, and favorite career memory.

"Who's your favorite current player?" Harris asked.

Troy didn't hesitate. "Scott Hunter."

Well. That was . . . unexpected. Scott Hunter was certainly one of the best players in the league, but he was also an openly gay man, and an activist. In short, Harris was impressed with Troy's choice. "He's pretty awesome."

"I'm also a big Ilya Rozanov fan," Troy added. "It's exciting to have the opportunity to play with him."

"Jesus. Don't tell him," Harris joked. "That guy doesn't need his ego any bigger than it already is."

Troy's lips twitched, just barely. "I won't."

Harris felt this was a good point to transition into personal preference questions. "Are you a dog person or a cat person?"

"Uh . . . dog, I think. I've never had a pet."

"Wow. Never?"

"Nope."

"Jeez, that's sad. I love dogs. I don't have one now, but I want a house in the country someday and, like, five dogs. Big ones."

"That's a lot."

"It's exactly the right amount of dogs."

Troy shook his head and made a noise that was almost a snort of laughter.

"Do you have any hobbies?"

Oddly, this seemed to be a difficult question for Troy. After a moment of racking his brain to reveal literally anything he liked to do besides play hockey, he finally said, "I play tennis sometimes."

Well, at least it wasn't golf or video games, which were the answers that Harris got ninety percent of the time. "Never played it," he admitted. "I like watching it, though." He didn't add that he mostly watched because tennis players were hot. He would bet that Troy looked *really* good playing tennis. "What's your favorite ice cream?"

"Um. Shit. It's been a while. Chocolate, I guess."

"Wait." Harris changed his tone to mimic a reporter asking a *very serious question*. "When was the last time you had ice cream?"

"I don't know. A few years ago?"

"How is that possible?"

Troy lifted one shoulder. "It's not something I crave."

"So what *do* you crave?"

Lord above, was Troy blushing? "I—"

"Like, what's a treat for Troy Barrett? If you could eat anything?"

Again, Troy seemed to struggle with the question. "I like salmon."

Harris laughed. He couldn't help it. "I was kinda looking for something that's not part of your trainer-approved diet plan."

"I don't really care about food. It's just fuel."

Harris didn't understand those words at all. "Food is the best thing about being alive! Like, I love fish, but if someone put a salmon fillet and a pile of my mom's apple fritters in front of me, that salmon is gonna get real cold."

"Cold salmon is good."

"You can have it. I'm stuffing myself with fritters."

"I don't have a sweet tooth, I guess."

"Nothing wrong with that. What about something savory, like poutine?"

"Always seemed kinda gross."

Harris blew out a breath. "I'll edit that answer out so the Ottawa fans don't know your shocking views of poutine."

"Cheese and gravy don't go together."

"The fuck they don't!"

Troy smiled properly at that. A brief and heart-stopping flash of teeth that made Harris light-headed. It changed Troy's whole face, and Harris wanted him to do it again.

"I'll take sweets over fries and gravy any day," Harris said, "but poutine is delicious. Who do you play as in *Mario Kart*?"

"What?"

Harris grinned. He found he got the best answers when he kept the questions random. "You've played *Mario Kart*, right? Please say yes, or I'll have to tear up my entire second page of questions."

"You have a page of questions about *Mario Kart*?"

"Answer the question."

The smile didn't fully return, but Troy's eyes glinted in a way that suggested he might be having an okay time. "I've played *Mario Kart*. I usually pick Mario."

"No imagination whatsoever." Harris sighed.

"He's the best one, isn't he? The game is named after him. Why? Who do you pick?"

"I've been a Yoshi man since I was, like, six years old."

"He's my second choice," Troy conceded.

"We're basically the same person!"

"Twins," Troy agreed flatly.

"What's your favorite place on earth?"

"It's really hard to follow these questions."

"But you're not bored, right?"

A slight quirk of Troy's lips. "No. I'm not bored." Again, he took his time considering the question. "Is *on the ice* a terrible answer?"

"It's the worst answer. Where do you spend your summers? Or have you traveled anywhere good?"

"I, um." All of the amusement left Troy's face. He looked tortured, like answering this question might actually kill him. Harris took pity.

"On the ice is fine. Don't worry about it."

"Thanks. Sorry. I'm not good at this."

"You're crushing it," Harris assured him, though it wasn't exactly true. "Next question: Mountains or ocean?"

"Why choose? I'm from Vancouver."

Harris grinned. "That's right! And the team is heading there this week. That must be nice for you."

Troy frowned. "Sure. Yeah. Of course." The way he said it implied that he would rather travel directly to hell than home to Vancouver.

Harris was fucking this up. Even the most basic questions were making Troy uncomfortable. Harris was usually so good at talking to people.

He decided to try a ridiculous question, to clear the tension out of the room.

"Okay. This one's important: What's your favorite type of apple?"

Troy's brow furrowed. "I don't know. Red?"

"Aw, man. Seriously?" Harris placed a hand over his heart, feigning being wounded.

"What? Not all apples are red. I like the red ones."

"I'm offended."

"Sorry I'm not a fucking apple expert like you."

It was a little mean, but it was also a little . . . warm. Troy's eyes once again glinted with something close to playfulness, and Harris liked it. "You're right," he teased back. "That was a really hard question."

Troy almost laughed. Harris was sure of it, and for some reason his stomach flipped in anticipation.

But Troy pressed his lips together in what was probably an effort to keep any displays of amusement from escaping. His eyes still sparkled, though. "How about McIntosh? That's an apple, right?"

Harris shook his head. "The disrespect. Unbelievable. Last

question: Would you rather skate sprints for half an hour, or answer questions for five minutes?"

"Sprints. Definitely."

Harris laughed. Probably too loudly, as usual, because Troy flinched and then quickly stood. "So, we're done?"

"Done."

"Okay." Troy walked to the door, clearly keen to get out of there.

"Wait," Harris said. Troy stopped, then looked back anxiously. Harris put a hand on Troy's shoulder, and he heard him inhale sharply. "You still have the mic on."

"Oh. Right." He stood perfectly still as he let Harris remove it, which Harris did quickly with as little contact as possible. He could smell the woodsy aroma of Troy's aftershave, or probably his bodywash since the shadow on his jaw suggested that he hadn't shaved that morning.

"Good to go," Harris announced cheerfully, holding up the mic. He took a giant step backward, needing to put some distance between them before Harris did something stupid like sniff Troy's neck. "You, uh, you might want to make sure you have noise-canceling headphones," Harris said. "For the flight. Those guys are pretty lively on the plane."

"You've flown with the team?"

"A few times. I usually go on a road trip or two each year to document stuff. It makes for fun content. I'm going on the trip south in January. There's a day off in Tampa, so it should be fun."

"Oh. Cool." It didn't sound like Troy thought it was actually cool that Harris would be on the team plane. He tried not to feel offended.

"Thanks for doing this," he said. "I'll let you know when I post it."

Troy nodded once, and then he was gone.

CHAPTER FIVE

Troy didn't know what was causing the loud banging noise, but he really needed it to stop. Gradually, he became aware that he was in a Vancouver hotel room, and that the banging was on his door. He groaned and pulled a pillow over his throbbing head, hoping the person would go away.

The person did not go away.

"Barrett. Wake up." The voice was unmistakably Rozanov's.

"What is it?" Troy's voice sounded like it had been sanded down to nothing. He tried to clear his bone-dry throat and said again, "What?"

"Open the door."

Defeated, Troy dragged himself out of bed and, after making sure he was wearing at least underwear, opened the door. Rozanov strode into the room, uninvited, and made a face. "Smells terrible. You got drunk last night."

"A little."

"Not good, Barrett." He thrust a bottle of Gatorade at Troy. "Drink this. Sit down."

Troy was more than happy to do both. He collapsed on the

bed and cracked open the Gatorade, wondering how Ilya even knew he had been drinking alone last night.

"I saw you in the lobby with a liquor store bag," Ilya said, as if he could read minds. "Heading for the elevators. You were in a hurry, it looked like."

In a hurry to not feel anything, Troy thought.

"This is something you do a lot?" Ilya picked up the mostly empty bottle of cheap vodka from Troy's dresser and frowned at the label.

"No."

"We play tonight."

"I know. It was stupid."

"Yes." Ilya studied him until Troy was forced to look away.

"It won't happen again," he said, though he wasn't sure that was true because now his reasons for drinking were all rushing back. After a long, lonely plane ride of listening to his teammates laughing and joking like the tight-knit friends they were, all Troy had wanted was to retreat to his boyfriend's arms. He missed Adrian so fucking much and he couldn't even call him. On top of that, he'd been ignoring his dad's phone calls and texts since yesterday because he could *not* fucking deal with that guy right now.

This was the first time in Troy's career that he hadn't enjoyed returning to his hometown. He'd never liked seeing his father, but until this trip, he'd been able to see his boyfriend, or his mother, or both.

Now his dickhead father was the only one left.

The shit with Dallas had happened so quickly after Adrian had dumped him, and then the trade, that the heartbreak had been kind of a vague emptiness that had hovered over Troy like a cloud. Now that he was in Vancouver, the cloud had descended, filling him with rage and despair. The breakup hadn't seemed real before now, because he and Adrian barely saw each other anyway. Being in the same city and not being able to hold him, kiss him, take him to bed and truly be himself for a few hours, was killing him.

And no one could ever know.

"I'm sorry. It was—"

If Ilya noticed the way Troy's voice broke, his face didn't show it. "This is your town, yes? Where you are from?"

"Yes."

"Your personal life is personal. If it does not affect your game, it does not matter to me. Coach will say the same thing."

Troy closed his eyes. "Are you going to tell him?"

"Not this time."

It was a warning, and one that Troy silently promised to heed. Hockey was all he had left. He needed to make the most of things with this Ottawa team or he'd fall apart completely.

"You look like shit," Ilya said. "Practice is optional this morning. You are opting out."

Troy almost protested because he had planned on skating this morning, but it would be ridiculous to argue. He was in no condition to do anything more strenuous than take a shower. "Okay."

"Also, your dad is in the lobby."

"What?"

"Yes. He introduced himself to me." Ilya made a sour face that Troy completely understood. "He is still there, but I can tell him you are . . ."

Fuck. "No. I need to talk to him. Otherwise he'll just—" Troy stopped himself. His messed-up family was none of Rozanov's business. "I'll shower and go downstairs. I'll text him. Let him know."

"Yes, okay."

Troy finished the Gatorade. "Thanks. For this." He held up the empty bottle.

"Rest today. Play good tonight. Don't do this again."

"I won't."

Ilya went to the door, then paused before opening it. "Family can be hard. Fathers."

It was a weird thing to say, and Troy didn't know how to respond. He went with, "Yeah. Sometimes."

Ilya nodded, then left. Troy blew out a breath and headed for the shower.

Troy did his best to make himself look presentable, but he shoved an Ottawa Centaurs ball cap on his head to partially obscure his face just in case his eyes were still red-rimmed. On top of being hungover, he felt dangerously close to crying.

Troy couldn't believe his dad was here. Except it also completely made sense; a rotten cherry on top of the trash sundae that his life had become.

He saw Curtis Barrett right away, lounging in one of the armchairs in the middle of the lobby. He stood when he spotted Troy, and the two men sitting in the chairs opposite him stood too.

Of course Dad had brought friends. He loved to show off his NHL star son.

"Troy! Jesus, you look like you were up all night." Dad clapped Troy hard on the shoulder. "I hope she was worth it."

Curtis's laugh was as aggressive as everything else about him, and Troy struggled not to flinch. As Curtis's friends joined in, braying like ignorant donkeys, Troy had a brief, wild urge to say, *"Actually my boyfriend dumped me for another man,"* but of course he didn't.

Instead, he settled himself into one of the chairs, done with standing. "Hi, Dad."

"This is Brad, he owns Condor Construction. And Darryl, from Harper Demolition. You remember Darryl, right?"

"Sure," Troy lied. "Of course." All of Dad's friends looked kind of the same: middle-aged men with builds that suggested they'd once been athletes, but had grown flabby over the years. Troy would probably look like that himself one day.

"So." Curtis inspected his son's Centaurs hoodie and ball cap. "You got downgraded to Ottawa."

"I got *traded*."

"You got punished, is what you got. I don't know what Kent did to get under your skin, but you've gotta watch your mouth, kid. Bad fucking luck having it caught on video." He made a face. "Practices should be private. What's said between teammates should stay there. I remember back when I was playing in Kamloops . . ."

And off he went, sucking all of the oxygen out of the room with tales of his glory days as a junior hockey player. Troy tuned him out. Troy being an actual NHL star had never stopped his father from trying to one-up his every hockey story. Eventually, Troy had just stopped sharing stories at all.

"Of course, you can't say anything these days," Dad was saying when Troy became aware that he was still talking. "Social justice warriors lurking everywhere."

"You got that right," Brad or Darryl agreed.

"Look at poor Dallas Kent," Dad said, as if Troy wasn't sitting right there. "People can say anything on the internet, trying to ruin a man's career. His reputation."

Troy wanted to say something, but he didn't know what. His head hurt and his throat was still precariously tight. Dad was now looking directly at him.

"Fortunately no one took what you said seriously," Dad continued. "Obviously Toronto had to get rid of you, which is a damn shame, but anyone who knows hockey knows that things get said in the heat of the moment."

Was that what people were telling themselves? That Troy

had lost his temper over something during practice and hurled a cheap shot at Kent? That Troy didn't actually *believe* that Kent was a sexual predator?

Dad chuckled. "If you'd been opponents instead of teammates, I think using the bullshit those women were accusing him of would be a smart strategy on the ice. Get in his head, y'know? But not your teammate. You two were like brothers. I hope you've at least tried to apologize to him. I don't blame him if he tells you to get fucked, but you've gotta man up and try."

Brad and . . . the other one . . . made noises of agreement.

Troy took a long, steadying breath. "You coming to the game tonight?"

"You bet. Bringing these guys with me. Not sure they'll be cheering for fucking Ottawa, though."

The three men laughed. Troy didn't. He almost asked why Dad wasn't bringing his new wife, but decided he didn't care. He didn't care about any of this, and he'd used up his ability to appear fine. It was time to seek refuge in his private hotel room so he could cry until he fell asleep. "Well, like you said, I didn't sleep much last night, so I should try to rest up before the game."

"You're not leaving already, are you? Here, I'll get you a coffee." Dad laughed. "You should be buying us coffees, with your millions of dollars."

Curtis Barrett also had millions of dollars. Maybe not as many millions as Troy, but the crane company he had started over twenty years ago had certainly made him a rich man.

"I think sleep would be better than coffee right now," Troy said. He stood up.

"I guess." Curtis frowned at his son, and Troy knew he'd been expecting him to do more to dazzle his friends than mumble a few words through the painful grip of a hangover. He did not look happy when he reluctantly stood and gave Troy another shoulder clap. "All right, well, good luck tonight."

"It's good to see you again, Dad." Troy was an excellent liar. "Enjoy the game," he said to Brad and Darryl, then turned quickly and left.

His eyes were already burning by the time the elevator doors closed.

Troy played terribly that night. Obviously. It had taken all of his focus to keep himself from bursting into tears in the locker room, or on the bench. Either would have been, of course, unthinkable. He wasn't known for his sunny disposition at the best of times, and his teammates didn't know him anyway, so it was easier to hide his agony than it might have been otherwise.

By the third period, Troy had been replaced on the front line by Luca Haas. Coach drastically reduced Troy's ice time, which only gave him more time to wallow in misery on the bench. His team lost.

In the dressing room, Troy's teammates didn't speak to him. They barely looked at him. Well, Ilya looked at him, but it was in a way that managed to say *you get to drink all night and play like shit the next day exactly once before I tell Coach* without any words at all. It was impressive. The rest of the team was probably only thinking one thing: Why the fuck did we sign this asshole?

Everything fucking sucked, and now hockey wasn't even working. What did Troy have left?

"All right, boys," Coach Wiebe announced. The room went silent, the air thick with shame and frustration. "We'll be practicing in Edmonton tomorrow after we land. Obviously, there are going to be some changes." He didn't look directly at Troy, but he didn't have to. "Edmonton has a stronger team than Vancouver, and we can't play like we did tonight against them. So get a good night's sleep—I don't want anyone going out tonight, I don't care what city we're in—and tomorrow get ready to work hard, okay?"

There was a chorus of "Yes, Coach," then Wiebe nodded and left the room.

Troy wished they were flying right now. He couldn't wait to leave Vancouver behind.

Troy wasn't on the top line when his team faced Edmonton. He'd been bumped down to the third line, which he couldn't blame the coaches for, but it still hurt.

He *needed* a goal. He'd never been so desperate for something in his life. As far as hockey players went, he wasn't particularly superstitious, but he thought maybe, if he scored a goal, things would turn around for him.

So he played hard every shift, using his speed to get to the net for a chance at a rebound or deflection. He played a physical game, taking his aggression out on anyone who got close to him. He *would* score tonight.

In the third period, Coach tried Troy out on the power play line. Edmonton was two goals ahead, and an Ottawa goal now would be a huge momentum boost. The face-off was in the Edmonton zone, and Rozanov won it, sending the puck back to Dykstra.

Troy darted to the net, right as Dykstra took a slap shot from the blue line. The Edmonton goalie made the save, but couldn't control the rebound. The puck landed on Troy's stick, inches away, just as the goalie fell backward on the ice. Troy fired it over the goaltender's sprawling body, into the wide-open net.

Troy celebrated like he'd won the Stanley Cup.

Then he registered that his teammates weren't celebrating with him, and he heard Dykstra yelling, "No fucking way that was interference, ref!"

But the ref was making the hand signal for "no goal," and Troy could not fucking believe it.

"I didn't touch the guy!" Troy yelled. "The clumsy fuck fell over!"

"No goal," the ref said. "You hooked the back of his skate, Barrett."

"The fuck I did."

One of Edmonton's defensemen, a giant doofus named Nelson, shoved Troy's chest, causing his back to slam into the boards behind the net. "We all saw it, you cheating little shit."

"How'd you see it? You were too busy doing fuck all to stop me. I walked right into your house and scored. Sorry you're bad at your job, you dumb fuck."

"At least I'm not a fucking traitor."

Troy shoved Nelson back, even though Nelson had about half a foot of height on him. Rozanov stepped in, face calm, and said, "You have to have friends to be a traitor, Nelson. So, no. You will not ever be one."

Nelson glared at him. "You better hope no chicks you bang make shit up about you online, Rozanov. This one will turn on you in a second."

"Yes. Could you ask your wife not to post about me then?"

"Fuck you, Rozanov!"

"Everyone back to your benches now," the ref barked.

Troy turned his fury on the ref. "That was a goal."

"No it wasn't."

"It was a fucking goal! Have you ever seen a hockey game before? He fucking fell."

The ref got up in his face. "Go to your bench. Last warning."

Troy was full of rage that had been simmering for over a week and he needed to let it out. The ref was probably the worst possible target but, well, he happened to be the one standing in front of Troy.

"Fuck you." And then he shoved the ref, and, yeah. That wasn't a good idea.

Troy was immediately handed a game misconduct. He continued hurling insults at the refs, the Edmonton players, the fans, and possibly God as he left the ice. In the tunnel, Troy smashed his stick to pieces on the wall, screaming profanity until he was holding a short chunk of carbon fiber in his glove. Then he threw the chunk at the wall.

He still hadn't showered or even undressed by the time the game ended. He'd just sat in his stall, seething.

Ottawa didn't score again, and ended up losing by three goals. The mood in the room was solemn after the rest of the team got there. Coach came in and gave another speech about how they needed to be better. Troy was starting to wonder if he only had one speech. Lord knew he only needed one, the way this team played.

After Coach left, and most of the guys were headed to the showers, Rozanov sat next to Troy. "Okay?" Rozanov asked.

"Fucking great."

"Yes, I can tell."

Troy didn't reply. He'd had his head down, but now he glanced over at his new captain. Ilya had stripped to his boxer briefs, and had his long legs stretched out in front of him. Troy's gaze caught on the famous tattoo of a snarling grizzly bear on Ilya's left pec. It was absolutely ridiculous up close. He noticed a second tattoo, less famous and probably more recent, on Ilya's arm, near his shoulder. It was a bird of some sort. A loon, maybe. Kind of a weird choice.

"You are a good hockey player," Ilya said.

It was so abrupt and unexpected that Troy fumbled his response. "Uh, okay. Thanks."

Ilya sighed and tilted his head back against the wall behind him. "I am tired of losing, Barrett."

"Well, you came to the wrong fucking team." Troy, like pretty much the entire NHL, had no idea why Ilya Rozanov had chosen to sign with Ottawa when he'd become a free agent. He could have gone almost anywhere. Instead he chose one of the worst teams in the league, in a quiet city that got about a billion tons of snow every winter. For a guy who loved sports cars, nightclubs and women, it seemed like a weird choice.

"I think we can win," Ilya said. "We have a good goalie. We have young talent, and solid defense. And we have me. Should be a good team."

Everything Ilya was saying was true. They *should* be a better team. "Then why aren't we?"

Ilya locked eyes with him. "Because we don't believe it. No one who comes here expects to win."

Well, Troy couldn't argue with that. He certainly didn't come here expecting to be a part of a winning team.

"Tonight," Ilya continued. "What did you want to do?"

"I wanted to score a goal."

Ilya nodded. "For you. Not for the team."

"I—" Okay. Troy couldn't argue *that* either. "I needed to score. I still need to, even though that goal should have—"

"Yes. I know." Ilya stood up, then turned and stared down at Troy. Even in his underwear, Ilya managed to make Troy feel embarrassed and ridiculous. He'd thrown a tantrum over a disallowed goal. A goal that wouldn't even have mattered, probably.

Also, Ilya looked really damn good in his underwear. But that wasn't a useful train of thought.

"Score a goal for you if you need to," Ilya said, "but think about what you can do for the team. You are, I think, what we have needed."

Without waiting for a reply, he turned and crossed the floor to his own stall, sliding his underwear off in the middle of the room. Troy huffed out a laugh. Rozanov was a piece of fucking work.

There were years of Troy's life when the locker room was the most stressful place in the world. When the conversation that had just happened, with a man as attractive as Ilya displaying himself as brazenly as he'd just done, would have been terrifying, because what if Troy gave something away? An involuntary glance or, god help him, an involuntary boner. He'd been miserable and alone, until one day, before he started his second season in the WHL at eighteen, he'd decided to start hiding behind a wall of aggressive macho bullshit. It hadn't been difficult; his dad had given him years of macho bullshit to emulate. So had most of his teammates and coaches.

And then he'd gone to Toronto and met Dallas Kent, the perfect loud, shithead shrub to hide behind. At some point, it had become easier to stay in character as a hetero bro who was, shamefully, pretty homophobic.

Troy had worn that mask full-time until he'd met Adrian. At that party two years ago, Troy had been utterly defenseless in the face of all of Adrian's beauty and charm. It had been difficult, every time, to put the mask back on after leaving Adrian's apartment, but Troy had needed to go back to his life as a hockey player, and he'd been nowhere near ready to be out and proud like Scott Hunter. He still wasn't ready.

But he didn't want to wear the fucking mask anymore either.

He thought about Ryan Price, a former teammate who had been on his mind a lot over the past year. Ryan had played with Troy in Toronto the season before last. He'd been traded a zillion times; Toronto had been, like, his ninth NHL team or something. Troy had been a complete dick to him because he'd been following Kent's lead. And because Troy was, admittedly, a complete dick.

Now Troy knew how fucking uncomfortable it was to be traded, and he was ashamed at how he'd treated Ryan when he'd been struggling to fit in. Instead of doing anything to help, Troy had laughed at how nervous Ryan had been on airplanes, and had made homophobic jokes right in front of him. Not after he'd learned Ryan was gay, but that didn't matter.

Ryan had been a perfectly nice guy. Shy, maybe. Awkward, definitely. But he'd been fierce as hell when he'd stomped on Dallas and Troy's immature jokes by clearly stating that he was gay, and that he wasn't going to stand for their homophobia anymore. That was a moment Troy would never forget.

It had been the single bravest thing he'd ever seen. And it hadn't even seemed like a big deal to Ryan, who had just calmly returned to his stall after and started putting on his gear like he hadn't just simultaneously humiliated and inspired Troy. Because Troy had been hiding behind homophobic jokes for so long that they'd become effortless to make. Effortless to laugh at. But Troy had had an actual gay teammate and he hadn't even tried to get to know him. To reach out. To help him feel accepted and welcome.

What a wasted fucking opportunity.

Troy liked that Ilya had taken a few minutes to talk to him just now, even if it wasn't exactly pleasant conversation. He knew Ilya was vocal about the importance of inclusion in hockey, and that he didn't just talk the talk. He and Shane Hollander ran charity hockey camps in the summer that celebrated diversity and had an inclusive staff to match. Troy heard that Ryan Price was one of the coaches. He'd also heard the rumors that Shane Hollander was gay. He wasn't sure if they were true, but he secretly thought it would be cool if they were. He certainly didn't blame Hollander for not announcing it.

He wondered if Ilya knew. Somehow those two rivals had

become tight over the past few years, and Troy would be impressed if Ilya was best friends with a gay man. Maybe when you'd hooked up with as many women as Ilya had, you didn't have to worry about having your own sexuality questioned.

Ilya would probably support Troy if he knew Troy was gay. If Troy wanted to come out and just . . . be himself. Finally.

Troy let out a long breath, and began tugging off his gear. This was a lot to be thinking about while still wearing sweaty, disgusting hockey gear. Troy needed food and sleep and to score a fucking goal and maybe get laid someday.

Maybe he should ask Ilya for Shane Hollander's number. Shane was a fucking babe.

The thought made Troy smile, and that was at least something.

CHAPTER SIX

Harris drove his truck under the hanging sign that read *Drover Family Orchards* late on Sunday afternoon. His family's home was about forty-five minutes outside the city, but he still tried to make it for Sunday dinner as often as possible.

Tidy lines of bare apple trees stretched out from both sides of the long unpaved road that led to the house, their branches twisting up into the white, late-November sky. The hard-packed frozen dirt crunched underneath his tires, loud and familiar. He loved coming home.

He drove past the newer road that ran from the main drive to the cidery his sisters had built on the property two years ago. He could see the fancy barn-like building in the distance, white Christmas lights lining its gambrel roof. He wondered if Anna and Margot were still working, or if they were waiting for him at home.

The dogs were already running to greet him when the house came into view. Mac—the youngest of the three—was first. Shannon and Bowser followed, barking happily.

Harris got out of the truck and laughed as all three dogs

jumped on him, tails slamming against his legs and against each other. "Hey, fellas, how's it going?"

He crouched to give each of them the rubs and scritches they deserved. Mac, an enormous brown beast, put his paws on Harris's shoulders. All of the dogs were rescues, and Harris could only guess what breeds they were made up of, but Mac must have some Newfoundland in him.

"Get down, you attention hog."

"Mac! Come!" Mom had appeared on the front porch, dressed in a plaid flannel shirt and jeans. She slapped her palms against her thighs and called for Mac again. Mac reluctantly released Harris and ran to her.

He grabbed a covered casserole dish from the floor of the passenger seat, then walked to the house. Shannon and Bowser followed, calmer now that they were convinced that Harris still loved and remembered them.

"What did you bring this time?" Mom asked when he reached the porch. She kissed his cheek, and he did the same.

"It's my brussels sprouts with bacon and balsamic. It just needs a few minutes to reheat."

Since Harris and his sisters had moved out, the Sunday dinners had more of a potluck structure. The whole family had always pitched in with the cooking when they'd all lived together, so it made sense to continue helping even if it was in separate kitchens.

"I was hoping that's what it was. Your father got experimental with the asparagus and I think we might need a backup green vegetable."

He followed her and the dogs into the house, which smelled like roast pork and possibly burnt asparagus. There was no sign of Anna, Margot, or their husbands yet. The Drover house wasn't large, but Harris couldn't imagine a better place to grow up in. Or come home to. It was an old farmhouse, white on the outside and mostly dark wood on the inside. Cramped and cozy and full of family photographs and antique furniture that had been in the house for generations.

Harris went to place his brussels sprouts in the oven. Dad was in the kitchen, frowning at a sheet pan of black asparagus.

"You used the broiler, didn't you?" Harris teased.

"Can't take your eyes off the damn thing for a second," Dad grumbled.

"It's okay, Dad. I've got the healthy green vegetable covered." He opened the oven door and slid his casserole dish in. "It has bacon, but it's still totally healthy."

Dad looked like he wanted to say something about bacon and cholesterol, but instead he asked, "You been feeling all right, Harris?"

"I feel great." Harris patted his chest. "Perfect working order."

Dad frowned at Harris's chest, where they both knew the ugly lines of multiple surgery scars marred his skin, then sighed and engulfed his son in a tight hug. "Glad to hear it."

"You worry too much. You know I'll go see Dr. Melvin if I feel even the slightest bit off."

"I know."

"Here," Harris said, reaching for the sheet pan. "I'll take that to the compost."

Dad gave the asparagus one last look, as if he might think of a way to revive them, then nodded.

Shannon, the oldest and smallest of the three dogs, followed Harris out the back door. The air was crisp and cold and the sun was setting fast. Harris loved this time of year, when the hockey season was in full swing and Christmas was getting close.

He dumped the asparagus into the compost bin while Shannon inspected a rock on the ground. He didn't like talking about his health. He didn't like thinking about it. He took it seriously—he hadn't been lying to Dad about that—but he hated the way his family looked at him sometimes. Like he was fragile. Like he could die at any moment.

Anyone could die at any moment.

Harris had decided a long time ago not to worry too much and not to feel sorry for himself. Ottawa had great hospitals, and he'd had the best of care since birth. There was no reason to assume he wouldn't live a long and happy life.

After a few minutes of scratching Shannon's ears and enjoying the quiet behind the house, Harris went back inside. The house was much louder than before, which meant his older sisters, Anna and Margot, had arrived with their husbands.

"Harris!" Anna called out. "What the hell. That Twitter war you were in with Edmonton was hilarious."

Harris hugged her. "Aw, well. They have a great social media person. Danielle is super funny."

"Fighting" with other NHL social media accounts was one of Harris's favorite parts of the job. He wasn't the kind of guy to trash-talk or say anything mean at all in real life, but when he played the role of the Ottawa Centaurs brand, he could really let loose.

"It was great," she said. "Jesus, Mac. Calm down. Here, take this to the kitchen for me, would ya?" She handed Harris a wrapped casserole dish.

"Is this apple crisp?"

"Of course it is. You put me on dessert duty, you're getting apple crisp every time."

Harris wasn't sad about it. He brought the dessert to the kitchen, and called for Mac to follow him. Now that everyone had arrived, the house would remain in a state of loud chaos until it was time to leave. Seven chatty adults and three friendly dogs crammed into an old farmhouse made for a lively time. Harris loved it.

There was a cat, too. Somewhere. Ursula wasn't a fan of the Sunday night dinners, and was probably upstairs on one of the beds.

And, of course, Uncle Elroy. But he wasn't a reliable presence.

The dinner was animated as always, with lots of teasing and laughter. Harris wasn't the only Drover with a booming voice and an unnecessarily loud laugh.

"How's that new guy fitting in?" Margot asked during dessert. "Troy Barrett."

Harris honestly wasn't sure. Despite Troy's prickly exterior, there was something appealing about the man. And not just his god-like beauty. Harris had enjoyed interviewing him. He'd enjoyed trying to make the man smile, even if it had barely worked.

But Margot hadn't asked about any of that.

"I'm not sure," he said carefully. "He's quiet. Keeps to himself, I think."

"He was kicked out of the game the other night in Edmonton," Dad said. "Shoved a ref!"

"Yeah," Harris said. He certainly hadn't missed *that*. Hockey media couldn't stop showing that clip and talking about how Troy had been spiraling out of control these past couple of weeks. "That wasn't great."

"I never liked him when he was with Toronto," said Mike, Anna's husband. "But he was talented. I hope he can get his shit together because we could sure use him."

Harris used to talk about hockey that way. The way all fans did, like he was part of the team, but only discussed the actual players as assets or tools. Now that he was working for an NHL team and had become friends with the players and staff, it annoyed him when they weren't acknowledged as human beings. He wanted Troy to play at the top of his game too, but mostly he wanted Troy to not be burdened by whatever was making him so miserable anymore.

Also, he wanted to stop thinking about him for five minutes.

"We put some more cases in the back of your truck, Harris," Margot said, snapping Harris out of what was about to be another Troy Barrett daydream. "Thanks for being our unpaid rep."

"Always. How's business?"

"Amazing. The new winter spice cider is selling like crazy. And the downtown taproom is booked solid for Christmas parties all month."

"Of course it is. That's great."

"Bring some of your NHL player friends when they get back. That makes us look cool."

"Conflict of interest," Harris joked. It wasn't really, unless he was using the place as a setting for promo stuff.

"Or you could bring a date," Anna said casually.

"I would *never* bring a date there. Oh my god. You guys would embarrass the shit out of me."

"We would not!"

"Nah. We totally would," Margot said.

"Are you dating anyone?" Mom asked.

"No."

"Well, that's a shame."

"I mean, I go on dates. But—you know what? I'm not talking about this."

"It's too bad Scott Hunter doesn't play for Ottawa. You two could have fallen in love."

"Mom!"

"And Ottawa might have a Stanley Cup," said Mike. "Y'know. If we had Scott Hunter."

"And Harris would be rich," Dad added, "if *he* had Scott Hunter."

Everyone laughed while Harris tried to glare at them all. "You know it's messed up to assume that two men would get together just because they're both gay and in proximity to each other, right?"

"Who could resist you, though?" Mom argued. "You're such a sweetheart."

"And you have nice hair," Mike said. "Good beard."

"You know a lot about apples. Men love that," said Margot. She turned to her husband, who was the quietest man Harris had ever met. "Right, Josh?"

"Super sexy," Josh agreed.

"Anyway," Harris said. "Scott Hunter does not play for Ottawa and is happily married, so I think I'll keep looking."

Truthfully, he was getting tired of looking. He wanted to have someone to bring to family dinners and cuddle up with at home later. He blamed the yearnings on his habit of spending too much time with NHL players in their twenties who were married with kids. He should probably make an effort to hang out with his other friends. His non-millionaire, normal friends. His queer friends, for sure. When was the last time he'd gone dancing? Or just met a bunch of friends for drinks at a gay bar, or karaoke? He used to be on a trivia team. Now he was obsessed with his job, and that job didn't have regular hours.

The dinner remained lively until the last bite of apple crisp, with everyone talking over each other as usual. Harris had been uncharacteristically quiet for most of it, his mind stuck on the possibility that he'd let his job consume his whole life. He really didn't get paid enough for that.

When he was leaving, Harris's parents both hugged him like they weren't going to see him again for months instead of days. The dogs jumped on him, as if trying to stop him from going.

"Take care of yourself," Mom said. "And tell Ilya Rozanov I said hi."

Harris laughed. Mom had met Ilya at a team fundraiser and Ilya had flirted shamelessly with her. "I will."

"And you'll call the doctor if anything feels . . . off, right?" Dad said.

Harris swallowed to contain the frustration that flared inside him. He'd been dealing with his busted heart his whole life, and he'd always been careful. "Of course I will. You know I will." He forced a laugh to cover his annoyance. "Don't worry so much."

Dad smiled sadly. "Can't help it. Sorry."

That took away Harris's annoyance in a hurry. "Love you guys. See you next week. Keep Mac out of trouble, all right?"

"Keep Troy Barrett out of trouble," Dad joked.

Harris turned away before Dad could see him blushing. "I'll do my best."

CHAPTER SEVEN

The day after the team had returned from their trip, Troy received an unexpected text message.

WYATT:

BBQ at Bood's tonight. You should come.

The address followed.

Barbecue? The fuck? It was snowing outside. Not a lot but, like, more than the amount that would suggest it was barbecue season.

TROY:

Is everyone going?

WYATT:

Most of the guys, probably. And partners. Bood and Cassie are great hosts.

Troy was not at all in the right headspace for a team party. He was surprised his teammates were either, given the fact that this team fucking sucked. Maybe you got used to sucking when you played for Ottawa and just made the most of things.

TROY:
Maybe.

WYATT:
Do you need a ride? Harris said he's going there straight from the arena so he could probably drive you.

Wait. Harris was going? The *social media guy*? This team was so weird.

Not that Troy couldn't see why Harris might be invited. He was . . . nice. Kind of annoying. Definitely too loud. Laughed too much. Smelled like apples, but that was probably Troy's imagination because it made no damn sense. Except when he'd been in Troy's personal space, removing that microphone after the interview, Troy could have sworn he got a whiff of something sweet and mouth-watering.

WYATT:
I'll get Harris to text you. Bring beer.

TROY:
I didn't say yes.

WYATT:
Get out of that hotel room, Barrett. Get to know your teammates.

Troy scrunched his nose. There was nothing wrong with his hotel room. He was, at the moment, lounging on a perfectly comfy bed. He had plenty of things to do tonight, like staring blankly out the window until he mustered up the energy to jerk off.

Harris texted him within twenty minutes. Wyatt said you needed a ride tonight?

TROY:

No.

He didn't need a ride. He drove his car here from Toronto instead of flying specifically so he'd have a car here. And because he'd felt like driving at the time and also getting the fuck out of Toronto as soon as possible.

Besides, Harris would probably ask him a bunch of weird questions during the drive. Or normal questions that Troy couldn't answer because he wasn't normal. Normal people didn't feel sick when they were asked about their favorite place on earth. It had been meant as an easy question, one that should have been pleasant to answer, but it had only made Troy think about Adrian's bed. Adrian's arms.

HARRIS:

You sure? I'm heading there from the rink anyway.

Troy rolled to his side, leaning on one elbow. Despite having a hard time answering some of Harris's questions, he had actually enjoyed the interview more than he'd been expecting. He liked Harris. He seemed like a good person, and Troy was trying to gravitate toward good people.

TROY:
What time are you going?

Not that he was seriously considering going. Even if he were, he would drive himself so he could arrive late and leave early. Harris would probably make sure he was the first one there.

HARRIS:
I'm swamped this afternoon. I probably won't get out of here until 7.

What the hell work was Harris doing? How hard could being a social media guy be, especially on an off day? Couldn't he post things on Twitter from, like, anywhere? Troy almost wanted to ask, but if Harris was busy he didn't have time to explain his job.

Seven didn't sound so bad. Not for a dinner thing. And Troy could get a cab back to the hotel anytime.

TROY:
Fuck it. Sure. You can pick me up.

HARRIS:
LOL love that enthusiasm.

HARRIS:
I'm actually working on a video of your top five career goals right now.

TROY:
You have to make that yourself?

HARRIS:

Yeah. It's, like, my job.

Now Troy felt stupid. He tried to think of something to say, but Harris sent another message.

HARRIS:

I need to get this done, then I have a conference call with marketing and a new sponsor who wants to do some sponsored content. And I've got some posts I have to schedule.

Harris: Sorry. You didn't actually ask for further info. I'm chatty when texting too. He added a happy face emoji to the end.

Harris was a really fast typer. Which made sense, Troy supposed, given his job.

TROY:

Ok. Just text me when you're leaving I guess.

He stared at the message after he sent it. It sounded rude as fuck. Did he always sound this rude? Probably.

Troy wrote, Looking forward to it, then deleted it because that seemed too far the other way. He wrote, Should be fun, but that didn't sound like him at all, so finally he landed on, I can get you a coffee from the Starbucks in the lobby, if you want. He sent it.

He'd *meant* that he'd get a coffee and give it to Harris when he picked him up. So he could drink it in the car or whatever. But Harris wrote back, What? Now? That would rule.

Um.

It wasn't like Troy was *busy*, but he wasn't a fucking errand boy either.

HARRIS:

Oh. You meant when I picked you up, didn't you? LOL

Troy should have been relieved, but instead he just felt shitty. Harris wanted a coffee, and Troy could easily fix that problem. He had nothing but time and money.

Like, literally. Nothing.

TROY:

I can bring you one now. What do you want?

Harris sent a string of excited face emojis, and then: Eggnog Latte.

TROY:

Isn't that a Christmas thing?

HARRIS:

It's November! Close enough! And it's a DELICIOUS thing.

TROY:

Way too early for eggnog.

Harris retorted with a row of Santa face emojis.

TROY:

Fine. Are you in your office?

HARRIS:

Yes. Wouldn't say no to a cake pop either if they have them.

😉

Troy didn't know what a cake pop was, but it sounded like the kind of thing that Harris would like.

TROY:

k. Be there soon.

Cake pops, it turned out, were even stupider than Troy thought they'd be. Especially since they were decorated to look like snowman heads, so apparently it *was* eggnog season. Troy had never really looked at any of the baked goods on offer at a Starbucks before. He always just ordered a black medium roast without observing his surroundings much.

He knocked on Harris's office door, balancing a tray with two cups and a paper bag with three cake pops because they seemed kind of small, so Troy bought a few.

"Come in."

Unlike the last time Troy had been here, Harris's smile didn't fade when he saw him. In fact, it grew wider.

"Coffee delivery from an NHL star. I could get used to this." He locked his fingers and stretched his arms over his head. It lifted the hem of his Carly Rae Jepsen T-shirt enough that Troy caught a glimpse of his fuzzy belly button area.

"Cake pops are supposed to be for kids, I think," Troy said, forcing his gaze away from the strip of exposed skin. He set the tray on the desk opposite Harris's, then handed him the paper bag.

Harris relaxed his arms and grabbed the bag with enthusiasm. He yanked out one of the pops and held it up, admiring it. "They're cute!"

"It looks like an impaled head on a spike."

Harris laughed way too hard at that. "It does! Yikes." And then he shoved the whole snowman head in his mouth, wrapping his lips around the base of the ball and tugging it off the stick. It was . . . something.

He swallowed the ball of whatever the fuck it was—cake, Troy guessed—and grinned. "I love these things. Holy shit, there are more in here!" He pulled a second one out.

Troy settled himself into a chair that was against the wall, near the end of Harris's desk. "I wasn't sure what a normal serving of cake pops was."

"No limit. Here," Harris said, holding it out to him. "You gotta try one."

Troy was conflicted. On the one hand, he didn't want to put that ridiculous thing in his mouth. On the other hand, he didn't want to watch Harris deep throat another one.

"I'm good." He took a sip of his black coffee to demonstrate how good he was, and promptly burned his mouth. *"Fuck."*

"You know what would cool your mouth down?" Harris asked, making the snowman ball dance around in the air. "A peppermint cake pop."

"No it wouldn't. And stop making it be, like, alive."

Harris turned the snowman so he was looking it straight in the eyes. "I'm naming him Gordon."

"Fuck off. Just eat it."

"I can't. We're friends now."

"Whatever. Your eggnog is there." Troy pointed to the paper cup on the corner of Harris's desk.

The small office was flooded with the sickly sweet aroma of eggnog and cake. Troy took a deep whiff of his own coffee to block it out.

He supposed he could leave. He'd only come here to deliver a coffee and a snack. Mission accomplished.

"When is your conference call?"

"Twenty minutes." Harris put Gordon the cake pop back in the bag and, absurdly, pulled out the third identical one and ate it. After he swallowed, he said, "Hopefully it won't go on forever like the last one."

"So do the sponsors, like, put their logo on the videos you post or something?"

Harris looked at him curiously. "Yeah. Have you never looked at your team's social media accounts? Not even in Toronto?"

"No."

Harris shook his head. "Well, I don't blame you. Whoever is doing Toronto's social media sucks at it. It has no heart at all. I don't know why anyone follows them."

Troy didn't know what gave a Twitter account "heart" but he just took a sip of coffee instead of asking. It was still hot, but his mouth was numb now anyway.

Harris took a sip of his latte and made a noise that Troy had only ever made during sex. "God, I needed this. Thanks for bringing it."

He licked his upper lip, and Troy watched with more interest than was warranted. He'd bet that Harris would taste disgusting right now—his mouth full of sugar and weird coffee.

"I guess I'll head back," Troy said, standing. Wondering what Harris tasted like was a definite signal to leave. "You can, um, text me. Later."

"Cool."

"Okay."

Troy hesitated a moment. He wasn't in a hurry to go back to his lonely hotel room, and he found he didn't mind being around this weird little apple farmer. He didn't mind looking at him either, which wasn't good.

He left.

Harris spotted Troy standing outside the hotel, wearing jeans and his black wool overcoat. Harris wished he'd had a chance to go home himself and change before the party, but he never looked any fancier than he did right now anyway.

"Hi," Harris said when Troy slid into the passenger seat of his Toyota pickup truck.

"You drive a truck."

"Farm boy, remember?"

"Right." Troy's cheeks were slightly pink from the cold, and he was freshly shaved. Without the dark shadow of stubble on his jaw, he looked younger. He blew on his hands and rubbed them together. "It's cold. Is Bood seriously barbecuing?"

"Oh yeah. No weather can stop that guy from grilling. He has a sweet deck with heaters and stuff all over it. Wait'll you see it."

"I probably won't stay long."

"I can drive you back after. I don't mind."

Harris had his eyes on the road, but he could sense Troy tense beside him. "I won't ask you to do that."

"You didn't," Harris said simply. "But the offer stands."

Troy didn't reply, and when they reached a red light, Harris glanced over and saw him chewing on his thumbnail, head turned toward the passenger-side window.

Harris had become used to palling around with NHL players over the past few years, so he wasn't intimidated by having Troy in his truck. Parties like the one they were going to had become a normal part of Harris's social life, and it occurred to Harris that *Troy* was the one who was uncomfortable right now. Who was probably nervous about hanging out with his new teammates, and was trying to hide behind a wall of indifference.

"It's a great group of guys," Harris said. "I've been working with and hanging out with most of them for a couple of years, and I don't think there could possibly be a better team in the league when it comes to personalities."

"Personalities don't win cups," Troy said bluntly. It sounded like he was repeating something a shitty coach had drilled into him.

"I don't know about that. Camaraderie counts for something. I'd think it would be hard to win games if you hated your teammates."

"Have you ever played hockey?"

A flash of embarrassment shot through Harris. "No."

Troy made a dismissive scoffing noise, and went back to gnawing his thumbnail.

Harris wished he could have said yes. The fact that he'd never played organized hockey was something he tried not to let bother him, and something he hoped everyone he worked with would ignore. Or not even know about in the first place. Harris had always loved hockey, and he probably *could* have played, but his parents had been nervous. He couldn't blame them; when your child's body is already struggling, hockey seems like an unnecessary risk.

So, as a kid, he'd thrown himself into being a fan, of hockey in general and the Ottawa Centaurs in particular. And now he got to feel like he was part of the team. And that feeling could mostly be attributed to how warmly he'd been accepted by the players as a friend. He'd talked to other NHL team social media managers, and he knew that his friendship with the Ottawa players wasn't the norm.

"Sorry," Troy said. It was so quiet, Harris almost missed it.

"For what?"

"I'm being a fucking dickwad. You're giving me a lift and I'm being . . . me. Sorry."

"You brought me coffee," Harris pointed out. "As far as favors go, we're even. In fact, since you also brought me cake pops, I'd say I still owe *you* a favor."

Troy didn't say anything for a long moment. Then he said, "Should we stop somewhere and get beer?"

"I've got it sorted," Harris said. "Got a few cases of cider in the back."

"Cider?"

"My sisters make it. One hundred percent Drover family apples. It's the best hard cider in Ontario."

"Is that your unbiased opinion?" Troy asked dryly.

"Absolutely."

"Can I pay you for some of it?"

"Nope."

"Then I guess that's your favor. We're even."

Harris grinned. "Fair enough."

There was another minute of silence, and then Troy said, "So, is, like, everyone going to be at this?"

"Probably not everyone. Ilya won't be there."

"He won't?"

"Nah. He's almost never around on days off."

"Where does he go?"

Harris shrugged. "No idea. If there's a team hospital visit or a community outreach thing, Ilya is always available. If not, no one can ever reach him on a day off. I figure it's his own time, so it's no one's business anyway. But the guys like to invent theories."

"You're right," Troy said after a moment. "It's no one's business."

★ ★ ★

Troy had been to plenty of team parties and outings over the years. Most had been at Dallas Kent's mansion, and Troy had usually enjoyed them. He'd always thought that Kent's taste level was questionable, though. His mansion was tacky as fuck.

Now he couldn't think of those parties without feeling sick. How many women had Kent forced himself on—or tried to—at those parties? Had Troy been in the next room, or one floor below? Had it been happening right in front of him and he hadn't realized it?

He reminded himself that Dallas Kent wouldn't be here tonight. This was a new team, with new people, and a very different vibe from the Toronto Guardians.

As soon as Troy followed Harris through Bood's front door, they were cheerfully greeted by Evan Dykstra.

"Harris! What's up, bro?" Dykstra wrapped an arm around Harris's head and pulled him against his chest. He was much taller than Harris or Troy—probably six-three or so—and he looked like a total redneck. When he wasn't in hockey gear or a suit, he seemed to always have his shaggy light brown hair stuffed into a camo snapback. Troy had only known him for a few days, but he'd already heard him talk about fishing, hunting, snowmobiling, and why his home province of Manitoba was the best place on earth.

"You brought the good shit," Dykstra said, taking the case of bottled cider from Harris. He frowned and nodded at Troy. "And you brought Barrett."

Right. No one wanted Troy here. He shouldn't have come.

Dykstra elbowed Troy and said, "I'm just joking, man. Good to see you. Rule one of being a Centaur: if Bood invites you to a barbecue, you go. Wait'll you taste his shit. Fucking incredible."

"Cool," Troy said. He held up the case he was carrying. "Where should I put this?"

"Bring it to the patio. Bood's got a beer fridge out there that might still have some room in it. I'll show you."

Harris had already wandered off to talk to a woman Troy was pretty sure was Wyatt's wife, so he followed Dykstra to the back of the house. They passed the living room, where a group of the younger players were engaged in a lively *Super Smash Bros*. battle.

Bood's back deck was enormous, with a slatted wood ceiling that was lined with lights. It gave the illusion of being indoors, except for the flurries of snow that caught in the light. Despite the weather, the space was warm with electric heaters, people, and the mouth-watering aroma of grilled meat.

People lounged on cushioned furniture, some in a circle around a firepit, some on the built-in benches that lined the perimeter of the deck. Most of the people were Troy's teammates, and some were women who were probably their partners. The party seemed very laid-back and intimate; nothing like Kent's ragers that were packed with young women, live DJs, and party drugs. Everyone was friends here.

"Bood!" Dykstra called out. "Harris brought cider."

Bood was standing at a massive grill, turning chicken parts with some tongs. "Awesome. I love that shit. Oh hey, what's up, Barrett?"

"Not much."

Zane Boodram was a little taller than Troy, a little shorter than Dykstra. He had warm, light brown skin and dark curly hair. His muscular arms were both covered in tattoo sleeves that incorporated nautical stuff, tropical flowers, and the Trinidad and Tobago flag.

"Make yourself comfortable. Grab anything you want from the fridge. I got a fuck ton of food out on the table over there."

He gestured with his tongs. "And this chicken is going to be done soon. You like spice?"

"Say no," Dykstra warned. "Bood takes it as a challenge."

Bood laughed. "Nah, you're just a lightweight, D."

Troy and Dykstra went to the beer fridge and unloaded the bottles of cider. Then they each took one and Dykstra said, "My wife, Caitlin, she's not here tonight, but she loves that you yelled at Kent. She volunteers at a charity that helps women who are, y'know. Victims. Of that sort of thing."

It made so many hockey players uncomfortable to talk about sexual assault. Troy wasn't particularly comfortable talking about it either, but he appreciated Dykstra making this unexpected effort to reach out.

"That's cool that she does that," Troy said, and Dykstra shuffled his feet uncomfortably for a moment, then nodded.

"I know a lot of the guys in the league don't believe what those women are saying about Kent, or don't want to. Not that long ago, I probably would have thought they were lying too, honestly. But I've learned a lot from Caitlin, and from, y'know. Reading stuff. Plus, I figure you know Kent pretty well, so if you believe those women, then I sure as fuck do."

Warmth filled some of the emptiness that Troy had been made of for the past week. "I believe them," he said firmly.

"Good enough for me." Dykstra took a sip from the bottle he was holding, and changed the subject. "You try this cider yet?"

Troy hadn't, so he took a sip from his own bottle. The cider was crisp and not as sweet as he'd been expecting. Refreshing. "It's good."

"Harris's sisters know what they're doing, that's for sure. But you can get surprisingly fucked up on this shit, so be careful."

Troy only planned on having one drink tonight. Given his mood, he knew two drinks could easily turn into too many. "I'll go easy."

Another defenseman—Nick Chouinard—called Dykstra over to the firepit area. Troy didn't follow, instead heading for the food table. He got there just as Bood plunked down a huge platter of grilled chicken.

"Okay," Bood said, rubbing his hands together enthusiastically, "I'm gonna give you a tour. We've got jerk chicken here, and that's the real shit, so don't fuck with it if you don't like spice. We've got chicken with my secret recipe barbecue sauce over here." He gestured to the platter he'd just added to the table. "It's more sweet and smoky than spicy. It'll go fast, so grab it now. Ribs, obviously, over there. Peas and rice, slaw, callaloo. Got some of my homemade pepper sauce. That's hot as fuck, but if you like it, I can give you a bottle. I make tons of it."

"Wow. Jesus. This all looks great." Troy grabbed a plate and a jerk chicken leg, which made Bood grin.

"Going for the heat. I love it." He clapped Troy on the shoulder. "And, listen. I played junior with Kent, same team, and I hated the little fucker. I'll be totally honest and say that I always thought you were a piece of shit too, by association."

What was Troy supposed to say to that? He *was* a piece of shit by association. And maybe just on his own too. "Makes sense" was what he came up with.

"I'm hoping you prove me wrong, is all I'm saying. We've got a good group here. Don't fuck that up."

"I won't," Troy said weakly.

"Cool. I gotta clean the grill." Bood grinned and nodded at Troy's plate of chicken. "Enjoy."

Troy found a quiet bench seat in one corner. The patio was filled with the happy chatter of a group of people who obviously knew each other well. Before he'd gotten here, Troy had assumed that the Ottawa players must be the most miserable bunch of people in the world. How could you have fun together—or even like each other—when you couldn't win on the ice? When your arena was only half full most games? How were you not completely embarrassed all the time?

But this group loved each other. Troy hadn't even been on this team for two weeks yet and he could see it clearly. He just couldn't see himself being a part of it, even if his teammates had been decent to him so far.

The food was delicious. Troy hadn't realized how hungry he was until he tore into the jerk chicken, and, yeah, it was spicy, but it was so fucking tasty too. He cooled his mouth with more of the cider.

As if summoned by the cider, Harris was suddenly in front of him. "Hey." He was holding his own plate of food and a bottle. "Mind if I sit?"

"Go ahead."

Harris sat next to him. "Having fun?"

"I guess. It's a nice patio."

"It's property porn, is what it is. I'm glad Bood likes to entertain so much." He picked up a rib and sank his teeth into it.

Troy went back to his own food, eating in silence until Harris asked, "You talk to anyone?"

"Um. Dykstra a bit. Bood."

"You meet Cassie yet? That's Bood's wife."

"No."

Harris gestured to a tall blond woman standing near the firepit. "That's Cassie. She's supercool." When she turned, Troy could see that she was pregnant.

"Is this gonna be their first kid?"

"Yup! They'll be the best parents." Harris nudged Troy. "Don't tell any of the other dads I said that."

"I don't even know who the other dads are."

"Dykstra has a daughter, Susie. She just turned one. Chouinard has three kids, Boyle has twins . . ." He went on to name every dad on the team, and all of their kids' names and ages.

Then he proceeded to list and detail everyone's pets. Troy tried to retain at least some of it.

"Wow. Do you know all their allergies too?"

Harris laughed. "I like people. And I like my job."

"What if the player is a fucking dick, but you still have to do promo shit to make him seem great?"

"It's never happened. This team only ever has good people."

He seemed awfully sure of himself, considering Troy was sitting right next to him as hard evidence that Ottawa did *not* only sign good people.

"Did you like being home for a couple of days?" Harris asked. "I've only been to Vancouver once. It lives up to the hype."

"It's not bad."

"Wyatt loves the Vancouver trips. His sister lives there with her wife and their son."

Troy's attention snagged on one word. "Wife?"

"Yeah. You didn't know? He talks about them all the time. I assumed he did in Toronto too."

Even if Wyatt *had* talked about his family when he'd played for Toronto, he wouldn't have talked to Troy about his queer sister. Not the way Troy had radiated homophobia. Given the culture of the Toronto team, there was a good chance Wyatt hadn't talked about his sister to anyone.

Maybe to Ryan Price. Wyatt had been friends with Ryan. Probably because no one else had been.

"I didn't know. That's cool, though."

"I've never met his sister, but she sounds awesome," Harris said.

They both finished their food, and then Harris stood and said, "I see seats available at the firepit. Let's check it out."

Troy glanced at the happy group of people who were chatting and laughing in the glow of the fire. He didn't need to intrude on that. "Oh, uh. That's okay."

Harris grabbed Troy's mostly empty paper plate and stacked it on top of his own. "Come on."

The plates got tossed into a giant garbage can that was strategically placed near the door. Then Harris headed for the firepit and Troy, not sure of what else to do, followed.

"Harris! Come sit," Wyatt said cheerfully. "Hey, Barrett."

"Hey."

Harris sat in the empty chair next to the love seat Wyatt was sharing with his wife. Troy sat in a chair across from them.

Bood was perched on the arm of the chair that his wife, Cassie, was sitting in. Nick Chouinard was next to them, and next to him was a woman who Troy had not met before but guessed was Nick's wife.

"Wyatt was talking our ear off about his nephew," Bood said to Troy.

"Yeah. Because he's amazing," Wyatt said.

"How old is Isaac now?" Harris asked.

"Three. Cute as hell too. I can't wait to see him again, but it won't be for a long time. Kristy and Eve, too. But mostly Isaac."

And there it was. Wyatt talking easily about his sister and her wife. Without fear of his teammates judging his family because no one on this team was a bigot. Once again, Troy felt like an intruder.

"You're from Vancity, right, Barrett?" Nick asked.

"Uh, yeah."

"Did your family go to the game?"

"Yeah." Everyone stared at him, probably waiting for him to elaborate, but Troy just stared at the fire.

He hadn't spoken to his father after the game. Dad had sent him a text that had basically made fun of how shitty the Centaurs were, and how terribly Troy had played in particular.

But Mom had texted too. She'd sent him a photo of his

little action figure on the table of a restaurant in Tokyo, and had also said, Next time you're in Vancouver I'll make sure I'm there too.

God, he missed her.

Loud laughter jolted Troy out of his thoughts. The conversation had clearly moved on without him.

"Oh, shit, Barrett," Bood said. "You haven't met my wife, Cassie."

Cassie waved at Troy from across the fire. She was stunningly beautiful, with hair and skin that suggested a lot of professional care. "Hi, Troy. Welcome to Ottawa."

"And this is Selena," Nick said.

"Hi," Troy said. Nick's wife was tiny compared to her husband, almost disappearing under the giant arm he had wrapped around her. She was blond and beautiful like Cassie, and Troy couldn't believe she was the mother of three children. Nick was only in his mid-twenties like Troy, and she looked about the same age.

"Nice to meet you," she said. She had a Quebec accent like her husband. "We know how hard being traded can be." She shared a look with her husband.

"At least you don't have kids, Barrett," Nick said. "Easier to move when it's just you."

"Are you with someone?" Selena asked. "Wife or girlfriend?"

Troy ignored the ache that pulsed in his chest at the reminder of being recently dumped, and of being different. "No one right now."

"You remember Lisa, right?" Wyatt asked, gesturing to his own wife.

Troy had completely forgotten her name. He'd probably only talked to her once in Toronto. "Of course. Yeah. Hi, Lisa."

"Good to see you again, Troy. You settling in okay?" Lisa looked very different from the other two women in the circle.

She had dark hair, cut short, and she didn't seem to be wearing makeup. She was very pretty, but where a lot of Troy's teammates' wives over the years had looked like models, Lisa looked more like a fitness instructor.

Or, he supposed, like a doctor. Because that's what she was.

"More or less. Never been traded before, so it's all kinda weird."

"Never Been Traded Club," Bood said, extending his arm and offering Troy his fist. Troy bumped it. "Well, I guess you're out of the club now."

"Yeah."

"Are you still at the hotel?" Lisa asked.

"For now. I need to figure out a place to live."

Lisa nudged Wyatt. "Give him the details of that building we lived in when you got traded here. You'll love it, Troy. Fully furnished, right downtown, concierge service for cleaning and laundry. It was perfect for us, while we were waiting to see if Wyatt would be staying in Ottawa after that season."

"I'll email you about it," Wyatt said. "You should definitely check it out."

"Okay. Thanks. Sounds good." It sounded perfect, actually. Although the proximity to the arena was nice, Troy was getting really sick of the hotel. And he needed something easy and temporary, just to last him until he could figure out how to get off this team.

"Okay, let me address something real quick," Bood said abruptly. "We need to talk about how last season, I scored the prettiest goal of the fucking year against Buffalo. Grabbed that puck from McCord, split Buffalo's D like a fucking knife, then faked out their goalie. Beautiful. Showed it like a thousand times on replay."

"I remember," Wyatt said. "Why are we talking about it, though?"

"Oh, Jesus," Cassie said. "I know exactly why. Let it go, babe."

"No. It *should* have been the highlight of the night." Bood's voice got louder, and he pointed a finger directly at Troy. "But then *this* fucker scores the goal of the fucking *century* against Philly on the same night."

Everyone laughed, and even Troy had to smile. "Sorry, man."

"Oh shit! *That* goal," Harris said. "I was just watching it again this afternoon when I was making that video of your best goals, Troy. How'd you even pull that dangle off? It was like magic."

Troy shrugged one shoulder. "Skill." The goal *had* been incredible. Even he couldn't believe he had done it when he'd watched the video.

"I wasn't impressed," Bood grumbled.

"He complained about it for *weeks*," Cassie said, then patted his arm. "Now you can score some pretty goals together."

"I guess. Hey!" Bood stood up and yelled in the direction of the beer fridge, "How many is that, Haas?"

Troy turned to see Luca Haas, frozen like a deer in headlights with his hand on the beer fridge door handle.

"I don't know. Five?" Luca said. His eyes were wide behind his glasses. Troy knew he was twenty, but he looked fifteen. He also looked flushed and tipsy.

"Uh-uh. There's iced tea in there. Drink that." Bood sat back down. "Fucking kids."

"You're gonna be a hell of a dad, Bood," Wyatt said.

"I'm tough but fair," Bood said. He gazed lovingly at his wife, then stroked her hair. "Besides. *Our* kid is going to be smart and cool as hell."

Cassie leaned in and kissed him quickly. Troy noticed that Lisa had snuggled in a little closer to Wyatt, and Nick had his arm wrapped even more tightly around Selena. Troy missed

Adrian so much in that moment, even though he had never done anything as public as snuggle next to him at a party. Would he ever be able to? With anyone?

Harris caught Troy's gaze from across the fire, and smiled. Troy managed to curve his lips a bit in a weak response.

Harris's golden hair and beard were glimmering in the firelight. He was handsome, even if he was a bit goofy. Rugged in an authentic way that Troy found surprisingly appealing. He was wearing a wool-lined corduroy jacket tonight, with a button that said *Ottawa Pride* and a pin in the shape of a hockey stick with rainbow tape.

Harris must not have a boyfriend. If he did, Troy was sure he would have brought him, or at least mentioned him by now. Harris wouldn't be ashamed to have his arm wrapped around a man at a party. He would probably stroke his hair and kiss him lovingly. Troy would bet Harris was absolutely disgusting in love, always touching his partner in fond, familiar ways. Smiling at them. Making them laugh.

For the past week, Troy hadn't been able to stop thinking about how things might have been different if he'd been brave enough to come out when he'd been with Adrian. Maybe they could have been a real couple. They could have gone to parties and movie premieres and the NHL Awards together.

Would Troy ever have that with anyone? Would he ever stop being such a fucking coward and be at least as brave as his team's social media manager? As brave as Scott Hunter, who had gotten married to the love of his life over the summer. As brave as Ryan Price, who Troy hoped was happy wherever he'd ended up.

He couldn't imagine it. Not really. Even the idea of it made his stomach twist. His father would never speak to him again, and even though that shouldn't bother Troy, it did. Curtis was a fucking asshole, and someone Troy probably should have cut out of his life years ago, but he was still his dad. And Troy was still scared of him.

The rest of the party, which until that point had been more enjoyable than Troy had been expecting, passed in a blur as he sank deeper into his private misery. By the time Harris asked if he wanted a drive back to the hotel, Troy was shocked by how late it was. He'd planned on leaving hours ago.

"Thanks," he said, when he was back in the passenger seat of Harris's truck.

"No problem. I like driving."

"I mean, yeah. Thanks for the drive. But also for getting me to go. And making me mingle a bit. It was a good idea."

Harris beamed at him. "I'm full of good ideas."

Quiet music played from the truck stereo as they drove. Troy didn't recognize the artist, but the songs were haunting and sad and not what he would expect Harris to listen to. "No country music?"

Harris chuckled. "Sometimes. I like all sorts of music."

The conversation distracted Troy from his misery, so he kept asking questions. "Who's this?"

"Fabian Salah. You don't know him?"

There was a note of surprise in Harris's question, as if he expected Troy to know who the random singer was. "Nope. It's nice, though. Pretty."

"He's Ryan Price's boyfriend."

"What?"

"Yeah. They've been dating since Ryan was playing with the Guardians."

Jesus. Troy didn't know a fucking thing about anyone, apparently. "I had no idea."

"Next time Fabian plays a show here, you should go. He's amazing live. Ryan usually travels with him, which is completely adorable. They must be super in love."

"Must be." Troy was happy to hear it, but it was also hard to hear about anyone being in love. Still, thinking about Ryan Price—a mountain of a man who was best known for punching hockey players—dating a musician with the voice of an angel was surprising. And nice.

They reached the hotel, which was a pretty long drive from Bood's and probably well out of Harris's way. He was way too fucking nice.

"Have a good sleep," Harris said. There was a note in his voice that suggested that he knew Troy wouldn't. That Troy hadn't had a good night's sleep in two weeks.

"I'll try."

Troy found it surprisingly difficult to leave the truck. It was warm and had pretty music playing and a handsome man smiling at him. Flurries danced into the lights of the hotel parking lot outside, reminding Troy that, once he opened the door, there would be nothing but cold and loneliness.

The world felt very still for a moment. Harris was studying Troy's face, green eyes glinting in the dim light, as if he expected Troy to say something important.

"Drive safe," Troy said. He opened the passenger door and stepped into the world he belonged in, closing the door firmly behind him.

CHAPTER EIGHT

After a whole pile of losses, Harris decided the best way to cheer up the team, and the fans, was with a puppy.

"Thank fucking god," Ilya said as soon as he spotted Harris and Chiron. "Bring him here."

Harris happily deposited Chiron into Ilya's arms. "He missed you."

"I know he did. Look at him." Chiron was already licking Ilya's face. "Were they good to you at the dog school?" Ilya asked the puppy. "Did you get to have fun?"

"He gets treated well at the facility. I promise. His trainer, Hannah, is awesome."

"I would like to meet this Hannah," Ilya said grimly, then softened when Chiron nuzzled his chin.

Harris snapped a couple of pictures of Ilya with Chiron, then held out his arms. Ilya very reluctantly returned the dog to him.

"He said I am his favorite," Ilya insisted.

"Only because you won't let him near anybody else." Harris set Chiron on the ground and let him run around the room a bit.

"He will be back," Ilya said confidently, but Chiron was already jumping all over Evan Dykstra.

"Just get a dog, Ilya."

"Can't. I live alone, and I am never home."

Harris couldn't argue with that. Between hockey, the charity Ilya had cofounded with Montreal's captain, Shane Hollander, and all of Ilya's other time commitments, he probably wasn't home often. Even his summers were taken up with charity hockey camps and . . . something. He was mysterious about his private life.

"Is Chiron coming on the ice?" Ilya asked.

"No, Coach told me to keep it to the dressing room only today."

"Fascist."

"Yeah. Wiebe's a real hard-ass." Brandon Wiebe was probably the most laid-back hockey coach ever.

"Team hospital visit on Wednesday, yes?" Ilya asked.

"Yup," Harris confirmed. "You gonna get your ass kicked at *Mario Kart* again?"

"No. I have been practicing."

Harris laughed. Ilya probably wasn't kidding.

Practice was starting soon, so the room was full. Everyone was putting their gear on and chatting in groups or pairs. Everyone but Troy Barrett, Harris noticed. Troy was already fully dressed and ready to go on the ice, but he was also crouched in front of his stall, offering Chiron his gloved finger. Troy didn't have his helmet on yet, and his black hair flopped over his forehead as he played with the excited puppy. When Chiron chomped down eagerly, a warm smile split Troy's face wide-open. Harris, who had been about to walk over, was suddenly frozen in place.

Troy was absolutely stunning when he smiled. And unlike the flash of smile Troy had teased him with during the Q and A, now Harris had time to admire it.

He raised his phone and quickly snapped as many candid photos as he could of Troy and Chiron. It would be good to show this softer side of Troy to the fans, Harris told himself. That was definitely what the pictures were for.

Troy glanced up at the same moment that Harris lowered his phone, and his smile faded immediately. Whether it was a reaction to Harris's presence or a general reaction to being watched at all, Harris wasn't sure. But he mourned the loss of Troy's smile.

"Hey," Harris said, crossing the floor to stand in front of him. Troy stood to meet him, and Chiron began pawing at Troy's leg.

"Hey."

Harris had been thinking about Troy almost nonstop since dropping him off at the hotel two nights ago, and now that he was faced with him, he wasn't sure what to say. He wanted to ask him if he was all right, or if he needed someone to talk to, but instead he said, "He seems to like you."

For a giddy second, Harris thought the smile might return. He could see Troy struggle to hold it back. But then Troy just said, flatly, "He likes chewing on me. Not sure that's the same thing."

Harris's answering smile was wide enough for both of them. "The video got a lot of likes, by the way. The Q and A one. I meant to tell you that the other day." He didn't mention the many replies that tore Troy apart for playing like shit and costing too much money. He was glad Troy didn't pay attention to social media much.

"Oh," Troy stepped back from the puppy, and from Harris, and Chiron pounced on his skate. "Cool."

"Most people agree with me, though. Salmon is not a treat."

"They're wrong."

Harris laughed, and gestured to where Chiron was still attacking Troy's skates. "Chiron has his own Twitter account now."

"Do you manage that too?"

"I share it with his trainer, Hannah. And with Chiron, of course."

Not even a fraction of a smile from Troy for that. His bottom lip was absurdly plump and luscious. Maybe the sharpness of the rest of his features made it seem softer by contrast. High, prominent cheekbones divided like an icebreaker by a narrow, straight nose. Severe sapphire eyes that glinted beneath heavy, dark brows. He looked menacing, or possibly even cruel, but that plush lip, like his secret, soft smile, hinted at the possibility of sweetness.

Or maybe Harris was imagining things. It wouldn't be the first time.

He wasn't imagining the deep lines under Troy's eyes, like he hadn't slept in days. Or weeks. He doubted Troy would want him to mention that, so instead Harris said, "You gonna check out that building Wyatt and Lisa told you about?"

"Yeah, I think so."

"Cool. It's not too far from me, actually."

"Oh." Troy did not seem to be excited about that news, which Harris tried not to be disappointed by. He wasn't sure what he'd been hoping for. Did he expect Troy to invite him over to watch movies or something?

Maybe Troy needed someone to watch movies with.

"If you want someone to show you the neighborho—"

"I'm gonna hit the ice," Troy interrupted. "I'll see you later."

Okay then.

"Come on, Chiron," Harris sighed. "Let's go to my office while the men do their important hockey stuff."

Troy knocked on Harris's office door, and didn't have to wait even a second before Harris called out for him to come in.

"It's just me." Troy held up the paper coffee cup he was carrying. "It's not Starbucks, but it's from the espresso maker in the player's lounge. It's a latte."

Harris looked stunned, but he smiled and waved Troy over. Chiron was asleep on the floor next to Harris's feet. "You made me a latte?"

"I hope so. I've never used that thing before." He placed the cup on Harris's desk, then realized he had no idea what his next move was. He didn't know what had compelled him to come here, except the best he'd felt in ages had been in Harris's office, watching him eat cake pops.

Harris took a sip. "You did good. That's definitely a latte. Thanks."

Troy felt absurdly thrilled by Harris's validation. "I'm sorry I was a dick to you in the locker room. When you offered to show me around. I—" He didn't know how to finish the sentence, so he stopped talking.

Harris waited for a moment, then said, "We should probably stop this cycle."

"Cycle?"

"You feeling bad about something you said to me, then showing up at my office to apologize. I don't mind the coffee deliveries, though." He pointed to a chair against the wall. "Bring that over. Sit. Unless you have somewhere to be."

Troy really didn't. He dragged the chair to the end of Harris's desk and sat. He wished he'd brought a coffee for himself, just to have something to occupy his hands.

As if reading his mind, Chiron lifted his head and immediately pushed to his feet when he noticed Troy. He trotted over, tail wagging.

"Can I pick him up?" Troy asked.

"I think he'll be sad if you don't."

Troy lifted the puppy onto his lap and scratched his ridiculously soft ears. He could see the appeal of owning a dog. It would be easy to become hooked on this level of adoration.

"What are you working on?" Troy asked.

"Making GIFs from the last game."

"How do you even make those? I've always wondered."

Harris gave him a curious look, like he thought this might be a trap. "You want me to show you? It's pretty easy."

"Yeah."

So Troy watched Harris make GIFs out of video footage of the last game. And then some from video Harris had taken during that day's practice. He didn't retain any of the process of making GIFs, but he did enjoy listening to Harris's cheerful, warm voice, and watching his green eyes dance whenever he looked at Troy. He knew Harris probably didn't actually smell like apples, but he couldn't get the idea out of his head. He swore he smelled apples whenever he was close to the man.

"Um," Harris said, "I posted a photo of you earlier that has gotten a lot of likes."

"From practice?"

"From before. Here, I'll show you."

Harris held out his phone, and Troy saw a photo of himself in the locker room, crouched down and smiling at Chiron.

"Oh," he said, because he hadn't seen many pictures of himself smiling like that. He couldn't believe he was *able* to smile like that these days. "People just like the puppy. Anyone can get likes with a cute puppy."

"That's not what the comments say."

"Don't tell me what the comments say."

"Okay," Harris said. Then he bit his lip, and Troy could tell it was killing him not to read them.

"I'm serious."

"Fine. I won't tell you that everyone thinks you're adorable and sexy."

Troy huffed. "I doubt it."

"I can read them if you—"

"No. That's okay." Troy felt his cheeks heat, and he ducked his head to hide it. "Adorable, huh?"

"Yup."

Troy was sure he'd never been called adorable in his life. He absently rubbed Chiron's belly, and wondered if Harris thought he was adorable. Or sexy.

For a few minutes, Harris worked while Troy kept his attention on the puppy in his lap. Then Harris swiveled in his desk chair and said, carefully, "How have things been going?"

Troy exhaled harder than he'd meant to. It startled Chiron. "You've seen the games. I'm playing like shit."

Harris looked like he wanted to argue, but obviously he couldn't. "Is there a reason? I mean, sorry. That's a really personal question. But I'm a good listener, if you want to talk."

Troy wasn't sure what to say. He hadn't come here to talk. Not really. He liked being near Harris, that was all. He was a calming presence. Something nice to distract Troy from all the shitty things in his life. And he didn't want to think about the shitty things right now.

"Or," Harris said with a shy smile, "you're welcome to stay here and cuddle Chiron while I quietly do my work."

It was staggering how Harris had just casually offered Troy exactly what he needed. Troy managed a slight smile. "Do you do *anything* quietly?"

Harris laughed—loudly, of course. "I'll try."

Harris found it distracting, having Troy Barrett in his office. It was hard to get any work done when one of the most beautiful men in the NHL was snuggling a puppy a few feet away.

Why was Troy Barrett in his office? Something was on his mind, obviously. And he clearly had no interest in talking about it. Maybe it was nothing more than the stress of being traded, of not being able to play at his usual level. Maybe it was the Dallas Kent stuff. Had Troy talked to *anyone* about that? Like, *really* talked?

Whatever was bothering him, it still didn't explain why he'd brought Harris another coffee. Why he was here at all.

After about half an hour of pretending to work, Harris pushed back from his desk and stretched. "I'm going to take Chiron for a little walk before Hannah comes to pick him up."

Chiron had almost fallen asleep in Troy's lap, but he perked up at the word *walk*. Harris grabbed his coat and Chiron's leash off a hook by the door, then turned to Troy. "You can come if you want."

Troy's face lit up as much as, Harris suspected, Troy's face ever lit up. "I'll get my coat."

The walking options near the arena weren't great, but the parking lot was huge and empty, so they strolled the perimeter of it. Troy held Chiron's leash and patiently let the puppy sniff every rock, puddle, and crumpled Tim Hortons cup they passed.

"I've never walked a dog before," he said.

Harris stopped dead. "Seriously?"

"Yeah. Never had one, never looked after anyone else's."

"Well? What do you think?"

"It's all right." The way Troy was looking at Chiron—not smiling, of course, but with definite amusement in his eyes—told Harris that he was enjoying the experience more than he was letting on.

It was a reasonably nice day for Ottawa in early December. Cold, but sunny and calm after a drizzly, windy night. Harris spent way too much of his life indoors these days. Mostly in front of a computer, or looking at his phone. "Has anyone ever said anything to you? About being gay?" Troy asked out of nowhere.

Harris had no idea why he was asking, or even *what* he was asking, but he said, "You mean given me shit about it?"

"Yeah."

"Of course. But no one I care about. Why?"

Troy didn't reply, seemingly as interested in a soggy McDonald's straw wrapper as Chiron was. Then he said, to the straw wrapper, "Anyone on the team? Or in the organization?"

"No one," Harris said. "Like I said, this is a good group. I've never hidden being gay, and no one here has ever made me feel like I needed to."

"That's good."

They walked to the end of one side of the parking lot, then turned the corner and started on the next. "I'm guessing things were different in Toronto?" Harris asked.

Troy's jaw clenched, and he nodded. "A lot of slurs and stuff. I can't pretend I wasn't contributing to it."

Harris was disappointed to hear it, but he wasn't surprised. "You gonna keep contributing to it?"

"No." Troy stopped walking. Chiron seemed confused, and walked back to bump his nose against Troy's sneaker. "I was a complete fucking asshole in Toronto. I know it. Everyone here seems so, like, *good* . . . I shouldn't be here."

Harris was tempted to put a hand on his arm, so he shoved his hands in his coat pockets instead. "Do you hate it here?"

"Not as much as I thought I would."

Harris chuckled at that. "Glad to hear it." He started walking again, and Troy joined him. "For what it's worth, I think you'll fit in just fine."

"You don't think I'm an asshole?"

Harris bit the inside of his cheek, then said, "Not as much as I thought I would."

Troy made a huffing sound—not quite a laugh—and Harris

nudged him playfully. Troy didn't return it, but his mouth was fighting a smile.

Then Troy handed him the leash. "I should go. Gotta nap, y'know. Before the game."

"Oh. Okay. Sure. I'll see you—"

But Troy was already jogging away, toward the hotel. And Harris was left to stare after him, wondering what exactly Troy's deal was.

CHAPTER NINE

Troy wasn't sure why he was doing this. The last thing hospitalized children needed was to be forced to spend even five seconds with him.

But here he was, at a children's hospital in Ottawa, wearing a Centaurs jersey and ball cap and holding a small stack of postcards of himself and a Sharpie.

He'd been paired up with Wyatt, which was good because the kids would probably be way too excited about meeting the star goaltender to even look at Troy.

"They're probably bored of me," Wyatt said, contradicting everything Troy was thinking. "The long-term patients anyway. I'm here a lot because Lisa works here."

Right.

Troy followed Wyatt into the first room they were visiting. It had two beds, both occupied by very young children who were hooked up to machines, and Troy wanted to leave immediately.

He focused on the parents who were standing beside the beds. They were smiling, obviously thrilled to see Wyatt and Troy, so maybe things weren't so bad, right?

"Jenny," Wyatt said, giving one of the women standing beside one of the beds a hug. Then he turned his attention to the little boy in the bed. "Danny. What's up, man?" He held out his fist, and Danny bumped it more heartily than Troy would have expected.

Wyatt went to the other bed, all smiles, and said, "We haven't met yet. I'm Wyatt. Would you like to tell me your name?"

"Nathan."

"Nice to meet you, Nathan. Would you like a fist bump?"

"Okay." The kid held out his fist—the one that didn't have an IV connected to it—and Wyatt gently bumped it. He turned to the father and shook his hand, chatting pleasantly with him for a moment before turning his attention back to both kids.

Troy was happy to linger near the door and just watch Wyatt put on a clinic on how to talk to sick kids. He noted the way Wyatt asked permission directly from the kids before he did anything.

"Would you like to meet my newest teammate?" Wyatt asked, and both kids nodded.

Nathan's dad said, "Yeah!"

Troy held up his hand in an awkward wave. "Hi."

"This is Troy Barrett," Wyatt said. "He used to play for Toronto like me."

"Boooooo!" said Danny.

Wyatt pointed at him. "Exactly! Boo, Toronto! Right, Troy?"

Troy managed something close to a smile. "Yep. Boo." He took a step toward Nathan's dad, because he seemed enthusiastic about meeting him, and extended his hand. "Troy. Nice to meet you."

"Greg. I'm a big fan. We're excited you're here in Ottawa now."

The pleasure that fizzed through Troy's body at this basic compliment was startling and ridiculous. "Excited to be here," he mumbled, then turned to the kid, Nathan. "Are you a hockey fan, Nathan?"

"Yeah," Nathan said quietly.

"Do you, um, want an autograph? I have postcards." Troy held up the stack. Christ. Could he have sounded more like he wanted to get this over with?

But Nathan looked thrilled by his offer. "Okay!"

Troy's handwriting was terrible, but he tried his hardest to write legibly when he scrawled *To my friend Nathan.* Then he added his mess of a signature and, after a moment's hesitation, a little happy face. Because maybe he could be the kind of guy who drew little happy faces next to his autograph.

He handed the postcard to Nathan, who smiled and immediately showed it to his dad, Greg. "Wow, that's awesome, Nate," his father said, as if he hadn't just watched Troy sign the thing. Jesus, what that man was probably going through.

"Would you like one?" Troy asked him.

"Oh." Greg looked embarrassed, but Troy could also tell he *really* wanted to say yes. "You should save them for the kids. Y'know."

"I have tons. Here."

Troy signed the next postcard. He wasn't sure if he should write anything else. He wanted to write a whole essay telling Greg he was a great father, and Troy was in awe of him. And he wasn't *jealous* of a hospitalized kid, but he couldn't imagine his own father looking at him so lovingly. His own father had, in fact, come to the hospital to detail all the ways Troy could have avoided breaking his leg when Troy had been hospitalized at eleven. He'd also had some racist things to say about the kid who'd accidentally caused Troy to fall on his twisted leg. Then he'd taken a work call and abruptly left.

Troy decided to add *Greg* with a cheerful exclamation mark before his signature, then handed the postcard to him. "Thanks so much," Greg said, beaming at the little piece of card stock like it would solve all of his problems. Troy wished it could.

Wyatt crossed over to Nathan's bed and reached into a large tote bag he'd brought with him. "Do you like comic books, Nathan?"

Nathan nodded.

"Who is your favorite superhero?"

"Ninja Turtles."

Wyatt grinned and rooted through the bag, producing two colorful *Ninja Turtles* comics. "You'll share with Danny, right?" he said as he handed them to him. "I gave him *Teen Titans Go!* comics."

"I love *Teen Titans Go!*" Nathan said, smiling at Danny across the room. "Who's your favorite?"

"Beast Boy," Danny said.

"Me too!"

"If Luca Haas comes in here, you should get him to draw you Beast Boy. He's a good drawer."

"Really?" Danny asked.

"Luca Haas is here too?" Nathan gasped.

"Oh yeah," Wyatt said. "We're just the opening act. Ilya Rozanov is here, and Zane Boodram. Evan Dykstra. All the important guys."

Troy huffed a laugh at the way Wyatt was selling them short. He and Wyatt were both at the All-Star game last year, and Wyatt was probably going to go again this year.

"And," Wyatt said in a theatrical whisper, "Chuck is here too."

The kids' smiles grew even wider. Chuck was the official Ottawa Centaurs team mascot, and he was, for whatever reason, a beaver. But, like all team mascots, he was a bigger celebrity with kids than the players.

"Did somebody say *Chuck*?" asked a cheerful, booming

voice. Troy turned and saw Harris standing in the doorway, a giant beaver wearing a hockey jersey standing behind him.

Troy stepped aside to make way for Chuck. Harris smiled at him, and Troy couldn't help but smile back. There were now way too many people crowded into the room, but no one seemed to mind. Chuck did his thing with the kids, silently offering high fives and doing big reactions that looked ridiculous with his huge, frozen, bug-eyed face.

"How's it going?" Harris asked Troy quietly.

"Not bad. Wyatt is good at this."

"He's the master."

"Chuck's good at this too," Troy said. He might be uncomfortable, but at least he wasn't wearing an awkward, heavy beaver costume.

"Oh yeah. I'll introduce you to Theo sometime. He's great."

"Theo?"

"The guy in the suit." Harris narrowed his eyes playfully. "You *do* know there's someone in that suit, right?"

"Shut up."

"We tried to hire a seven-foot beaver for the job but, let me tell you, it did *not* go well."

Troy snorted, then tried to cover it up. "You suck."

Harris nudged him. "Let's take some pictures."

Troy smiled—really smiled—in every photo Harris took at the hospital that day. Harris found himself hesitating to return the phones to the parents, hoping they appreciated the rare gift of Troy Barrett's full, effortless smile.

It was a hectic couple of hours, Harris darting from room to room to help with photographs, and capturing some candid shots and videos for the team's social media as well. He wanted to make sure he got at least one photo of each of the players.

But he kept gravitating to the rooms where Troy and Wyatt

were. Sometimes he would watch silently from the door for a minute, sneakily observing Troy with the kids. He was doing great, despite being unpracticed in this sort of thing.

Harris remembered the Ottawa Centaurs visiting the hospital when he was twelve. It had been thrilling to meet real NHL players. It had been thrilling to do *anything* other than sleep, or read, or stare at the ceiling. At least one of his family members had been beside his bed at all times, usually more. Friends had visited too, but meeting his heroes—in particular the team captain, who he'd had a bit of a crush on—had given him a high that he'd ridden for days after. He knew now that NHL players were just people, but back then they'd seemed like gods. He couldn't believe they were actually in his hospital room, talking to him.

Now, in the patients' lounge, Harris watched Troy and Ilya battle each other and two kids at *Mario Kart*. Ilya was trash-talking—without profanity—and making everyone laugh. Troy had just barely stopped himself from swearing several times.

"I have a present for you, Barrett," Ilya said.

"F—" Troy cut himself off. "I don't want it, Rozanov."

"It's red."

"Shoot it at a computer player!"

"Nah. It's for you." Everyone laughed as a red Koopa shell slammed into Troy's car. Mario went ass over teakettle and Troy, again, struggled not to swear.

"You're the worst," Troy grumbled.

"Didn't I hit you like that last year?" Ilya teased. "In Toronto. You did the same thing Mario just did." He rolled one hand in a tumbling motion, then quickly returned it to the controller.

"No," Troy said.

Within seconds one of the kids found the hit on YouTube and gleefully showed everyone her iPad so they could see it.

"Thank you, Grayson," Ilya said. "See, Barrett? Just like Mario."

Ilya won the race, and he stood with his arms above his head in victory. "Undefeated!"

Gloating about beating a bunch of hospitalized kids at video games should be rude, but somehow Ilya made it charming.

Troy stood and handed his controller to Wyatt. He shuffled awkwardly to the side, and glanced around the room as if unsure what to do now. When his gaze landed on Harris, he smiled in that same genuine way that Harris had been enjoying all day.

This time, Troy's smile was just for him, and Harris couldn't help the way his stomach flipped in response. Developing a crush on Troy Barrett was a terrible idea, but Harris was way past the point of being able to stop it.

Late in the afternoon, the players boarded the team bus that would take them back to the arena. They'd left directly from their morning practice.

Harris caught Troy before he boarded the bus. "I'll see you tomorrow, I guess."

"Before the game. Definitely."

Harris wanted to ask him what he was doing tonight, but that wouldn't do anything to help quell this ridiculous crush. So instead, he offered some reassurance. "You did great, by the way. With the kids."

Troy's lips curved into a soft smile at that. "Yeah?"

"Trust me. I'm an expert."

Something warm glowed in Troy's sapphire eyes. "You drove yourself here?"

"I got a ride in the van with Theo and Rebecca." Troy's blank expression told Harris that he didn't know who he was talking about. "Chuck, I mean. That's Theo, like I said earlier. And Rebecca is basically his handler. She's a marketing intern."

"Ah." Troy glanced around. "Does Chuck—I mean Theo—have to get changed somewhere or . . . how does that work exactly?"

Harris laughed. "Very carefully. We can't let anyone see him half dressed, y'know? Ruins the magic. He'll wear the costume in the van until we're out of the parking lot at least."

"Sounds complicated."

"Theo's got it down to a science."

Troy glanced at the bus, which seemed to have everyone but him on it now. "Well. I should . . ."

"Yeah. See you tomorrow."

For a moment, both men just stared at each other, Harris beaming and Troy's lips curving slightly upward. His gaze dropped to Harris's mouth, then back to his eyes.

Then he blinked and said, "See you later, Harris."

He got on the bus without looking back, and Harris sauntered over to the van, where a giant beaver was probably waiting for him.

CHAPTER TEN

Over the next week, Harris was visited by Troy three times. He felt like Ebenezer Scrooge, except instead of spirits, he got a sullen hockey player who was, like, the Ghost of Christmas Mixed Messages.

He appeared and disappeared as suddenly as a ghost, that was for sure. But he always brought coffee, and Harris didn't mind having him around. Even though he continued to be distractingly hot.

Sometimes Troy would ask questions. Sometimes he would ask *weird* questions out of the blue that had nothing to do with Harris's job.

"Have you ever brought, like, a date to any hockey stuff? Team parties or whatever?"

That was today's random question. Harris paused, mid-email. "Usually I'm pretty busy working at official team events, but there were a couple of house parties where I brought someone."

Troy didn't reply, so Harris went back to writing his email.

"Like, a boyfriend? You brought a boyfriend?"

Harris turned in his chair. "More like guys I was hoping would be my boyfriend. Why?"

"Everyone was cool with it?"

Troy seemed to ask a lot of variations of this same question. "As far as I could tell. It's not like we were making out wildly. I might have kissed them quickly. Maybe sat with an arm around them."

Troy was absolutely destroying his coffee cup lid. He'd folded it in half twice somehow, and Harris was worried he was going to cut himself on the jagged plastic. "Do you worry about it? People judging you. Like, when you're in a group of straight people?"

Harris wanted to say that he didn't worry about it at all, but it wasn't exactly true. "Sometimes, I guess. I've been lucky with the support I've gotten from my family and friends, so I don't worry about it as much as some people, but sure. There's always something in the back of my head that puts me on edge a bit. Especially if I don't know everyone in the room."

Troy let the coffee lid pop back out into a rough-looking circle, then began folding it again. "How do you—" He sighed. "Do you just tell that thing in the back of your head to shut up or something?"

"Basically." Harris carefully reached out and took the lid from Troy's hands. He tossed it into the trash can by his desk. "I try to do what feels right to me. What's honest, y'know? And if someone has a problem with it, well, we were never going to be friends anyway."

Troy was staring at his empty hands, frowning. "That's good," he said, though he sounded miserable. "Why didn't they want to be your boyfriend?"

Harris was beyond confused now. "Who?"

"The guys that you brought to parties. That you said you'd hoped would be your boyfriend."

"Oh." Harris flushed. "I don't know. Different reasons, probably."

"You should have a boyfriend." Now it was Troy's turn to blush, which was so cute Harris couldn't stand it. "I mean. There's no reason why you shouldn't. Um." He chewed his lip nervously, and Harris was going to die. "You're, like, nice. And not, y'know, ugly."

Harris laughed. "Jesus. Thanks."

"No, I mean—" Troy's eyes were wide with horror, like he couldn't believe he'd just said that. Harris kept laughing until suddenly, miraculously, Troy joined him. It started as a shaky exhale that formed into full-blown laughter. Troy's eyes crinkled and his wonderful, rare smile spread across his face.

"Forget I said anything," Troy said, though he was still smiling. "I don't know what I was trying to say."

Harris didn't either, because at the moment he was completely dazed by Troy's smile and couldn't remember any words at all. It wasn't until Troy's face fell back into its usual blank frown that Harris was able to say, "I've had a couple of boyfriends. Real ones. But not for a while now. I mostly use a dating app, but not many of those dates have led to a second one lately."

"Oh." Troy looked like he'd really like his coffee cup lid back. "Are they mostly for, um."

"Sex?" Harris offered. "Sometimes. I like talking to people, though, as you've probably noticed. I like getting to know someone. So I'm usually hoping for more, but if it's just a hookup, that's cool too. Sometimes that's all I need anyway."

Troy looked like he had something lodged in his throat. Harris watched his Adam's apple bob as he swallowed hard. He had no idea why Troy was asking him all these questions about his gay dating life if it made him uncomfortable.

Well, there was one possibility, but Harris was trying not to think about it too much. If Troy was working out his own sexuality, Harris didn't want to push him. He also didn't want to get his own hopes up.

"What about you?" Harris asked carefully. "Do you date much?"

Troy stood. "I should let you work."

"No, it's fine. I'm almost—"

"I need to—"

Troy didn't even finish his sentence. He just darted out the door, as he always did, leaving Harris to replay the conversation and wonder what exactly Troy wanted from him.

Troy opened his browser on his phone and typed *fun things to do in Ottawa*. The results were mostly museums, tours of Parliament and other historic buildings, and going to an Ottawa Centaurs game. Not great.

The team was heading out on the road tomorrow morning, starting with a game in Toronto.

Toronto.

It was early in the evening now, but Troy could already tell he was going to have trouble sleeping. He needed a distraction.

He tried *Ottawa nightlife* instead. There were clubs, live music venues, sports bars, and several other places Troy didn't want to be. He didn't know what he wanted. Maybe just a chill pub where he could sit alone and nurse a beer. Somewhere he could people watch without having to interact with any of them.

He chewed his lip, then typed *Ottawa gay bar*. He didn't know why he did it; there was no way he was going to one. If he went to a gay bar alone in a city he would definitely be recognized in, he may as well start wearing Pride pins on his jacket like Harris did.

Harris was probably at one of those bars right now, surrounded by friends and laughing that earsplitting, bellowing laugh that Troy should hate way more than he did.

Maybe Harris was on a date. Using that app of his. Troy had never tried online dating, or a hookup app, or anything like that.

It would probably be a good idea, if he ever got brave about his sexuality. He was going to have to figure *something* out, because he hadn't had sex in months, and while he was used to droughts, at least with Adrian there had been regular FaceTime sex.

Troy put his phone on the nightstand, then paced the hotel room. He needed to get out of here. He knew he wasn't going to get laid tonight, but he could do *something* to distract himself from his churning stomach.

He wasn't ready to face his old team. Tomorrow he would travel to Toronto, walk into his old arena, and go to the visiting team dressing room. He would put on his Ottawa gear and skate out onto his former home ice in front of his former home crowd and compete against his former teammates. Against Dallas Kent.

Troy would be booed by the fans who used to love him. He expected that. He would be taunted and roughed up by men who had, until very recently, been his family. He would need to trust his new teammates to have his back, and he wasn't sure he had earned that yet. He wasn't sure he ever would.

He shouldn't text Harris. He'd bothered that guy enough this week, and he was aware of how weird it was. Troy's brain was a whirling mess and it only ever settled when he was sitting in Harris's office, listening to him type. Soaking up his smiles and enjoying his implausible apple scent that Troy was definitely imagining.

What time was it in Singapore right now? That's where his mom was. Yesterday she'd sent a photo of his figurine in front of that giant building with the park on top. He picked up his phone to Google the time difference and found a text message.

HARRIS:

Are you nervous about tomorrow night?

Troy sat on the bed, staring at the message. On the one hand, it was kind of a stupid question; of course Troy was nervous. On the other, the fact that Harris had been thinking enough about him to send this text made his throat tighten.

He decided to be honest.

TROY:
I'm a wreck right now.

HARRIS:
Wanna drive around and look at Christmas lights?

"What the fuck?" Troy said into the empty room. He wasn't seven years old. Why would he want to look at Christmas lights?

Except he liked the idea of being in Harris's truck, listening to whatever music Harris was in the mood for and seeing what his eyes looked like with Christmas lights reflected in them.

TROY:
Ok.

When Troy got into the truck half an hour later, he definitely smelled apples. But Harris had an explanation ready.

"Brought some warm cider for you." He gestured to the two travel mugs nestled into the cup holders between the seats.

"Drover family apples?" Troy asked. When was the last time he'd had warm apple cider? Probably around the last time he'd taken a drive explicitly to look at Christmas lights.

"You know it." Harris's smile was wide and bright, and Troy knew he was staring, but he couldn't look away. He was so *cute*, bundled into a festive dark green scarf that was patterned with white snowflakes. Quiet Christmas music played from the stereo.

"You're really into Christmas, huh?" Troy said.

"Buddy. You have no idea." Harris pulled out of the hotel parking lot. "You're not?"

"Not really. I don't think I've ever voluntarily listened to Christmas music."

"You can turn it off if you like. I don't mind."

Troy was already being a massive dick. Great. "No, it's nice. Festive, y'know?" It *was* nice. To make up for being an ass, he took a sip of the cider. "Shit. This is good."

"Mulled it myself!"

"Is that, like . . . what is that? What's mulling?"

"Basically just warming it with spices and stuff."

Troy took another sip. It was sweet, but it was also spicy and comforting and wonderful, and it soothed him like medicine.

"I do it in the slow cooker," Harris explained. "Then I come home to an amazing-smelling apartment. Do you have a slow cooker?"

"No. I live in a hotel room."

"Yeah, I know but, like, will you have one when you move into an apartment? Did you used to have one?"

"I barely even know what a slow cooker is."

"Oh man, they're great. They cook stuff slowly."

Troy was really glad he'd agreed to come. He felt better already, listening to Harris say stupid, adorable things. "Why is that good? Don't you want things to cook faster?"

"So you can come home to a meal that's been cooking all day! It's like a little husband."

That actually made Troy laugh. "That's bleak."

"Said like someone who's never known the love of a slow cooker."

"I don't want to hear how you thank the slow cooker for dinner."

Harris laughed so hard Troy thought they were going to drive off the road. "It's the best relationship I've ever been in. Easily."

They got on the highway, which Troy thought was weird but didn't say anything about it. Frankly he didn't care if they saw a single Christmas light. He was just enjoying the ride.

Harris hummed along to "Winter Wonderland" while Troy sipped his cider and tried not to find everything about Harris painfully charming.

"Is this what you do for fun?" Troy asked. "Look at Christmas lights?"

"Well, not in the summer," Harris said dryly.

Troy checked himself. He was being a dick again. "What do you do normally? For fun."

"Lots of stuff. I go out a lot. Or at least I go out as much as I can these days. This job keeps me pretty busy. Wyatt hosts a monthly board game night at his place, so I go to those usually."

Troy almost laughed. Did his new teammates really get together to play board games? "Like, what? Monopoly?"

"Usually games like Settlers of Catan or Ticket to Ride."

Troy had not heard of those, but they sounded nerdy as hell. "Where do you go when you go out?"

"Lots of places. I like live music, so I go to a lot of shows. I go to gay bars. Not clubs very often. I'm more of a pub guy. How about you?"

"Pubs, I guess. I don't go out much."

"Unless some weirdo invites you to look at Christmas lights?" Harris teased.

Troy's lips twitched. "Apparently."

"Are you going to see your family at Christmas?"

"Nope." Troy didn't like talking about his family, but for

some reason he said, "My parents are divorced. Kind of a messy one. Mom is traveling and Dad is basically a giant asshole."

"Oh."

"He has a new wife, too, and she's barely older than me. So."

"Awkward Christmas."

"Yeah. I'm not sad to miss it. I haven't cared about the holidays in years." It wasn't exactly true. Last year Adrian had surprised Troy in Toronto on Christmas Eve, and they'd had a really excellent couple of days together. Their celebrations weren't exactly traditional, though.

There was a silence for a few seconds, and then Harris asked, "Did you see your dad when you were in Vancouver?"

"Yup. He still sucks."

"Sorry."

Troy could imagine what Curtis Barrett would say if he saw his son riding around Ottawa with a gay man, looking at Christmas lights. "Whatever. Fuck him."

"That's a good attitude," Harris said. "Toxic people aren't worth your energy."

"I'm starting to figure that out," Troy said to the window. The highway was dark, and he actually wouldn't mind some festive lights to look at right now.

"What about your mom? Is she cool?"

"She's great. She's . . ." Troy sighed. "She was miserable, after Dad left her. And I was too busy with hockey to do much except give her money. Buy her a new place to live in Vancouver. That sort of thing."

"That doesn't exactly sound useless."

Troy knew she'd appreciated the help, but he'd wished he could have done more for her. "Anyway. She's good now. She met a nice, quiet guy named Charlie who treats her well and makes her smile. So now they're traveling the world together. Been gone for almost three months."

"That's awesome. I'll bet you miss her, though."

"Yeah. A lot."

There was silence between them for a moment, then Harris said, "Can I ask you something? About that dickbag you used to be teammates with?"

Troy almost laughed. "Sure."

"I can't really—like, he doesn't exactly hide the fact that he's—"

"A dickbag?" Troy offered.

"Right. Why were you friends with him?"

Troy sighed. He didn't want to talk about this, but he also kind of did. There was something about Harris that made him want to share. "We were rookies the same year. Roommates. I knew he was a dick, but he was also exactly the kind of guy my dad loved. So part of it might have been me recognizing him as a guy I should want to be friends with."

"You must have liked him, too, though. At least a bit."

"I did," Troy admitted. "He was fun. Liked to party, liked to spend his money. Loved hockey, and being an NHL star. We would talk about all the cups we were going to win together. All the records we were going to break. The cars we were going to buy." Dallas had also talked about sex and women a lot, while Troy had awkwardly tried to contribute, but he didn't tell Harris about that. "We were close. Until a few weeks ago, he was my best friend. I know it's fucked up, but that's how it was."

"Have you talked to him since?"

Troy huffed. "No."

"Jeez. I've never liked that guy, and I think you did the right thing and are better off without him, but I'm sorry you lost your friend. That's rough."

"Thank you," Troy said quietly. It was nice to have someone acknowledge the loss he felt for his former friendship, and to make it seem less shameful. "I didn't witness anything. I never actually saw him assault anyone. I feel stupid, but it didn't even occur to me that he would do that. Until I read those posts."

"You believed them right away?"

"Yeah. It was a punch in the fucking gut, but yeah. I believed them."

"Sorry," Harris said again.

Troy exhaled and released some of the tension that was making his jaw ache. "So where are we going?" he asked, wanting to change the subject.

"Taffy Lane."

"Taffy Lane? Where's that? Is that a real street name?"

"Oh man. Just wait. It's in Orleans and they go *all out* every year. It's a total Christmas wonderland."

Troy couldn't wait to see what that meant. So he drank his cider and let a jolly bearded man take him to Christmas wonderland.

Taffy Lane was *hideous*. But also, kind of great.

"How much are these guys spending on electricity?" Troy asked as they slowly drove past a house that must have had tens of thousands of lights all over their house and front yard. There were also several generators running, keeping the cartoon characters on the lawn inflated.

"A lot," Harris said, grinning.

"Why is there Darth Vader? What does he have to do with Christmas?"

"His lightsaber is candy cane striped. See?"

"Yeah, but . . ."

"Don't question someone's Christmas vision. Just enjoy it."

Troy frowned at the allegedly festive Darth Vader. Troy wasn't a *nerd* or anything, but he knew enough about *Star Wars* to say, with authority, that Darth Vader was not an appropriate Christmas decoration.

"He blew up a planet," Troy argued.

"Yeah, but he felt bad about it after. Eventually."

It was such a ridiculous debate, but Troy couldn't let it go. "Too little too late. He should have tossed the emperor into that pit sooner."

Harris laughed. "You are such a geek. Wow. I had no idea."

"No I'm not. I saw those movies, like, twice. That's fucking normal."

"I prefer to applaud Vader's heroic decision to stand up to his evil friend, no matter how long it took him," Harris said. He caught Troy's eye after he said it, as if making sure Troy got his point.

Troy shifted uneasily in his seat. He got it.

"Still a stupid Christmas decoration," he grumbled.

They drove to the end of Taffy Lane, which took a while since they were in a line of cars that was crawling along. Then Harris drove them around some other nearby streets, which also had some decent decorations but nothing on the level of Taffy Lane.

"I don't like the light projections," Troy declared when they were halfway down their fourth or fifth street. "It's lazy."

"I hear ya. But combined with other lights, they look pretty cool."

"It's too much. I like houses like that one." Troy gestured to a small house with a pointy roof. Lights outlined the gables, windows, door, front porch, and the sides of the front of the house from ground to roof. There was a big wreath with a red bow hanging on the door. "That's classic, right there. Like, that's the kind of house I'd want to spend Christmas in."

"That's sort of how my parents decorate our house," Harris said.

Troy could imagine the Drover family farmhouse, sitting perfect and pretty in the middle of a snow-covered apple orchard. That house was probably bursting at the seams with overly loud laughter and love during holidays. "Sounds nice."

"You should come over on Christmas. The dinner is always

amazing. My folks would be happy to have you." Harris made the offer easily, as if it wasn't one of the kindest invitations Troy had ever received. But there was no way someone as miserable as Troy should be tainting anyone's Christmas festivities, much less a family's as perfect as Harris's probably was.

"I can't. I'm moving into that apartment two days before Christmas and I'm going to just, y'know, get myself settled in there."

"Offer stands if you change your mind."

"Thanks." They were at a stop sign, and their gazes locked for a moment. Harris's eyes reflected the twinkling lights all around them, and his smile was so warm and lovely that Troy felt a sudden and intense desire to kiss him.

Instead, he looked away. "I should probably get back. Long day tomorrow."

"Sure," Harris said. "Hope this helped a bit with your nerves."

"It did." Troy knew as soon as he was alone again, all of his anxieties about tomorrow would come rushing back, but that wasn't a good enough reason to keep taking up Harris's time. Also, he needed to get his urge to kiss him under control.

As they merged on to the highway, Mariah Carey's "All I Want for Christmas Is You" started playing, which didn't help. The situation was made worse when Harris started singing along.

Troy hadn't even known Harris for a month. In fact, he barely knew him at all. Why was he so drawn to him? He was nothing like any of the men Troy had been secretly attracted to before. He was nothing like Adrian. He wasn't even the kind of guy Troy would normally be *friends* with.

But as he watched the absolute goofball in the driver's seat cheerfully dueting with Mariah Carey, he couldn't deny how badly he wanted him. For his own. More than Harris could ever, ever, *ever* know.

CHAPTER ELEVEN

Troy had never been in the visiting team's dressing room in Toronto before, and he didn't like it. Everything about being in this building—this city—again was unsettling. He sat in his stall, wearing his Ottawa Centaurs uniform, and tried not to let his face show the panic that was tearing him up inside.

He couldn't do this. He couldn't go out there.

Maybe if he hadn't been playing like shit since he'd been traded. Maybe if Dallas Kent hadn't been on fire all season. Maybe if Troy wasn't returning as a member of the Ottawa fucking Centaurs.

God, he felt sick.

"Walk with me." Troy glanced up and saw Ilya standing over him.

He obeyed his captain, standing and following him into the hallway.

"You are nervous," Ilya said as soon as they were alone.

"A little."

"No. Not a little. What do you need?"

Troy shook his head. "I don't know. I'm not ready."

"You are not facing them alone. We are with you. We have your back, Barrett."

Troy managed to hold his gaze for a few seconds before looking away. In truth, he wasn't confident that his new team did have his back. "Thanks."

"You don't believe me."

Troy shrugged one shoulder. "I wouldn't blame you if you didn't have my back."

Ilya stared hard at him, then let out a huff of exasperated laughter. "Cheer the fuck up, Barrett. We don't hate you, you know."

"No?"

"No. Everyone on the other team hates you. Dallas Kent hates you. Everyone in the crowd hates you."

"All right, I get it."

"No one on our team hates you. And we want to beat Toronto as much as you do."

Troy stared at his skates, embarrassed and a little bit touched.

"Okay?" Ilya asked.

"Okay."

Ilya punched Troy's padded shoulder. "I have been looking forward to knocking Dallas Kent on his ass. It has been a while."

Troy managed a bit of a smile. His stomach felt calmer than it had before their talk. "I've been wanting to do it for years."

The crowd booed every time Troy touched the puck.

They fucking *booed* him. And they cheered on a sexual predator. What the fuck was wrong with the world?

His former teammates were even worse, snarling insults at him every chance they got. Dallas seemed to be on a mission to spend as much of this game as possible attacking Troy. Dallas's gray-blue eyes flashed with hatred every time he looked at him, and it made Troy furious. How dare this fucker feel anything but shame?

By the middle of the first period, Troy was channeling all of his rage into his game. He played fast, aggressive hockey, the kind he was known for. He went hard to the net, took bodies in the corners, and never stopped battling.

It didn't matter. Toronto was still all over them. Dallas had a goal and an assist already.

"Merry Christmas, bitch," he sneered at Troy after he scored.

Dallas had practically spat every word he said to Troy during the game. And then he'd punctuate it by literally spitting.

"How's it feel to lose everything, traitor?" Kent asked him after a whistle in the second period.

"You're going to *really* lose everything, one day," Troy warned. "I can't fucking wait."

Dallas shoved him. "Your dad must be pissed. He likes me way more than he likes you."

Troy shoved him back. "Because you're both shitheads."

The ref broke them apart, but Dallas got one last dig in. "You fucked yourself, Barrett. Was it worth it?"

Troy skated away without answering.

In the third period, Troy *scored a fucking goal.* Finally. It was off a perfect pass from Ilya, and watching the puck sail past the goalie felt fucking incredible. The crowd booed louder than ever, but Troy didn't care. He was too busy hugging his new teammates.

"Tell your dad I said hi," Dallas said as Troy skated past him.

"That sounds like you want to fuck my dad," Troy shot back.

Dallas looked horrified. "Blow me, fuckhead."

"That sounds like you want to fuck *me.*"

"You wish," Dallas yelled after him. "That's probably why you're so mad, right? You wanted this dick, you disgusting fucking—"

He didn't get the last word out because Ilya had laid him out on the ice. Dallas was on his back, stunned. Then he started flailing his arms, gesturing wildly toward Ilya. "Hey, ref! What the fuck! You see this fucking psychopath?"

"Shut the fuck up, Kent," Ilya said in a low, dangerous tone.

"Why? Is Barrett your boyfriend? Did you take a break from fucking Hollander to shove your dick in Barrett's—"

Ilya hauled Dallas up by his jersey, yanking him roughly until he was fully standing. Then Ilya shook his other glove off and punched him in the face.

"Holy shit," Troy muttered.

The refs, who had been taking their time breaking things up between Ilya and Dallas considering this was all during a stop in play and very illegal, came rushing in. Ilya was swiftly handed a game misconduct, but he didn't seem to mind. He winked at Troy before he left the ice.

During the final minute of play, Troy was battling Dallas in a corner for the puck. He could already see the bruise forming on Dallas's cheek where Ilya had punched him.

Troy shoved up against him, hard, trying to knock him off the puck. Dallas shoved back and said, "*You're* the piece of shit, Barrett."

"Cool. You finally came up with a comeback."

Dallas rammed his shoulder into Troy's chest. "You're such a fucking asshole."

"Yeah? How many accusations have there been so far? There was a new one yesterday, right?"

Dallas cross-checked Troy with his stick, then dropped it and shoved him again with both hands. "They're liars."

Troy snorted and shoved him back. "All of them?"

"Yes." And then Dallas tackled Troy to the ice, the puck forgotten.

Troy tried to roll Dallas off him, but Dallas was hitting him wildly with one gloved hand, while holding him down with the other.

"You were my *friend*!" Dallas screamed. His eyes were wild with fury and hurt as he kept hitting Troy.

"I shouldn't have been," Troy spat back. The refs finally showed up to haul Dallas off him. Troy raised himself up to his knees and yelled, "You're disgusting, Dallas."

Dallas shot him one last look, over his shoulder, and Troy was shocked to see tears in his eyes.

Good. Fuck him.

The game ended with Ottawa losing 4–2. Ilya was already showered and changed into his suit when the rest of the team returned to the dressing room. Troy went to him right away.

"You didn't need to do that," he said. "But thanks."

"I loved it. Why play hockey if you can't enjoy it, right?"

Troy's lips curved up. "Right."

Ilya nodded at him. "Nice goal. Feel better?"

"Yeah. Thanks for that pass."

He went to get undressed. The thing that didn't sit well with Troy was that Ilya had gotten angry when Kent had accused him of doing gay shit. Troy had known, when he'd been suggesting that Dallas wanted to fuck his dad, that it would make Dallas angry because he was a homophobic trash bag. It was disappointing to see Ilya get so offended from the same kind of taunts.

But that was exactly why Troy had kept his sexuality a secret all these years. Accusing an opponent of being gay was still the lowest insult you could hurl.

He tried to focus on positive things. His first game against Toronto was over with, he'd finally scored a goal, and his teammates had supported him, especially Ilya.

It would have been nice to win this one, though. To rub Dallas's face in it. Not just Dallas, but the entire team, especially Coach Cooper. And every fan who booed Troy. Fuck them all.

It was over. The two teams wouldn't meet again until February, and Troy would make sure he was less of a mess by then. For now, he would put this one behind him, and focus on their next game in New York.

Troy knew it was Ilya Rozanov knocking on his hotel room door before he opened it. There was a confidence to his knocking that matched the confidence he did everything else with.

"Get your coat," Ilya said.

"Why?"

"We are in New York and we are going out. I am meeting friends and you should come."

"Where? Why?"

"A bar. And because you need to have fun."

Well, Troy could think of worse things than going to a bar in New York with Ilya Rozanov. "Okay. One sec."

The taxi took them a short distance into a neighborhood that had a *lot* of rainbow flags.

"Is this . . ." Troy started, then stopped. "Where are we going?"

"The bar that Scott Hunter and Eric Bennett own. Is nice, sort of."

Okay. Wait. Troy knew that Hunter and Bennett bought a bar together, but . . . "Isn't it a gay bar?"

Ilya frowned at him. "Is that a problem?"

"No! No, I didn't mean—I'm just—" Troy shook his head. He wasn't *against* gay bars, obviously. He'd just never *been* to one. And now he was going to go to his *first* gay bar with Ilya Rozanov, apparently. "Just surprised. I didn't even know you liked Hunter."

Ilya made a face. "He is okay. But you are in love with him, so I thought you would like this."

"I'm not in love with him," Troy grumbled as the cab came to a stop in front of a pub called the Kingfisher. A minute later, Ilya was holding the door of the bar open, and Troy had to force his feet to move, and to not let his panic show on his face.

The bar didn't look much different inside from any other tavern Troy had gone to. A little nicer, maybe, and decorated for Christmas. There were flat-screen televisions showing sports, pop music playing, and pitchers of beer sitting on dark wood tables surrounded by people talking and laughing. Regular bar stuff. The patrons were mostly men, which wasn't unusual for a sports bar, but the fact that most of those men were probably *attracted* to men was kind of blowing Troy's mind. And making him feel queasy.

There were a few flags and decals around the bar that designated it as a queer-friendly space; not just the rainbow Pride flag, but a few others that Troy had seen before, but wasn't sure exactly what they represented. Because no one knew less about his own community than he did.

Ilya led him to a round table in one corner with a reserved sign on it. Troy hoped the table was meant for them because he wouldn't put it past Ilya to claim it anyway. As soon as they sat down, a very attractive blond man who looked about Troy's age came over.

"Hey, boys," the man said. "Eric said he and Scott will be here soon." He smiled at Rozanov. "Hi, Ilya."

Ilya nodded at him. "Kyle. The place looks better."

"All the bar needed was a little hard work and some rich new owners who gave a shit. Here." He slid something across the table to Ilya. "New cocktail menu. Changes monthly."

Ilya glanced at it. "You still have beer, yes?"

They both ordered lagers, and Kyle left to fetch them. Troy

had already told himself that he was only going to have one beer, first because they were playing a game tomorrow night, and second because there was no way he was getting anywhere near drunk when he was in a gay bar for the *first time*. With a group of his fellow NHL players.

He still didn't understand why they were here. Sure, Scott Hunter, the superstar captain of the New York Admirals, owned it with recently retired superstar Admirals goaltender, Eric Bennett, but hockey players owned lots of ridiculous businesses. If Troy patronized them all he'd never drink anything except terrible wine from their vineyards.

Troy's gaze kept traveling over the room. There were a lot of handsome men in the bar tonight. Tall, fit men. Distinguished-looking older men. Young pretty men. Big burly men. It was a tantalizing buffet. And one that Troy wasn't going to pay any attention to.

Kyle brought their drinks just as Scott and Eric arrived. A man who Troy recognized as Scott's husband, Kip, was with them.

"I'm just saying hi," Kip told the table. "I'll let you hockey boys have your private time." He turned to Troy. "You're new." His gaze traveled over Troy in a blatantly assessing way. "Damn. How do you play hockey and stay that pretty?"

"Hey!" Scott said with mock offense.

Kip laughed and offered Troy his hand. "Kip. Nice to meet you."

Troy shook his hand. "Troy."

"Oh shit! You're Troy *Barrett*, right? You're my new hero."

"Same," Scott said, which made Troy's eyes go wide. Scott Hunter—his *idol*—was looking at him with so much approval and warmth that Troy couldn't stand it.

"I'm not a hero," Troy mumbled, ducking his head to hide his darkening cheeks. Especially not compared to Hunter, who had bravely kissed his boyfriend on live television after winning the Stanley Cup a few seasons ago, and had been an activist ever since. All Troy had done was get mad at someone who deserved it. It's not like he accomplished anything by it.

The last time Troy had spoken to Hunter was during the All-Star weekend in January. He'd been so nervous, when he'd approached Scott at the hotel bar, because he knew that Scott hated Dallas Kent, and probably hated Troy by association. Scott had seemed wary at first when Troy had awkwardly introduced himself, but had quickly relaxed when Troy had congratulated him on his engagement, and, in the clumsiest way possible, attempted to articulate how inspiring it was for Scott to have come out as gay. Without, y'know, actually saying that.

He wondered if Scott had understood what Troy had been really trying to say. The way he was looking at him now—considering, *knowing*—suggested that he probably had.

Kip waved goodbye to the table full of hockey players, then kissed Scott. Troy held his breath, waiting for disgusted reactions, but of course no one was bothered or even interested. There was a whole world of people that had no problem with men kissing each other or falling in love. Troy had just been hanging out in the wrong circles.

Then Kyle, the bartender, kissed *Eric Bennett* full on the mouth. They smiled at each other when they broke apart, eyes full of adoration, and Troy was *floored*. He glanced around the table to see how everyone else was reacting, but again, no one seemed to care.

Wasn't Eric straight, though? He'd been married to a woman for years, until recently. Maybe he was bisexual? Whatever he was, he definitely seemed to be fucking a very hot—and much younger—man. So, go Eric.

Eric sat, and Ilya said, "Enjoying retirement?" with a knowing little smirk.

"I really am," Eric said, then took a sip of the cocktail Kyle had left on the table for him. He turned to Troy. "Good to see you again, Troy. How's Ottawa treating you?"

"Fine, I guess."

"I was impressed that you stood up to Kent. Scott was too."

"Damn right," Scott confirmed. "That took guts."

Troy shifted in his chair. "It's not like it did anything."

"Change needs to start somewhere," Scott said with authority. "I know nothing's happened to Kent, so you probably feel like your words meant nothing, but I'll bet they meant a lot to his victims."

Troy's cheeks heated. "I doubt it."

"It's one thing to stand up for yourself," Eric said calmly. "But standing up for others, for people who aren't even there and you've got nothing to gain from it? That's shows courage, and it shows you're a good person."

There were murmurs of agreement from everyone, even Ilya. Troy hadn't been prepared for this level of attention at all, and he didn't like it.

"I'm gonna hit the men's room." He stood quickly and darted away before anyone could see the uneasiness on his face.

And then Troy was in the men's room at a gay bar. A place that had been the punch line of countless awful locker room jokes.

If only Dad or Dallas Kent could see him now.

The bathroom honestly seemed pretty normal. There was only one other guy in there and he took care of business quickly and left without even looking at Troy. There didn't seem to be any orgies happening in the stalls, or whatever his former teammates had imagined went on in these places.

Troy took a few deep, settling breaths after he washed his hands. *Nothing is weird. You're at a normal bar with three NHL stars because you are an NHL star. At least two of them are queer, but guess what? So are you, buddy, so pull yourself together.*

He felt, he realized, the same way he did when he was around Harris. Overwhelmed and disoriented because he'd found a small space where his two worlds existed together peacefully. He was a hockey player, and he was a gay man, but he'd never tried to be both at the same time.

Scott and Eric both seemed so happy. Completely relaxed and comfortable in their own skin. Would Troy ever be like that? Would Troy ever overcome the effects of being burdened by years of, first, denial, then self-loathing, shame, fear, jealousy, and longing? He *wanted* to be comfortable here. To be comfortable *everywhere*. To be himself and not give a shit who had a problem with it.

It occurred to him, suddenly, that he could come out. Right now. To the group he was with. He barely knew any of them, but they would all accept him and support him.

Troy's heart pounded as he stared at his reflection in the bathroom mirror. Holy fuck. He could come out.

Someone entered the bathroom and shot Troy a curious look before heading to one of the urinals. Great. Now *Troy* was the one being weird in a gay bar men's room.

He left, mind racing with possibilities. He could do this. He could just . . . *do it.*

He could not do it. As soon as he saw Scott, Eric, and Ilya, he lost his nerve. He pivoted and went to the bar instead.

"Hey, handsome," Kyle said with a flirty smile. "What can I get you?"

"Can I just get some water?" It felt like the room's temperature had increased twenty degrees in the last five minutes.

"No problem."

Troy leaned on the bar, needing the support. He wished,

suddenly, that Harris were there. Harris would love this place, and he would love knowing that Troy was here, with these guys. He'd be so excited about it.

Troy was grounded a bit by the thought. He could tell him all about it when he saw him again.

"Here you go." Kyle set the water in front of him. "Anything else?"

"No," Troy said. "But, um . . . are you dating Eric Bennett?"

"Been together for months. Why?"

"I didn't know he was . . . uh . . ."

"Spoken for? Sorry."

Troy knew Kyle was teasing him, but he still flushed with embarrassment. "No! I meant—"

"I know what you meant."

Troy gave a nervous laugh, which was a testament to how much the whole evening was fucking with his head because he *never* did that. "Sorry. I'm just a little, um, out of my element here."

Kyle's eyebrows shot up. "First gay bar?"

"Uh, yeah. Actually."

"Don't worry. As long as you leave by midnight. That's when the floor opens up to reveal the sex pit."

Troy's laugh was a little less nervous this time. He liked this Kyle guy. "Thanks for the warning."

"If you wanted to stick around for the sex pit, though, I'll bet Cutie over there wouldn't be sad about it." He nodded subtly to Troy's left, and when Troy turned to look he spotted a very attractive man with olive skin and stylish glasses checking him out.

Oh.

Troy looked away. Then looked back. Then away again. What if he talked to him? What if he just went over and talked to him? And flirted with him? And went home with him? Jesus,

Troy could have sex tonight. He could pick up a man in a gay bar and have sex with him.

He downed half of his water in one go and forced himself to look anywhere but the handsome man who was trying to catch his attention. His gaze landed on a bulletin board behind the bar that was neatly displaying flyers for various upcoming events. In one corner, there was a small enamel pin in the shape of an apple with a rainbow flag heart in the middle.

Holy shit.

"Hey," he asked Kyle. "Where can I get one of those pins?" He pointed to the bulletin board.

Kyle looked confused. "That's just an old New York Pride pin. I think I have a few under the bar here still. You want one?"

"For a friend," Troy said, probably too quickly. "I know someone who would love it."

Kyle ducked below the bar and came back with an identical pin. He handed it to Troy. "All yours."

Troy held the pin like it was something precious, stroking his thumb over the raised metal ridges. His face must have given everything away, because Kyle smiled at him knowingly.

"He's an apple farmer," Troy explained, trying to sound cool, but unable to keep the uncharacteristic giddiness out of his voice. "And he's gay. And he loves pins. So this is, like, perfect."

"Sounds like it."

"Thanks."

"No problem. Tell your gay apple farmer to come visit the Kingfisher the next time he's in Manhattan."

"I will." Troy tucked the pin carefully into the pocket of his jeans and tried to ignore the weird fluttery things *your gay apple farmer* did to his stomach.

He returned to the table, where Scott was frowning and Ilya was grinning, so Ilya must have been making fun of him.

"Was Kyle flirting with you?" Ilya asked Troy cheerfully.

"Uh." Troy glanced uneasily at Eric.

"Probably," Eric said. He didn't sound bothered.

"You would be an attractive couple," Ilya continued. "Both very pretty. And the same age. Kyle would probably like that for a change."

"Shut it, Rozanov," Scott said.

But Eric just smiled. "I don't think Kyle is looking for a *change*, but if Troy was interested, I'm sure Kyle would be more than willing to—"

"Nope." Troy put up his hands. "Not interested. Your boyfriend is hot, but—" He froze. Had he really just said that? "I mean, he's probably considered to be attractive. And it's cool that you, um, are open-minded about, uh." He needed to shut up. Right now. So he did.

Ilya cracked up. "Your face!"

Troy knew how red his cheeks must be right now. He took a big gulp of his water, trying to cool his burning flesh.

"That goal you scored last night must have felt good," Scott said, changing the subject in a very obvious way that Troy was grateful for.

"Yeah. It felt great."

They talked about hockey for a while. In fact, nearly two hours had passed before Ilya pushed back from the table and said, "Time for bed. Game tomorrow."

"Yeah," Scott agreed. "Same."

"You should have been in bed hours ago, old man," Ilya said. "You'll feel it tomorrow on the ice."

"Against you guys? I doubt it."

Eric glanced toward the bar, and Kyle. "I'm going to stick around for a bit. Because I don't have a thing to do tomorrow."

Ilya clapped his shoulder. "I miss scoring on you, Eric."

"And I miss shutting your ass down."

When Ilya and Troy left the bar, Ilya said, "We could walk. Let's walk."

It was a weird suggestion, but it *had* seemed like a short cab ride so, sure. They could walk. Plus, walking around New York City was neat.

"You seem like you want to ask something," Ilya said once they started walking. "Or tell me something."

"No," Troy lied. Then he blurted out, "Why did you punch Dallas Kent?"

Ilya laughed. "Many reasons."

"I know, but why *exactly* did you punch him? Because I thought it was because he insulted you by saying that you were, like, gay. Or whatever. But then you took me to a gay bar, so I'm pretty confused right now."

"I did not punch Kent because of that. I am not so fragile."

"Oh. I just thought, because most hockey players would rather be accused of murder than be accused of liking dick—"

"I am not most hockey players." There was an edge to Ilya's tone. "And I have not ever said I was straight."

Troy stopped walking. *"What?"*

Ilya turned back to face him. "People assume things. They are idiots. Dallas Kent said something hateful about something that is—about something he does not know anything about."

"That's sort of his whole deal, yeah."

There was a visible tightness to Ilya's jaw, and anger burned in his eyes. "People like Kent stand in the way of other people being happy. For no reason. I am always glad to punch people like that."

Troy wanted to throw his arms around him. It was a wild, ridiculous impulse, like when he'd wanted to kiss Harris in his truck the other night. Why had Troy wasted so much energy on the worst people?

"Can you keep a secret?" Troy hadn't even realized he was

asking the question before the words were out, hanging between them with their clouds of breath on a Manhattan sidewalk.

Ilya's lips curved into a wry smile. "Yes. Very well."

Troy's heart pounded against his ribs. He might throw up. Or he might collapse. But he was going to say these words, dammit. "I'm gay."

For a moment, Ilya didn't react. He just surveyed Troy calmly. Then he said, "You have not told anyone."

"Not really, no."

Ilya tilted his head in the direction they needed to go and resumed walking. Troy fell into step beside him.

"That must have been very hard. In Toronto," Ilya said.

"It wasn't easy."

"I'm sorry." They walked a few more steps, and Ilya brightened and said, "Was that your first gay bar?"

"Yeah, it was."

Ilya burst out laughing. "Incredible."

Troy shook his head, but the absurdity of the whole night hit him all at once, and he started laughing too.

"What did you think?" Ilya asked.

"It had more NHL players than I was expecting."

Ilya's laugh was a high, delirious-sounding giggle that only made Troy laugh harder.

"But it was okay?" Ilya asked, more seriously despite his grin.

"It was okay," Troy assured him. "I liked it. Maybe I'll even go to another one someday."

Ilya's smiled faded. "It would be okay, I think, if you told the rest of this team. When you are ready."

"I know. I don't know if I want to, though."

Ilya nodded. "I can understand that very well."

"I'm not really into that kind of attention. So I probably won't tell anyone."

"There is *someone* you would like to tell, though, yes?"

Ilya's teasing smile had returned. How the fuck did he know? "I don't know what you're talking about."

"Okay." Another few steps, and Ilya said, "Is very normal for an NHL player to spend most of his free time in the social media guy's office."

Troy wanted to die. Who else had noticed? "I was just—oh god. Does everyone know? Is it obvious?"

"No. Not everyone is as, um, notices things?" Ilya furrowed his brow, and Troy helped him out.

"Perceptive?"

"Yes. I am the most perceptive."

Troy hunched his shoulders against the cold and against everything he was feeling. "I like him."

"I know. We all like Harris. But you want to kiss him."

Troy didn't bother denying it. "I won't. He deserves better, and there's probably a work conflict thing that makes it wrong."

"Yes. Maybe the social media guy will give you a Twitter advantage if you blow him."

Troy let out an uncharacteristic yelp of shocked laughter. "Oh my god."

"You will get all the good GIFs."

"Okay. Enough."

Ilya turned so he was directly in front of Troy, walking backward with that irritating grin on his face. "He likes you too, I think."

"Come on."

"He does not think he has a chance with you."

"Are you psychic or something?"

"No. Just per—fuck. I forget the word already."

"Perceptive."

"Perceptive," Ilya repeated. Then said it three more times,

drilling it into his brain. "Good word." He returned to walking beside Troy instead of in front of him.

Jesus, Troy had just come out to his team captain. And his team captain had . . . sort of come out to him?

"So, you're not straight?" Troy asked carefully.

"I am bisexual. It is not anyone's business, but, yes."

"I heard the rumor that Shane Hollander is gay. I don't know if it's true, but . . . that's what I heard."

"Did you."

Something clicked in Troy's head. "You guys are close, huh?"

Ilya started walking faster. "That is enough sharing for tonight, Barrett."

CHAPTER TWELVE

Ilya Rozanov was wearing a Santa hat and a snowman sweater, and was holding a puppy. Harris loved his job.

"Stand closer to the tree," Gen instructed.

Ilya took a step toward the giant, illuminated Christmas tree in the corner of the meeting room. He was unfairly handsome for someone dressed so ridiculously. Chiron had a festive bandanna tied around his neck and looked adorable as he nuzzled Ilya's face. Harris hadn't needed to twist Ilya's arm at all to agree to this photo shoot.

"Ah!" Ilya yelped. "He's got my pom-pom!"

Chiron had indeed chomped down on the big, fluffy pom-pom on the end of Ilya's hat and was tugging aggressively at it while Ilya laughed. Harris, thank god, was capturing the whole thing on video with his phone while Gen took rapid photos.

The fans were going to love this.

"Maybe some where you're kneeling or sitting, Ilya?" Gen suggested. "In front of the presents under the tree."

Ilya lowered himself until he was sitting cross-legged, which was super cute, and Chiron stood on the floor beside him with his little paws on Ilya's thigh.

"Ugh, that's adorable," Gen said, snapping pictures. "Stay like that."

"Whoa. What's this?"

Harris didn't need to turn around to know that it was Troy who was asking, but he still turned so quickly he nearly gave himself whiplash. Troy was standing in the doorway wearing workout clothes and an honest-to-god smile.

"Hi," Harris said. He hadn't seen Troy since their drive together before the road trip, and, damn. He was still very hot. "We're, um, doing a little holiday photo shoot. It's like a virtual Christmas card that we'll post to our accounts."

"Ah. Looking good, Ilya."

"I know."

Troy glanced uneasily between Harris, Gen, and Ilya, then said, "I, uh, brought you an eggnog latte, Harris. But I can just leave it."

"No!" Harris said, too quickly. "You can stay. And thanks. For the latte." He took it from him, the warmth of the paper cup seeping into his fingers as warmth from something else glowed inside his chest.

Gen let out a huff of laughter that Harris knew meant *you are into this guy and being very obvious about it.* To Harris's alarm, Ilya made an almost identical sound.

He tried to ignore both of them. "We're almost done, if you want to sit, or . . ."

"There are other sweaters," Ilya said, then nodded at the table loaded with Christmas costume pieces. "You should get in here."

"Oh. No. I was going to do a workout and, um." Troy gestured to his gym shorts.

"Sweater, hat, shoot from the waist up. Come on, Barrett."

Harris loved this idea, but only if Troy was into it. "It would be awesome to have two of you in the photo."

"The fans will like you more," Ilya said bluntly. "You, me, puppy, Christmas shit. No one can resist that."

Troy glanced at the table, then at Harris, then back to the table. "Okay. Sure."

"Harris, help him pick a sweater," Ilya said, because he was apparently in charge of this photo shoot now. "No! Chiron! Come back."

Chiron had lost interest in Ilya and was bounding over to Troy.

"Hey, buddy," Troy said, crouching and scratching Chiron's ears. "I missed you."

Troy glanced up and locked eyes with Harris. His lips parted like he wanted to say something, but then he looked back down at the puppy.

Harris went to the table and selected a blue sweater with a Christmas lights design knit into it. "Try this one," he said. He did not say that it would make Troy's eyes look amazing. Not that his eyes needed the help.

Troy gave the sweater a rueful look, but accepted it and put it on over his performance T-shirt.

"Is there an elf hat?" Ilya asked.

"No," Troy said flatly.

"I think you mean *yes*," Harris said, holding up a felt elf hat with bells dangling off it. He placed it carefully on Troy's head then, boldly, he tucked an unruly tuft of black hair behind his ear. Troy's eyes blazed into him for a moment, brighter than any holiday lights.

"How do I look?" he asked quietly.

Harris didn't see anything but those eyes. And those lips. "Perfect."

He swore Troy had started blushing before he'd quickly turned toward Ilya. Chiron trotted after him, tail wagging.

"I hate you for this," Troy grumbled to Ilya.

"I don't think you do. Now look cute for Gen and Harris."

Jesus, Troy *was* blushing. And smiling. And elbowing Ilya playfully. Who was this guy?

They took a bunch of photos of the two men standing together, holding the puppy between them. They looked like an absurdly attractive couple, but Harris kept that to himself. Troy smiled for the camera, and even laughed a few times, thanks to Ilya. It was nice to see the two of them getting along. They must have bonded on their recent road trip.

Ilya handed Chiron to Troy and said, "Take some photos with just Troy, yes?"

Harris wasn't sure they needed those, but Ilya was already pulling off his Santa hat and sweater, and Troy did look irresistibly silly.

Ilya squeezed Troy's shoulder before he walked away, which made Troy blush again for some reason. Then Ilya tossed his hat and sweater on the table and left quickly. It was kind of strange, the sudden departure, but Ilya was generally strange.

Without Ilya there to tease him, Troy's face fell into its usual blank stare, which looked hilarious set against an elf hat, a loud sweater, and a puppy. Harris couldn't wait to see the photos later.

"Okay," Gen said. "I think we're good."

Troy carefully set Chiron on the floor, then removed his costume pieces. "Those were probably terrible photos. Sorry."

"They're great," Gen said as she scrolled back through the images she'd captured on her camera. Harris could tell she was barely suppressing a giggle. "Very festive."

Harris took Troy's sweater and hat from him. "Thanks for helping out."

"No problem. Um. Does Chiron need a walk?"

Chiron let out a happy bark at the word *walk*. Harris laughed. "Sounds like it. You want to take him?"

"Sure. Can you come too? Or if you're busy I could—"

"I'm not busy. Just give me a few minutes, okay?"

"Okay."

"I can clean up here," Gen said. "You boys go on your walk."

It was a blatant attempt to get Harris and Troy alone together, and Harris tried to shoot daggers at her but probably failed because he'd never shot daggers at anyone in his life. "You sure?"

"Oh, I'm *definitely* sure." Gen seemed to be under the ridiculous assumption that Harris's weird friendship with Troy was going to blossom into something more. As if *Harris* could turn the head of an *NHL player*.

"I'll get my jacket," Troy said. "And, uh, my pants."

"Probably a good idea," Gen said. "It's December."

Troy walked quickly out of the room, and Harris rounded on Gen. "What the *hell*, dude?"

"What?"

"Why not just wear a T-shirt that says *Harris is into you*?"

"Oh, come on. He's a hockey player. He doesn't pick up on stuff like that."

"He's smart!"

She made a face that said *Is he, though?*

"You're mean."

She laughed. "Seriously, I like him. And he's sweet to you, which I also like. So even if he just wants to walk dogs with you and bring you coffee, I support it."

Harris relaxed. "Thanks." He grabbed his latte off the table and went to the door. "See you in a bit."

"I'll send you the best Troy photos."

"Yeah. Because it's your *job*."

"And your job is to walk a puppy with Troy Barrett. Go."

Harris was going to argue that this wasn't his job at all, but that would waste valuable walking-a-puppy-with-Troy time, so he left.

* * *

"So is it acceptably eggnog season now?" Harris asked. They were halfway down the first length of the arena parking lot, Troy holding Chiron's leash. Harris was holding the latte, trying not to drink it too quickly.

"Yeah. It's Christmas next week."

"Eggnog has a one-week window?"

"It has a zero-week window for me."

"There must be a Christmas treat you like, though."

Troy shrugged. "Turkey?"

Hoo boy. Harris decided to change the subject. "The Toronto game seemed intense."

"It was pretty rough."

"I couldn't believe it when Ilya punched Kent."

Troy's lips curved up. "That was awesome."

"What did Kent say to him to make him lose it like that?"

Troy's jaw worked for a moment, then he said, "Nothing really. Just typical bullshit."

Harris wasn't sure he believed that, but he let it go. "Was it awful, being back in Toronto?"

"It was weird. And pretty terrible. I thought I was going to be sick before the game. Ilya talked me down, actually."

"He's good at that."

"Mm."

They finished a lap of the massive parking lot, and Harris was about to start a second one after tossing his empty cup into a garbage can, but Troy stopped walking.

"Um," Troy said.

Harris waited. Troy handed him the leash, then reached into his own jacket pocket.

"I got you something." He said it like one word, then thrust a small, shiny object at Harris.

"You did?"

Harris took the object and saw that it was an enamel pin in the shape of an apple. With a little rainbow heart in the middle.

His own little rainbow heart fluttered in his chest. He beamed at Troy. "Where did you find this?"

"New York. It's, y'know. The Big Apple. And that pin was from Pride, I guess. So. Yeah."

"Big Gay Apple."

Troy huffed. "I thought you'd like it."

"I love it!" Harris pinned it on to his jacket immediately, then smiled at it. Troy had been *thinking of him* on his trip.

"Ilya took me to that bar Scott Hunter and Eric Bennett own. That's where I saw the pin. And the bartender gave one to me when I asked about it."

Harris's mouth dropped open. "You went to the Kingfisher? Shit, I'm so jealous. I love that there's a gay bar in New York that's owned by two NHL players. Who would have ever thought, huh?"

"I know, it's kinda unbelievable. But it's a nice bar. And the bartender who gave me the pin is, uh, Eric's boyfriend, I guess."

"Oh yeah. I heard Eric Bennett was dating the manager of the place. They met there, before Eric and Scott bought it. They were regulars, apparently, which is adorable. Christina told me his boyfriend is super hot."

"Christina?"

"The Admirals' social media manager. We're friendly. So is it true? Is the boyfriend hot?"

Harris enjoyed the color that bloomed on Troy's cheeks. "He's a good-looking guy."

Harris was sure he had nothing on the good-looking guy who was standing in front of him right now. Harris admired his new pin, and made sure it wasn't crooked on his jacket. He wondered how difficult it had been for Troy to ask the bartender for it. How difficult it had been for him to be in a gay bar at all.

When he turned his gaze back to Troy, he found the man smiling shyly at him. He looked pleased with himself, which was so cute Harris couldn't stop himself from hugging him. "Thank you."

For a few seconds, Troy's arms hung stiffly at his sides. His whole body seemed to freeze. Then, slowly, he placed one hand on Harris's back, then the other. "No problem," he said. His breath tickled Harris's cheek. His arms tightened, holding Harris closer.

Harris tilted his head, just slightly. Just enough to inhale the spice of Troy's aftershave.

Then Troy took a step back, and stumbled because Chiron had managed to wrap his leash around their legs as if he was doing his own matchmaking.

Harris reached out and grabbed the front of Troy's jacket to keep him from falling backward. Momentum brought Troy close again as he was pulled upright. His nose brushed against Harris's own, and for an endless moment, they just stared at each other. Troy's eyes were wide and bright and maybe a bit scared.

Harris wanted to kiss him so badly. He couldn't remember any reasons why he shouldn't.

But Troy laughed nervously and bent to untangle their legs from the leash. "Shit, Chiron. What did you do?"

Harris didn't bend to help. He used the distance to clear his head and take a few deep breaths. What the hell had he been thinking?

Troy got the leash sorted, then stood and took a few steps backward. "I'm gonna go work out. But, um, thanks for the walk."

"Oh. Okay." Harris didn't want him to leave, but he couldn't think of a way to make him stay. "Thanks for the pin. And the latte."

Troy glanced at the pin, and his mouth bent into that rough-hewn smile of his. "Merry Christmas."

Then he left without another word. Again.

"I know what you were trying to do there with the leash, buddy," Harris said to Chiron. "I appreciate the effort, but I think we need to let this one go."

No boyfriends showed up at Troy's apartment to surprise him on Christmas Eve, but at least he was in an actual apartment and not a hotel room.

The apartment was nice enough. It was a spacious two-bedroom, fully furnished, and everything looked fairly new, if slightly bland. He'd had some of his stuff shipped from his storage unit in Toronto—clothes, mostly—so he was officially no longer living out of a suitcase. The building had a pool and a gym, and underground parking, basically everything Troy needed.

Except maybe some company.

This was the first Christmas that Troy would be spending completely alone. He didn't *care* about Christmas much, but it felt weird to spend it by himself. Part of him hoped for a text from Harris, inviting him to look at more Christmas lights. Or maybe a second invitation to dinner at his family's farm. Troy wasn't sure he'd say no this time.

He couldn't stop thinking about the way Harris's face had lit up when Troy had given him that apple pin. He wanted to keep giving him things so Harris would keep smiling at him like that. Not that it took much to get a smile out of the guy.

Troy frequently found himself wondering what it would take to get a moan out of him. Or a gasp of pleasure. What would fill those green eyes with heat?

He realized he was lazily brushing his fingertips over his stomach as he lay on the leather couch that had come with the apartment. His dick twitched with interest, and Troy's hand slid lower, seemingly on its own. He gave his thickening cock a squeeze through his loose-fitting gym shorts, and grunted softly into the empty room.

Troy *could* make this Christmas Eve even sadder than it already was by jerking off to fantasies of the total sweetheart who was way too good for him, or he could find something distracting to quickly cool his blood.

With a lot of effort, Troy removed his hand from his dick and grabbed the television remote off the coffee table. He found a sports highlights show that was counting down the top NHL goals of the year.

Dallas Kent's face filled the screen, and that quashed Troy's boner in a hurry.

"Fuck you," Troy said to the man on his television. And then felt silly about it.

Troy remembered the goal they were showing. It'd been epic, the way Troy had gotten around both San Jose defensemen, then knocked the puck over to Dallas, who took it and flew to the net. He'd faked out the goalie perfectly and scored the game-winning goal.

On the television, Dallas was jumping into Troy's arms, and they were both smiling and yelling and hugging. Like friends. Like brothers.

He changed the channel, and after some rapid flipping, stumbled upon an episode of Adrian's superhero show. Because Troy's life was an endless parade of shit. On the screen, Troy's ex-boyfriend was shirtless, battle-ravaged, and breathtaking.

Troy turned off the television. For a long time, he stared at the ceiling, not moving. His brain ran in circles, trying to work out how exactly his life had gotten to this point. What had made him so mean? Why had he always been so quick to make fun of other people? Was it only a defense mechanism, or a way to protect his secrets, or was he just a total dick like his father?

Why did he gravitate toward people whose senses of humor were based entirely on putting other people down?

And, most importantly, could Troy change that? Could he actually be friends with someone like Harris, who seemed determined to see the best in people? Who, when he teased Troy, made it feel like a hug, rather than a jab.

Eventually, Troy got himself off the couch. He ordered sushi and ate it at his kitchen counter while he, for the first time, checked out the Ottawa Centaurs Twitter account.

He wasn't sure what made him do it, but he found it comforting, reading things Harris had written. He could hear Harris's voice when he read the posts, and recognized his sense of humor in them.

Harris posted a *lot*. Maintaining the team's social media accounts seemed like a ton of work. Each day had dozens of posts, and they were all *fancy*, with graphics and GIFs and videos and clever emojis. All of the posts were written in both French and English, and it hadn't even occurred to Troy that Harris could speak French. He supposed it would be a job requirement, though, in a bilingual city like Ottawa.

The most recent post was one of the photos of Troy and Ilya posing in front of the Christmas tree with Chiron. Troy looked ridiculous in the picture, but he also looked . . . happy. Or at least not miserable.

There were quite a few posts about Troy. Pictures of him at the children's hospital, and with Chiron in the locker room. Pictures of him during practice—including one where he was laughing at something Bood said. Troy stared at that one for a long time, barely recognizing himself with his eyes crinkled in amusement.

It occurred to Troy, later when he was in bed for lack of anything else to do, that Harris probably had a personal Instagram account.

It didn't take long at all to find it. His profile picture was the apple pin Troy had given him. Troy could have sworn he felt his heart inflating like a balloon when he saw it.

The posts had almost nothing to do with hockey. There were lots of photos of his family's farm, and of dogs that Troy assumed lived there. There were photos of live bands and of friends in crowded bars. A few selfies, but almost always with his arm around another person. Troy wasn't surprised; Harris seemed like a person who was rarely alone.

When Troy looked at pictures of Harris—when he thought of Harris at all—he felt the opposite of the anger and shame that surged through him when he'd seen Dallas and Adrian on his television. His stomach twisted in an entirely different way, full of a nervous energy that was fueled by excitement and anticipation, instead of dread and anxiety.

Maybe Troy would never be as good a person as Harris, but he could at least try to be as good a person as, like, *Ilya*. That guy made fun of people all the time, but he was just so damn likable. And he balanced it by genuinely caring about people, and starting a charity, and being an impressive team leader in his own weird way.

The kind of leader who was able to make Troy comfortable enough to *come out to him*, which Troy still couldn't quite believe he'd actually done.

Troy slept in the next morning, because there was no reason not to. He awoke to find "Merry Christmas" messages on his phone from both of his parents, and a third, more surprising one.

HARRIS:

Merry Christmas!

Troy's heart lifted. He was sure Harris had sent the same message to everyone on the team, and probably everyone he had ever met in his life, so it would be silly to reply. Besides, if he replied, he would only spend the rest of the day hoping for a reply that would definitely never come. It was Christmas morning and Harris was with his family, busy and full of festive cheer.

TROY:
Thanks. You too.

He cringed at himself, then put his phone down on the bed. Then picked it back up again.

HARRIS:
How's the new place?

Oh. That was a question specifically for Troy.

TROY:
Fine. Quiet.

HARRIS:
Ha. This house is the opposite of quiet.

Troy smiled at that, and wished Harris was with him, filling his lonely apartment with earsplitting laughter. While he tried to think of something to write back, Harris wrote, I actually just stepped outside for a moment. It's totally calm and peaceful out here.

Then he sent a photo. Snow was gently falling on a giant yard, with trees behind. Troy could see Harris's truck off to one side.

He wanted Harris to send a picture of himself. He wanted to see him with snowflakes in his hair. He just wanted to see him.

TROY:
Looks nice.

HARRIS:
Perfect Christmas weather.

HARRIS:
But I'm looking forward to being in Florida next week.

That message was followed by a string of palm tree emojis. Troy had almost forgotten that Harris would be joining the team on their road trip down south. The thought warmed him more than the Florida sun probably would.

TROY:
Me too.

In an attempt to be cute, Troy added a flamingo emoji.

Harris didn't reply, which meant Troy spent most of his Christmas Day staring at that damn flamingo. Finally, around nine o'clock at night, Harris wrote, Just got home. Did you do anything fun today?

Troy sat up from where he'd been lying on the couch, grinning like a loon, and wrote, I called my mom, which was true and sounded cooler than *I spent the whole day hoping you'd text me again*.

HARRIS:
Aw. Where is she today?

TROY:
Brisbane. Australia.

HARRIS:

Holy shit, really? I've always wanted to go there.

Troy had never given much thought to going to Australia himself. The few times he'd traveled for non-hockey reasons, it had been to Mexico or the Caribbean with teammates. He and Adrian used to make vague plans to go to Hawaii together one day.

HARRIS:

I love Australian accents.

Troy smiled and wrote, G'day, which was close to flirting without being too obvious about it.

HARRIS:

If you're trying to seduce me, it's working.

Heat raced up Troy's neck, but he laughed and wrote, LOL to let Harris know that he wasn't taking that seriously. His dick was, but *Troy* wasn't.

They texted back and forth for over an hour, and in that hour Troy saw at least eight emojis that he hadn't even known existed.

All in all, it was one of his best Christmases.

CHAPTER THIRTEEN

"Stop working so fucking much!"

Harris grinned up at Bood from his plane seat. "I can't! A big win like that means I have a ton of work to do."

Bood clapped him hard on the shoulder and continued down the aisle, already yelling something at Luca Haas.

It was the first week of January, and the Centaurs had started their road trip with a huge 4–1 afternoon win in Raleigh and were now headed to Tampa Bay. Tomorrow would be a day off they were all looking forward to, away from the frigid winter weather of Ottawa. Despite the fact that everyone who'd played in the game was probably exhausted, the plane was a party at the moment.

Harris was joining in as best he could, but he also had his laptop in front of him, and was working hard updating the team's various accounts, replying to fans, and taking phone videos of the celebrations happening on the plane. He'd edit them so nothing too personal was posted online.

He was sitting alone because he wasn't being much fun at the moment, but he was enjoying the whooping and hollering all around him. Some people liked listening to rainfalls or birds chirping to relax, but Harris always felt most at ease when surrounded by happy people.

"First star of the night: Troy B-B-B-Barrett!" Bood called out.

Harris turned his head to look behind him and saw Troy walking up the aisle toward him. Troy waved Bood's revelry aside and sat in the empty seat next to Harris. "Hi."

"Hey," Harris said. "You must feel pretty good right now. Two goals."

Troy nodded solemnly, like he was thinking about whether or not scoring two goals was good. "Yeah," he finally decided. "It was a good game."

So everyone was in a party mood except, of course, Troy Barrett.

Who was sitting with Harris. Watching him work.

"Lots to do?" Troy asked.

"I'm afraid so. No one ever thinks of the poor social media guy."

"That's not true," Troy said, then looked like he immediately regretted it. "I mean, sorry. For making you work harder."

"No you're not."

The barest suggestion of a smile from Troy. "Not really, no."

The plane lurched suddenly, which caused a lot of the guys on board to yelp in alarm, and then laugh. It also caused Bood to fall down in the aisle, which made everyone laugh harder. Harris craned his neck to see if Bood was okay, and when he turned back, he saw that Troy had placed a steadying hand on his laptop.

"Thanks," Harris said. Troy pulled his hand away quickly, like he hadn't realized he had accidentally done something thoughtful.

Harris closed the laptop. "I can finish this at the hotel later anyway. We must be getting close to landing."

Troy, still wearing most of the suit he'd left the arena in, was fiddling with the end of his necktie. "You were right," he said quietly.

"Usually. But what about?"

"This team. It's a good group."

Harris elbowed him. "I *told* you!"

Troy's lips curved up a bit. "I'm not a great judge of character. I always pick the wrong people to be friends with. Or trust. I, um." He rolled the end of his tie up into a tight cylinder, and then released it. "I want to fit in here. With this team. I like them, and I think for once I'm not wrong about wanting them to like me."

"They do like you," Harris said. "And so do I."

Troy's blue eyes were full of anguish, which was a weird way to react to that statement. Harris tried not to take it personally.

"I like you, too," Troy finally said. He glanced around them nervously, then dropped his voice even lower. "Harris, I—"

There was a loud bang, and then the plane lurched again, more violently this time.

"Jesus! What the fuck?" Troy yelled at the same time everyone else on the plane yelled a variation of the same thing.

And then the plane dropped.

It was an awful, sickening sensation, made worse by the screams that filled the cabin. Harris didn't scream because he couldn't find the breath to do it. They were going to die. They were all going to die, tumbling through the dark somewhere over Florida.

Harris closed his eyes and hoped they crashed far away from any other people.

The plane shuddered and leveled out, with another stomach-lurching swoop. There was total silence on the plane as everyone waited for whatever was about to happen.

A voice came over the speakers. "We've lost an engine, but still have control over the aircraft. We have been cleared for an emergency landing in Tampa, but expect it to be a rough descent. Please stand by for further instructions from your flight attendant."

He heard Troy suck in a breath beside him, then Harris realized that his own hand was being held in Troy's tight grip. Harris squeezed back and said, as calmly as he could manage, "It's going to be okay."

There were panicked cries all around them, and Harris hated that he knew who was making each one. He knew these guys so well and loved them like family, and he didn't want them to be scared.

His heart was hammering in his chest, and he should be worried about that, but one thing at a time.

"There's fire out here!" It was Nick Chouinard. "The plane is on fire!"

"Fuck," Troy muttered. *"Fuck."*

Across the aisle, Ilya was frantically typing something on his phone. Harris should probably try to message his parents, but what would he say?

God, his parents. They'd be devastated.

His laptop had crashed to the floor at some point. He put his foot on it to keep it from being tossed around. The flight attendant—a young woman who had a brave face on but Harris could tell was barely holding it together—was coming down the aisle with instructions. "Tables up. Remove your ties, glasses, chains. Anything like that. Get into a position to brace for impact. Duck your heads and rest them against the seatback in front of you. Feet firmly on the floor."

Harris released Troy's hand and put the table up while Troy removed his necktie. Then they both braced for impact, as instructed. Harris closed his eyes again and focused on Troy's heavy breathing beside him. He thought about everyone else on board. About Bood, who was about to become a father.

About Wyatt's wife, Lisa. About Coach Wiebe's wife and three daughters. About Luca Haas, who had just turned twenty. About Dale, the equipment manager, who had just celebrated being eight years cancer-free.

He turned his head, just slightly, against the hard plastic of the seat in front of him, and found Troy's face inches away, staring at him with wide, fearful eyes. Harris placed his hand over Troy's, where it was pressed, palm-down, on his knee. Troy flipped his hand and curled his fingers around Harris's, holding tight.

Harris managed a weak smile. Either they would live through this, or they wouldn't, but there was nothing they could do about it now. All he could do was wait, and offer as much comfort as he could. In return, he could enjoy the view of Troy's beautiful face, which, if it was going to be the last thing he ever saw, well, there were worse options.

The plane was so quiet. Maybe it was because Harris's heart was pounding in his ears, drowning everything else out, but it seemed like no one was making a sound. He'd bet some were praying—Chouinard, probably. He was Catholic. Or maybe everyone was just concentrating together, as if their combined mental energy might safely guide the plane to the ground.

It felt like the plane was descending faster than usual, but Harris couldn't be sure. It was shakier, much more turbulent. He tried not to think about the fire. He'd heard that plane engines could put out fires automatically. Maybe it was out already. Maybe it had spread to the wing. Maybe the whole plane was about to explode.

Harris swallowed hard. He needed to stay positive, for himself, and for Troy, who was still staring at him from a few inches away, eyes wild with fear.

"When we land," Harris said, just loud enough for Troy to hear, "I'm getting ice cream."

There were tears in Troy's eyes, but he managed a small smile and said, "What kind?"

The plane shuddered and jerked, and Troy squeezed his eyes closed, his lips pulled tight in a grimace.

"Cookie dough. Definitely," Harris said quickly.

Troy opened his eyes. They were still wet. "That sounds gross."

Harris laughed, but it sounded like a sob, and suddenly Troy's face was very blurry.

The plane made a whirring noise, and oh thank god, was that the landing gear? Maybe they'd survive this. Maybe this would be an adventure they'd talk about for years after. Harris was going to have so much work to do after this. The Ottawa Centaurs would be getting a lot of media attention.

The wheels touched the ground, and Harris had never felt anything so wonderful in his life. It wasn't even a particularly rough landing. The plane slowed, and an earsplitting cheer rose up from everyone. Even Troy.

Their hands separated—Harris wasn't sure who let go first—and they both joined in the applause for the pilot, and for their good fortune.

There were emergency lights flashing outside the plane windows, but Harris couldn't stop looking at Troy. He was wiping his eyes and grinning from ear to ear.

Maybe it was the adrenaline talking, but Harris realized he was maybe a little bit besotted.

"Your laptop is broken," Troy said, smile disappearing.

Harris followed his gaze to the cracked plastic of the laptop on the floor. "Yeah, I can't bring myself to care about that right now."

Troy should have been completely drained by the time the bus finally reached the hotel in Tampa, but he was buzzing with adrenaline. He'd really thought he was going to die. That they were *all* going to die. That *Harris* was going to die.

And during those horrible minutes when he'd been grappling with his impending death, he'd kept thinking one thing, over and over:

I want to kiss him.

He wanted it so badly he'd nearly done it. Nearly leaned in and closed those few inches and let the last thing he felt be Harris's lips brushing his own. What would Harris have done, if Troy had kissed him? Would he have kissed him back? And if so, would it have been out of panic? Would it have been an act of charity, giving Troy what he needed because Harris was a nice guy? Or would Harris have kissed him because he'd wanted it as much as Troy did? Because if they had to die, at least they could have this first?

He hadn't done it, but he'd taken Harris's warm hand in his and gripped it like the connection would somehow keep them safe. Taking comfort from Harris had become a habit, and Troy had selfishly needed to do it then, even if giving comfort was the last thing Harris ever did.

He still wanted to kiss Harris. That was the thought that was bouncing around his brain as he followed his teammates into the hotel lobby. It would be easy to say the urge had been a heat-of-the-moment thing, and that it wasn't something he actually *wanted*, but it wasn't true. He wanted. He wanted so fucking much that he could barely stand to look at him.

"Well," Coach Wiebe said, "I don't know about you guys, but I could use a drink."

There were murmurs of agreement, and some scattered laughter that sounded like relief. They had survived together, and now they would get drunk together.

They filled the bar area. Every available table was taken up by players, coaches, trainers, doctors and other team staff. Harris sat at one of the larger tables. Troy went to the bar and took one of the empty stools. He needed to think.

He sat for a while with his whiskey and his thoughts. If the plane had crashed, how would Troy have been remembered? An NHL All-Star? The guy who got in an argument once with Dallas Kent?

Who would even mourn him? His mother, definitely. He expected he would be hearing from her as soon as the news got to her. His dad might care. Adrian would at least feel weird about it.

Jesus, what if he and Adrian had still been together? If the plane had crashed and Troy had died, Adrian wouldn't have been able to mourn him. Troy had never imagined a scenario where one of them died while they'd been together, but now his stomach twisted thinking about how devastating it would have been if he had lost Adrian when no one even knew what they'd been to each other. How awful it would be to have to hide his grief. It had been hard enough when Adrian had broken up with him.

It wasn't fucking fair that this was how Troy felt he had to live. To love in secret, to feel *everything* in secret.

Someone took the bar stool next to him, and he saw in the mirror behind the bar that it was Ilya.

"What are we drinking?" Ilya asked, his words a little slurred. His accent a little heavier, and he smelled faintly of cigarette smoke.

"Whiskey."

"Perfect." He got the bartender's attention, then pointed to Troy's empty glass and then to the empty space in front of himself. "How are you?"

Troy huffed. "Alive."

"Yes."

Their whiskeys were delivered, and Ilya immediately tossed

half of his down his throat. He grimaced, set his glass down, and said, "When you think you are going to die, there is . . . what is it? Important things. In your head."

"Like a clarity," Troy said. "Yeah."

Ilya nodded slowly. "Makes you think about things. What is important. What is not."

"It does." Troy found Harris in the mirror again. He was at a different table now, leaning in close to Luca Haas with a hand on his arm. Listening, offering comfort in that effortless way Harris always did for everyone.

Who was taking care of Harris?

"I think," Ilya said, "that what you think in that moment . . . it is correct, yes?"

Harris caught Troy looking at him. Their eyes met in the mirror for a second, then Troy looked away. "Maybe."

"I think so." Ilya downed the rest of his whiskey, then clapped Troy on the shoulder. "What you wanted on that plane. Go for it."

Ilya left, seemingly headed for his hotel room. Troy should probably do the same. He needed to get out of this suit, at the very least.

He got to his feet and grabbed his suit jacket off the back of the stool, then stole another glance at Harris.

His heart *hurt* when he looked at him. He was everything Troy wanted, and everything he didn't deserve. All Troy had done so far was take from him, but maybe tonight he could give something back.

CHAPTER FOURTEEN

An hour later, Harris was mourning the death of his laptop.

He couldn't sleep; he couldn't even keep his eyes closed for more than a few seconds before all of the screams and sobs from the plane came back to him.

He'd gotten checked out by one of the medics who had been on the scene at the airport. The medic had assured him his heartbeat and blood pressure were only slightly elevated, which, of course, was normal for anyone who had been through something so terrifying. But she'd suggested he take it easy, and to go to a hospital if he felt off later.

Harris felt a lot of things, now that he was alone. He was rattled and still buzzing with a restless energy despite feeling drained at the same time. He was also startlingly horny. And that was why he wished he had a working laptop. Not that he *needed* porn, but he would welcome the distraction right now. He didn't want to look at his phone, though. In fact, he had turned it off, and buried it in his suitcase.

He turned on the television instead, and found a reality show about house flipping that was exactly the level of drama he could take right then.

There was a knock on his door just as the episode was ending. Harris knew who he *hoped* it was, but was still surprised to see Troy when he opened the door.

"Hey." Troy had changed into black sweatpants and a soft-looking gray T-shirt. His hair was damp, and his skin was still rosy from what must have been a very hot shower. He looked dangerously sexy, especially when Harris was already so keyed up.

"I can't sleep," Troy said.

"Me neither." Harris stepped back, and Troy walked past him into the room.

"I brought you something." Troy turned and thrust a plastic CVS bag at Harris with so much nervous anticipation that Harris wondered if it might be full of condoms.

He took the bag from Troy, and when he looked in it, nearly burst into tears. It probably had more to do with his emotional state after the whole plane ordeal, but goddamn. Troy Barrett was going to kill him.

"Cookie dough ice cream," Harris said, pulling the small container out of the bag. "You went out and got this for me?"

"Yeah. I got a spoon from the bartender. It's in the bag there."

He really had. He'd left the hotel at . . . whatever the fuck time it was . . . and tracked down some cookie dough ice cream.

"So it is." Harris managed to keep his voice steady, just barely. "Only one?"

Troy shrugged. "It's not for me."

Harris didn't know what to say. His poor heart had already been through so much today, and now Troy was standing in his hotel room, inches away, smelling so good and watching Harris with wide, uncertain eyes. It was too much.

Harris gestured to the bed. "Have a seat."

Troy sat on the edge of the bed. The room was dark except for the television, and the blue, flickering light danced across his face.

"What are you watching?" Troy asked.

"A real estate show. I was only half watching." Harris stretched out on the half of the bed where he'd been before, then patted the other half. Troy hesitated a moment, then moved until he was beside him. Harris peeled off the seal on the ice cream and dug his spoon in.

"Mmm," he moaned around his first bite. "You're my hero for getting this, buddy."

Troy was propped on one elbow, watching him eat. "You deserve it."

"Yep. I definitely earned my treat today. Jesus fuck." Harris laughed, and Troy, miraculously, did too.

"What a fucking nightmare," Troy said.

"No kidding. I don't ever want to experience that again."

They both stared at the television for a few minutes. Harris wasn't really watching at all, his attention divided between the ice cream and the gorgeous man who had brought it to him. The man who was reclining beside him, close enough that Harris could feel the warmth from his skin.

"I used to make fun of Ryan Price on planes," Troy said quietly. Unexpectedly. "Because he was scared of flying."

Harris didn't say anything. He hated hearing things like that, but he waited for Troy to continue.

"He was such a wreck, every time he flew. We thought it was hilarious."

Harris knew that by *we*, Troy meant himself and Dallas Kent.

"And now," Troy said, "all I can think about is how we have to get on another plane in a couple of days. I don't know if I can do it."

"Yeah," Harris said. "I've been thinking about that too."

"I owe Ryan a thousand apologies. Jesus fucking Christ. I was such an asshole." Troy turned on his side to face Harris. "He's the bravest person I've ever met. Seriously. Dallas liked to laugh at what a baby he was about flying, but how much fucking courage do you need to have to face your fears, like, at least once a week? Usually several times a week. For *years*. I can't even fucking imagine."

"It's impressive," Harris agreed.

"And he's gay, too."

Okay. That seemed like a non sequitur. "I don't think being gay makes flying scarier."

"No, I mean, like, that's fucking brave too. Two things Dallas thinks are weak, being afraid and being gay, but they aren't. I wish I'd . . ." He sighed. "I wish I'd done everything differently. I should have supported Ryan and told Dallas to go fuck himself."

"Probably," Harris said. He wanted to say something more substantial, but his brain was in tatters and Troy's mouth was very close to his.

Troy flopped onto his back, creating some distance, but not removing the temptation. "I have so many regrets."

Harris was about to create a regret of his own if he didn't stamp out the burning need to kiss Troy. Because, yeah, it had been a weird night, and, yes, they had been holding hands on the plane, and, sure, Troy was lying beside him now in the dark after coming to his hotel room with *cookie dough ice cream*.

But none of that meant that Troy wanted anything from Harris besides some companionship. Troy was straight, as far as Harris knew, and even if he wasn't, he was the most beautiful man Harris had ever seen. He could do better than an apple farmer with a busted heart.

"So what's on your mind?" Troy asked. "I'm unloading on you like a selfish jerk over here."

"You're not a jerk. I like it when you talk to me. And I don't know what's on my mind right now. A million things, but I'm too tired to figure them out." Harris laughed. "I was thinking about watching porn earlier, if you want total honesty. But my laptop is broken and I turned my phone off and shoved it to the bottom of my suitcase. Don't want to look at it until I have to."

"Same," Troy said quietly, eyes fixed on the ceiling. "Porn, huh?"

Harris probably shouldn't have mentioned that. "Yeah. Just thought it would be a good distraction."

"It would be." Something bright was on the television screen, and for a few seconds, Harris got a clear view of Troy's cheekbones, his full lips, and the shadow of stubble on his jaw.

Harris needed to change the vibe. Immediately. "Do you want some ice cream? You should at least try it."

Troy turned his head to glance up at Harris. "Is it good?"

"It's the best thing I've ever tasted. Here." He held out a spoonful of ice cream, hovering it over Troy's lips. Troy stared at the spoon, as if unsure if it was safe. Then, slowly, he leaned forward, and parted his lips. Harris slipped the spoon inside and watched Troy's face as the sweet, silky ice cream hit his tongue.

Troy's eyes fluttered closed for a moment, those long, raven-wing lashes brushing his cheekbones. The tip of his tongue peeked out from between his plush lips, as if seeking any stray drops that he may have missed.

It did *not* change the vibe. At all.

"Oh," Troy said quietly. "Shit, that's really good."

"Yeah," Harris said distantly. If he kissed Troy right now, he would taste like ice cream. "More?"

A painfully shy smile curved those soft lips. "Okay."

Harris, realizing that it would be weird to continue spoon-feeding Troy, handed him the container and the spoon.

It was also weird to be sitting in the dark, so he turned on the bedside lamp. Troy settled back against the pillows with the ice cream, while Harris sat, cross-legged, next to him, trying like hell to focus on the television. It was difficult when Troy kept sighing happily around each mouthful of ice cream.

Harris gave his thigh a playful shove. "I told you ice cream is awesome."

"Mm" was all Troy said, because he'd just shoved another spoonful of ice cream into his mouth.

They watched TV while Harris's hand twitched with the urge to touch him again. He often craved physical touch and loved cuddling possibly even more than sex. He found it comforting, and at that moment he desperately needed comfort. Nothing inside him felt right; his brain couldn't settle, his skin prickled, his stomach was in knots and his throat was dry.

He didn't want to think about his heart. He was sure it was beating normally, medically speaking, but it felt . . . fluttery. Anxious.

He heard the spoon scrape against the bottom of the ice cream container and smiled. "That didn't take long."

"It's a small container."

Harris turned to look at him, and huffed out a laugh when he saw how relaxed Troy seemed. His hair was mostly dry now, but it was messy and fell in his eyes. He had one arm stretched over his head, which gave Harris a nice view of his biceps, and also of a strip of skin above the waistband of his sweatpants. A hint of his muscular abs.

"I'll take that," Harris said, grabbing for the empty container. "I'm going to the bathroom anyway."

He needed distance. Now.

In the bathroom, he rinsed out the container, then brushed his teeth, drank some water, and examined himself in the mirror. He looked exactly like he felt: wired, exhausted, on edge. He wondered if Troy would go back to his own room now. He didn't want him to.

Troy was curled up on his side, facing away, when Harris returned to the bed. The change in position gave Harris an eyeful of Troy's muscular ass, his broad back and shoulders, and his oddly adorable socked feet.

Cautiously, Harris approached the bed. He wanted to drape himself over Troy's gorgeous body and breathe him in, but instead he left some distance between them when he lay on the bed beside him.

Harris faced the ceiling with his hands folded on his stomach, avoiding all temptation. "You can stay," he said.

There was a long pause before Troy murmured, sleepily, "You sure?"

"Yeah. Stay."

"Thanks."

He couldn't stop himself from gazing helplessly at the slow rise and fall of Troy's back. At the short hairs on the back of Troy's neck. At the absolutely normal, yet somehow precious curve of his ear.

He allowed himself a few moments of furtive admiration before turning off the television, then the lamp. They were both on top of the duvet, and maybe that was fine for tonight. It would be safe.

He rolled to his side, away from Troy. He still couldn't sleep, but he liked listening to Troy breathe. It was nice to have another body close, even if he couldn't touch him.

In the dark, memories from the plane came racing back, playing in a horrible, looped clip package in Harris's brain. He tried some deep breathing.

"You okay?" Troy's voice was low and scratchy, and Harris stopped breathing altogether at the sound of it.

"Yeah. Sort of. I don't know."

There was movement behind him, and then Troy's big, warm hand was on Harris's arm. "Can I help?"

Harris gnawed on his lip, deciding what to say. "I'm glad you're here."

More movement, and then Troy's body was almost touching

his. He could feel Troy's breath on the back of his neck when he said, "Me too."

For a moment, everything was very still and quiet. And then Troy's hand slid, very slowly and gently, down Harris's arm to his wrist. Harris was sure every hair was standing up in its wake.

Troy stopped at his wrist, fingers lightly stroking the sensitive underside, and Harris would swear it was the most intimate touch he'd ever received. He stifled a gasp, not wanting to make a sound in case Troy realized what he was doing and stopped.

But Troy didn't stop. He stretched his fingertips and brushed them over Harris's palm, making him shiver.

Touch me, Harris thought. *Touch me everywhere.*

Warm breath tickled his nape. "I'm sorry you were on that plane."

Harris exhaled. "Could've been worse." He curled his fingers until they met Troy's in the middle of his palm.

"I know." And then Troy pressed his lips, just briefly, to the back of Harris's neck. It was the softest of kisses, almost nothing, but Harris couldn't hold in his gasp this time.

"Sorry," Troy said, and he began to pull away. Harris laced their fingers together and pulled him close, wrapping Troy's arm firmly around his chest.

"I wouldn't hate it if you did that again," Harris said.

For a moment, Troy did nothing. Then Harris felt the wonderful tickle of his lips against his neck again. Then another kiss, just below that spot. Then another, to the right. Painfully gentle and perfect.

The mattress shifted, and Troy must have raised himself up a bit because now his lips were caressing Harris from a new angle. He trailed kisses up the side of his neck, behind his ear, making Harris shudder happily.

Troy sighed against Harris's skin, then Harris felt the wet warmth of a tongue, just under his ear where his beard started.

"Yes," Harris breathed. There were a bunch of questions flying around in his head, but he didn't want to worry about them because he was already hard and he really fucking wanted whatever was happening right now.

He took a chance and rolled over so he was facing Troy. He couldn't quite see him, in the dark, but he found his face with his fingers. He felt the scratch of stubble, the sharp line of his jaw, and then his thumb brushed over Troy's wet lips.

"Harris." Troy's voice was worn thin, making the name sound like a dying wish. He captured Harris's hand with his own and kissed his knuckles, flicking his tongue gently against the tight skin. Harris let out a long, shaky breath, unable to believe this was really happening. He'd dreamed of this, fantasized about Troy countless times over the past several weeks, but he never thought it would ever be real. And even in his fantasies, he'd never expected Troy to be so devastatingly sweet.

Finally, Troy leaned in and kissed him. Their lips found each other in the dark, brushing shyly together. It was gentle for only a few seconds, and then Harris threaded his fingers into Troy's silky hair and kissed him back, hard and hungry.

He was kissing Troy Barrett. Unbelievable.

Troy moaned into his mouth and rested a hand on the side of Harris's face, stroking his beard with his thumb. His tongue stroked over Harris's, and he applied the slightest amount of pressure to the hinge of Harris's jaw, urging him to open more for him. Harris did, wanting as much as he could have of this man. Wanting Troy to take whatever he needed from him.

Somehow, despite the perfect wet heat of Troy's mouth and the ache of Harris's rigid cock, Harris was able to form a responsible thought. Was Troy really okay with this?

Harris broke the kiss, but only left enough distance between their lips to pant, "Is this—are you—"

"Can we talk about it later?"

Harris nodded, his forehead bumping against Troy's. Later.

He kissed him again, and for several minutes lost himself in the exquisite pleasure of kissing someone he really liked. It had been a long time, and Troy's mouth was lovely. So was his body, which Harris couldn't see, but he could smooth his palm over the soft fabric of Troy's T-shirt, mapping the hard muscles beneath.

Feeling daring, he rolled Troy to his back and straddled his waist. Troy let out a huff of surprise, then gasped when Harris kissed under his jaw, then down into the hollow of his throat. Harris angled his hips, letting Troy feel his erection through his pajama pants. Letting him know that Harris was a thousand percent on board with this, and that he wasn't always the goofy guy who hung out with hockey players.

Troy responded by jerking his hips up, and they both groaned when their hard cocks bumped together. Harris was fully gone now. He wanted Troy to make him forget everything.

Troy rolled them over, covering Harris with his solid, heavy body and kissing him again. Harris writhed underneath him as Troy ground their erections together. Even with barriers of fabric in the way, Harris was losing his mind. He loved being pinned down like this. Loved that Troy was so hard for him. Loved every soft sound Troy was making.

"Fuck, that's so good, Troy. Don't stop."

"Want this. Want you," Troy rasped.

God, Harris needed more information. How long had Troy wanted him? Would he still want him tomorrow?

Fuck it. Nothing mattered right now except the pressure building in Harris's balls. He needed release more than he needed answers. But also . . .

"We should," he panted, "get our pants out of the way."

"Yeah, okay." Troy yanked down Harris's waistband, just enough to free his erection, then did the same with his own pants. Troy's dick brushed against Harris's, solid and smooth and hot.

Had Troy done this before? Was this his first time with a man? He seemed confident, but if he'd been with other men and wasn't straight, then why hadn't he mentioned it to Harris? He must have known he didn't need to hide that from him.

Later. These were questions for later.

"Kiss me," Harris said, needing the distraction.

Troy was on him immediately, kissing him with all the urgency that Harris felt. Rutting against him like a teenager, which was so much hotter than it had any right to be. Harris had never seen Troy just let go before, and he wished the lamp were on because he wanted to see his face.

Instead, Harris cupped his cheek and murmured encouraging words against Troy's lips. "So good. Fuck, I'm close. Want you to come."

Troy grunted and wrapped a hand around both of their dicks. Harris arched into the touch. "That's perfect. Holy shit, Troy."

He put his hand over Troy's, helping him stroke them both off. He brushed his fingers over Troy's tight balls and enjoyed the way Troy shuddered and moaned.

"I—fuck, Harris. I'm gonna come. I'm gonna—"

"Yeah. Me too. Me too. *Fuck*."

Harris cracked open, every part of him bursting with pleasure as he unloaded between their bodies. He cried out, probably too loudly because Troy pushed three fingers against his lips. It didn't do much to quiet him. Fuck, he hadn't had an orgasm like that one in ages.

For a minute, they stayed where they were, Troy braced over Harris, both men breathing hard. Then Troy blew out a breath and flopped onto his back beside Harris.

"Holy shit," Troy said. "I fucking needed that."

"Me too, buddy." Harris should have had the foresight to lift his own T-shirt out of the way, because now the cotton was soaked with their mingled releases. He couldn't be mad about it.

After a couple of minutes, Troy left the bed and went into the bathroom. Harris scrubbed a hand over his face as the reality of what they'd just done started to set in. He never would have predicted this happening in a million years, and now that it had he felt a bit anxious. He hoped they hadn't just fucked up their fledgling friendship, because he really liked Troy.

He turned on the lamp and looked down at himself. When he saw the state of his T-shirt, he started laughing.

"What?" Troy asked, returning from the bathroom.

"Nothing. I'm a mess, is all." Harris waved a hand over his shirtfront.

"Oh. Sorry."

"It's at least half my fault," Harris joked.

He couldn't read Troy's expression, but he seemed . . . uneasy. Harris knew they needed to talk, but sleep was probably more important. "I'll get cleaned up, then we should get some sleep."

"Right, um."

"You can still stay here. If you want."

Troy's face relaxed a bit. "Okay."

Harris grabbed a clean shirt from his suitcase and headed into the bathroom. He was self-conscious about baring his chest, so he changed in private. When he returned to the bed, Troy was already under the covers, facing him. Harris crawled in beside him, but kept some distance between their bodies.

"That wasn't my plan," Troy said, "when I came to your room. I wasn't expecting . . . that."

Harris smiled. "Me neither. But, um, thanks. It helped."

Troy yawned, which made Harris laugh and Troy smile slightly. "Yeah."

He closed his eyes, and Harris allowed himself a moment to admire his handsome, peaceful face, before turning off the light.

CHAPTER FIFTEEN

Troy woke up first.

For a few wonderful moments, while his brain was still foggy with sleep, he was happy. He had Harris's warm, solid bulk under his arm, and when he inhaled, he smelled apples.

Then reality set in.

He shouldn't be in Harris's bed, and he certainly shouldn't have rubbed off on Harris last night. Shouldn't have kissed him, shouldn't have thrust into their joined hands. Shouldn't have soaked Harris's shirt with his release.

Troy was a monster. Harris was so good and sweet, and Troy kept feeding from him like a vampire.

Fuck, the things Troy wanted to do to him. He wanted to absolutely take him apart, but then he wanted Harris to be there for him when it was over. Comforting him. Caring about him.

Troy was so fucking selfish.

He nuzzled into Harris's thick hair, breathing him in. Trying to memorize everything about this perfect moment before he forced himself to leave.

Harris let out a long, content sigh and wiggled slightly

against him. His ass nudged Troy's morning wood, causing a soft moan to escape.

"G'morning," Harris slurred sleepily.

Troy jerked his hips away from him. "Hi."

Harris placed a hand on Troy's forearm and pressed it tighter against his chest. "I could stay here all day."

So could Troy. He was utterly, wonderfully cozy and relaxed in a way he didn't even think was possible for him.

Which was exactly why he couldn't stay.

He retrieved his arm, then left the bed while he still had the willpower to do so. Harris rolled to his back and blinked at him, sleepy and confused. His hair was rumpled, and one side of his face was pink from where it had been pressed into the pillow. Troy wanted to eat him alive.

"You're leaving?"

"Yeah. I, uh, I should get back to my own room. Y'know." The last thing Troy wanted was for anyone on the team to know that he'd spent the night with Harris. For Harris's sake, more than his own.

"Right." Harris sounded dejected.

"So, okay. See you later, I guess."

Harris sat up. "Are you sure we shouldn't talk first?"

God, he looked so hurt. But the kindest thing Troy could do for him was leave.

"Nah. I'm gonna—" He pointed to the door, then after one last glance at Harris's miserable face, left.

Well.

Harris certainly wasn't going to let *this* stand.

He would give Troy some room, let him enjoy his day off in Florida as much as he still possibly could, and then he would talk to him. Because they *needed* to talk.

There was a chance that last night had been Troy's first sexual experience with a man. If it had been, then Harris knew his brain must be a mess of confused thoughts now. Everything about last night, from the plane to falling asleep in each other's arms, had been overwhelming and surreal. Harris wouldn't let Troy deal with all of that alone, no matter how self-sabotaging the guy was.

Harris eventually left the bed to take a shower. He'd have to get in touch with his boss, figure out a plan for today after the airplane incident. Let her know that he needed a new laptop. This was still a work trip, even if everything was fucked.

God, he didn't want to look at his phone. He was sure the team had released an official statement, and would have posted that to the social media accounts themselves. He probably had a million worried texts and voice mail messages from his family.

At least he could honestly tell them that his heart was doing its job. Props to the surgeon who installed his mechanical aortic valve three years ago. Props to whoever invented the mechanical aortic valve too. Holds up during near death experiences on airplanes, and hot and heavy make-out sessions with NHL hunks.

When Harris was dressed—excited to be wearing shorts and a T-shirt in January—he retrieved his phone from the bottom of his suitcase and turned it on. As he suspected, there were a ton of messages. He sent a group text to his parents and his sisters, assuring them he was fine and that he would call them later. He sent an email to his boss, Theresa, to let her know about the laptop situation and to see what she wanted him to do today now that no one on the team was in the mood for fun videos.

There was a text from Gen. What the fuck!!!! Are you ok?????

HARRIS:

I'm fine. A bit shaken up. Everyone is, I think.

GEN:

No shit. This team can't even win at days off.

Harris laughed out loud at that.

HARRIS:

I wonder if they'll be ok playing tomorrow night.

GEN:

We'll see. Also . . . you have to get on a plane again!

HARRIS:

Or we could stay here forever.

He added some palm tree emojis.

GEN:

Fuck you. It's minus twenty-five here today.

HARRIS:

Can't relate.

Gen didn't reply, which was normal for her. She often abruptly vanished during a text conversation. Harris decided to go see about some breakfast. It was almost noon, but he was sure there was an IHOP or a Denny's or something around. He could crush some pancakes right now.

He hated to eat alone, so he texted Wyatt. He got a reply almost immediately.

WYATT:
Hell yes.

HARRIS:
See if anyone else wants to go. I'll meet you in the lobby.

WYATT:
I'll try to get Roz to go. I think he needs it. Haas, too.

Half an hour later, Harris was sharing an IHOP booth with Ilya Rozanov, Wyatt Hayes, and Luca Haas. Luca, the rookie, was bleary-eyed behind his glasses. Too much to drink last night or not enough sleep. Wyatt seemed more or less his normal, cheerful self. Ilya barely spoke, and had been staring at some spot over Harris's shoulder for several minutes.

"I texted Barrett but didn't hear back," Wyatt said. "Not a surprise, I guess."

"He probably is tired," Ilya said mildly. He glanced quickly at Harris with raised eyebrows.

Harris blushed into his coffee mug. How did Ilya always know everything?

The server brought their ridiculous piles of food. They'd all ordered massive breakfast combos, except Ilya, who had ordered black coffee and toast.

"What are the kids doing today?" Wyatt asked Luca.

"We were going to rent scooters, but after last night I don't know. Everyone is . . ."

"Blah?" Harris offered.

"Yes. Exactly."

"Too bad Chiron isn't here," Harris joked. "That would cheer everyone up."

Ilya's head shot up, eyes burning with shock and indignation. "Then Chiron would have been on the *plane*. What the fuck, Harris? He would have been so scared!"

Harris put his hands up. "I was just saying. A puppy would be nice right now."

Ilya took an aggressive bite of his toast, his eyes still full of warning. Harris changed the subject. "Well, at least the team got a bus for the trip to Ft. Lauderdale on Friday."

"Thank fuck," Wyatt agreed.

"We still have to get on a plane on Sunday. Back to Ottawa," Ilya pointed out.

Silence hung over the table, thick with the anxiety of men who weren't used to being terrified. Or at least weren't used to talking about it.

Harris came to a decision. "We should have fun today."

Ilya snorted. "Doing what?"

"I don't know. Let's go to the beach. Let's . . . play mini golf."

Ilya looked like he had something to say about that, but Wyatt cut him off. "Sure. I'm in. Better than sitting around worrying about the flight home."

Luca glanced at Ilya, as if waiting for guidance. Ilya sighed. "Fine. Yes. Let's lie on the beach."

Luca smiled, and it made him look even younger than his twenty years. He worshipped Ilya and everyone knew it. "I'll go too."

This time Harris got to raise his eyebrows at Ilya. The Centaurs captain shut down his silent teasing with a glare and one sentence: "Did Barrett pack a bathing suit, do you think?"

Troy's sneakers pounded the sand as he pushed himself one more mile. The sun was hot, the air humid, but he didn't want to stop running. Not yet.

It felt great, being able to run outdoors like this. On an endless beach with the sun beating down on his chest and back. His sweat-soaked T-shirt hung from the waistband of his shorts, brushing his thigh with each stride.

Finally, when his lungs couldn't take any more, he slowed to a jog, and then a walk. He could see the hotel ahead, not too far. He pulled his shirt from his waistband and wiped his face.

He couldn't stop thinking. About Harris. About the plane. About the game they were supposed to somehow play tomorrow night. About the impending flight home. About Dallas Kent. About Ryan Price. About how many years Troy had spent being mean, so full of anger and fear that he'd been incapable of making a good decision.

He also thought about the way Harris had cried out Troy's name when he'd climaxed, so loudly that Troy had frantically tried to silence him. And about how wonderful it had felt to wake up with Harris in his arms. He shouldn't have left him the way he had that morning. He should have talked to him. Harris probably never wanted to talk to him again, after that, and Troy couldn't blame him.

He sat down hard on the sand, and called his mom.

"Troy? Oh my god, I just heard about—"

"I'm okay. I'm fine. It was scary, but we're all okay."

"*Are* you okay? You sound a little rough."

"I just finished a run."

"Oh."

Troy pulled his knees up and fixed his gaze on the ocean. "Sorry. Where are you? Did I wake you up?"

"I'm in New Zealand. Auckland. Just got here yesterday. It's about six in the morning here, so don't worry about it."

New Zealand. Jesus. It hit Troy suddenly just how far away his mom was, and how desperately he wanted her with him.

"I miss you," he said, sounding as wrecked as he felt.

"Oh, honey. You don't have to act brave for me. You must be traumatized."

"It's not that." Troy exhaled. "I don't know, it's probably partly that. But it's everything. I keep fucking up." He grimaced. "Sorry. *Messing* up."

She laughed gently. "I've heard that word before. Talk to me."

Troy wasn't sure he could. Not without telling her *everything*. And if he was going to come out to his mom, he didn't want it to be like this.

Except, fuck. He'd almost died yesterday. He could have died without her ever knowing, and for some reason he hated that thought.

He took a breath.

And went in a completely different direction.

"I feel useless. Like, with Dallas. Nothing bad has happened to him. I can't stop thinking about his victims and no one else seems to give a shit. He was just named Player of the Week! Like . . . I don't know if there's anything I can do, but maybe there is."

Mom was silent a moment, then said, "That's a lot to carry."

"Like, I wasn't a witness to anything, but only because I wasn't paying close enough attention. I should have been. I could have stopped him. I could have—"

"First of all, I understand what you are saying and why you feel that way. But, Troy, you know it's not your fault, right? Dallas was the one who assaulted those women. Dallas is the bad guy."

"He was my best friend."

"I know," she said quietly. "I'm sorry."

"I just . . . want to be better. I want to be, I don't know, proud of myself. I want to be worth looking up to."

"Well, you're not bad at hockey."

Troy huffed. "I know. But that's not enough."

"As far as Dallas goes, there's not much you *can* do. None of his victims are pressing charges, and, like you said, you're not a witness. But you can help in other ways."

"Like what?" God, Troy would do anything. "What ways?"

"Off the top of my head, and remember, it is *very* early in the morning here, but you could donate to charities that help victims of sexual assault. You could use your social media to promote those organizations, and to provide general support for victims."

"Okay. Yeah, I could do that." Troy was getting excited. "What else?"

"Pay closer attention. I was with your father for nearly thirty years, so I know all about seeing someone through rose-tinted glasses and overlooking bad behavior. I'm more careful about who I spend time with now."

Troy hoped he was already ahead of the game on that one. "I've made some new friends here. Kinda. Good guys. *Better* guys."

"You can be friends with women, too, Troy. Don't forget that."

Troy flushed. "I know. I'm just around men mostly."

"That might be something worth changing."

It seemed easier said than done since Troy wasn't even great at making friends with his *teammates*, but it was something to consider. He'd add it to his homework list. "All right."

"It sounds like you're feeling better already."

"I am. Thanks." He decided to end the call before he started crying on a public beach. "I've gotta go. I love you."

"I love you too. I'm proud of you."

"Bye, Mom."

He sat with everything Mom had suggested to him for a few

minutes. He'd never been afraid of putting in hard work when it came to improving himself physically. It was time to be brave about improving the rest of him.

Harris was a professional, first and foremost, and he would never use his access to the team as an opportunity to ogle NHL stars.

But.

He was, at that moment, on a beach surrounded by very fit, very attractive hockey players, most of whom were only wearing swimming trunks. It wasn't terrible.

The beach excursion had proven to be more popular than the IHOP breakfast, and there were about a dozen members of the Ottawa Centaurs gathered on the sand in a loud and happy cluster. It was nice to hear them laughing, and to see them looking almost relaxed.

Harris was one of the only ones wearing a shirt, but it was a tank top, so he felt practically naked. He was tossing a Frisbee with Bood and Dykstra, which was a physical activity he was actually good at.

He'd engaged in another physical activity he was good at last night, so he was on a real fitness kick lately. Practically a decathlete.

He'd been trying to go about his day as a normal guy who'd been forced to face his own mortality, and not a guy who had faced his own mortality and then gotten off with Troy Barrett. It was difficult because he kept hearing the way Troy had gasped his name. The way he'd gently stroked Harris's wrist. Those first careful, precious kisses to the back of Harris's neck.

And, whoops. He missed the Frisbee.

"My fault." He jogged after the Frisbee, which had landed a few yards behind him. He picked it up, and when he stood he spotted something that nearly made him drop it back in the sand.

Troy Barrett. Shirtless and sweaty. Walking toward Harris.

"Oh. Hey," Troy said, when he got close. He glanced around at his frolicking teammates. "What's going on? Beach party?"

"Beach," Harris said faintly. It was the best he could manage. He hadn't actually seen Troy bare-chested in person before and, wow. It was a whole experience.

His gaze traveled over Troy's wide chest with its smooth, sculpted pecs and dark nipples, down to the ridges of his six-pack abs and the dark trail of hair that disappeared into the waistband of his shorts.

Troy looked toward the ocean. "I should take a dip. I'm a mess."

"Yeah." There was sand clinging to Troy's glistening skin, on his thighs and calves, on his forearms. There was some on his neck. Harris knew that, in practice, it would be awful, but he really wanted to lick it all off.

Then Troy was removing his socks and sneakers, leaving them in a pile with the T-shirt he removed from his waistband. "Wanna come?"

"Uh." The waves looked really inviting, and Harris couldn't remember the last time he'd gotten to swim in an ocean, but he also didn't want to take his shirt off.

He wasn't ashamed of his body or anything. Sure, it didn't quite stack up to the Adonises he was surrounded by, but that didn't really bother him. It was that there were things he didn't want Troy to see. Things that would lead to questions that Harris didn't feel like answering right now.

Troy was already walking toward the surf, shorts clinging to his muscular ass. "Fuck it," Harris muttered, and followed him. He'd leave the shirt on. It would dry.

The water was warm and wonderful, and Harris laughed when the first wave crashed over him, nearly knocking him over. Troy dived into the next wave, using perfect form. When he surfaced he shook his head, flicking droplets of water into the sunshine like a merman.

The next wave did knock Harris over, but only because his legs were basically jelly at that point.

"Are you okay?" Troy asked. He waded over to him, gripping Harris's bicep with one strong hand.

Harris coughed a couple of times, and grimaced at the taste of salt water. "I'm fine. Thanks." He realized he had a hand on Troy's shoulder, using him for balance. He took a risk, and said, somewhat seductively, "My hero."

There was a flash of something in Troy's eyes—heat? fear?—and then he stepped back. "Watch out for sharks."

"It's not the sharks you should be worried about. It's the Portuguese man-of-war."

"The what?"

"Jellyfish. Their stingers are deadly, and they can grow over a hundred feet long!"

Troy stared down into the water around his body. "They have those here?"

"Yeah. Sometimes."

Troy glared at him. "Why'd you have to say that, man?"

Harris laughed. "Sorry. I mean, I think they're more a South Florida thing."

"Then why'd you fucking mention them? Jesus, now I can't think of anything else." Troy glanced warily out to sea, and Harris couldn't resist reaching out and gently brushing the back of Troy's calf with his toe.

To his delight, it made Troy *scream*.

"Fuck! What the fuck? Was that you?"

Harris was laughing too hard to answer.

"Oh, fuck *you*." And then Troy was tackling Harris, both men landing hard on the sand under the shallow water. Harris sat up, still laughing, Troy kneeling between his sprawled legs.

Troy was laughing too, really laughing, eyes crinkled, as water dripped from his hair and off the tip of his nose.

He stopped laughing when he noticed the way Harris was staring at him. For a few seconds, they held each other's gazes, both breathing hard. Obviously Troy wasn't going to kiss him here, in public, in front of half of his team, but damn. Maybe he wanted to?

Instead, Troy playfully splashed water in Harris's face and stood up. He offered Harris his hand and pulled him to his feet. There was definitely heat in Troy's gaze, but Troy looked away before Harris could get lost in it.

Oh yeah. They definitely had some things to discuss later.

Troy was exhausted, slightly sunburned, and a little bit tipsy by the time he returned to his hotel room that night.

It had been, all things considered, a very fun and relaxing day. Ilya had mentioned to Troy that it had been Harris's idea, getting everyone to go to the beach. Troy wasn't surprised.

By the end of the afternoon, nearly all of the players, and most of the coaches and other staff, had joined in the fun. At six o'clock, Bood announced that he had managed to book them a bunch of tables at a Mexican restaurant, so the party had moved there.

The only stressful thing about the day was Troy's struggle to stop himself from openly staring at Harris. He tried to keep some distance from him, especially after he'd been nearly overcome with the need to kiss him in the ocean. He'd looked so adorable, soaked and laughing with the sun highlighting all of the shades of green in his eyes. His wet tank top had clung to his chest, and Troy had seen the outline of chest hair and firm nipples pressed against the fabric.

Troy hadn't sat at the same table as Harris at the restaurant, but he'd kept stealing glances at him. He'd been able to hear his cheerful voice and ridiculous laugh throughout the meal, and he'd been a bit jealous every time he heard one of the other guys laughing at one of his jokes.

God, Troy had such a crush on this guy.

He was determined to stay in his own room tonight. He could feel the pull from Harris's room down the hall, but he would resist it. Harris deserved someone way, way, *way* better than Troy.

Which reminded Troy of his plan to start an official Instagram account, for real this time. He knew he was going to get shit on in the replies, especially if he actively posted in support of sexual assault victims, but fuck it. He could handle it. It was such a small discomfort, in the grand scheme of things.

He wondered how to get one of those little blue checks. Harris would know. He could text him and ask. Or walk down to his room and see if he—

No. Troy could figure this out.

He was several minutes into a tutorial video on getting verified when there was a knock at his door.

He opened it, hoping it was anyone but Harris, but also really wanting it to be Harris.

It was Harris.

"Hi. Am I interrupting anything?"

"Nope." Troy, against his better judgment, let Harris into his hotel room.

When the door was closed, Troy leaned back against it. "What's up?"

"I think we should talk, maybe."

Troy wasn't enough of an ass to ask *about what?* so he just nodded. "Okay." He tried to keep his expression blank, not exposing the way his heart was racing, or the way he really wanted to pull Harris into his arms.

"So, about last night," Harris said with a nervous smile. "Was that your first time? With a man, I mean?"

Even though Troy had already kissed Harris, gotten off with him, and held him in his arms all night, he still had to force the admission out. "No."

Harris's eyes widened. "Wow. Okay. So, um . . ."

Troy crossed the room and sat on the bed. "I'm gay." He let that hang there a moment. Harris didn't say anything, just stood in front of him, waiting patiently. "I had a boyfriend. We were together, secretly, for almost two years."

"Oh. Jesus, that sounds hard."

"It was, I guess. But neither of us wanted to come out, so it worked. I thought it did anyway. But then he dumped me and now he's . . ." Troy sighed. "I guess I can just tell you. It was Adrian Dela Cruz."

Harris's mouth dropped open. "Wait. *What?*"

"Yeah."

"The *actor*?"

"Yeah."

"But when were you dating? Because I thought he said in his Instagram post that he'd been with Justin Green for months. They're engaged!"

"He dumped me in November. So, yeah. You can do the math."

Harris sat beside him and placed a hand on his arm. "Aw, Troy. I'm sorry."

Troy swallowed thickly. He had never talked about Adrian to anyone before. "It sucked, seeing that post. I was in love with him, I thought. I mean, I still think I was."

Harris took his hand, rubbing his thumb over Troy's knuckles. "Damn. I was so excited when I saw that post. So happy for him. I had no idea he was a total scumbag."

Troy huffed. "He found someone better. I don't know why I was surprised."

Harris looked at him sternly. "Don't say that."

His thumb was still brushing over Troy's knuckles, steady and soothing. "I was thinking about coming out for him, if he wanted," Troy said quietly. It was something he hadn't ever admitted to himself, really, let alone said out loud. He'd only considered it when he'd been in Adrian's arms, behind the safety of a locked door, but in those rare, perfect moments, Troy had felt brave.

"Do you have people you can talk to about him?" Harris asked quietly.

"No. I've never told anyone about him."

Harris's thumb stilled. "You've been dealing with a broken heart all by yourself?"

Troy shrugged one shoulder.

Harris squeezed his hand. "Oh, Troy. Jeez, you've had a rough couple of months."

Troy gazed into Harris's warm eyes and offered a small smile. "It hasn't been all bad."

Harris's smile in response was so sweet, it took all of Troy's self-control not to kiss him.

He straightened his shoulders. "So, yeah. It wasn't my first time, so don't worry about, um, that. And obviously we both needed some release after . . . everything. It's not a big deal."

Harris let go of his hand, and his smile faded. "Got it. It was just convenient."

Troy should have been relieved that Harris understood, but he wanted to grab his hand back. Instead, he nodded and said, "Exactly. I liked it a lot, don't get me wrong, but I'm not sitting here thinking it means more than it does." *Please tell me it means more.*

"Right," Harris said. He laughed, but it sounded forced. "Me neither."

Troy stood, because the proximity to Harris, especially while on a bed, was too much. "So, I should get to bed, probably. Game day tomorrow."

"Yeah. Okay." Harris stood, and Troy could tell he was hurt. Had he been hoping to stay? To go another round with him? Maybe this time with their clothes off? God, Troy wanted to throw him on the bed and just fucking wreck him. Or maybe just hold him all night and breathe in his scent.

"Good night," Harris said. He had one hand on the door handle, but he was twisted around to face Troy, like he was hoping Troy would stop him.

"Good night," Troy said, and turned away. The door opened and clicked shut behind him.

CHAPTER SIXTEEN

Troy was sure he looked at least as bad as Ryan Price always used to on planes. His whole body was gripped with an intense feeling of panic that he was just barely keeping in check.

Fortunately, based on the ashen faces and white knuckles of his teammates around him, everyone was battling their own inner wars, so Troy couldn't feel too embarrassed about it.

The plane hadn't even taken off yet. They'd just closed the door, and already everyone was on edge.

The games in Florida hadn't been great, but had been okay considering. They'd lost 3–2 to Tampa, and then 2–1 to Florida, so not the blowouts that people were probably expecting. Troy thought Harris's insistence that they have fun on their day off probably helped the team mentally.

But it wasn't helping now. Not when they were sealed inside a death trap exactly like the one that had burst into flames a few short days ago.

The silence on the plane was eerie; the absence of chatter and laughter was only adding to the tension. By the time the plane was racing down the runway, about to lift off, Troy was swallowing a lump in his throat.

He was sitting alone. He wished he was sitting with Harris, but that would only make him fall into bad habits. He knew he'd be grasping Harris's hand right now if it were anywhere near him.

Ilya was sitting across the aisle, also alone. His head was down, eyes closed, and Troy thought he'd pre-emptively gotten himself into the brace for impact position. Then he noticed his lips moving, forming silent words, and he realized he must be praying.

Weird. He knew Ilya wore that cross around his neck, but he'd never thought of him a religious man. Troy supposed if you prayed at all, though, now was the time.

Just let us get home safe, he thought to no one in particular. His own lazy version of a prayer.

Statistically, he told himself, it was extremely unlikely to be on two planes in a row with mechanical failures. But half an hour into the flight, Troy's muscles were aching from his tense posture. He glanced over at Ilya and saw him staring hard out the window, as if watching the engine to make sure it stayed together. There was something very unsettling about an anxious Ilya Rozanov.

Troy closed his eyes, tipped his head back, and wished he'd taken some sort of sleeping pill. That would have been smart. Since he hadn't, he tried to think about something pleasant.

He'd been trying *really* hard not to fantasize about Harris, but desperate times called for desperate measures, and the sexy images in his head were extremely effective as far as distractions went.

So he let himself drift into a lovely diversion where Harris was rubbing that soft beard all over Troy's balls while he sucked him off. In this scenario he could actually see Harris, and they'd both taken off their clothes. Damn, he wished they'd at least gotten naked for that one and only hookup.

Troy liked him way too much. He'd *come out* to him. Maybe in a very backwards kind of way, where he had sex with him first and then told him he was gay, but that was how he'd told Adrian too.

"All right, everyone. It's story time."

Troy's eyes shot open at the sound of Harris's extremely well-projected voice. He was standing in the aisle, right in the middle of the plane, grinning at everyone like this was a totally normal thing to do. "Have I told you guys about my sister Anna's first date with her husband?"

"No!" someone shouted.

"Yes!"

"Tell us anyway!"

"Okay, so Anna had been crushing on this guy, Mike, for months. I can let you know now that he's a super-nice guy and we all love him, but at the time all I knew was he was the reason I couldn't borrow our parents' truck that night."

There were some scattered chuckles already. Troy would bet that Harris had the attention of every person on board. He even turned as he talked, making sure everyone at the front of the plane could hear him too.

"Anna and I never fought much, but that night it got vicious. I'd been invited to a party, and I'd offered to give a lift to this supercute boy in my geography class, so I needed that truck."

Troy's heart raced at the easy way Harris had said *cute boy* in front of an audience of NHL players.

The story went on, and everyone hung on Harris's every word. Troy found he was on the edge of his seat for a reason that had nothing to do with fearing for his life. Even Ilya was smiling and laughing, and he groaned along with Troy when Harris told them that Anna had won the truck that night, and Harris hadn't gotten to woo his cute geography boy.

"So Anna's got her man in the passenger seat, and they're

driving to the movie theater, talking and flirting, and he asks her if she hears anything weird. Like, maybe something wrong with the truck. They both stay silent for a few seconds, and hear nothing, so he decides he was imagining things."

"Harris," Ilya warned, "if this story is about a fucking vehicle breaking . . ."

"It's not! I promise. Okay, so they drive some more, and this time Anna hears it. Like a weird scratchy sound. But then it stops. The truck is driving fine, doesn't seem to be any issue. No warning lights or anything. So she pulls over into a parking lot because she just wants to check the rear part of the cab, and when she peeks behind Mike's seat, she sees a *skunk*."

"No!" someone yelled.

"Swear to god."

"Did you put the skunk in there? As revenge for taking the truck?"

"I didn't!" Harris laughed. "But she still doesn't believe me. But now she's on this date with this guy she's been into forever, and there's a fucking skunk in the back, which is obviously a precarious situation because they have to get it out without, y'know, setting it off."

"What the fuck did they do?"

"They were smart. They got out, left the doors open, and went to sit on the curb a few meters away. Eventually the skunk left on its own, no harm done. But the cute thing is that Anna and Mike had their first kiss sitting on that curb, waiting for that skunk. So the skunk is, like, a matchmaker. But man, she was still so fucking mad at me when she got home."

"I think you did it," a voice that was definitely Bood's said.

Harris put his hands up. "I really didn't. How would I even have managed that without getting sprayed? But I'll tell you what, I'm glad it wasn't me driving around trying to impress a boy that night."

"Did you ever hook up with that boy?" Ilya asked, which was exactly the question Troy wanted to ask but was scared to.

"Yeah. We went to get McFlurrys after school a few days later. Then we went back to his bedroom."

There were a few whoops and catcalls, which Harris waved away. "It wasn't *that* great."

Laughter filled the plane. The mood had shifted so drastically since Harris had begun his story, it was staggering. And really impressive. Troy felt a swell of unearned pride.

"So who else has a story?" Harris asked. He pointed to Evan Dykstra. "D, I know you've got a million."

"Well," Dykstra said slowly as he stood up, "since we're talking about disaster dates . . ."

Everyone cheered. Harris caught Troy's gaze and winked at him. Troy smiled back, easy and effortless. He'd bet he could smile all the time if he had enough of Harris in his life.

Eventually, they landed safely in Ottawa, and everyone on board breathed a collective sigh of relief. Troy caught up with Harris once he reached the tarmac.

"How'd you do that?" he asked.

"Do what?"

"Get everyone to loosen up. Stand up and tell that story like you weren't terrified too."

Harris huffed out a white cloud into the frigid winter air. "It was going to be a really long flight if we all sat there white-knuckling our armrests. And, I dunno. I figure, if we're all going to die in a plane crash, then there's nothing we can do about it anyway. May as well enjoy life while we can, right?"

"I guess."

Harris bumped him with his shoulder. "I know this trip was a shit show, but I had fun with you."

Something bubbled up inside of Troy. Happiness, he supposed. "Me too."

"Holy shit."

Gen didn't look up from her computer. "What?"

"Troy Barrett has an Instagram account now, and it's, um. You should look at it."

"Okay," she said slowly, and held out her hand for Harris's phone. Harris walked across the office and handed it to her.

"Holy shit," she said after she looked at Troy's first couple of posts.

The bio for TroyBarrett17 sent a clear message: *NHL player for the Ottawa Centaurs. I believe victims of sexual assault.*

He'd made three posts so far. The most recent was an infographic with some statistics about sexual assault that he'd gotten from a national organization's timeline (and, Harris was pleased to see, he had credited them properly for it and encouraged people to follow them). The second post was a graphic that listed the phone numbers and websites of organizations that helped survivors of sexual assault. The first post was a selfie, taken in the team gym. Troy's face was flushed, and his hair was damp with sweat. You could see sweat darkening the top of his gray T-shirt as well. He was almost smiling. Almost.

The caption read: *Working hard. Always room for improvement.*

It *could* just be referring to Troy's physical fitness, and his on-ice performance, but Harris didn't think that was what Troy meant. Not entirely anyway.

"He's not fucking around," Gen said. "I'm impressed."

"Yeah," Harris said distantly, still staring at Troy's selfie. He was also impressed. Impressed, surprised, proud, and a little bit infatuated.

Also, did Troy know what a thirst trap that selfie was? He must, right?

"How are the replies?" Gen asked. "Does he even have followers yet?"

"He has over five thousand followers so far," Harris said.

He hit the follow button, then scrolled through the replies on each post. They were mostly positive, some welcoming him to Instagram, showing their support as fans. A few were explicitly supportive of his last two posts. And a few fucking dickbags who seemed delighted that Troy had given them a place to trash him directly. Some of the negative replies even tagged Dallas Kent. Jesus.

"Well," Harris said, sitting back in his chair, "time to promote his posts." He made a show of cracking his knuckles, then got to work.

He hadn't spoken to Troy since they'd returned from the Florida trip two days ago, though they'd parted on friendly terms. Harris had just assumed that Troy, like everyone else on the team, wanted some alone time after that road trip.

It was so hard to read Troy. He'd told Harris, clearly, that their hookup hadn't meant anything. But Harris also got the impression that the only other man Troy had been with was his ex-boyfriend, Adrian. Which, to Harris, meant that their hookup must have meant *something*.

It had meant something to Harris. He'd had plenty of hookups—guys he met in clubs or at parties or online—and he usually enjoyed them. He liked meeting new people, however briefly, and he liked sex. He liked comforting people and making them happy, and sex, he'd found, made a lot of people happy.

The encounter with Troy hadn't been the stuff of erotic legend—they hadn't even removed their clothes, and there hadn't been any real skill involved. It had just been burning, unchecked need and desperation, and Harris had never experienced anything quite like it before.

And those kisses. Wowzers. Troy knew how to use those pillowy lips of his. Harris would bet they'd feel great on his—

"Why wasn't Rozanov at practice yesterday?" Gen asked.

Harris blinked as he followed his coworker's voice back to reality. "Huh?"

"Ilya wasn't at practice. Unusual for him. It wasn't an optional practice, and he wasn't doing therapy either. Do you think he's sick?"

Ilya had seemed a bit off since the airplane incident. Everyone had, really, but Ilya was always cool and unflappable, so his anxiety was more noticeable. "I don't know."

"I hope he plays tonight. The Admirals are going to wipe the floor with us if he's out." She rolled her neck, stretching it. "They'll probably destroy us either way, but it'll be worse without Rozanov."

"They might surprise you."

Gen huffed. "When has this team ever surprised me?"

The mood in the locker room was heavy. The Centaurs were fresh off the harrowing, and disappointing, road trip where they'd lost two out of their three games, and now they were about to face the top team in the East, the New York Admirals.

It felt like they'd already lost.

Coach Wiebe came in and tried to pump them up. He was, Troy had decided, a good coach. He didn't have a lot of experience, but he had a good sense for what each of his players needed at any time. And he was nice, which some people might see as a flaw in a hockey coach. Troy might have felt that way too, not long ago, but he liked Coach Wiebe a lot, and wanted to win for him.

Easier said than done.

After Coach left, the mood lightened a bit. There was no confidence in the room, though. In Toronto, the Guardians' locker room had always been loud and often aggressive before games. There'd always been an assumption among the players that they were going to win. That anything less was unacceptable. Here in Ottawa, the locker room energy felt more like an acceptance that they probably wouldn't win, but maybe they wouldn't embarrass themselves completely.

It was fucking annoying.

"Everyone listen."

Troy's head shot up and he was surprised to see Ilya standing in the middle of the room. He was team captain, but he wasn't one for speeches.

"The New York Admirals are not a better team than us." There was some scattered scoffing and laughter. Ilya cut it off. "They are *not*. They have Scott Hunter, we have *me*. They have Tommy Andersson—a good goalie. Young, talented, yes. We have Wyatt Hayes—a *great* goalie." He grinned at Wyatt. "Old, talented."

There were some enthusiastic whoops and claps around the room.

"Experienced," Wyatt corrected him jovially.

"They have Carter Vaughan, Hunter's right-hand man and one of the best forwards in the league. We have Zane Boodram *and* Troy Barrett." Ilya stretched his arms out. "I have *two* hands. Who is on Scott's left? Does anyone even know his name?"

It looked like Luca Haas wanted to supply the name of New York's top-line left wing forward, but he wisely kept his mouth shut.

"New York has Matti Jalo, but we have Evan Dykstra and Nick Chouinard." More cheering. Sticks were being drummed against the floor with each name that Ilya listed. "We've got Boyle, Holmberg, LaPointe and Young."

He proceeded to name every player in the room, sometimes adding something that was specifically impressive about them. "I am fucking tired of losing," Ilya said. "Enough. We are going to win this game tonight, and we are going to keep winning. We are going to fill every seat in this fucking arena. We are going to surprise *everyone* and we are going to the playoffs this year. Not next year. Not in the future. *This fucking year.*"

Everyone roared their agreement. Troy was astonished. This was exactly the energy he was looking for.

"We went through something together," Ilya said, more soberly. "It was fucking scary. But we are alive. We are all alive and I don't plan on wasting another second of it. Let's fucking go."

"Fucking right, Roz!" Dykstra yelled, over the deafening noise of cheering and banging sticks.

"Hell yes," Bood agreed. "Let's fuck up some Admirals!"

Troy bent for the puck drop to start the game. He was back to regularly playing right wing on the top line, and he was going to make sure he fucking stayed there.

He was facing the starting left wing player for New York, and he did, in fact, know who he was, but Ilya had inspired him.

"Hi. I'm Troy. What's your name?"

The man—Cale Wagner—narrowed his eyes. "Fuck you."

"Nice name. Pretty."

"Do you know how embarrassing it is that we even have to play against your shitty team?"

"Gonna be more embarrassing when you lose."

The puck dropped, and the game started with Wagner trying to knock Troy down. Troy was too fast, though, and was already charging toward the Admirals' zone, because Ilya had won the face-off.

There were no goals on the first shift, or even the second, but the Centaurs' third line came through and deflected the puck past Tommy Andersson less than two minutes into the game.

"Yeah!" Troy yelled, hammering the boards with his stick. "That's how you fucking do it!"

The crowd, which was a little bigger than usual—possibly as a show of support for their hometown players managing to not die in a plane crash—was on their feet. It was a great start.

Later into the first period, Scott Hunter tried to tie the game with an incredible wrist shot that Troy was sure was going to go in, but Wyatt gloved it down.

Ilya burst out laughing. "Wow, Hunter. That sucks. That should have gone in, right?"

Troy bumped Wyatt's blocker pad with his glove. "That was beautiful, Hazy."

"I'm not sure how I did that," Wyatt said.

"Because you're awesome."

Wyatt grinned at him from behind his goalie mask. "I almost forgot. Thanks for the reminder, Barrett."

Troy smiled as he skated toward the face-off circle. It was nice to feel like he might be friends with Wyatt now.

Ilya grabbed his arm outside the circle. "We're going to score on this play, okay?"

Troy laughed. "Sounds good. You got a plan?"

"Yes. Keep up with me."

Troy shook his head, still grinning as he bent down across from Cale Wagner. "Hi again," Troy said. "Wilson, right? Or Wagon? Sorry, I keep forgetting your name."

"Why don't you ask your mom?"

"Nah. There's no way she's heard of you."

The puck dropped and Ilya knocked it over to Troy. "Let's go!" Ilya yelled, and took off down the ice.

Troy had no problem keeping up, leaving Wagner in his dust. He made sure he entered the New York zone first, carrying the puck, then passed it to Ilya, who dropped it back to Bood while Ilya got himself past the Admirals defenseman. Bood passed to Troy, and Troy found Ilya in front of the net. The goaltender never had a chance.

The goal made it 2–0 for Ottawa. Troy jumped on top of Ilya against the boards, and Bood crushed up against both of them.

"Good job," Ilya said, tapping each of them on the forehead with the front of his helmet. "Let's do it again."

"No way," said Bood. "Next one's mine."

The next one, it turned out, came from Luca Haas in the second period. Unfortunately, it was after the Admirals had scored two goals to tie it up, but Haas's goal gave Ottawa the lead again.

By the third period, things were pretty intense. The Admirals were desperate for a goal to save their pride, and the Centaurs were determined to keep them from getting it.

There was some shoving after Wyatt made an easy save midway through the third period. Tempers were high, and Ilya had, as usual, been antagonizing Scott Hunter all night.

"I'm going to fucking kill you, Rozanov," Scott growled in Ilya's face. Troy was sort of holding Scott's arm, but it was mostly for show. Scott was roughly twice his size.

"You have been saying that for years," Rozanov said with a big grin. "But I am still here."

Scott turned away from him, briefly locking eyes with Troy, who let go of his arm immediately. Then Troy noticed Scott fighting a smile as he began to skate away.

"I think he likes you," Troy told Ilya.

"Of course he does. I'm great."

The score stayed at 3–2 for Ottawa for most of the third period. New York battled hard, hungry for the tying goal. But the Ottawa team worked together like they never had before, and kept their one-goal lead. It was stressful, trying to keep the Admirals from scoring, and the Ottawa bench was nervously watching the clock tick down the final minutes of play.

With three minutes left, getting close to the point where

New York was probably going to pull their goalie for the extra attacker, Troy got a breakaway. Dykstra put the puck on his stick in the Ottawa zone and Troy took off. He was one of the fastest skaters in the league, and a skilled stick handler. He poked the puck between the legs of the New York defenseman in his way, picked it up on the other side, and then he was all alone, closing in on the goalie.

Tommy Andersson was a good goalie, but Troy faked him out easily, dangling the puck and getting it over Andersson's outstretched leg.

It was a highlight reel goal for sure.

His linemates were on top of him a second later. Bood jostled his helmet and said, "I like those show-off goals of yours a lot more when we're on the same team."

After the game, most of the team went to celebrate at a bar called Monk's that Troy learned was a team favorite. It was an older tavern in the Glebe, not far from Troy's apartment.

Troy was sitting at a table with Evan Dykstra, Wyatt, and Wyatt's wife, Lisa. Quite a few wives and girlfriends had shown up at the bar, which Troy thought was cool. In Toronto, there'd been an unspoken no-partners rule for most team celebrations.

"I just ended my shift and I've never needed a beer more," Lisa said after her first sip. "If I fall asleep in a minute, just ignore me."

Wyatt wrapped an arm around her and kissed the top of her head. "Let me know when you want to leave, champ. We can continue the celebrations at home."

She shoved his chest lightly. "My celebrations involve a shower and bed."

He waggled his eyebrows. "Mine too."

Evan laughed. "I think Caitlin fell asleep hours ago. She said she was going to watch the game, but her texts stopped after the first period."

"I don't blame her," Lisa said sympathetically. "How is Susie doing?"

Evan lit up and started talking at length about his one-year-old daughter. Lisa smiled as she listened, but Troy noticed her snuggling closer into Wyatt, her eyelids growing heavier.

Troy scanned the bar to see what everyone else was up to. Ilya was loudly trash-talking Bood as they played pool. A rowdy table full of the younger players was littered with empty pitchers, which probably wasn't good.

Then he spotted Harris at the bar, and he stopped looking anywhere else. He hadn't noticed Harris come in, but he wasn't surprised that he was here. He was wearing a denim shirt, the sleeves rolled up to show off his forearms.

And he was talking to a very tall and attractive dark-haired man. Smiling at him. Laughing. And the other man was smiling and laughing too.

Troy's jaw clenched. He had no claim on Harris, obviously, but seeing him with another man made Troy realize that he'd been hoping to go home with Harris himself tonight.

He pushed back from the table and went to the bathroom. Maybe by the time he returned Harris would already have left with Johnny Handsome.

The bathroom was empty when he walked in. He parked himself at a urinal, and as he was opening his fly, the door opened behind him.

"Barrett," said Ilya Rozanov's voice.

Ilya sidled up to the urinal next to Troy, which was . . . cozy. Ilya was a weird guy, though, so it made sense.

"Having fun?" Ilya asked.

"Um."

"At the bar. Not in here."

"Yeah, sure." Troy tried to finish up as quickly as possible, but he'd drunk a lot of beer.

"Feels good to win." Ilya finished first, zipped himself up, and headed for the sinks. "To have something to celebrate."

"Hey, uh." Troy got himself tucked away and followed Ilya. "That speech before the game . . . I don't think we would have won without it."

"Everyone worked hard tonight," Ilya said as he inspected himself in the mirror. "You did a good job today."

"It was a pretty nice goal," Troy admitted.

"Not the goal. The posts you made. Instagram. It was good shit, Barrett."

"Oh. I didn't know you saw those."

Ilya's lips quirked into a teasing half smile. "I follow you. Did you not see?"

"I didn't really check after I posted those."

"You should. People like them. Especially after *I* shared them."

Oh god. Didn't Ilya have like hundreds of thousands of followers? Troy knew that the point of social media was to get your thoughts and photos seen by as many people as possible, but he still felt anxious. "So lots of people have seen them then?"

"Yes." Ilya clapped him on the shoulder. "Like I said. Good job."

Ilya left the bathroom, and Troy stared at the door, unsure if he was ready to go back out there. Unsure of who he even was anymore. He'd never felt so uncomfortable in his own skin. It had been easy, being an asshole. It had been safe. Now he was suddenly standing up for shit, and putting himself out there online, and thinking about publicly coming out as gay, and maybe seeing if Harris wanted to kiss him again.

He had no one to hide behind anymore, and the mask was so full of cracks he may as well throw it out.

Troy left the bathroom and, though he knew it was a bad idea, made a beeline toward the bar. And Harris. And the hot man Harris was probably flirting with.

"Troy!" Harris called out happily as soon as he spotted him. "Amazing goal tonight. Holy shit."

"Thanks." Troy's gaze was fixed on the smoke show Harris was practically holding hands with. *How many amazing goals did* you *score tonight, buddy?*

"This is Alain," Harris said. "Alain, this is Troy Barrett."

Alain stuck out his hand and Troy, after frowning at it for a second, shook it. Alain's hand was warm and strong, and his dark eyes were so beautiful they were hard to look at directly.

"Hi, Alain," Troy mumbled.

"It's an honor to meet you," Alain said with a heavy Quebecois accent. "Gen was telling me about your Instagram."

"Oh?"

"Alain is Gen's boyfriend," Harris supplied.

It was embarrassing how relieved Troy was by that. "That's cool. Gen seems great."

At that moment, Gen came up behind Alain. "Gen *is* great. Oh, hi, Troy. Nice goal tonight."

"Thanks."

"The GIF I posted of it has a zillion likes already," Harris said.

"Oh yeah?"

"Yup. And so do your Instagram posts now that the team accounts've shared them."

Troy felt a confusing mixture of embarrassment and pleasure. "You saw those, huh?"

"No thanks to you." Harris punched his arm playfully. "You

didn't tell me you created an account! Or that you were going to use it to be a fucking hero."

"As if." Troy's cheeks heated. "I had to, um, watch some tutorials, figuring out how to do some stuff, but I think I'm getting the hang of it."

"I love your posts, Troy," Gen said. "That's how you be an ally. Keep it up."

An ally. Troy supposed that's what he was, or what he was trying to be. Not a hero, certainly. "Thanks. I will."

Gen turned to Alain and said something to him in rapid French. Then she said, to Harris and Troy, "We're going to head out."

Harris gave each of them a hug while Troy stood awkwardly to the side.

"So," Harris said, after they left, "you want a drink?"

"Nah, I had a couple of beers already. I think I'm good." He gestured to Harris's pint glass. "Is that your sisters' cider?"

"You bet. They have it on tap here."

"Nice."

An awkward silence fell between them. It had been a pretty excellent day all around for Troy, and he couldn't help but think that the perfect way to cap it would be pinning Harris to a wall somewhere and kissing him breathless.

If Harris was into that.

"We haven't talked really. Since we got back from Florida," Troy said.

"I noticed that too."

"I haven't been avoiding you or anything. It's not because we, uh. Y'know."

Harris's eyes twinkled. "You sure?"

Troy couldn't lie to him. "Maybe it is. I'm kind of embarrassed about it."

Harris huffed. "Well, that's not what I want to hear."

"No! I mean, I'm not embarrassed about . . . what we did. It's because I kind of dumped a bunch of stuff on you and bolted."

"You did," Harris agreed. "But to be fair, it was a weird couple of days."

"Yeah, well." Troy ducked his head. "I also said that what we did wasn't a big deal. But the thing is, it kind of . . . was."

Harris's eyes widened.

"For me, at least," Troy said quickly. "I don't usually . . . do that. I've only ever done that with, um . . . well, you know." He hoped someday he'd be able to talk about being gay, about dating men, in a public place, but today wasn't that day.

"I know," Harris said gently. "When I left your hotel room after saying all that stuff, I spent the rest of the night thinking about what a big deal it must have been for you. All of it. What we did. What you were able to tell me. And I'm honored you trust me enough to share that with me."

Troy nudged the leg of a bar stool with his toe. "I do. Trust you. And, um. I liked what we did. A lot."

Harris put a hand on his arm, warm and steady. "Troy. Would you like to do what we did again?"

Troy's heart sped up, but he managed to nod.

"Would you like to do it . . . right now?"

Troy couldn't answer. He just stared, stunned at Harris's easy proposition. His gaze focused on Harris's lips, glistening with his last swig of cider.

Harris stepped slightly closer. "Because I would *really* like to."

Troy felt light-headed and couldn't think of anything except crushing their mouths together. His cock was already firming up, which was going to be noticeable in the snug jeans he was wearing.

"Yeah," he whispered, then, more loudly and steadily, said, "Yeah. Let's go."

Harris stepped back, and Troy damn near fell forward trying to chase his warmth. Harris steadied him with a helpful hand and laughed. "You sure you only had two beers?"

"I'm not drunk," Troy promised, straightening. "I'm just . . . eager."

Harris leaned into him, his breath brushing Troy's ear. "I can work with eager. Let's get our coats and get out of here."

CHAPTER SEVENTEEN

"You wanted to kiss me in there," Harris said as soon as they were alone on the snowy sidewalk.

"Was I obvious?"

Harris didn't think he'd ever forget the hungry way Troy had been staring at his lips back in the bar. And he didn't think he'd ever get *used* to Troy frigging Barrett wanting him. "A little."

"Well, if I'm being honest, I still want to kiss you."

Harris stopped walking and turned to face him. "Yeah?"

A car drove by, and Troy stepped away from him. "I'll wait."

Harris tried not to feel disappointed. Was he really expecting Troy to kiss him on a busy street, right outside a bar that was full of his teammates? That wouldn't be good for either of them.

"I parked at home and walked here," Harris said.

"Me too."

"Should we go to your place then? We're close to both."

Troy chewed his lip. "Let's go to your place, if that's okay."

"Definitely."

Troy's mouth curved into one of his rare and adorable little smiles. "I've been wanting to see where you live."

That warmed Harris. "It's not a palace, but I like it."

Snow was falling all around them, gentle but fluffy enough to pile up on the sidewalk. It was a beautiful, quiet night. Once they turned onto Harris's street, they were the only ones around. Harris took a chance and reached for Troy's hand. He was thrilled when Troy tangled his gloved fingers with Harris's without hesitation.

He was surprised, a minute later, when Troy tugged on their joined hands, pulling Harris close, and then kissed him. It was quick, and not exactly passionate, but it was so sweet and unexpected that Harris thought his legs might melt.

"That was cute," Harris said when they resumed walking.

"I can be cute."

"Is that how you imagined kissing me, back in the bar?"

"No. I'm waiting until we're behind a locked door for that." Troy's low voice was full of filthy promise, and Harris picked up the pace.

Finally they were at Harris's front door, and he managed to remember how to use a key despite the way Troy kept touching him. His fingers were gently brushing along Harris's nape, then he kissed under Harris's ear.

"Can't wait," Troy said in a low voice. "Been thinking about this so much."

"Really?"

Troy nudged his crotch against Harris's ass, letting him feel how turned on he was. "Mm. Open the door."

Harris shoved the door open, hauled Troy through, and was immediately pinned against it as soon as it was closed again. Troy took his mouth the way they both wanted, hard and possessive and hungry. Harris moaned and went boneless against the door, letting Troy hold him up with a knee between Harris's thighs, a hand on the back of his neck, and another on his hip.

"You taste like apples," Troy murmured against his lips.

"Cider," Harris rasped.

Troy dived in again, kissing him more slowly this time, as if savoring the taste. Harris was in heaven. If he could just stay here, exploring the slick velvety heat of Troy's mouth with his solid body pressing against him, he'd be happy for the rest of his life.

Except his erection was grinding against Troy's enormous thigh, adding some urgency to the situation. They needed to get to the bedroom.

"We should—" Harris tried.

"I know." Troy dropped to his knees and practically ripped open Harris's fly.

"I meant—" Harris gasped desperately.

"I know. Just let me—" He shoved the bottom of Harris's coat up and out of the way, and dived in. Harris's dick was encased in Troy's warm, wonderful mouth, and he stopped caring about the bedroom. They could fuck right here in his tiny kitchen, or in a snowbank outside. He really didn't care.

Troy was taking him deep, bobbing his head and sucking hard in a way that was almost aggressive. There was nothing gentle about it, and Harris fucking loved it. He let out a loud blissful moan and tangled his fingers in Troy's silky hair.

Troy pulled off long enough to ask, "You like that?" His voice sounded wrecked already. "It's not too much?"

Harris could only shake his head, mesmerized by how beautiful the man kneeling before him was. Troy's eyes were dark with lust, his lips swollen and glistening.

Those lips curved into a shy, boyish smile. "I'm sorry if I'm being . . ."

"Eager?"

Troy wrapped his lips around the head of Harris's cock and hummed an affirmative noise.

"Just—just so we're clear," Harris said unsteadily, "you don't have to be gentle with me."

Troy pulled back and stared at Harris as if he couldn't believe what he'd just said. "I won't hurt you."

"I know."

Troy sucked in a breath. "Shit. We need to get to your bedroom. Holy fuck."

He stood, which allowed Harris's head to clear a bit. "Let's take our coats and shit off first. Feels weird to be wearing a parka with my dick out."

Troy raked his gaze over him. "Looks good, though."

Harris laughed and tucked his erection back into his underwear, then unzipped his coat. They dumped their outerwear and boots in a pile in front of the door. They didn't get any closer to the bedroom because Troy immediately crowded Harris against a wall and kissed him again.

"Bedroom," Harris said, laughing.

"Right. Yeah. Sorry."

Harris took his hand and led him through the kitchen and toward the bedroom at the back of the apartment. "How about I give you the tour later?"

"Deal."

Harris crossed his bedroom in the dark and turned on his bedside lamp.

Troy Barrett was in his *bedroom*.

The room was chaotically decorated with lots of photos of friends and family—including a whole cluster of framed photos of the dogs and cats the Drovers had owned over the years. There was also Centaurs memorabilia, concert posters, various prints that he'd bought on Etsy, Pride paraphernalia, and a lot of pillows on his bed. One was shaped like an apple.

"Wow," Troy said. "This is . . . kind of exactly what I was expecting."

"Really?"

"Yeah. It's very you. Shows your love of . . . everything."

"I don't love *everything*."

Troy wrapped his arms around Harris from behind, and kissed down the side of his neck while Harris shivered with happiness and anticipation.

"I love this, though," Harris sighed. He *really* loved that he never knew what to expect from Troy. It was exciting and a little bit scary, and that was exciting too.

Troy could probably give him exactly what he wanted, if Harris asked. If Harris could find the brainpower to form words now that Troy's hand had dipped into his unzipped jeans, and was massaging his cock through Harris's briefs. He groaned and tipped his head back, searching for Troy's mouth. They kissed messily and awkwardly, until Harris turned so they could do it properly.

He slid a hand under Troy's T-shirt, over the hard ridges of his abs. Troy took it as a hint, and swiftly yanked his shirt off. And, wow. There was Troy's ridiculous torso again. Right there for Harris to play with.

"You are so fucking hot," Harris said. "Thought I was gonna die on that beach. And not from the waves."

"From the mile-long killer jellyfish?"

Harris laughed. "No. From how much I wanted you to push me down on the sand and straddle me."

Troy caressed Harris's beard. "Is that what you want? You wanna be pushed down and taken?"

Harris's mouth dropped open because *yes*. "God yes. So fucking much."

"You don't want me to be gentle with you. That's what you said."

"I don't. I want you to . . ." Harris couldn't finish his sentence for some reason. Possibly because the reality of the situation was catching up with him. He'd never actually had someone treat him exactly the way he craved. He needed to be with someone he trusted, and who was willing and able. He may have found the perfect person.

He swallowed, and squared his shoulders. "I want you to be rough with me. I'm not a masochist but, just, don't treat me like I'm delicate, okay?"

Troy brushed a thumb over Harris's cheekbone, his blue flame eyes dark and intense. "You're not delicate, Harris."

Harris felt light-headed. Hearing those words, spoken so plainly by a man he was extremely attracted to, was almost too much. He'd waited so long for someone to say them. "I'm not."

"I've been fantasizing about taking you apart," Troy said.

There was no way any of this was real. It was too good. "You have?"

"I want to give you whatever you need. Will you let me?"

Harris didn't answer. He just kissed him with no finesse whatsoever. It was pure need and lust because that was all that was left of him. His hands roamed over Troy's hard, naked chest and stomach, around to the muscles in his back and shoulders. Troy walked them back to the edge of the bed, then broke the kiss.

"Your turn," he said, fingering the top button of Harris's shirt.

Right. Shit.

He watched as Troy opened the shirt, one button at a time. He slid it down Harris's arms, and Harris shook it to the floor. He was wearing a plain white T-shirt underneath, and he supposed he'd need to take that off too. He let out a slow breath, then tore the shirt off quickly, like a Band-Aid.

And waited.

"Shit, Harris." Troy brushed his fingertips down the long, vertical scar on Harris's chest. "What—"

"Not now, okay?"

"But—"

"You promised." Troy hadn't exactly, but Harris didn't want his scars to change Troy's mind about how delicate he was.

Troy looked like he wanted to push it, but instead trailed his fingers into Harris's chest hair, away from the marred flesh that Harris hated so much.

"Love all this hair," Troy murmured. "So fucking sexy."

Harris sighed with relief and pleasure. "That's good. I've got plenty."

Troy pulled him on the bed, then rolled so Harris was under him. Troy's weight pressed him into the mattress while he kissed Harris's throat, his clavicle, his chest, all while carefully avoiding the scars. Harris gasped when Troy captured his nipple with his teeth, almost too hard, which was exactly perfect.

"Fuck yeah," Harris exhaled. "Just like that."

Troy bit it again, tugging at the sensitive flesh with his teeth. Harris whimpered and squirmed, and Troy murmured, "God, look at you." His words danced across Harris's skin in a hot rush of air. "I could eat you alive."

"Do it," Harris pleaded mindlessly. He wanted Troy to hold him down and fuck him hard. He wanted whatever Troy had fantasized about.

Troy pushed himself up, straddling Harris's waist and gazing down at him. In the dim light of the bedside lamp, Troy's smooth skin glowed. Shadows pooled in the grooves between his muscles, accentuating them. Harris ran his thumb over one dark, firm nipple, fascinated. He heard a soft chuckle, and was startled to find Troy smiling at him. A bright, dazzling smile that fully reached his eyes.

"Wow." Harris had lost any ability he might have once had to be cool. "What's making you smile like that?"

"I'm happy."

It was such a simple, obvious answer, but it made Harris beam back at him. "Yeah?"

"I'm gonna have sex with a hot guy."

Harris's stomach was an absolute mess of giddy excitement. "Do you want me to leave, then?"

Troy shook his head. "If you don't know how hot you are, then maybe I need to show you."

"Maybe."

"Let's start by taking these jeans off," Troy said in a low, delicious rumble. "I want to see all of you."

He stood beside the bed and watched as Harris removed the rest of his clothing. Then Harris was naked, sprawled out on the bed and trying not to cover himself while Troy inspected him.

"God, you're even better than I imagined, Harris," Troy said huskily. "I love your cock. Stroke it for me. Lemme see."

Harris did as he was told, more than happy to give his dick some attention. He moaned with relief as he gave himself a few slow strokes.

Troy opened his own jeans and slid a hand down to fondle his erection through his underwear. "So fucking hot, Harris."

Harris still couldn't believe that someone who looked like Troy found him attractive. Thought he was *hot*, even. But now was not the time to protest because Troy was sliding his jeans and underwear down his hips and holy fuck.

Troy's cock was as stunning as the rest of him: long, solid and uncut, jutting out from a dark, neatly trimmed patch of hair like an offering.

Harris waited, still stroking himself, waiting to see what Troy would do next.

* * *

Troy exhaled slowly as his gaze raked over Harris's body. He was entranced by every inch of him, from his broad, furry chest to his soft belly with its trail of hair leading to his plump, uncut cock.

And that scar. The one Harris didn't want to talk about but Troy's eyes kept returning to.

He forced his gaze away, back to where Harris's hand was still obediently working his own cock. It had been too long since Troy had done this—*really* done this, without clothes and with enough light to see his beautiful partner. He didn't know where to start.

"Come here," Harris said.

Troy went, stretching out on top of Harris's solid body and taking his mouth. Their cocks rubbed together as they kissed wildly. It felt so fucking good to be pressed against a man's naked body. If it were up to Troy, he'd never be anywhere else.

But mostly it was incredible to be pressed against *Harris*. To be in his bed, making him gasp with pleasure. Kissing him.

"Want you to fuck me," Harris panted against Troy's lips.

Oh fuck. Troy had guessed that was where this was all heading, but hearing Harris say those words was unreal. "Yeah?"

"Yeah. Want it hard."

"Fuck." Troy rubbed his cheek against Harris's beard, trying to ground himself. "Mind if I suck your dick some more first?"

"N-no."

Troy slid down his body. He grabbed both of Harris's thighs, gripping hard, and pulled them apart and back, spreading Harris wide, stopping, he hoped, before the stretch became uncomfortable.

Harris groaned and rolled his head on one of the thousands of pillows piled on his bed. "Troy. Fuck."

Troy dug his fingers into his meaty thighs, just enough pressure to make Harris squirm. "Okay?" he asked.

"So fucking good. Holy fuck."

Troy dipped his head and licked up Harris's shaft. God, he'd missed sex, and he'd missed giving head more than anything. It had been too long since Troy had gotten to do this, despite being twenty-five and horny most of the time.

Stupid long-distance relationship. Not that it had stopped Adrian.

Troy didn't want to be thinking about that now. He wanted to focus on the man underneath him, and enjoy the musky scent of his crotch, the salty beads of his precome, and the sexy way he was moaning—overly loud, like he did everything.

He took him deep, because that was something Troy *was* good at. Hockey and deep throating, his top two skills.

"Wow. Holy. Troy, that's—wow."

Troy hummed in response, and removed one of his hands from Harris's thighs so he could squeeze and caress his balls. He loved the way Harris was writhing on the bed, already out of his mind. He deserved to feel this good. Troy wanted to give him everything he deserved.

With that goal in mind, Troy trailed his fingers down to Harris's hole and began to lightly stroke and circle it. He slid his lips up to the head of Harris's cock, suckling and teasing out more precome.

"Shit," Harris rasped. "You gotta stop."

Troy released him, and stilled his fingers. "Need a break?"

"If you don't want me to come already, yeah."

"Maybe I do. Maybe I've got a few rounds in me."

"You played a game tonight. There's no way you do."

"Is that a challenge?"

Harris just laughed, which Troy deserved. He knew he was

probably going to fall asleep as soon as he came. Harris would be lucky if Troy didn't crash out on top of him.

"Here . . ." Harris reached into his nightstand and pulled out a bottle of lube. "I think it's safe to touch me again."

Troy took his time opening Harris up. He liked doing this and, again, it had been a while since he'd had the opportunity. He and Adrian didn't have set roles in the bedroom; they'd both been figuring out what they liked with each other. Troy preferred topping, and he hoped he was experienced enough to make this good for Harris. It was intimidating being with someone new when he'd only ever been with Adrian before. What if they had done everything wrong?

"God, that's so good, Troy. So fucking good." Harris moaned as Troy slowly penetrated him with three fingers. So maybe Troy *was* doing this right.

Harris's dick was so cute. Troy wasn't sure how to express that without sounding weird, so he kept it to himself. Troy's own dick was decent looking, long and lean with, he thought, a good shape to it. Harris's dick was chubby and a little shorter than Troy's, and had a single freckle on the head that Troy was already obsessed with.

"Buddy," Harris gritted out. "Gonna need you to fuck me now."

Troy stroked his index finger over Harris's prostate, making Harris jolt and moan. "Condoms?"

"Drawer. With the lube. Fuck. Hurry."

Troy grinned as he withdrew his fingers. His own dick had barely been touched yet, and that was probably for the best. He already felt like he might come as soon as he entered Harris, and that would be tragic.

He got the condom on while Harris watched him with glazed eyes.

"You want it hard?" Troy asked, making sure.

"Hard as you've got. I can take it."

Troy sucked in a breath. "Roll over. I'm gonna break the fucking bed fucking you."

Harris flipped over so quickly it almost made Troy laugh, but he was trying to be intimidating here. Or at least macho and sexy. He knelt behind Harris, gripping his ass cheeks with both hands and digging his fingers in. Harris's back bowed, lifting his ass in invitation.

Impulsively, Troy lowered his head and sank his teeth into the left cheek. He enjoyed the surprised gasp Harris let out. "Troy. Please."

Troy lined himself up, took a slow, steadying breath, then carefully pushed in. Harris might want it hard, but Troy was going to make sure he didn't hurt him.

"Good?" he asked when he was fully inside. He was breathing hard, as if he'd just finished a long shift on the ice, trying to stay in control.

"You're killing me, pal," Harris said. "I said I liked it rough, not that I like torture."

Troy bit back a smile, then took firm hold of Harris's hips and gave him what he wanted.

Troy pounded into him, as hard as he could while Harris made loud, encouraging sounds. Troy enjoyed exercise and working out, but even if he hated it, the daily hours of work he put into his body would all be worth it for this moment. He loved being strong and having the stamina to fuck Harris like this.

"Ah," Harris panted. "Fuck, Troy. Don't stop."

He wouldn't. Not until Harris had had enough. He slid his hands onto Harris's back, and Harris's arms gave out, dropping him to the mattress. Troy followed, bringing his body low over Harris's, holding him down with a firm hand splayed between his shoulder blades as he jackhammered into him.

"Yes," Harris gasped. "Love that. Holy shit."

Troy kept it up, losing himself in the bliss of fucking someone. Of fucking *Harris*. He wanted to do it forever, except he was getting close to his own orgasm, and didn't want to come first.

"You," he gritted out. "Want you to—"

He lifted his palm and stared in amazement at the angry red patch he'd left on Harris's skin, then wrapped an arm around Harris's chest and roughly hauled him up. He pulled Harris back so he was seated in Troy's lap, back to chest. "Stroke yourself," he growled into Harris's ear. "Need to see you come."

Troy thrust up into him while Harris jerked himself frantically. It was becoming a struggle to keep up the pace Harris wanted because Troy was about to explode inside him. He needed Harris to come. Now.

"Come on," he panted. "I'm so fucking close, Harris. Fuck."

"Me too. Keep going."

Troy wasn't sure what came over him, but suddenly he was biting into the flesh between Harris's neck and shoulder like a fucking dog. It was a strange impulse, but it seemed to do it for Harris because he cried out and shot his load all over his furry stomach.

"Holy shit, Harris. I'm coming. I'm—" Troy couldn't speak. His orgasm ripped through him in a blinding, wonderful blaze as Harris's ass gripped him tight.

When he could think again, Troy realized he was peppering Harris's shoulder with gentle kisses, as if apologizing for going feral on him. Harris was breathing heavily, his chest heaving against Troy's arm.

"That was perfect," Harris wheezed. "That was—holy god. I've never—"

Troy kept kissing him. He couldn't stop. Anywhere he could reach: shoulders, neck, back, hair.

"Thank you," Harris sighed. "I needed that."

"I needed it too."

He carefully released Harris and pulled out. Harris collapsed on the bed, sprawled on his back, and grinned lazily up at Troy.

"Jesus," Troy huffed. "You look annihilated."

"There's nothing left of me." Harris spread his arms out on the mattress. "They'll need to hire a new social media manager."

"Gonna be awkward explaining why."

"Mm." He closed his eyes, which meant he couldn't see the way Troy was smiling helplessly at him. Harris's hair was a mess, his skin flushed and glistening with sweat, and his face was relaxed and content, like Troy had given him exactly what he'd needed.

"Don't fall asleep yet. Where's your bathroom?"

Harris waved a hand in the direction of the door without opening his eyes. "Out there."

Troy snorted and removed the condom. "I'll be right back."

"Mmff."

When Troy returned from the bathroom, he cleaned Harris with a facecloth he'd found. "Are you okay?"

"I'm amazing," Harris said. "Probably won't ride a horse tomorrow, but . . ."

"Seriously, though? I didn't hurt you?"

Harris sat up. "I promise you didn't. I loved it."

"Okay." Harris's dick was even cuter when it was soft. "Do you want me to leave?" Troy really hoped not, because he was crashing hard.

"No! Of course not. Stay."

"Good. Thanks." Troy tossed the facecloth into the laundry hamper in the corner. Harris pulled back the blankets in invitation, and they both got under them. Several pillows tumbled to the floor as the two men got comfortable.

"I can't believe you thought I was gonna kick you out," Harris scolded.

"I didn't want to assume."

"What happened to going all night, stud? Isn't that what you said?"

"Fuck off," Troy murmured sleepily. He was struggling to keep his eyes open.

"A few rounds. That's what you said."

Troy closed his eyes. "Jus' gimme a second," he slurred.

Harris laughed, then turned off the lamp. A moment later, he snuggled against Troy, warm and soft and very welcome. Troy wrapped an arm around him, pulling him close so they could spoon together. Troy was pretty sure there was a throw pillow or something under him, but he didn't care. He was more comfortable than he'd ever been in his life.

"Good night," Harris said.

"Yeah," Troy agreed.

CHAPTER EIGHTEEN

Troy woke up late the next morning feeling well rested and perfectly comfortable.

Almost.

"What the fuck am I lying on?" He reached under his back and pulled out what appeared to be an extremely battered and worn-out stuffed . . . giraffe?

"Oh," Harris said, reaching for it. "That's Mr. Neck-Neck."

Troy held it away from him, examining the well-loved toy. "Jeez. Mr. Neck-Neck has been through it."

"Yeah," Harris said, dropping his hand. "I've had him since I was a baby. We used to be inseparable."

"Cute."

"He was comforting, y'know, when I was . . . Well, I was in the hospital a lot as a kid. And as an adult, I guess, but mostly as a kid."

Troy turned on his side so they could face each other. "You wanna talk about it?"

"Sure. Why not?" Harris frowned, and Troy held his breath. He was terrified that Harris was about to tell him he had a month to live or something. "I was born with a heart defect.

It's called truncus arteriosus, but basically my arteries were all fucked up, and I've gotten a few operations over the years to sort it out. The most recent one was three years ago."

"Jesus." It seemed so wrong, for someone as warm and loving as Harris to have anything wrong with his heart. "I'm sorry. How are you now?"

"Fine." Harris said it quickly, automatically, the way someone would who had been asked about his health far too many times. "Really, I'm good. I get it checked by doctors all the time. But that's why I never played hockey as a kid. I probably *could* have, but my parents were worried. I don't blame them."

Troy couldn't blame them either, because even now he wanted to wrap Harris in a blanket and keep him safe. But Harris would hate that, so instead he handed Harris his stuffed giraffe. "I'm glad you have good doctors. And good parents. And Mr. Neck-Neck."

Harris laughed. "Mr. Neck-Neck was with me through thick and thin. He's true blue."

"I'm sorry he had to witness what we did last night. Um. On top of him." Troy propped himself up on an elbow and grinned. "Was that a threesome, technically?"

Harris hit him with the giraffe. "No! What the hell is wrong with you? And it's not the first time Mr. Neck-Neck has seen that sort of thing."

Troy felt an unwarranted pang of jealousy that there had been other men in this bed, but he shoved it down deep. "Mr. Neck-Neck is a pervert."

"No way, man. He's just chill and sex positive."

They both laughed. Troy found it shockingly easy to laugh with Harris.

"We should take a shower," Harris said.

"Can we both fit?"

"I'm willing to try." Harris kissed him quickly, then rolled out of the bed. "Fuck, it's cold. Come on."

They both managed to fit in the shower, but barely. It was okay because Troy didn't feel like being more than an inch apart from Harris anyway. They kissed for a long time, wasting water, as their erections bumped together.

Eventually they got down to the business of getting clean. Harris handed him a bottle of shampoo, and Troy laughed when he read the bottle.

"What?" Harris asked.

"It's apple scented."

"Is it?"

"Yes! Oh my god. I thought I was losing my mind. I kept smelling apples whenever you were close and I told myself I was imagining it. Jesus."

Harris grinned. "I think my laundry detergent might be green apple scent too."

Troy poured some shampoo on his palm and began working it into Harris's hair. "Unbelievable."

Harris gave a happy sigh and seemed to quietly enjoy Troy massaging his scalp for a few seconds, and then said, "Did you think I just naturally smelled like apples? Because that's adorable."

"No! I thought it was, like, psychosomatic. Or whatever."

"You *wanted* me to smell like apples?"

"We can drop this, y'know."

"Are you turned on by the smell of apples, Troy?"

"I didn't used to be." He took a step back from Harris. "Rinse."

Harris tilted his head back under the spray. "Did I give you an apple fetish?"

"Maybe." Troy dropped to his knees and kissed the head of Harris's bobbing cock.

"Oh shit," Harris said, opening his eyes in surprise. "I was kidding."

"Yeah, well, I want you to shut up about apples." Troy took him into his mouth and palmed both of his ass cheeks, squeezing them as he worked his cock. Harris stopped talking about apples or anything else for a few minutes.

"You are," Harris panted, "so good at this." He stroked Troy's wet hair, watching everything he did. Troy pulled back a bit so he could give the head more attention.

"Ah, fuck," Harris gasped. "I'm super close."

Troy didn't stop. He wanted everything he could have from this man.

Harris came within seconds; his cries sounded even louder than usual in the confines of the small shower. Troy swallowed his release, moaning at the thrill of getting a man off with his mouth.

"Get up here," Harris said huskily. "Kiss me. Wanna touch you."

Troy took his time, slowly sliding his lips off Harris's cock and kissing his way up his stomach, his chest, past the scars that guarded his resilient heart.

Their mouths crashed together and Harris wrapped his hand around Troy's erection. It didn't take long at all for Harris to take him to the brink of orgasm, and then over, pleasure exploding throughout Troy's body as his release splattered Harris's stomach.

Even as he was catching his breath, Troy kept kissing him. He couldn't get enough of him. It wasn't good.

"So," Harris said, pressing his forehead to Troy's, "did I taste like apples?"

Troy snorted. "Shut up."

Harris laughed, and Troy couldn't stop himself from joining him. Being able to laugh effortlessly like this was a different kind of release, one that was possibly more exhilarating than the orgasm he'd just thoroughly enjoyed.

Eventually they got clean, then left the shower and dressed. Troy was starving by the time they went into the kitchen.

"Do you like oatmeal?" Harris asked. "That's what I normally have for breakfast. I'll make coffee too, of course."

Panic started to claw its way into Troy's unusually happy brain. Maybe it was Harris's mention of what he *normally* had for breakfast, the reminder that Troy had managed to insert himself into his morning routine. Maybe it was the sudden realization that Troy was standing in Harris's kitchen, in his *home*. Maybe it was the more frightening realization that he didn't want to leave. Whatever it was, Troy reverted to his usual, cagey self.

"I should go, probably. You don't have to feed me."

"But you haven't eaten," Harris protested. Then he smiled. "Well, you've *barely* eaten."

"Gross."

"It's just as easy to make two servings of oatmeal as one. Have a seat. Stay for breakfast at least. Or, if you'd rather, there's a diner not far from here that—"

"I'll stay. Oatmeal is fine." The only thing that would be worse right now than staying here with Harris would be spending time in public with him. Anyone who saw them together would know that Troy was crushing hard on the guy, and he wasn't ready for that.

Troy didn't sit. He wandered around the small kitchen, probably getting in Harris's way. He was full of nervous energy and should probably go for a run or head to the gym as soon as he was out of here.

"If you're going to bounce around like that, maybe you can make coffee," Harris suggested.

"Okay."

Harris pointed to a cupboard and then to the coffee maker on the counter. Troy got to work. When the coffeemaker was gurgling and coffee began trickling into the pot, he leaned back against the counter, watching Harris stir the oatmeal. He was wearing jeans and a blue plaid shirt and his hair was still damp. Troy wanted to pull him into his arms, back to bed, and never leave.

Two months ago, he couldn't imagine ever feeling happy again, much less finding a man who he could be himself with. He'd thought Adrian had been his one chance at happiness, but now, in Harris's kitchen, Troy realized that he'd never felt this comfortable with Adrian. Their relationship had been hot and exciting, but it had been held together by fear and anxiety. They'd both been so scared of being caught, and their stolen times alone together had been full of desperation and relief. Troy had been so thrilled to have *someone* to fall in love with that he'd clung to Adrian with both hands, not daring to look at other options. Adrian, meanwhile, had been reaching his hands in two different directions. Until he'd let go of Troy completely.

It hadn't all been sex. They'd shared parts of themselves with each other, but Troy had never gotten the impression that Adrian had ever been particularly interested in Troy's life. Adrian had never been overly interested in *anyone* who wasn't Adrian. He doubted he was even very interested in his new fiancé.

In short, Troy was experiencing all sorts of new feelings with Harris, and it was fucking him up.

Harris spooned oatmeal into two bowls. "You want maple syrup on it?"

"Sure." Troy pointed to the corner of Harris's kitchen counter. "Is that the slow cooker you told me not to worry about?"

Harris laughed. "I swear there's nothing going on between me and the slow cooker."

"Hm."

"But," Harris said cautiously, "if the slow cooker asks about you, what should I tell him?"

Troy's heart skipped. "I don't know. What do you want to tell him?"

Harris glanced at him quickly, then returned his focus to the bowls of oatmeal. "I'd like to tell him that I met someone, and I really like him. And I think he likes me too. And I'd like to see where things go with him, if he also wants that."

Troy didn't reply. He couldn't. It wasn't shocking, what Harris was saying. Obviously they were both into each other, but Troy still couldn't believe what was being offered. And he wasn't sure if he could allow himself to accept it.

"Um," Harris said, his cheeks darkening. "Maybe I'm assuming too much. With this guy. That I like."

"You're not," Troy said quietly.

"No?" Harris turned to face him, his expression hopeful.

"But," Troy said, because he had to make this clear, "I'm not sure what I can offer. You know I'm not out, and I won't ask you to hide with me."

"I don't think I *could* hide," Harris admitted. "I'm kind of an open book. I'm no good at sneaking around."

No, Harris was the most honest and sunny person Troy had ever met. He didn't belong in the shadows. "I know. And you shouldn't." Troy sighed. "I like you a lot, Harris, but I need some time to figure my shit out. Maybe until then we should just, y'know, be friends."

Harris's smile didn't look effortless. Or real. "Sure. Makes sense."

Troy nodded, his head feeling suddenly heavy. "It does. Thanks."

For a moment, neither man said anything. Then Harris handed Troy one of the bowls. "Oatmeal's getting cold. Let's eat."

Troy wanted to throw the oatmeal into the sink and kiss Harris against the fridge. He wanted to take him out for breakfast, and hold his hand while they waited for their food. He wanted to make coffee for him every morning.

Instead, he silently took his bowl to the table, and awkwardly sat across from his new friend.

CHAPTER NINETEEN

Now that Troy had let himself have a taste of Harris, his body burned with sexual frustration. He told himself that he was distancing himself from Harris for the right reasons, and that it wouldn't be fair to sleep with him if Troy wasn't brave enough to hold his hand in the light. Troy needed to *earn* Harris. Maybe he would never deserve him, but he needed to try.

Truthfully, he wasn't distancing himself from Harris at all. Over the past two weeks he'd seen as much of the man as their busy schedules would allow. Harris had even helped Troy with his Instagram posts, giving him a list of activists, shelters and organizations to follow, and showing him how to share their posts to Troy's stories. Harris had been excited about the number of followers Troy had gained, but Troy continued to avoid looking at his account beyond creating new posts.

He felt good, though. He'd been making sizable donations to the organizations he'd been promoting and, though he wanted to do more, it was a start. For once in his life he was using his privilege for something worthwhile, and, even though he was still a bit terrified, he was excited.

Ottawa had also won every game since their big win against New York. That didn't hurt.

And Harris seemed to be proud of Troy. That didn't hurt either.

But Harris's proud smiles and enthusiastic compliments did nothing to shut Troy's body up. Every time he was near Harris, he ached to kiss him, to pin him against a wall and tear his clothes away, to go to his knees and suck him off in his office.

His body had lots of terrible ideas, so Troy was punishing it now in the team gym. He pushed himself through one more set of barbell squats, determined to keep going until he could almost forget the heated look Harris had given him in his office three days ago. It was one that made it pretty clear that he wouldn't mind being ravaged by Troy.

"Whoa," Bood said, grabbing the barbell so Troy wouldn't have to support it alone with his trembling arms. Together, they set it back in the rack.

"Thanks," Troy said. He dropped to the floor, sitting in a heap with his chin against his chest.

Bood sat beside him. "Is your goal to lift a Zamboni or something?" he teased.

"No. Just felt like pushing it a bit today."

"Did it help?"

"A little."

A phone rang nearby, and both men turned their heads toward the sound. "Is that you?" Bood asked.

"I think so. Hand it to me? It's there." Troy gestured lazily toward the shelf where he'd left his phone. "My legs are toast."

Bood laughed as he stood and grabbed the phone. "Unknown number," he said.

Troy took it from him. It was probably a telemarketer or something, but he answered it anyway. "Hello?"

"Troy Barrett?" The voice was gruff and male and vaguely familiar.

"Yeah?"

"This is Roger Crowell. I was hoping you might have a few minutes to talk."

Suddenly Troy found the ability to walk again and was on his feet. Roger Crowell, the commissioner of the entire NHL, was calling *him*. Troy had never spoken to him in his life beyond a handshake on his draft day. There was no way this phone call was for a good reason, though.

Troy walked quickly out of the room, ignoring Bood's questioning glance. "Yes, sir. Of course."

"Good. How are you, Troy? How's Ottawa?"

The questions were bland and friendly, but Crowell made them sound like a trap, and Troy's chest tightened as he walked. "Fine. Ottawa's good."

"Beautiful city," Crowell agreed. "Cold, I'll bet."

"Yeah." Troy found a quiet spot at the end of a hallway, and leaned back against a wall, waiting for Crowell to reveal his reason for calling.

"Probably doesn't have the nightlife Toronto did. Nothing to amuse you during your free time."

Troy didn't know what to say to that, so he only swallowed.

"You're causing quite a stir with your Instagram account, Troy."

Oh god. "Am I?"

"It's a noble effort. The league wants its players to be engaged in the community, and of course the cause you're bringing attention to is important."

Troy knew better than to relax at this apparent praise. He'd had too many years of experience talking to intimidating men like Crowell to fall for that. "I think it is, yes."

"If any other player had been posting about sexual assault,

I'd be nothing but pleased, but with you, Troy . . . Well, I have to wonder about your motivation here."

"Motivation?"

Crowell sighed somewhat theatrically. "I don't know why you and Kent stopped being friends, and frankly I don't care. Shit happens, right? Maybe he slept with your girl. Maybe you were jealous of his talent. But this personal vendetta you have against him isn't good for anyone, Troy. Not the league, not your team, and certainly not for you."

"I—that's not why—" Troy stammered.

"Those women, the ones who have been saying things about Kent, I can see why you might jump on that opportunity, if you were mad at your friend. You don't have a clear head right now because you're angry. But . . ." Crowell laughed, and it sounded cold and cruel like Troy's father's laugh. "You know those girls are only looking for their five minutes of fame. People can say anything on the internet and they don't even have to sign their names. It disgusts me because there's no integrity in it. In the hockey world, and in the business world where I've been for decades, integrity is important. I don't know about you, but I don't have much respect for anyone who won't own up to the things they say. Hurling accusations in the dark is cowardly, and creating lies to ruin a talented young man at the pinnacle of his career is monstrous." Crowell paused, and Troy could imagine a slow, sickening smile creeping across his face. "At least, that's my opinion."

Troy's heart was racing in his chest. His palms were so sweaty he worried he would drop his phone. He knew every word Crowell was saying was wrong—twisted—but he didn't know how to defend himself. To defend the women he hadn't been able to stop thinking about.

"I don't think they're lying," he managed to say. He hated how small his voice sounded.

"Did you see Kent do any of the things they accused him of?" Crowell asked. His voice was calm, but Troy suspected that this question was the exact reason he was calling. Crowell needed to know if Troy was a real danger.

"No," Troy admitted quietly.

"So you don't know if these girls are telling the truth."

"I think he—"

"You don't," Crowell said slowly and clearly, *"know."*

Troy couldn't argue. He didn't know. He didn't know anything. He just . . . oh god. What if Crowell was right?

Except no. He *did* know. He knew Dallas and he understood enough about how the world treated victims of sexual assault to know that Kent's accusers had nothing to gain from speaking out.

"The problem is," Crowell continued, "that your posts, while admirable, have the appearance of being personal attacks at Kent. Little digs. Obviously the best thing for the league is if this whole ridiculous business faded away, but your posts keep fanning the flames. I need you to stop."

Some of Troy's fear solidified into anger. He was so tired of being pushed around by men like Crowell. "I'm not doing anything wrong. I'm trying to help people who need it."

"There are plenty of causes you can promote, Troy. Homelessness, or poor kids having access to sports. I can have my assistant send you a list of charities and initiatives the league supports."

"Okay," Troy said, because it seemed safer than refusing. "Thank you."

"Good," Crowell interrupted. "I'd hate to have to take this matter further."

Further? Jesus, Troy didn't want to find out what that meant. "No, sir."

"I'll let you go now, Troy. It was nice speaking with you. Good luck tomorrow night against Montreal."

"Thank you." Troy sounded like a child being forced to speak to a stranger.

Crowell ended the call, and Troy slid down the wall until he was sitting on the floor. What the fuck was he going to do?

"You surprised yet?" Harris asked Gen the morning after another Ottawa win, this time on the road against Detroit.

"They should almost die in a plane crash more often," she said dryly. Then she grimaced. "Sorry. I keep forgetting you were on that plane."

Harris waved a hand dismissively. "I'm alive."

"Alive and grumpy," Gen muttered.

Harris only grunted in response.

Ottawa was enjoying the team's longest win streak in over ten years, which should have put Harris in a good mood. But instead he couldn't stop thinking about Troy. He knew the team had flown back late last night after the game, and he'd felt a ridiculous stab of longing for Troy to drive straight to Harris's apartment. He wanted to be the man Troy went home to, and he was frustrated by how close he'd possibly gotten to being that.

Or maybe he was kidding himself.

"To be fair," Gen said, "your grumpy is like my very best mood."

"Maybe I'm not grumpy."

Gen scoffed. "Something is bothering you. The team is on a hot streak and you're miserable."

There was no way Harris was going to tell Gen about Troy. For one thing, it would mean outing Troy. For another, it was too embarrassing to talk about. What had Harris been expecting? For Troy Barrett to want to be his boyfriend? Men who looked like Troy didn't date men who looked like Harris. Troy's last boyfriend had been a stunningly beautiful television star with, like, a sixteen-pack.

Troy probably only saw Harris as a convenient fix. Someone he was comfortable enough to come out to, which was nice, but also someone who wasn't much of a risk. He'd known Harris was gay the minute he'd first met him, and he also likely assumed that Harris wouldn't reject him.

"I'm going take a walk," Harris said. "I need a break from the computer."

He needed a break from these dark thoughts. He knew they weren't true. Troy had fixed that intense, cobalt gaze on him enough times to let Harris know that he saw something he liked. He had, in fact, *told* Harris that he liked him when they'd decided to end the physical side of their relationship. He just needed space, and Harris needed to give it to him without pouting about it. And, besides, being friends with Troy was . . . nice. They got along well, and Troy seemed happier lately, laughing and smiling more easily, and throwing himself into helping victims of sexual assault however he could. In short, he was continuing to be wonderful and handsome, while also maintaining a commitment to friendship without benefits. It was basically killing Harris.

"Tell Troy I said hi," Gen said.

"I'm not going to see Troy."

"Sure."

Troy probably wasn't even in the building. Maybe. Harris supposed it was the usual time for him to be working out in the team gym.

He wished he could stop thinking about their last night together. God, the way Troy had fucked him. He'd given Harris exactly what he'd needed and it had been incredible.

And then he'd held him all night, and talked to him while

they'd relaxed in bed together the next morning. He'd washed Harris's hair, blown him in the shower, teased him about his slow cooker.

Harris liked him so much.

Of course Harris walked past the entrance of the team gym, and furtively peeked inside. He wouldn't go in, but he wanted a glimpse of Troy. Just a taste.

Troy wasn't there.

Probably just as well. Harris kept walking, pulling his phone out to check Twitter as he rounded a corner.

And crashed right into Troy.

"Shit! Sorry," Harris said. "I wasn't looking where I was going."

Troy had his hand over his heart, and he exhaled loudly. "Jesus. Wasn't expecting that."

Harris held up his phone sheepishly. "You know me. Addicted to my phone."

Troy just stared at him, and that's when Harris noticed how upset he looked.

"What's wrong?" Harris asked.

Troy's eyes darted from side to side. Then he nodded his head in the direction behind him. "This way."

They walked to the end of the hallway, putting distance, Harris noticed, between them and the gym where Troy's teammates were. Then Troy turned to face him and said, just above a whisper, "The commissioner called me."

"The commissioner?" Harris didn't understand. "Crowell?"

"Yeah. Like, he actually called me. Roger Crowell himself. On the phone."

"When? Why?"

"A few minutes ago. He's *concerned*."

"About what?" Harris had a sinking suspicion that he already knew. The NHL's commissioner was not, in Harris's opinion, a force for good.

"About my Instagram account. About, y'know, everything. Starting with what I said to Dallas." Troy scrubbed a hand through his hair. "*Fuck!* I don't want . . . I was trying to be *good*. Instead I'm just pissing people off."

Harris put a hand on Troy's arm. "You *are* doing good, Troy. Tell me what he said exactly."

"He asked me some questions about Dallas, to make sure I hadn't actually witnessed anything. And based on that, he said I shouldn't be fanning the flames of . . . shit. I forget what words he used. But basically he wants me to stop talking about sexual assault victims. He said it was, like, admirable, but also that I shouldn't do it. I don't know. I'm really fucking confused now. Have you ever talked to him? He's intimidating as fuck."

Harris had never heard Troy babble before and he didn't like it. "No, I haven't. But I get the gist of what he's like from interviews and press conferences and stuff. Did he threaten you? Offer an ultimatum if you don't stop posting like you have been?"

"He said he hoped the matter was settled because he didn't want to have to take things further, whatever that means."

"Fucker," Harris grumbled.

Troy blanched like Harris had just blasphemed.

"Listen to me," Harris said, placing his hands firmly on Troy's biceps. "You are playing incredible hockey, and that's all you owe this team or this league. You aren't doing anything harmful or illegal. You're using your fame and influence to help people who often don't have a voice, and there's nothing bad about that. Fuck Crowell if he says otherwise."

Troy swallowed. "He said Dallas Kent is one of the league's biggest stars, and that it reflects badly on the entire league if we give credit to his accusers' stories."

Harris felt a very rare urge to punch something. "What else?"

"He was laughing about it, like we were old friends having a beer or something. Laughing about women trying to get their five minutes of fame or whatever. Can't believe what they say. Fuck, Harris. The way he says things, he had me doubting myself. Doubting everything."

Harris shook his head. "He's wrong. You know he's wrong."

"Do I? I didn't see anything. Maybe I just wanted to believe them because Dallas was getting on my nerves."

Harris kept his voice steady. "Is that really what you think?"

Troy took two slow breaths. "No. I think Dallas did it. I know he did it. All of it."

"Okay."

"It's not like he's the only one. I'll bet this league has been protecting predators for a hundred fucking years."

"Probably," Harris agreed.

"I know I can't fix everything, but I just want to help. A little. If I can."

Troy slumped back against the wall, looking so defeated Harris wanted to hug him. So he did. Troy returned it immediately, pulling Harris close.

"I keep dumping all of my shit on you," Troy said into his shoulder, his arms tight around Harris's back. "Sorry."

"Don't be sorry. I want to help. We're friends, right?"

Troy took a slow breath that tickled Harris's neck. Then another, as if he was inhaling Harris's scent.

"Apples?" Harris teased gently.

"Mm."

Troy stayed there for a minute, then pulled back. Their mouths were inches apart. It would be wrong to kiss Troy here, especially now that he was so vulnerable.

"I should get back," Troy said, stepping back.

"Right. Okay." Harris regained his senses. "But we should talk more about this when you have time."

"All right. If you don't mind."

"I don't mind."

"I might stay off Instagram for a while."

"Makes sense."

Troy nodded, then took a step toward the gym.

"What are you doing Friday night?" Harris blurted out.

Troy turned back. "I don't know. Nothing. Why?"

"Fabian Salah is playing a show in town that night."

Troy's brow furrowed. "Who?"

"The musician. We were listening to him in my truck once. He's dating Ryan Price."

"Oh. Right."

"I have two tickets. I bought two because I knew it would sell out and I wanted to make sure I could bring someone, and it just occurred to me that you might like to go. Maybe." Harris was lying. He'd bought the second ticket with Troy in mind. "Anyway, you should come. If you want. With me."

"It's this Friday?"

"Yep. The first night of your week off."

Troy seemed to think about it. "Sure. Okay."

Harris lit up. "Yeah?"

"Yeah. It will be, um, nice. Hanging out with you, away from here. I've kind of been . . . wanting to." Troy's shy smile was devastating.

"Me too," Harris said.

Troy looked at him seriously. "I honestly don't know how I would have dealt with anything this season without you."

Oh.

Harris managed a shaky smile. "Happy to help."

"I know. It's one of the things I love about you." His eyes went wide. "I mean—thanks."

He jogged away before Harris could reply.

"Oh man," Harris muttered to his patched-up heart. "I think this guy might destroy us."

CHAPTER TWENTY

Shane Hollander shoved Ilya hard against the glass, and Troy almost laughed at the way Ilya was grinning about it. Ilya shoved Hollander back, which made Hollander's linemate, Hayden Pike, step in.

Which made Troy join the pile. He got there just in time to hear Ilya roasting Pike.

"You still play hockey?" Ilya asked.

"Don't even start, Rozanov."

"Why are you even here?" Ilya pushed Pike's chest, forcing the other man away. "I am talking to my friend Hollander."

"Leave him alone, Rozanov," Shane growled. "And back the fuck up."

Troy was holding Pike's arm, but Pike wasn't making any moves toward Ilya. Troy heard him mumble, "I'm so sick of this weird bullshit."

Troy wasn't sure what that meant.

Ilya moved away from Hollander and said, "We can catch up at the All-Star game this weekend." He turned to Pike. "The All-Star game is a special match played between the best players in the league."

Troy snickered, and Pike gave Hollander a look that Troy would call *pleading*. "Can I please stab him?"

"No one is stabbing anyone," the ref barked.

"Not yet," Ilya said, somewhat silkily and in Hollander's direction.

Hollander's eyes narrowed, but he didn't say anything. Just skated away, taking Pike with him. Ilya watched him go.

"I thought you guys were friends," Troy said.

"Off the ice, yes."

Troy supposed it wasn't that different from how Ilya treated Scott Hunter when they played against each other. Maybe it was a sign of respect if Ilya gave you shit on the ice. He mostly used to ignore Troy, when they'd played against each other.

In the end, Ottawa beat Montreal 5–3, adding another win to their streak that was now a team record: nine straight games. It felt incredible. Once again, the dressing room was a party, this time with the added excitement of a whole week off ahead of them.

"Ilya's in a good mood," Troy observed.

Ilya was sort of half dancing to the loud hip-hop music that was playing in the dressing room, randomly clapping his hands and cheerfully congratulating everyone.

"Oh yeah," Wyatt agreed. "He's always in a good mood when we beat Montreal. I guess being Shane Hollander's friend doesn't stop him from loving to destroy him on the ice."

"Guess not."

Ilya and Wyatt were heading to the All-Star weekend in Anaheim tomorrow. Troy hadn't been invited to the All-Star game this year, obviously. Based on the commissioner's feelings about him, he'd probably never be invited again. But he really didn't care. Harris had basically asked him on a date, and that was a much more exciting invitation.

In truth, Troy didn't even want to *watch* the All-Star game, let alone participate in it. Dallas Kent would be there, and the commissioner. And probably a bunch of players who thought Troy was a traitor.

"Looking forward to the All-Star game?" he asked Wyatt.

"I am. I know a lot of guys hate it, but I never thought I'd be invited, y'know? Now I'm going for the second year in a row. Plus, I'm heading to Vancouver for the rest of the week to hang out with my nephew. I can't wait. Lisa is going to meet me there."

"Nice. Is Ilya excited, do you think?"

"He seems to like All-Star games," Wyatt said. "I think he enjoys the opportunity to annoy all of the biggest stars at once."

Troy smiled at that.

Later, when he was walking to his car, Ilya caught up with him. "Big plans for the week off?" Ilya asked.

"Not really."

"Just hanging around Ottawa?"

"Yep."

Ilya smirked. "Interesting."

Troy narrowed his eyes. "No it isn't. It's the opposite of interesting."

"You could make it interesting. With Harris."

"Shut up!" Troy glanced around frantically, but they seemed to be the only ones in the garage. "I'm going out with him tomorrow night."

"Holy shit, Barrett. That is adorable."

Troy scratched the back of his head nervously. "It's a date, I guess. I mean, I think it is. I hope it is."

Ilya poked his shoulder. "He is a good guy. Treat him well."

"I know. I will."

"Yes," Ilya agreed sternly. Then his face softened into a crooked smile. "Where are you taking him?"

"He's taking *me* to a concert. Fabian Salah."

"Fabian! I did not know he was in town."

"You know him?"

Ilya stared at Troy like he was an idiot. "Yes. He is Ryan Price's boyfriend. Ryan Price who coaches at my camps."

"Right. I forgot."

"I saw Fabian play once," Ilya said. "In Montreal. He is very good. Very . . . pretty."

"Oh yeah?"

Ilya grinned. "Fabian and Ryan is like Beauty and the Beast. Wait until you see."

Troy nodded, and hoped his face didn't show how anxious he was about the possibility of seeing Ryan Price again.

"Speaking of beasts, I will be making Dallas Kent's weekend very uncomfortable."

Troy huffed. "I can't believe he's a fucking All-Star this year."

"I know. I am sorry you weren't invited."

"I'm fine with it. I don't want to see Dallas, and the commissioner is pissed at me, so—" Troy cut himself off. He hadn't meant to tell Ilya—or anyone besides Harris—about the call from Commissioner Crowell.

"Crowell? What do you mean he is pissed?" Ilya asked.

"Nothing. Forget it."

Ilya's expression turned serious. "No. What did he say?"

Troy sighed. "He called me, and he warned me about, y'know, implying that Dallas Kent was guilty. He doesn't like the stuff I've been posting on Instagram."

"You are serious?"

"He called my cell phone. Talked to me for like fifteen minutes. I was scared shitless."

"I don't like this," Ilya said grimly. "This is bad."

"I know. That's why I stopped posting."

"No. Is bad that Crowell said these things to you. I might talk to him in Anaheim."

Panic surged through Troy. "Please don't. Seriously. Don't. It will only make things worse, and then you'll get dragged into it."

Ilya's jaw tightened, and he was quiet a moment before saying, "Don't stop posting. Unless it is your choice, and not Crowell's."

And just like that, Troy felt like a coward. He had, once again, been bending to the will of aggressive, overbearing men with questionable morals. "I just need some time to think."

"You will have a whole week to think. Use it."

"I will."

Ilya pulled his phone out, glanced at it, and smiled. "I have to go."

"Sure. Have a good time in Anaheim. And a good week off."

"I will." Ilya began walking toward his Mercedes SUV, then called over his shoulder, "Harris could use a break from work. Maybe you can distract him."

Troy let out a weird sputter of laughter, which probably gave more away than he wanted to. "Whatever."

Ilya's laugh was much more dignified and controlled. He winked as he got in his SUV and drove away, leaving Troy standing alone in the garage with a lot to think about.

Troy thought he was doing a remarkably good job of remaining cool, all things considered.

On the outside, at least.

He was on a date, sort of. With a man. In the city where he played hockey. With someone who *worked* for that hockey team. At a performance by an openly queer musician who was dating his *former teammate*.

Oh god.

Harris's arm brushed his. "You okay?"

Troy had noticed that Harris had been carefully not touching him since they'd walked into the packed club. Troy pressed back against him, just slightly, to silently let him know that he wanted to be brave. That he really wanted this to be a date. He wanted to hold Harris's hand tonight, or maybe even kiss him, here in this club. He just needed to find the courage.

"I'm okay," Troy said. "I haven't been to this kind of concert in a long time. In a club and, like, standing up."

"It's my favorite way to hear live music. I love being part of a crowd."

Troy didn't normally mind it, but he felt like everyone was staring at him. Plus, it didn't really seem like his usual crowd. He couldn't spot any obvious jocks. Everyone looked artsy, with loud hair colors and outfits that were maybe ironic? Definitely ugly, but probably intentionally so. Others were dressed very stylishly, but in a way that Troy's former teammates would have scoffed at. They would have used slurs to describe the people here. And, not long ago, Troy might have used them too.

Someday, he hoped, he would be among openly queer people and feel that he belonged. Because, yes, he was a jock, but he was also gay, and he needed to figure out a way to be both.

"Can we get a drink?" Troy asked. The room was already so warm.

"You read my mind. Let's go."

They squeezed through the crowd, Harris pausing to smile and say hello to several people. Not for the first time, Troy wondered why Harris had invited him and not one of his many friends who wouldn't stick out like a sore thumb. Unless this was a date, which it might be.

The bartender—a very attractive young man with dark hair and light brown skin—gripped Harris's hand and pulled him in for an over-the-bar hug. "What's up, Harris?"

"Not much. Looking forward to the show."

"It's going to be amazing," the man agreed. Then he turned

his attention to Troy. His gaze was blatantly assessing, and Troy had difficulty not squirming. "Who's your friend?"

"This is Troy. He moved here from Toronto. Troy, this is Manu, a friend from college."

Troy almost laughed at Harris's dull description, but he was also grateful that he hadn't mentioned his last name or that he played for the Centaurs. He shook hands with Manu. "Nice to meet you."

"You too. Damn, Harris always gets the pretty ones."

"No I don't," Harris scoffed. "I mean," he glanced nervously at Troy, "we're not togeth—"

"*Always*, huh?" Troy teased.

Harris blushed adorably. "I barely have time for dating! You know what my life is like. Manu is exaggerating."

Manu laughed. "Whatever you say, Harris. What can I get you? Wait. Let me guess."

"Drover Cider, please."

"I don't know why you pay for them here when you could get it for free."

"Because I want to support my local economy," Harris said with a grin.

"What about you?" Manu asked Troy.

Troy glanced at Harris. "Would you be mad if I ordered a beer?"

"Of course not. Do you like pilsners? My buddy Johnathan runs Portage Brewery and they make a killer pilsner."

"Are you friends with *everyone*?"

Harris shrugged. "I like people and I've lived here my whole life."

"Sure," Troy said to Manu. "I'll try one of the pilsners."

Manu went to get their drinks, but not before a parting glance at Harris that seemed to say a lot of things Troy couldn't translate. He recognized Harris's bashful smile, though.

"Is this a date?" Troy blurted out.

Harris's eyes went wide. "Huh?"

"You said you just had an extra ticket, but . . . is this a date?"

"Do you want it to be?"

Troy narrowed his eyes. "Do *you* want it to be?"

Harris leaned one elbow on the bar. "This game sucks. Let's just be honest."

"Okay," Troy said, as if that were an easy thing to do.

"I'm trying to give you space, like you asked. But I lied about the ticket. I bought it for you. I want this to be a date."

Troy's heart did a little shimmy. "So do I."

Harris beamed. "Well, okay then. We're on a date."

Troy smiled back at him. "Let's do it."

Fabian Salah knew how to put on a show. Troy had never seen anything like it. Fabian stood alone on stage, but somehow created a wall of sound all by himself using his violin, various pedals, an electric piano, a laptop and who knew what else. You could hear a pin drop in the packed club when he was singing, his voice clear and ethereal.

He was also wearing wings. Huge, black, elaborately feathered wings. And a black minidress. And gold, strappy sandals that went all the way up to his knees. And, like, a *lot* of makeup.

This was Ryan Price's boyfriend. *Ryan Price.* One of the fiercest enforcers in NHL history. Quiet, socially awkward, enormous Ryan Price.

It was blowing Troy's mind.

But mostly he was watching Harris, who was watching Fabian with rapt admiration. Troy understood; the music combined with the spectacle of a man performing it was pretty incredible.

And sexy as hell. There was something profoundly erotic about the entire experience, though Troy's confused brain couldn't quite sort out exactly what it was. Maybe it was Fabian's confidence—his courage to present himself so openly and shamelessly. The lyrics were sexy, too. Were they about *Ryan*? Jesus.

In the middle of one of Fabian's songs, Troy brushed his fingers over the back of Harris's hand. He'd been wanting to touch him all night, and Fabian was inspiring him to be brave.

Harris smiled at him and then, suddenly, they were holding hands. A warmth seemed to radiate from their joined palms and it filled Troy's whole body. He could do this. He could hold this man's hand in public because he wanted to. Because Harris made him happy and Troy was so fucking tired of being miserable.

They stayed like that, fingers tangled together, for the rest of the song. They broke apart to applaud, then automatically took each other's hand again.

After the encore, and the applause had died down, Troy tugged Harris toward him. "Thank you for inviting me. That was amazing."

"Right? He's, like, life changing. I can't believe he's a real person."

"I can't believe he's dating Ryan Price."

"I know!" Harris glanced around. "I wonder if Price is here. He usually travels with him."

Troy glanced around too, and found Ryan near the back of the room. He was easy to spot, since he was the tallest person in the room, and had very red hair.

Troy made a decision. "I want to talk to him."

Harris nodded. "Then you should. You want me to stay here?"

"Maybe. I won't be long." He locked eyes with Harris. "I'll find you."

"You'd better."

Impulsively, Troy leaned in and kissed him on the cheek. Then he darted away before he could see Harris's reaction.

Ryan was standing alone when Troy approached him. He could see the exact moment Ryan recognized him, because his expression shifted from someone who was probably fantasizing about his impressive boyfriend to one of wide-eyed anxiety.

"Hey," Troy said when he was in front of him.

"Barrett? What are you doing here?"

"I came with a friend."

Ryan's eyes darted around anxiously as if he expected to see Dallas Kent. "Why are you in Ottawa?"

That question surprised Troy. "I play here now."

"Oh." Ryan looked embarrassed. "Sorry. I don't follow hockey too closely anymore."

"It's okay." Troy tilted his head toward the now-empty stage. "Is that really your boyfriend?"

Ryan's face shifted again into a proud smile. "Yeah. I know, I can't believe it either."

His hair had always been long and he usually had a thick, sometimes unruly, beard covering his face. Now his hair had been cut shorter than Troy had ever seen it, and his beard had been reduced to dark red stubble. It turned out that Ryan had been hiding a very handsome face and a nice smile under all that hair.

"You look good," Troy said, because he owed this guy a compliment. And so many apologies. "Look, um, I know this probably won't mean much to you, but I want to apologize. I was a complete asshole to you when we played together, and I'm sorry. It makes me sick thinking about how I treated you."

Ryan had clearly not been expecting any of that, the way his mouth fell open. "Uh, okay. No problem."

"Especially about the fear of flying thing. I can't believe how horrible and immature I was. And I kind of got a taste of how you must have felt."

"Right. I heard about the plane thing. I didn't know you were on that plane because I didn't know you played for Ottawa, but, um, it seemed like a nightmare."

"It was pretty fucking scary."

"I don't even want to think about it. I haven't been on a plane since I quit hockey."

"Really? I heard that you travel with your boyfriend when he tours."

"We drive. Or he flies alone. I don't go on every trip." His eyes narrowed. "Wait. Who's telling you all of this?"

"Uh . . ." Okay, so this was the other thing Troy wanted to talk about. "My friend Harris. He's a big fan of Fabian's and he does the social media for the Centaurs. He's . . . gay."

Ryan's eyebrows shot up. "You have a gay friend now?"

"Yeah, uh. That's the other thing I wanted to apologize for. I said a lot of homophobic shit when I played for Toronto and I shouldn't have. I don't want to make excuses, but I was kind of . . . hiding behind it, if you know what I mean. That doesn't make it less shitty. But it's why I did it."

He could see Ryan putting things together in his head. "Wait. *You're* gay?"

Troy swallowed. "Yes."

Ryan blew out a breath. "Didn't see that one coming."

"I know."

Troy couldn't tell from Ryan's expression if he actually cared about any of this.

"Does your friend know you're gay?" Ryan asked.

"Who? Harris?"

"No, Dallas."

Troy's stomach clenched the way it always did when he heard Dallas's name. "Wow. You really haven't been following hockey. We're not friends anymore."

"Oh. Good."

"I know."

Both men shared an awkward silence, then Ryan said, "I should go meet Fabian backstage. But, um . . ."

"Yeah. Of course. Go." Troy hesitated, then said, "I'm glad you're happy, Ryan."

Ryan nodded. "Good luck with, y'know, figuring everything out."

He left quickly without a glance back, which Troy couldn't blame him for. He was glad he'd gotten a chance to apologize, but he didn't expect Ryan to want to talk to him for any longer than he needed to.

But there was someone here who did want to talk to Troy. Who always had time for him, and seemed to really care about him. And Troy wasn't going to keep him waiting.

Harris had found friends to talk to while Troy was busy with Ryan, so he hadn't been bored. But a thrill shot through him when he spotted Troy walking toward him.

"You found me," Harris said.

"I said I would."

Then he placed a hand on Harris's cheek, tilted his head, and *kissed him*. Full on the mouth. With people all around them.

And suddenly, there was no one around them. At least not as far as Harris was concerned. All that existed in the world was the firm, warm press of Troy's lips against his own, and the slow, gentle tangle of their tongues.

Troy began to pull away, but Harris nipped at his bottom lip, pulling him back in for another long, luxurious kiss.

"Wow," Harris said, dazed, when they finally broke for air. He hadn't been expecting anything like this when he'd invited Troy out tonight. He hadn't expected, but he'd *hoped*. "What was that all about?"

"I don't know. I've been wanting to do it all night, and—"

Troy's smile was wider and brighter than Harris had ever seen it, and his eyes shone with an excited energy. "I don't do things I want to do very often. I like kissing you."

"Oh," Harris said. "Good."

Troy was still cradling Harris's face. "Come home with me?"

"Okay," Harris said, still light-headed from the kiss.

Then Troy kissed him again. It was quick, but sweet because he was still smiling.

"Sorry," Troy said. "Last one, I promise."

"I hope not." Harris took his hand. "Let's get our coats."

CHAPTER TWENTY-ONE

"Your place is nice," Harris said breathlessly as Troy pressed him against a wall.

"It's boring. And it's not mine." Troy kissed him, hard and possessive and perfect.

Harris couldn't argue, both because his mouth was full of Troy's tongue, and because the apartment really was boring. It was basically an extra-large hotel room.

But it probably had a bed, and that was all Harris was interested in at the moment. He'd been fired up since Troy had first held his hand at the club, the gesture unexpected and exhilarating. Then there'd been the kiss on the cheek, which was such a small, silly thing, but Harris knew it hadn't been either of those things for Troy.

And then there'd been the *real* kisses. Hungry, like this one was, as if they contained every secret longing Troy had ever had. As if he'd forced them down for so long that the pressure had become too great and now they were erupting out of him, hot and messy and potentially devastating.

Eventually, they made it to the bedroom, and Troy immediately began removing his own clothing. He opened just enough buttons to haul his shirt over his head, taking the undershirt with it. Harris was enjoying the show so much he forgot to get himself undressed.

"Come on," Troy said, already fully naked. "Off. Wanna see you."

Harris started unbuttoning his own shirt, but he wasn't fast enough for Troy, who stepped close to help. In seconds, all of Harris's clothing was in a pile on the floor, and he was back in Troy's arms, being kissed like he would evaporate if Troy stopped.

"You want me to fuck you again?" Troy asked. "Like last time?"

Harris shuddered happily thinking about it. "Yeah. Just like last time. If that's what you want."

"It's exactly what I want."

Harris was shoved backward on the bed, Troy looming over him. Harris gazed up in amazement at his hard, beautiful body and his intense eyes, bringing to life every fantasy of being ravaged by a jock that Harris had ever had.

"Jesus," Harris said on an exhale. "You can't be real."

Troy gripped his own rigid cock and slowly guided it toward Harris's lips. "Is *this* real?"

Harris took him eagerly into his mouth, moaning at the first taste of him. Troy straddled his thighs as Harris propped himself up on his elbows—a little awkward and slightly uncomfortable, but for some reason it only made it hotter. Like they couldn't even wait to get in a position that made sense. Harris certainly didn't feel like moving.

He couldn't take him deep like this, so he focused on the sensitive head of Troy's cock, flicking his tongue and probing the slit. Troy swore through gritted teeth, and Harris could see the tension in his muscles as he fought to hold still.

Except Harris wanted him to thrust. He wanted him to use all that strength to fuck his mouth.

Harris let Troy's cock drop out of his mouth, and heard Troy's disapproving grunt. Then Harris slid off the bed to the floor, settling on his knees beside Troy.

"Let's try it this way," Harris said, head tilted back to see Troy's expression. Troy nodded, eyes hooded and lips parted, and offered Harris his cock.

"Don't hold back," Harris instructed, then wrapped his lips around him, taking him deep to show him he could. He bobbed his head and ran his palms over Troy's thighs, and around to his ass, spelling it out for him.

Troy jerked his hips forward, just once, and stopped to meet Harris's gaze. His eyes asked permission, and Harris nodded slightly, hoping his own eyes showed how much he wanted this.

They must have, because the next thrust was harder. And the next one. Harris kept his jaw slack and his head still, and let Troy plunder him.

"Fuck, Harris," Troy growled. "So fucking good to me."

He gripped the back of Harris's head, fingers tight in his hair. His thrusts were so hard and fast that Harris could barely even groan his approval. He could only gaze up with hazy, damp eyes and focus on the sparks of excitement that were shooting through his body. He loved everything about this. He loved making people feel good, and he loved being handled so roughly. He always wanted to be useful, but right now he wanted to be *used*.

Troy's skin was flushed, from his face, down his neck, and across his chest. His abs clenched with each snap of his hips, and Harris watched, mesmerized.

"God, look at you take it," Troy panted. "So hot. Fucking beautiful."

Harris relaxed his throat, inviting Troy deeper. Troy pushed in and stopped, gasping and moaning as Harris swallowed around the swollen head of his cock.

"Harris, I—" Troy inhaled sharply, and huffed it out. "I shouldn't—fuck, I'm too close. You gotta stop me."

He meant it, Harris could tell, so he pulled back and Troy released his grip on his scalp.

"Ah, shit." Troy wrapped his hand around the base of his cock, squeezing tight. He closed his eyes and took a few deep, shaky breaths while Harris watched from his knees, amused by Troy's struggle.

"Okay," Troy sighed after a tense few seconds. "I'm good." He laughed unsteadily. "Fuck, that was close."

Harris playfully leaned in and parted his lips. Troy took a step back.

"Don't you dare," he laughed. "Stand up. I want to kiss you."

Well, that was an easy order to obey. Harris's knees were killing him anyway. He hadn't noticed until Troy had pulled his cock free.

"You could have, you know," Harris said, looping his arms around Troy's neck. "Finished, I mean. You don't *have* to fuck me tonight."

"I *definitely* have to fuck you tonight," Troy growled, and kissed him.

Harris's lips were swollen and bruised, but he couldn't get enough of Troy's kisses. They kept kissing as Troy lowered himself to the bed, pulling Harris down with him. Troy lay back, and Harris followed, settling his body on top of all that firm muscle. Letting their legs tangle together as he kissed Troy's chin, neck, nose, ears, shoulders, then back to his lips.

"God, you're sweet," Troy murmured as Harris kissed his collarbone. "When you offer yourself like that, on your knees with your mouth open, I can't resist. I hate how much I love being rough with you, when all I want is to take care of you."

Harris lifted his head so their eyes met. "You *are* taking care of me. You're giving me what I want, and I love how you don't hold back with me, Troy."

"I don't want to hurt you."

"And that's why you won't."

Their mouths crashed together again, and they rolled on the bed until Harris was on his back, under Troy.

"I want to do it like this," Troy murmured. "Want to look at you."

Harris really hoped the bouncy things his heart was doing weren't related to his medical condition. "I want that too."

Harris usually preferred to be taken from behind, or some position that didn't put his scars on display, but he wanted to see Troy's face when he entered him, when he lost control, and when he came. Harris wanted all of his senses to be full of this man.

Troy grabbed lube and a condom from his nightstand. He took his time opening Harris up, maddeningly careful after everything they'd just discussed, but Harris knew it was for the best. He squirmed impatiently, wanting more than Troy's strong fingers. When Harris was on the verge of begging, Troy gripped his thighs and pushed his knees toward his chest. He was so open and exposed, and Troy was admiring his entrance like he'd found treasure.

"Keep your legs there," he ordered. He removed his hands and Harris obeyed, keeping himself spread wide-open while he watched Troy roll a condom on.

Troy drizzled lube on his sheathed cock, then stroked himself slowly. "Don't deserve all this," he said huskily. "This gorgeous man waiting for my cock. So fucking hot."

"You deserve it," Harris said. "Please. Give it to me."

Troy hauled him roughly to the end of the mattress, then planted one foot on the bed. He lined himself up and slowly pushed in, making Harris groan with relief.

Harris was so hard. His cock had been mostly ignored tonight, and it was demanding attention now. Troy was buried to the hilt inside him, panting and squeezing his eyes shut.

"Fuck," Troy gritted out. "You feel too fucking good."

Harris began stroking himself, because it seemed that Troy wasn't going to be able to last very long tonight. "Take your time," he said. "Or come if you need to. Just want you to feel good."

Troy watched the movement of Harris's hand. His tongue poked out to wet his bottom lip. "Get yourself close." He gave a few shallow thrusts, each one sending waves of pleasure through Harris's body. Getting close wouldn't be a problem for Harris.

Troy moved faster as Harris's hand sped up, and finally he rasped, "I can't—I have to—" and then he was *really* pounding into him. Hard and relentless, slamming the headboard against the wall, making Harris cry out with pleasure.

"Fuck. *Fuck!*" Troy gasped, then he stilled and his mouth went slack. He pulled out so quickly that Harris yelped, then he swallowed Harris's cock down, sucking hard. It was a matter of seconds before Harris erupted into Troy's mouth with a loud moan. Hopefully the soundproofing in Troy's fancy building was decent.

"Holy shit," Harris panted. Troy flopped beside him, also breathing hard.

"Yeah. Sorry I went off so fast."

"Don't be. It was hot as hell."

They lay together quietly for a minute or two, letting their breathing return to normal. Then Harris turned his head and could see Troy fighting a smile. "What?"

"Nothing. Just that I always feel ridiculous after sex."

"Oh." Harris traced a finger over the curve of his shoulder, then over to the grooves around his pecs. "I get that. It's a pretty weird activity, really."

Troy snorted and then shook with laughter, which made Harris laugh.

"Now that you said that, I can't stop thinking about how weird it is," Troy said.

"Yeah, it's like, we can have dinner, or watch TV, or you can stick your dick in my ass."

Troy was full-on giggling now. It was a joy to listen to.

"I would like those other things," Troy said, once he'd gotten himself under control. "With you, I mean."

Harris's heart pounded. "You would?"

"Definitely. I'd . . ." Troy trailed off, gaze fixed on the ceiling. "Do you think people saw us kissing? Like, who recognized me?"

Ah. Here we go. "I don't know," Harris said honestly.

"Maybe there are photos of us on Twitter."

"It's always a risk these days, but you could always deny that it's you in the photos."

Troy was silent a moment, then said, "No one would expect me to be at a concert like that." Harris translated it as *no one would expect me to be surrounded by queer people.*

"Probably not."

Troy abruptly sat up and grabbed his phone off the nightstand.

"What are you doing?" Harris asked.

"Posting something."

Harris propped himself on one elbow, craning his neck to see the screen. Troy pulled it away.

"Be patient," Troy scolded.

Harris enjoyed the line that appeared between Troy's black eyebrows as he concentrated on typing. A few seconds later, he handed Harris his phone.

Harris gasped theatrically. Troy had posted a photo he'd taken of Fabian Salah onstage, tagged the location, and written *An incredible night.*

"I figure there probably weren't any homophobes at that show," Troy said. "So if anyone saw us, they'd be, y'know. Cool about it."

Harris kissed him, touched by this small but significant act of bravery, then said, "At worst they'd be jealous. Of you, I mean. Obviously."

Troy laughed and wrapped an arm around him, pulling him close so Harris's head was resting on his chest. "I want to take you somewhere. Another date."

Harris beamed. "I'd like that."

Troy kissed the top of his head. "When?"

"I'm working this weekend. All-Star game and all that. But it's quiet at work for the rest of the week because of the break."

"Okay. I'll think about it over the weekend. It'll be epic. Best date ever." Troy kissed him quickly and said, "I should, um, deal with the condom and stuff. But you'll stay tonight, right?"

Harris rolled to his back and stretched his arms out. "Buddy, I might never move again."

CHAPTER TWENTY-TWO

TROY:

Can our date start Tuesday morning and end Wednesday afternoon?

The text had been left unanswered for twenty minutes, and Troy was milliseconds away from calling Harris when he finally saw the three dots.

HARRIS:

Sounds like a hell of a date.

Troy smiled and wrote, It's going to be amazing. And it's a surprise, so don't ask.

HARRIS:

Do I need to pack anything?

TROY:

Is that a yes?

HARRIS:

I'm curious now! Of course it's a yes!

Alone in his apartment, Troy pumped his fist triumphantly. Since Harris had left on Saturday morning, Troy had been frantically trying to think of the perfect date to take him on. He wanted it to not only be something that Harris would enjoy, but something that would give him a real break from work. Something that would allow Troy to take care of him.

They had never discussed the fact that Troy was a millionaire, but Troy got the impression that Harris wasn't interested in fancy restaurants or lavish gifts. Troy still wanted to spoil him a little, though.

Then he'd gotten an idea. It took some internet searching, but Troy found the perfect place: a spa retreat in Quebec, less than two hours away, that had private chalets. He knew it was a long shot when he'd called, because it was extremely short notice, but he'd gotten lucky: there had been a last-minute cancellation. The woman he'd spoken to had apologetically told him that he would have to book the exact same package that had been canceled, and Troy had laughed when she'd told him what it was.

The Lovebird Getaway.

She hadn't sounded the least bit surprised or offended when Troy had given her Harris's name as the second guest. It was the first time Troy had ever indicated his sexuality to a stranger, and, once the butterflies in his stomach had calmed down, he'd felt a wave of relief surge through him. He'd booked a romantic getaway for himself and his boyfriend, and it was fine. He'd used his real name and everything.

TROY:

Pack a bathing suit and comfy clothes.

HARRIS:

How am I supposed to tweet about the All-Star Game now?

Troy had, wonderfully, forgotten about the All-Star game. He decided to leave Harris alone for now, and wrote: **I'll pick you up at 10am on Tuesday.**

Harris replied with a string of excited-face emojis.

"Oh my god," Harris squeaked.

"Okay, so the thing is—"

"Oh my *god*. I have *dreamed* of coming to this place."

Troy pressed his lips together to keep from laughing at Harris's excitement as he took in the stunning interior of the main lodge. "I was only able to book it on short notice because someone canceled, so I had to book the same package they had."

"Unless it was the You Have to go Home Immediately package, I don't care."

"It's the Lovebird Getaway. So it might be a bit . . . much."

Harris's eyes went even wider. "Is this our *honeymoon*?"

Troy elbowed him. "Calm down."

He went to the desk and got them checked in. The woman working there turned out to be the same woman he'd spoken to on the phone, Cora.

"Our last-minute lovebirds," she said warmly in her Quebecois accent. "You can leave your bags here, and we will bring them to your cabin. Just take your bathing suits out first, and you will start your day with a soak in our hot tub."

Harris was bouncing on his toes, grinning like a kid on Christmas morning. As a pro athlete, hot tubs, saunas and steam rooms were an almost daily necessity for Troy, but he had a feeling this would be a more enjoyable soaking experience than most.

They were led to a change room with lockers and left alone to put on their bathing suits. "So far this is a lot like a typical day at work," Troy said. "Hot tub, locker room."

"So far this is the best day of my life, so shush."

One thing that was different about this locker room and the ones Troy was normally in was that this time he openly ogled the man who was undressing next to him.

"Already?" Harris teased when he noticed Troy's semi-erect cock.

"I missed you."

Harris pulled his swim trunks up, then wrapped his arms around Troy's neck. "I missed you too." He kissed him, and Troy wondered how important it was that they did any of the spa treatments. The cabin had a bed that could probably provide all the relaxation and rejuvenation Troy needed.

But Harris looked so damn happy. And adorable, now that he was bundling himself into the fluffy white bathrobe the spa had provided.

There were some medical forms that they both needed to fill out. Troy finished his quickly, and it occurred to him that Harris might have more boxes to check.

"There's nothing here that's unsafe for you, is there?" Troy asked.

"Not unless we're skydiving."

Troy huffed. "God, I hope not."

Harris kissed him quickly on the cheek. "I think I'm safe then. I need to be careful about the hot tub, but I'm fine with them if I don't stay in too long. Let's go get pampered!"

The hot tub room was fancy as hell. The tub itself was the size of a small swimming pool, recessed into the dark granite floor. The lighting was dim and dramatic, and soft music reverberated off the stone walls.

"Wow," Harris whispered. "I feel like I'm in ancient Rome."

"Yeah. This is not my usual hot tub."

They removed their robes and stepped into the hot water. Harris moaned as soon as he got himself seated, the echo of it bouncing off the walls. "Oh man. This is the best."

Troy grinned and sat next to him in the same corner. "Soaking in hot water rules."

"Mm." Harris closed his eyes and tipped his head back. "My body isn't going to know what hit it. I never treat it this well."

"You work too hard."

Harris scoffed. "Compared to you? Hardly."

"Well, how about we make our time here hockey-free?"

Harris smiled without opening his eyes. "Sounds perfect."

His skin was already deep pink from the hot water, and it made the white line of his scar stand out more. Troy tried not to stare at it, but he couldn't help but worry about the heart behind it.

"Still beating," Harris said mildly. Troy noticed that his eyes had opened, and he flooded with embarrassment.

"Sorry. I wasn't staring."

Harris brushed his foot against Troy's. "Yes you were. It's okay. I get it. That's why I don't lounge around in a bathing suit very often."

"I'm sorry," Troy said again. He wanted to tell him he didn't need to hide his scars, but he was the last person who should be telling someone not to hide. Instead, he reached under the water and pulled Harris's foot onto his lap. He lightly caressed the hills and valleys of his ankle.

Harris sighed happily. "Do I get a massage before my massage?"

"I just want to touch you."

Harris's eyes went a little gooey. "Are you nervous, being here with me?"

"No," Troy said, then corrected himself. "Not as nervous as I thought I'd be anyway."

"That's good."

"I mean, there's nothing to hide at this point. We're two men enjoying a couple's retreat at a romantic spa. No one can misinterpret that. There's something freeing about having that worry taken away."

Harris inched a little closer to him. "That's true."

"Was it scary for you, when you came out?"

"Of course. Even when you're sure your friends and family will be cool and supportive, it's still scary. But most of my fear was, like you said, around the possibility of someone finding out my secret. Once it wasn't a secret anymore, I didn't have to worry about that."

"I'd like to know how that feels. I've been fucking terrified my whole life that someone would find out. I didn't touch another man until Adrian, when I was twenty-three. So if I'm doing anything wrong in bed, that's my excuse."

"You're definitely not doing anything wrong in bed, stud."

Troy smiled and ran his palm up Harris's shin, then back down. When his hand returned to Harris's knee, Harris, gave a shaky laugh and said, "Don't go any higher or I'm going to have an awkward time leaving the bath."

Troy's own dick perked up. He wished he could haul Harris out of the water and take him right here on the fancy stone tiles. He would love to hear Harris's moans echoing in the quiet, cavernous room. "Is this too high?" he asked, walking his fingers up Harris's thigh.

Harris swatted his hand away. "Fuck off. I mean it. Don't make this weird for the poor staff."

"Serves them right for making this place so sexy."

Harris grinned and sank deeper into the water, retrieving his leg from Troy's lap. "It *is* sexy. But I can wait until we're in our cabin. The waiting makes it sexier, right?"

"You know, we don't *have* to get the massages . . ."

"No way, superstar. Some of us don't get daily rubdowns. I haven't had a massage in ages."

"Fine."

"And Troy?"

"Mm?"

"This is already the best date I've ever been on."

Troy's heart flipped. "Me too."

The hot stone massage turned out to be far more enjoyable than the often painful deep tissue massages Troy got from the team therapist. It also had more loud, filthy moaning than Troy was used to. All of it from the table next to his, and all of it making it very difficult for Troy to relax.

"Unf. Why don't I always have hot stones on my back?" Harris said, his words sleepy and slurred with pleasure.

Both of the massage therapists were laughing. Harris had barely shut up the entire massage. Troy had been mostly silent, since he was entirely focused on not getting a boner, but he was grinning into his face rest. He'd never expected to be so charmed by such an unrepentant goofball.

Lunch was served in a private room where they ate healthy and delicious grain bowls and drank fresh-pressed juice in their bathrobes. It felt decadent, even with the high nutritional value.

After lunch, they had some procedures that were as exciting to Troy as they were to Harris: facials, followed by manicures and pedicures. Troy had always taken care of his skin—he had often been roasted by Dallas Kent for his daily regimen when they'd roomed together. But Dallas's forehead was always covered in helmet acne, so fuck him.

Again, Harris had all of the practitioners laughing while Troy sat silent, smiling as he continued to fall hard for the walking ray of sunshine he'd managed to snag for himself.

The day finished with one more soak in the hot tub, and then showers before putting their clothes back on.

"I hate wearing clothes," Harris complained. "Now that I know how good a day spent in a bathrobe can be, clothes feel like prison."

"It's just until we get to the cabin," Troy assured him. "We can order room service for dinner."

Harris kissed him, then grabbed his hand and pulled him out of the change room. "This date keeps getting better."

The new person at the front desk directed them to their cabin. It was a short, scenic walk through snow-covered evergreen trees to their tiny log cabin, and Harris loved it immediately.

"It's so cute!" He squeezed Troy's hand. "Too bad we're going to destroy it."

Troy chuckled. "Maybe I have other plans."

"No way. You promised sex and naked eating."

The cabin interior was even more charming than the outside. There was a woodstove in one corner, with a small stack of firewood next to it. A leather couch and chair faced it because there was no television. Harris was fine with that; he'd left his phone in a locker all day and he was happy to continue his break from screens.

There were cozy blankets neatly folded on the furniture, and a thick, soft rug in front of the stove. It was absurdly romantic.

Things got even more romantic in the bedroom. The bed had a welcome basket with chocolates, fresh fruit, an assortment of teas, and two of the spa robes rolled up. There was a bouquet of roses on the dresser, and an ice bucket with a bottle of champagne on the nightstand.

"Oh my god, I feel like a princess!" Harris started poking

through the basket immediately. "Chocolate-covered strawberries!"

"It's a bit much."

"No, I love it. I'm going to feed these to you later."

Troy stepped close behind him and kissed his neck. "I could eat now."

Harris turned and kissed him. This time they let it linger, Troy tipping Harris's head back slightly so he could kiss him as deeply and thoroughly as he'd been wanting to all day.

"Robes?" Harris said huskily when they broke apart.

"Robes," Troy agreed.

Within twenty minutes, they had a fire built in the stove, and were lounging on the rug with flutes of cold champagne and a coffee table full of treats.

"All we need is a dog," Harris mused.

"How would a dog make this better?"

"Dogs make everything better."

Troy leaned in and kissed him as he ran a hand up Harris's thigh, under the hem of the bathrobe. "Not everything," he said in a low, seductive voice.

And, no. Not everything.

Harris plucked one of the strawberries from the coffee table and hovered it in front of Troy's lips. Troy smiled and opened, taking the berry in his mouth and closing his lips around Harris's fingers.

It actually wasn't as sexy as Harris was hoping. He had to remove his fingers so Troy could chew the slightly-too-big berry that was making his cheeks bulge. Once Troy swallowed, he coughed and said, "That was a sour strawberry."

"Was the chocolate good?"

"Could've used more of it." Troy took a gulp of champagne.

Harris laughed. "Sorry. I thought it would be, y'know, sensual."

"I have an idea." Troy set his flute on the table. "How about I lay you out on that rug and kiss every inch of you?"

Harris immediately tipped backward on the rug, arms and legs spread wide. "I'm in."

He thought Troy would pounce on him, but instead he sprawled out on his side next to him, gazing at him with those piercing blue eyes. Harris almost squirmed under the scrutiny, but then Troy gently placed a hand on the side of Harris's face and kissed him.

He kept kissing him. He kissed the corner of his mouth, his cheek, his eyebrow. His soft lips teased the shell of Harris's ear, and down to his throat. Each kiss was soft and unhurried, savoring Harris like fine whiskey.

He didn't even notice Troy untying the belt of his bathrobe until it fell open. Troy positioned himself between Harris's spread legs, kneeling as he trailed his fingertips over Harris's chest and stomach. The gentle brush against his skin was almost ticklish, but it also sent delicious shivers through him.

For an eternity, Troy didn't do anything except caress Harris's skin. His fingers explored everywhere—torso, legs, arms, throat, face. Everywhere except Harris's now rigid cock. Harris just lay there like a puddle of mush, perfectly relaxed and blissful after a day at the spa with the man he—

The man he definitely had some significant feelings for.

"I don't know if you've noticed," Harris said dreamily, "but I'm a bit aroused."

"I noticed."

"Okay. Just making sure."

Troy's lip curved up in one corner, then he pulled one of Harris's hands to his lips and kissed his palm.

"Little lower," Harris quipped.

Troy kissed the inside of his wrist.

"Meanie," Harris grumbled.

A low rumble of laughter shook Troy's shoulders, then he lowered his head and snatched Harris's right nipple between his teeth.

"Getting warmer," Harris sighed. He watched Troy as he kissed a path across his chest, over his scar, to his left nipple. God, Troy was beautiful. He was always beautiful, but now, in the glow of the firelight and with Harris's brain fizzy with champagne and lust, he was breathtaking.

And if he wanted to spend the rest of the night tormenting Harris with soft kisses, well, Harris shouldn't complain.

Eventually, however, Harris had to complain.

"You're gonna kill me," he said raggedly.

"Shh. Let me take care of you my way."

"Your way is torture."

Troy chuckled against Harris's inner thigh, sending ripples of pleasure up to his balls.

"If you're not gonna touch my dick, at least let me touch yours."

With an exaggerated sigh, Troy shifted until he was kneeling beside Harris's shoulder. His erection was peeking out from the front of his loosely tied bathrobe. Harris pulled one end of the belt, and the knot fell apart.

"Let me suck it?" Harris asked. He had no idea why he was asking permission, except it felt like Troy was fully in charge here and Harris wanted to go with it.

"I was just about to suck *you*," Troy said, letting his robe drop to the floor.

"Oh, were you really?" Harris drawled. "After, what? Two hours of forgetting where my dick is?"

"Brat." Troy turned himself so he was facing Harris's feet and straddled his face. Harris had noticed before how meticulous Troy's personal grooming was. His balls were smooth and hairless, and the hair around the base of his cock was a neatly trimmed dark patch. Harris kept on top of his own manscaping, but Troy was at a level that rivaled porn stars.

And now those smooth, heavy balls were dangling over Harris's face, brushing his lips.

"Well?" Troy asked.

Harris huffed. "Listen, pal. You don't get to be impatient after all that." But he didn't make Troy wait; he licked and then sucked one of his balls into his mouth, and enjoyed the soft gasp Troy let out.

Troy didn't move, so Harris stayed focused on his balls, rolling one carefully on his tongue, and then the other. He licked behind them, pressing his tongue firmly against Troy's perineum.

"Oh," Troy said quietly. "God, that's—"

Harris kept going, inching his tongue slowly back to Troy's ass. He reached up and spread his hands on his ass cheeks, pulling them gently apart to give Troy a clue about his plans.

For a moment, Troy's whole body seemed to freeze, and Harris stilled too. Then, Troy shifted forward, just a bit. Just enough to bring his hole closer to Harris's mouth. Harris grinned at the offering, and wondered if anyone had done this to Troy before. It wasn't something everyone was keen to do, but Harris was a fan.

He pressed his tongue flat against Troy's hole, not moving. Just letting Troy feel the warm wetness of his tongue against the sensitive nerve endings there.

"Holy—" Troy gasped.

Harris licked a few slow strokes, then changed to a circular motion with the tip of his tongue. Within seconds, Troy was rocking against his mouth, moaning and swearing wantonly while Harris used every rimming trick he knew.

He wondered if Troy wanted Harris to fuck him. Harris would definitely be into that. He liked being taken hard, but he certainly had nothing against being on top. Especially when sex was like this: tender and sensuous and indulgent. When no one was in a hurry and it was all about exploration and discovery. He would love to slide into Troy, bury himself in him and rock together until they both shattered.

"Fuck, that's good." Troy panted. "Love your beard against my skin."

Troy's entrance was still closed tight like a fist, but Harris managed to wiggle the tip of his tongue inside.

"Ah!" Troy cried out. "Jesus. I need to—" Then he fell forward, pulling his ass away from Harris's mouth and wrapping his lips around Harris's cock.

Now Harris cried out, partly from the relief and surprise of finally having Troy's mouth on his long-suffering erection, and partly from frustration. He'd wanted to see if he could relax Troy's hole with his tongue, and now he couldn't quite reach it.

But he could reach Troy's dick, so he opened his mouth wide and let Troy slide inside.

Troy moaned, and the vibrations made Harris's back arch. He hadn't done this exact thing in a while, and he'd *never* done it next to a fire, being pressed into the floor of a cabin by a huge, heavy NHL player.

He hummed and moaned and sighed while he sucked Troy, because Harris couldn't even be quiet when he had a dick in his mouth. He slid his palms over Troy's thighs and hips and ass, unable to decide if he wanted to fuck this man, or be fucked, or just do this for now. After another minute, the decision was taken away from him when he realized he was on the brink of orgasm.

He made a loud, muffled hum to warn Troy, but Troy stayed on him, and seconds later Harris exploded into his mouth. It hit him so hard that he had to pull away from Troy's dick. He cried out as intense pleasure ripped through him again and again. Through it all, Troy kept sucking, taking every drop and giving Harris as much pleasure as possible. Harris frantically tried to get his mouth back on Troy's dick, knowing he was close, but was astonished when Troy started shooting into the air, spattering Harris's chest with his release.

Even after all that, Troy kept peppering Harris's spent cock with light kisses, eventually moving to Harris's thighs and then, finally, pulling away. He lifted his leg so he wasn't straddling Harris and turned so he could lie next to him on the rug.

"Thank you," Troy said, his voice low and battered.

"Thank *me*?" Harris said with a tired laugh. "I was just trying to keep up."

A wide, unguarded smile stretched across Troy's face, and it sent a jolt through Harris that felt more powerful than his orgasm. Because he did that—*he* made Troy Barrett smile like that. Somehow, Harris had earned that, and he realized, in that moment, how fiercely he would protect that smile. How fiercely he would protect *Troy*.

Because he might be falling in love with him.

"What?" Troy asked, smile fading because Harris's face must have shown some of his anxiety.

"Nothing," Harris said quickly. "I'm just . . . hungry. We should order room service."

Troy's smile returned. He kissed Harris quickly and said, "I hope they have salmon."

They did have salmon, and Troy ate his with gusto because he'd realized, as soon as their dinner had been delivered, that he was famished.

"Still not as good as chocolate cake," Harris said, setting his empty plate on the end table. They were sitting on the sofa together, still wearing only bathrobes, and still enjoying the fire.

The champagne was gone.

"You're wrong," Troy said, "but good thing we got chocolate cake too."

Troy let Harris feed him cake off his fork, which was something he would find revolting in other couples, but no one could see them now so he didn't care. Besides, he had a pretty good buzz on from the champagne.

When they finished their dessert, Harris snuggled against him, and they watched the fire together. "What are you doing Sunday?" Harris asked.

"I have a practice in the morning, but nothing after that," Troy said.

"Wanna come to the farm for dinner?"

Troy tensed. "With your family, you mean?"

"Of course," Harris said, as if it wasn't the biggest deal in the world. "They'd love you."

This was . . . a lot. "What would we tell them? About us?"

"Whatever you're comfortable with. They certainly won't judge if we tell them we're . . . whatever we are."

"Really?" Troy couldn't even imagine.

"They've always loved and accepted me. The worst they'll do is embarrass me by being so thrilled that I've brought someone home."

Troy relaxed a bit. "You don't bring people home very often?"

"I invite friends for dinner sometimes, but not men I'm dating. Or, y'know. Whatever."

They were both quiet a moment, and then Troy said, bravely, "Are we dating?"

Harris glanced up at him. "Kinda feels like it maybe."

Troy smiled. "It does." He was so wonderfully happy in that moment. If this was what dating Harris felt like, he wanted to keep doing it. Whatever it took. "You should tell your parents," he said.

"You sure?"

"Yeah. But maybe tell them before Sunday? I'd rather it not be a whole thing."

"I can do that. And it won't be a big deal. Not to them. I promise. And they'll keep it a secret, if I ask."

Troy shifted so he could pull Harris more onto his lap. He wanted to see his face properly. "Maybe just for a bit. I said I wouldn't make you hide, and I won't. I need a little time to figure some stuff out, though."

Harris studied his face, then smiled. "I need a little time to believe this is even real."

CHAPTER TWENTY-THREE

The Drover family farm was even more absurdly picturesque and charming than Troy had imagined. The long road took them past snow-laden apple trees until they reached a perfect white farmhouse.

"Are you nervous?" Harris asked as they parked the truck.

"No," Troy lied.

"Good. They'll love you. Just wait."

They both got out of the truck, and Troy immediately heard barking.

"Uh-oh," Harris said cheerfully. "Here they come."

Several dogs of various sizes were running toward them, barking excitedly. Troy took a step back, but his back hit the side of the truck, leaving him trapped between hard metal and a tornado of dogs. Because of course they'd all made a beeline for Troy.

"Aw, come on, guys. You're embarrassing me," Harris laughed. He whistled and two of the dogs immediately went to him, leaving Troy with one very large dog pinning him against the truck with its paws on his stomach.

"Uh, hi," Troy said. He realized that he had his hands in the air, as if he were surrendering. He lowered them slightly.

"Mac, you too. Get off of him, you demon." Harris smacked his thigh, which got Mac's attention. After a moment's consideration, Mac seemed to decide he preferred freaking Troy out to hanging with Harris.

"Okay," Troy said slowly. "Um . . . down?"

"Just start walking," Harris said. "He'll move."

Troy took a step forward, and Mac dropped to all fours and wiggled between Troy's legs.

"Mac's the problem child," Harris said, then knelt to scratch Mac's head. "The little one is Shannon, and the white one is Bowser. They're total sweethearts. Not like *this* boner." Harris said the last part in an affectionate voice directed at Mac.

"Harris, don't make your friend stand in the cold all afternoon!" The voice came from the house, and Troy turned to see a woman who must be Harris's mother standing in the open door.

"We're coming," Harris said. He started walking toward the house, then stopped and said, "Shit! The pie."

As Harris jogged back to the truck to retrieve the pie he'd made, his mom beckoned for Troy to come inside.

"I'm Marlene," she said, extending her hand as Troy reached the top of the steps to the front veranda.

"Troy," he said, shaking her hand. She had silver hair cut into a shoulder-length bob, dark-rimmed glasses, and the same compact build as her son. She was even wearing a plaid flannel shirt. She looked pretty hip, actually. Like a celebrated farm-to-table restaurateur.

"I'm glad to finally meet you," she said as they went inside. "Harris has been talking you up."

"Mom." Harris groaned as he followed them with the pie and all three dogs.

Troy's stomach flipped at the thought of Harris saying anything about him to his parents. It was touching and terrifying at the same time.

"He talks a lot," Troy said, then realized it sounded more like a complaint than a gentle ribbing. "I mean, he's friendly." Then he realized he was talking about Harris as if he wasn't there. "*You're* friendly. And chatty. So I'm not surprised that you were talking about me." He could feel the back of his neck heating as Harris and Marlene stared at him. "I can take that pie . . . somewhere . . . for you?"

Harris burst out laughing. "Glad you're not nervous."

The heat crept around from Troy's neck to his face. "Sorry." Excellent. He'd been here a few minutes and had basically cowered away from one of their dogs, then babbled some nonsense about Harris being chatty. Great first impression.

Troy glanced around at the old house that was obviously packed with family history and pride. It was so homey and pleasant and unfamiliar that Troy felt an urge to cast himself out into the cold like a monster.

"Is that Harris?" a new voice asked.

A man stepped into the front entrance from an adjacent room who looked a *lot* like an older version of Harris. The same eyes, the same full beard and thick hair, but both mostly gray, and the same warm smile and booming voice. The biggest difference was that he was several inches taller than Troy.

"You must be Troy. I'm Sam."

They shook hands. "Thank you guys for having me. I haven't had a home-cooked meal in a long time."

"It's been a long time since Harris has brought someone home that he's sweet on," Marlene said. Troy's stomach fluttered.

"Oh my god, Mom. Way to make Troy think we live in the thirties or something."

Marlene laughed. "Make yourself at home. We've got a fire going in the living room. That's why the dogs are already back in there." And that seemed to be the end of the Troy-is-gay-and-dating-Harris conversation. It had been barely anything, and Troy felt almost giddy.

"You saying you're not sweet on me?" Troy murmured into Harris's ear as they walked into the kitchen.

"You're the bee's knees, sweetheart."

The kitchen was surprisingly large and smelled amazing. Harris set his pie on the counter and said, "Want something to drink?"

"Whatever you're having."

Harris opened the fridge and grabbed two bottles of his sisters' cider, then handed one to Troy. "Maybe this will take the edge off."

"I'm fine," Troy said, though it was another lie. He was trying very hard to ignore how surreal this all felt. His relationship with Adrian had been based on a mutual fear of discovery. They had certainly never met each other's families. It hadn't even been discussed. He wasn't quite sure what he was doing with Harris, but he knew he didn't want the same sort of arrangement he'd had with Adrian. He *wanted* to get to know Harris's family, and he wanted them to like him.

Which was a *lot*.

"Wanna see my old bedroom?" Harris asked, waggling his eyebrows.

Troy managed a half smile. "Are you allowed to have boys up there?"

Harris took a step toward him. "You'd be the first one."

Oh. "Really?"

"Yeah. Wanna see it?"

Hell yes, Troy did.

* * *

Troy Barrett was in Harris's childhood bedroom, sitting on his old, creaky twin bed, and Harris was trying very hard to be cool about it.

"This is a lot of Ottawa Centaurs stuff," Troy observed.

He wasn't lying. There were posters, pennants, and knick-knacks everywhere. Harris had hockey cards shoved in the frame of his mirror. Even the bedside lamp had a Centaurs branded shade.

"I was a bit of a fan."

"I'm a little concerned. This feels like you might have lured me up here to add to your collection."

Harris grinned. "I was thinking about chaining you to my bed."

Troy's lips curved up. "*This* bed?" He bounced a couple of times, making it squeak loudly. "I think the detectives would find me."

"Stop bouncing!" Harris hissed. "Mom and Dad will think we're *doing it*!"

"Like this?" Troy bounced some more.

"Oh my god." Harris lunged at him, and seconds later he had Troy pinned on his back and was sprawled on top of him.

"Be awkward if they walked in right now," Troy said. Their lips were so close together that Harris could feel his breath tickle.

"We should get up, probably," Harris murmured.

"Mm." Then they were kissing. Harris had probably started it, but Troy was definitely into it, kissing Harris in that slow, exploratory way that absolutely melted Harris every time.

There was a loud crash behind them, which broke them apart.

"What the hell?" Troy asked.

"Uncle Elroy," Harris said, dipping his head for another kiss.

Troy sat up, nearly knocking Harris to the floor. "Fuck off. It's not a fucking ghost. What was it really?"

Harris glanced behind his shoulder and spotted the culprit on top of his dresser. "Ursula."

"Who's Ursula? The ghost of your great-grandmother?"

Harris laughed. "The cat. She was probably under the bed."

Ursula swished her enormous fluffy tail and knocked a hairbrush to the floor.

"Oh," Troy said. "And how many cats do you have? Eight?"

"Nope. Just one. If she treats you like garbage, don't be offended. She's not into people."

"That makes two of us, Ursula."

Harris shifted off Troy and sat on the edge of the bed. Troy moved to sit beside him.

"This seems like an okay house to grow up in," Troy said.

"It was the best."

"It would be nice, out here in the country, I think. I grew up in the suburbs of Vancouver."

"I like being downtown, but I miss the quiet sometimes," Harris said. "I'll probably move back here someday. Not to this house, exactly. I mean, I don't think so. Anna and Margot built the cidery on the west side of the orchard, and they more or less run the farm now. I assume one of them will get the house eventually. It's been in the family for four generations so far. I'm glad my sisters are passionate about the farm."

"You're not?"

"I love it, but I don't know if I want to run it." Harris shrugged and gazed out the window. The sun had almost set over the snow-covered orchard. "I like my job a lot. I think I'd like to see how far I can go doing marketing and communications stuff."

"And you get to work for the team you're obsessed with."

"True."

"And you get to bone down with the hottest guy on the team."

Harris elbowed him. "You're making me feel unprofessional."

At that moment, amazingly, Ursula hopped off the dresser and walked directly over to Troy. She paused a moment, glancing up at him, before jumping onto the bed beside him.

"Holy," Harris said. "She never does that."

Troy cautiously stroked Ursula's head with a gentle hand. She leaned up into his palm, seemingly as fond of Troy's touch as Harris was. Within seconds, she was purring loudly with her front paws on Troy's thigh.

"Wow. She loves you."

"Because she has great taste," Troy said as he stroked under her chin.

Harris watched in astonishment for several minutes as Ursula shamelessly soaked up as much of Troy's attention as she could get.

"Should I leave?" Harris asked.

"Are you still here?"

Harris laughed and kissed Troy's cheek. "We should go back downstairs."

"Okay." Troy stood, and Ursula meowed angrily. "Well, come downstairs then," Troy told her. "Jesus, it's a pretty simple problem to fix."

"She hardly ever comes downstairs. This is her domain up here."

But as they grabbed their cider bottles off the nightstand and walked out of the bedroom, Ursula followed. "She can't get enough of me," Troy said.

Harris grinned. "That makes two of us, Ursula."

"I like him," Harris's mom whispered to him when they were alone in the kitchen.

He smiled as he sliced the Dutch apple pie he'd made. "Who? Troy?"

She swatted his arm. "Of course Troy. He's quiet, but he's very polite. And he can't take his eyes off you."

Warmth bloomed in his belly. "Come on."

Troy hadn't said much during the meal, but it had barely been noticeable because everyone else—besides Josh—talked so much. He'd eaten heartily, though, and complimented the food, so everyone was charmed by him.

"He's nuts about you. It's very cute."

"Well," Harris said slowly. "I'm pretty nuts about him. I know it's new, but I think—"

Troy's deep voice cut him off. "Can I help?"

They both turned toward the kitchen entrance, where Troy was standing. His expression was blank, so Harris had no idea if he'd heard any of the conversation.

"Good idea," Mom said cheerfully. "You help Harris with the pie, and I'll . . ." She didn't even bother inventing a task that she needed to do before darting out of the kitchen.

"Still can't believe you made this," Troy said, moving to stand beside Harris.

"Old family recipe."

"I can barely cook anything."

Harris smiled. "I know."

Troy's hip brushed Harris's, and Harris leaned into it, relishing the contact, however chaste.

"How can I help?" Troy's lips were close enough that Harris felt his breath tickling his ear.

"You can, um." Harris couldn't even remember what they were supposed to be doing, and now his dick had other ideas.

Right. Pie.

"Hold the plates, and I'll put pie on each of them."

"Okay."

They worked quickly and silently as Harris tried to will his erection away. He couldn't go to the dinner table with it.

Sheesh. He couldn't even plate dessert with Troy without getting all hot and bothered. This honeymoon phase was going to be a wild ride.

"Hell yes," Anna said when Harris returned to the dining room. "Pie!"

It took a few minutes, but eventually pie had been distributed to all eight people around the dining table. Harris's sisters and their husbands had been eyeing Troy curiously all night. He knew Margot for sure was silently evaluating her brother's new boyfriend.

"So you're the guy from the skunk story?" Troy asked Anna's husband, Mike.

Mike laughed. "Yep, that's me."

Anna scowled at Harris. "Jesus, Harris. Could you stop telling everyone in the world that story?"

"Would *you*?"

"Do you finally admit that you're the one who put the skunk in the truck when you tell the story, at least?"

Harris gasped. "I can't believe you think so little of your adoring baby brother."

"Raise your hand if you think Harris did it," Anna said.

Anna, Mike, Margot, Dad, Mom, and, reluctantly, Margot's quiet husband, Josh, raised their hands. Harris turned his head to share a *can you believe these people* look with Troy, and saw that he'd raised his hand too. Harris shoved him, which made Troy and everyone else laugh.

"The way you're all willing to gang up on a young man with a heart condition," Harris said with mock affront. "Unbelievable."

"You can't play the heart card this time, buddy," Anna said.

"Your heart was working fine when you shoved a skunk in the truck."

Harris laughed. He'd always appreciated the way Anna, especially, was able to joke about his condition. He was happy to see, when he glanced around the table, that his parents were laughing too.

"So, back to work tomorrow, boys?" Dad asked.

"Yep," Troy said. "Kind of a brutal schedule this month."

"You guys head to St. Louis tomorrow, don't you?" Mike asked.

"Yeah."

"Is getting on a plane hard?" Margot asked. "After the whole . . . thing?"

"It's getting easier. Just have to keep doing it until we feel normal about it again, I guess."

Harris was certainly glad *he* didn't have to get on a plane again for a while, but he would miss Troy when he was gone. The Centaurs had three road trips this month.

"Well," Mom said, leaning back in her chair, "that was an excellent pie, Harris."

There were murmurs of agreement all around. Troy said, "I still can't believe you made that."

"Dude, you *watched* me make it."

"I know. Still seems like magic."

"Aw," Anna said. "He thinks every little thing you do is magic, Harris."

Troy turned redder than any apple Harris had ever seen.

They stayed long enough to help clean up, and then Troy loaded a few gifted cases of cider and a giant bag of apples into Harris's truck. When Harris walked outside, he found Troy staring into the rear part of the cab.

"What's up?" Harris asked.

"I'm checking for skunks."

Harris laughed. "I do that every time."

Troy knew he was being quiet during the drive back into the city, but he had too many things in his head. Being at the farm, among Harris's warm, loving family, had been almost too much. Especially since they had all known that Troy was dating their son. They'd been so welcoming, treating him like he was part of the family. Troy had never experienced anything like it.

"So," Harris asked. "Did you have an okay time?"

He sounded nervous, so Troy shook himself out of his thoughts. "Your family is awesome. I had a great time. Thank you for inviting me."

Harris smiled and looked relieved. "You're welcome anytime. We have dinner together most Sundays. They loved you."

"You think?"

"Definitely."

The other thing Troy was contemplating was what it would take to keep this thing with Harris. What he would need to give up in exchange for unlimited Sunday dinners and cozy mornings. Unlimited kisses and sex that was both hot and fun. He needed to stop hiding.

"I want to come out," Troy said. "Like, all the way out. Maybe on Instagram or something."

Harris glanced away from the road for a moment. "Yeah?"

"When's our Pride Night game?"

"The end of February, but—"

"I want to come out before then. Maybe the same day." Troy was excited now. "Every Pride game I've ever played in has felt so weird. Like I was hiding in plain sight or something. I hated it. But this time I can just . . . be proud. Actually be proud."

Harris, for some reason, wasn't smiling. "That's awesome, and I want that for you. But you should know, the Pride game is against Toronto."

A heavy silence hung in the air as all the joy drained from Troy's body. Finally he managed to say, "Well, that's stupid."

Harris smiled sadly. "I know. I wish it was against any other team."

Troy could not believe that the Pride game was against Toronto. "I don't care," he decided. "I still want to do it. But I need to come out to my mom first. I'll do that soon. I wanted to do it in person, but phone will have to do."

"What about your dad?" Harris asked carefully.

Troy had told himself for months that he didn't care if he never spoke to Dad again, but was that true? Because coming out really would end his relationship with his father. He had no doubts about that.

"I guess that's up to him. But I don't expect he'll talk to me again once he knows." He sighed. "It's for the best. I know not everyone is going to accept me, but I can't live like this anymore." He huffed out a surprised little laugh. "I almost can't wait to do it, actually. It's weird because I never thought I would want to do this, but if it wasn't for the fact that I want to tell my mom first, I'd probably post something on Instagram right now."

"Yeah, don't do that. But I'm glad you feel that you're ready. And . . ." Harris reached over and squeezed Troy's hand. "I'm going to make sure this is the best Pride Night ever."

Troy squeezed back. "I'm glad you'll be a part of it." He stared at their joined hands in the dim light of the truck. "I'm glad I met you. That you're here. With me."

"Me too." Harris retrieved his hand. "We're going to have sex when we get back, right?"

Troy laughed. "I fucking hope so."

* * *

They went to Harris's place because Troy wanted to keep the homey good vibes going. He wanted to make love to Harris under a homemade quilt and surrounded by colorful pillows. And a weird stuffed giraffe.

Now they were both naked in Harris's bed, and had been taking their time kissing and warming each other's bodies up.

"I really like you as a person," Harris said in between the kisses he was peppering Troy's belly with. "I like everything about you, including the weird way you smile and the way you pretend not to like sweets."

Troy huffed. "Okay."

"I just want to make that clear, so you don't get any wrong ideas here. Because, holy hell, Troy. Your body is ridiculous."

"*You're* ridiculous."

"What exercises do you even need to do to get this muscle here?" Harris trailed a finger over Troy's right oblique.

Troy shivered. "You have that muscle too, you know."

"It's probably buried in there somewhere, yeah. But yours are so . . . bumpy."

"I work out for a living."

Harris kissed Troy's hip, and then across to his belly button. "And I appreciate it."

"Good. It's hard work being . . . bumpy."

They both laughed. They'd been laughing a lot since they'd stumbled into Harris's apartment, barely able to stop kissing long enough to unlock the door. Troy felt like he was drunk, although he had gone easy on the cider at the farm.

"Come here," he said, and Harris crawled back up so their faces were level. Troy stroked Harris's hair for a moment, and lost himself in his green eyes. "I'm going to miss you."

"I'll miss you too. But I'll be here when you get back."

"I'll probably text you a lot," Troy warned.

"You'd better." Harris kissed his nose. "I take a mean dick pic."

Troy cracked up, which made Harris crack up. "What does that even mean?" Troy gasped.

"You'll see."

Troy got himself under control and said, "I wouldn't mind a dick pic. Your dick is adorable."

Harris thunked his forehead against Troy's chest. "Adorable?" he groaned.

"I like it." Troy kissed the top of Harris's head and said, "I'd like to have it . . . in me."

Harris's head shot up. "Tonight?"

"If that's okay."

"Super okay. You've done it before, right?"

"Yeah. Been a while, but I like it."

Harris sat up, straddling Troy's thighs, and rubbed his hands together excitedly. "This is going to rule."

Troy laughed, and then moaned when Harris took his dick in his mouth. Troy had only been half hard, due to all the laughter and conversation, but he went rigid in seconds.

It took a while for Troy to get relaxed enough to take even Harris's fingers comfortably, but Harris was patient and encouraging, and, frankly, skilled. He was giving Troy's prostate more attention than it had ever gotten before, and Troy was losing his mind, writhing and gushing precome. He'd never come from prostate stimulation alone before, but in that moment it felt possible.

"Good?" Harris asked, checking in.

Troy could only give a strangled laugh, and a slurred, "So fucking good."

"I have an awesome vibrator I could use on you. It makes me come so hard it almost hurts."

Fuck, Troy really wanted to do that. Someday. Not now.

"Not tonight. Want you, Harris. Please."

Harris kissed his knee. "Okay."

He slowly withdrew his fingers, and Troy did some deep breathing to deal with the temporary sensation of emptiness. Harris got a condom and lube on, and finally lined himself up.

"You are so beautiful," Harris said. His voice was quieter than Troy had ever heard it. "How are you even real?"

"I'm real. Please fuck me," Troy practically whimpered.

Troy's back arched at the first press of Harris's cock against his entrance. Harris entered him in one slow, sweet slide until Troy felt wonderfully stretched and full.

"Still good?" Harris asked.

Troy nodded. "Kiss me?"

Harris leaned down, and they kissed so tenderly it was somehow more overwhelming than being penetrated. Then Harris began to thrust. He kept it slow, and that was okay. Troy just kept kissing him as a warmth spread through him that had nothing to do with sexual release. He'd bottomed before, but he'd never felt *this*. He felt cared for, in the way Harris was kissing him, touching him, fucking him. Like nothing bad would ever happen to Troy again if Harris could help it.

And god, Troy hoped Harris knew it went both ways. He hoped Harris could feel how important he was in the way Troy was kissing him back, and the way he was clenching around Harris's cock, reluctant to let him go.

They rocked together for a blissful, immeasurable stretch of time, Harris murmuring sweet things that Troy couldn't quite process.

"I'm close," Harris eventually rasped against Troy's lips. "Stroke yourself. Come with me."

Troy reached between them and did as he was told. He realized, as soon as his hand was wrapped around his dick, that he was close too.

"Fuck, hurry," Harris panted. His thrusts sped up, and Troy tried to match him.

"Okay," Troy said. "I'm close. I'm—shit. I'm coming. Harris, fuck, I'm—"

They both cried out—Harris louder, as usual—and Troy's release shot on his own chest as Harris finished with a few fast, frantic thrusts.

For a moment, Harris stayed where he was, hovering over Troy, his slightly damp hair falling in his eyes. His lips were wet and bruised from their kisses, and his emerald eyes were bright and beautiful.

Harris smiled at him. "That went well."

Troy laughed and hoped Harris never stopped being such a goofball during sex. "Agreed."

Harris pulled out, then kissed Troy quickly before leaving to clean himself up. Troy spread his arms out on the bed, and found Harris's stuffed giraffe in one corner. He grabbed the toy and held it over his face.

"I think I'm in love with him, Mr. Neck-Neck."

CHAPTER TWENTY-FOUR

Troy paced his living room, waiting for his phone to ring. He'd texted Mom last night and asked her to call him this morning before practice. Today was the day he'd come out to her.

He was ready. For the past two weeks, Troy was spending every possible moment with Harris. There were road trips, and plenty of time-consuming obligations for both of them in Ottawa, but whenever neither of them was busy, they were together. He wanted to tell his mom about his boyfriend. He wanted her to know how happy he was.

He was also so nervous that he nearly jumped when his phone finally rang.

"Hi," he said.

"Is everything okay?" Mom sounded worried, and Troy felt terrible. He should have assured her in his text that nothing was wrong.

"Yeah. Sorry, I should have—everything is fine. Great, actually. I just, um, wanted to tell you something."

"Okay . . ." She said the word slowly, and he could hear the curiosity in her voice.

"Where are you?" he asked.

"Troy! Who cares? Don't make me wait!"

He laughed a little at that. "All right. So the thing is . . ." He sighed, and started pacing again. He'd practiced this in his head a million times, but he couldn't find the words now. "I need to tell you something about myself. It's not a big deal. I mean, it's kind of a big deal. I hope it's not something that—"

"Troy," she said gently. "You can tell me anything."

He closed his eyes. "I'm gay."

There was silence, and then a soft whoosh of air from her end, like a sigh or a huff of disappointment. But then she said, "Oh, sweetie. Thank you for telling me."

Troy sat on his sofa. "I've been wanting to, but I was scared."

"Your father," she said, and her voice broke. "I'm so sorry."

"It's okay."

"It's not. I already felt so guilty for the way he treated you, and now . . ." She sniffed. "It must have been a nightmare, hiding this from us."

He couldn't deny it, but he said, "I'm not hiding anymore."

"I thought—" She stopped, as if ashamed of what she'd been about to admit.

"What did you think?" Troy asked gently.

"I thought you were going to be like Curtis. Every year you seemed to be more and more like him. And you were friends with Dallas Kent, who reminded me so much of Curtis when he was young."

Troy grimaced. He hadn't known his dad when Curtis was young, of course, but he wasn't surprised to learn he'd been like Dallas.

"When he left me," Mom continued, "I worried that I was going to lose you both. That you'd take his side because . . ." She trailed off and sobbed, and Troy's eyes welled up.

"I would never take his side, Mom. I'm sorry I acted like him. It just seemed . . . safe. I was scared of people finding out

I was gay, so I tried to be someone else. Someone he would respect."

"I know. I understand now. And I've known for years that you aren't like him at all. Since he and I split up, you've been there for me. You've been such a good friend to me, which is something I could never say about Curtis."

"I'm glad you're happy now. I'm glad you got away."

"So am I. God, I love you so much. I wish I could hug you right now."

"Me too. I love you."

She sniffed again. "Are you going to tell him?"

"Wasn't planning on it. He might find out, though. I'm going to come out publicly, I think."

"Oh wow. Like Scott Hunter?"

"Well," Troy scoffed. "I'm not going to kiss my boyfriend on live television, if that's what you mean."

"Do you . . . do you have a boyfriend?" She sounded excited.

Troy smiled. "I do, actually."

"*What?* Tell me everything about him! Can you send me a photo?"

So Troy told his mother everything he could think of about Harris. He didn't stop smiling the entire time he told her about how they'd met and gotten to know each other, about Harris's ridiculously loud laugh, and his wonderful family.

"I can't wait to meet him," Mom said. "He sounds adorable."

"He is. I really like him. You'll like him too. Here, I'm sending a pic."

He texted her one of his favorite photos of Harris. One that he had taken while Harris had been making the apple pie in Troy's kitchen two weeks ago. He had flour on his shirt, and his hair was a little rumpled, but he was grinning like Troy was the best thing he'd ever seen.

"I love him!" Mom squealed. "Look at how cute he is! I'm so happy for you."

"I'm happy for you, too. We both found nice men."

"We did. I'm glad you found yours when you were much younger than I was."

"I got lucky. So where *are* you anyway?"

"Hawaii. We're on Kauai."

"Shit. It must be the middle of the night there."

Mom laughed. "Time has no meaning to me anymore. We're in a different time zone every week, almost."

"Still having fun?"

"We're having the best time. I can't thank you enough for helping us be able to do this. It's been incredible. You'll have to do it yourself someday. Maybe after you retire, with your man."

Troy flushed a bit, but smiled. The idea of spending his life with Harris was overwhelming and exciting. And probably a bit much to be thinking about this early into the relationship. "Maybe I will. Someday. But right now I have to get to practice, and you should go to bed."

"I love you, Troy. And I'm so proud of you."

"I love you too. I miss you."

"Me too. I'll see you and Harris soon, okay?"

Troy loved his mom so much. He should have come out to her years ago. "Okay."

He ended the call, and was so excited to get to the arena he almost forgot his coat. He couldn't wait to tell Harris.

Before Troy got a chance to find Harris at the arena, he got called into Coach Wiebe's office.

"Just need to talk to you for a sec, Barrett," Wiebe said. He looked anxious, but not angry. Troy had no idea what this would be about.

"What's up?" he asked, as calmly as he could manage.

Wiebe nodded at one of the leather chairs in front of his desk. "Have a seat."

Shit. This couldn't be good.

"I just had a meeting with management. Apparently you've upset Commissioner Crowell."

Troy's stomach dropped. God, he was about to be suspended. Or tossed down to the AHL. Or worse. "I wasn't trying to," he said.

Coach smiled wearily. "It doesn't take much, I don't think."

Troy relaxed a bit. It seemed his coach was on his side.

"I'm supposed to discipline you. To be honest this whole thing makes all of us very uncomfortable: the GM, the owners. Everyone."

Troy swallowed. He had no idea what to say. Was he supposed to apologize? Defend himself? He'd known, when he'd decided to start posting about sexual assault again, that he was going against the commissioner's instructions. He'd expected some sort of backlash, so he should be able to face it now that it had come.

"I'm sorry if I made your job harder," Troy said carefully, "but I don't regret using my voice to address something important."

Coach raised his eyebrows. "It's not you who's making us uncomfortable, Troy. We agree with you. Even the owners have said they're impressed with what you're doing. We want our players to be good role models, and to contribute to the community. It's Crowell who's causing us problems."

Wow. Troy had not been expecting any of that. His throat felt tight. After coming out to Mom less than an hour ago, and now receiving this unwavering support from his employers, he was a little overwhelmed. "Oh," he said.

"To be honest, Crowell kind of has it out for this team. He

hates that we don't draw big crowds, and it's no secret that he wants to move us to a larger American market."

"We've been getting bigger crowds lately," Troy said, as if that would be reason enough to change Crowell's mind.

Coach smiled. "That's what happens when you're on fire." His smile faded. "Crowell's on a warpath, though. He really doesn't like you."

Troy shifted in his chair. "I got that impression."

"He's not a fan of Rozanov either. Or me."

"Really? Why? Rozanov is one of the biggest stars in the league. He's one of the most entertaining players to watch ever."

"Yep. And then he voluntarily went to the smallest market team in the NHL."

Ah. Right. "Okay. Why doesn't he like you?"

"When I used to play, I filed a few complaints against one of my coaches for using slurs and generally being an abusive prick. He was bullying some of the rookies in particular. I didn't like it."

Troy's mouth fell open. "I had no idea."

"Because the complaints never saw the light of day. The league remembers, though, and I heard Crowell was pissed when I got this coaching job. I think I was hired just to spite him."

Troy shook his head. "No way. You're a great coach."

Wiebe leaned back in his chair, smiling. "Well, there *is* that franchise-record win streak."

"Did anything happen to that coach?"

Wiebe's smile tightened. "Sure. He's in the Hall of Fame now."

Troy's heart sank. "Oh."

Coach shrugged. "I don't regret trying. It's hard to change anything in this league, though. Anyone who tries tends to get squashed." He leaned forward. "So here's what we're going to do, Troy."

Troy braced himself. He could withstand whatever the punishment was, he told himself. Especially since he knew the Centaurs organization was on his side.

"Absolutely nothing," Coach finished. "We're going to keep winning, and you can post whatever you want, and Crowell can get stuffed. Everyone in management agrees: he can't really do anything. If he does, we'll back you up and he'll look like a monster. Stalemate, I'd say."

It sounded risky to Troy, but he was still thrilled. "Seriously?"

"Dead serious. Now go get your gear on."

Troy stood up. "Thanks. And, um, I really like playing here. I know it probably didn't seem like it for a long time, but I'm glad I'm here."

"I thought you might be," Coach said. He put his head down and began scribbling some notes on a lined pad of paper. "Oh, and you should probably disclose your relationship with Harris to management."

Troy froze halfway to the door. "What?"

Coach glanced up, smiling. "I saw you smooching in his office last week."

Jesus, had Troy really been that sloppy? Had he really kissed Harris with the *door open*? He felt like he might combust. "I, uh—we were—um—"

Coach chuckled. "I'm happy for you. I'm just trying to keep you out of trouble."

"Thank you," Troy said. Oh god, he really was going to cry if he didn't get out of there. This day was too much.

He left the office in a daze. There wouldn't be time to find Harris before practice now, but he was certainly racking up a long list of things to kiss him about.

"Holy smokes!" Wyatt yelled. "When did Chiron turn into an actual horse?"

Harris grinned at the team puppy, who had grown into a decently large dog, and was looking like he might end up around the size of a Bernese mountain dog. "He did some growing over the past month, that's for sure."

"No shit." Wyatt took a knee on the dressing room floor, still wearing his giant leg pads. "Let me get some pets in before Rozanov sees—"

Wyatt was cut off by a banshee scream coming from Ilya's stall. "What the fuck, Harris? Why is he huge?"

"Dogs grow, Roz."

Ilya had already crossed the room and was kneeling next to Wyatt, bumping the goalie out of the way. "Chiron! You are such a big boy now! You are like two Chirons!" He thoroughly scratched the happy dog's ears and neck.

While Ilya and Wyatt warred for Chiron's affection, Harris glanced at Troy's empty stall. He'd told Harris last night that he was planning to come out to his mom today, but Harris hadn't heard from him since. "Was Troy not here today?"

Ilya didn't look up from Chiron. "He is here somewhere. Showers probably."

Well. Harris should probably wait then.

"Chiron got some bad news this week," Harris said. "I mean, maybe he's not too sad about it."

Ilya's head shot up, his eyes wide and horrified. "What news? What is wrong?"

"Turns out he's not therapy dog material. At least according to the trainers."

"Impossible," Ilya said.

"Aw." Wyatt rubbed Chiron's back. "We love you anyway, buddy. I sucked at school too."

"What will happen to him?" Ilya asked.

Harris couldn't help but smile at Ilya's concern. "Nothing bad. He's still going to be the official team dog, but he'll need a home away from the arena."

"You will adopt him." Ilya didn't make it sound like a suggestion.

Harris let out a startled laugh. "Well, maybe. I mean, I was thinking maybe that would be a good idea. Then I could bring him to work with me and you guys could see him all the time." And, Harris added privately, Troy would get to cuddle him at home, and join Harris on walks with him, and maybe one day they'd get a house in the country with a big yard . . .

He'd gotten *way* ahead of himself with his fantasizing when he'd first learned about Chiron not making the therapy dog cut. For now, he had to be realistic about his small apartment and this very large dog, but he'd probably be able to bring Chiron to work every day, and he could bring him out to the farm all the time, if he got along well with the other dogs. And he'd bet Ilya wouldn't mind having Chiron hang out at his giant house sometimes.

Ilya smiled at Chiron. "You are going to be the happiest dog ever."

Harris would make sure of it.

At that moment, Troy emerged from a back room, but he was still wearing some of his gear. Not much of it. Just a few select pieces that, combined with Troy's exposed skin and sweat-slicked muscles, basically made him a walking fantasy.

He was wearing his jock and garters, but the socks and shin guards had been removed, leaving his muscular legs bare. His skin-tight performance T-shirt was rucked up just above his belly button, and he still had his elbow pads on, which was weird, but Harris was extremely into it.

"Troy." Harris realized he'd said the name as if Troy was

a magical being who he had only before seen in dreams. He forced himself to snap out of it. "Hi."

"Hey. I didn't know you were here."

Harris could not stop staring. He knew it. And he knew Troy, Ilya, and Wyatt probably noticed. But he could not. Stop. Staring.

"Um," Troy said. He ran a hand through his damp hair, pushing it back off his forehead. "Are you, uh . . ." He glanced down. "Oh. You brought Chiron."

"Harris is Chiron's new dad," Ilya said.

"What do you mean?" Troy asked.

"Um." Harris had planned to surprise Troy with this announcement later but, well, Ilya. "I think I might adopt Chiron. He's not going to be a therapy dog, but he's still the team dog, and, uh . . ." Jesus, Troy looked like an amalgam of Harris's entire jock fantasy porn playlist.

"He's big now," Troy said.

"Uh-huh."

Then Troy smiled at him, seeming to notice the effect his appearance was having on Harris. He nodded in the direction of his stall, then walked toward it. Harris followed helplessly.

Troy's garter straps were hanging loose and bouncing off his massive thighs as he walked. He had fancy athletic underwear on under the jock that looked like little black booty shorts. They clung to every inch of his ass, showing off the ripple of his muscles.

When they got to his stall, Troy said, "You're really adopting Chiron? That's awesome."

"I thought you'd like that." Harris stepped close, and fought the urge to put his hands on Troy's chest. "This is completely unfair," he murmured.

"What?"

"This!" Harris waved a hand over Troy's body. "Tell me you have a spare jock at home."

Troy smiled wickedly. "Why? You got a fetish for hockey gear?"

"Uh, yeah." Harris said it like it was obvious. "Like, you have no idea. Look!" He gestured toward the bulge that had appeared in his jeans.

Troy looked, and when he met Harris's gaze again, his eyes were dark and full of heat. "This is interesting."

Harris felt hot everywhere. "It's just a fantasy or whatever. You don't have to make a big deal about it."

Troy's gaze dropped back to Harris's crotch. "Looks like I already did."

"Oh fuck." Harris shook his head. "Nope. Okay. We've got serious stuff to discuss."

Troy's eyes lost some of their heat. "We do."

"How'd it go with your mom?"

"Amazing. She was super supportive and great."

Harris beamed, and nearly kissed him right there in the locker room. "That's awesome!"

"Yeah. And when I got here, Coach called me into his office to tell me that Crowell is mad that I'm posting again."

Harris rolled his eyes. "Oh fuck. Are you serious?"

"But listen, Coach said management supports *me*. And so does he. They aren't going to do anything to discipline me, even though Crowell asked them to."

God, Harris loved this team. "I'm not surprised. I told you we only have good people here. Sounds like you got a lot of love today."

"I wouldn't mind a little more," Troy said seductively. Then his eyes went wide. "Oh! And Coach knows about us! He caught us, uh, *smooching*, as he put it, in your office."

Whoops. "Shit, Troy. Sorry. Are you okay?"

Troy nodded. "I'm okay. I feel great, actually. I think I might come out to the team. Like, maybe right now?"

"Right now? Here?"

"Yeah. What do you think?"

"It's okay with me, but are you sure you—"

But Troy had already stepped up to stand on the bench in his stall.

"Hey, everyone," he announced loudly.

The room got slightly quieter. Then Ilya said, "Everyone shut up and listen to Barrett," and the room went silent.

"Just one thing," Troy said. His voice was surprisingly steady. "I'm dating Harris. We're together. I'm gay."

Well, it wasn't poetry. But it still made Harris's eyes fill with tears.

There was another seemingly endless moment of silence, and then there was applause. And whistling. And cheering.

Troy slumped back against the wall, as if he couldn't believe he had just done that. He stared wide-eyed at his teammates until a wide, elated smile stretched across his face.

"I'd like that to stay in this room for now," Troy said, still smiling. "Please. Okay. Thank you."

He stepped down, into Harris's waiting arms. Harris hugged him tight, not caring at all that he was drenched in sweat and smelled like a gym bag. "That was weird. I loved it."

"It was okay?"

"I said I loved it."

"We still have to, like, officially disclose the relationship," Troy said.

"I know. It's just a formality. No one will care."

"Okay. Can I kiss you?"

"Everyone is probably watching."

"Then I'd better make it a good one."

Troy placed a firm hand on Harris's back, dipped him slightly, and went for it.

Everyone whooped and clapped around them, as Troy kissed Harris like he'd just returned from the war. Harris did his best to return it, and not just get swept away. He was so fucking proud of Troy, and still more than a little overwhelmed that somehow Troy thought Harris was worth all this upheaval. That he wanted to be with Harris enough to face his deepest fears.

When they broke apart, Troy straightened and waved awkwardly at his rowdy teammates.

"Way to go, Harris!" Bood yelled.

Harris knew he was blushing, but he also couldn't stop smiling. "See you later?" he asked Troy.

"If these guys ever stop making fun of me, yeah."

He said it as if he was annoyed, but Troy's smile and misty eyes said he was anything but.

CHAPTER TWENTY-FIVE

Troy was getting used to waking up next to Harris's warm, naked body. Whether they were at Harris's place or Troy's, greeting the day with gentle, sleepy kisses while bundled comfortably in sheets that smelled like last night's sex had quickly become Troy's favorite thing in the world.

This morning, when his eyes fluttered open, he found Harris sitting up, and grinning at his phone. For a moment, Troy just watched him, his heart swelling with affection.

"What is it?" Troy finally asked in a raspy voice.

"Bood and Cassie had their baby last night. A boy. They named him Milo."

"That's awesome. Cute name." He kissed Harris's elbow, because it was there.

"No pictures yet, but I can't wait." He typed something.

"Are you talking to Bood?"

"No, Wyatt."

"Ah." Troy kissed a path down Harris's flank, then nibbled his sensitive hip bone, making him squirm.

"What are you up to down there?"

In reply, Troy took Harris's soft dick in his mouth.

Harris inhaled sharply, and put his phone on the nightstand.

Some amount of time later, they were both sated and tangled up together. Troy never wanted to leave the bed.

Except.

"Shit. What time is it?"

Harris grabbed his phone. "Quarter to ten."

"Fuck!" Troy scrambled out of bed. "I have a video meeting at ten! I'm fucked."

"Whoops. Sorry. You want me to write you a note?"

Troy didn't bother answering that. He didn't have time. He brushed his teeth, splashed some water on his face and threw some sweats on. Harris met him at the door wearing only boxer briefs as Troy shoved his boots on.

"Not going to work yet?" Troy asked.

"No, I have an appointment with my doctor today. I'll work from home. You mind if I let myself out later?"

"Of course not." Troy's gaze snagged on Harris's scars. "Everything okay?"

Harris folded his arms over his chest. "Oh yeah. Just a routine checkup. I feel great."

"Good." Troy was super late, but he spared a moment to give Harris a proper goodbye kiss. "See you later. Dinner tonight?"

"Yeah. There's a Lebanese place I want to take you to."

"Sounds good."

One more kiss, and Troy began his mad dash to the arena.

Troy was late, of course, but Coach just waved him in without comment. Again, Troy marveled at how different he was from every coach he'd ever had.

The meeting was mostly positive, and Troy could feel the excitement buzzing in the room; there was a very good chance that the Ottawa Centaurs were going to the playoffs for the first time in over a decade. Even a couple of months ago no one would have believed it.

Despite Coach Wiebe's upbeat energy, Troy had a hard time concentrating on the video clips he was breaking down. Lately Troy's brain seemed to be full of nothing but Harris, little floating hearts, and creeping anxiety about Pride Night. The game was in three days, and he still wished it were against anyone other than Toronto.

But he was also determined. He knew he didn't need to come out publicly, and he certainly didn't have to announce it with the video Harris was helping him put together, but he felt it was the right decision. Once he did this, it would be over. Everyone would know, and he wouldn't have to worry about people finding out anymore. That energy could be spent on creating positive change in hockey, and in himself. It could be spent on loving Harris. Because he was pretty sure he had a lot of energy for that.

When the meeting was over, Wyatt turned around in his chair and, with a big grin, asked, "Did you hear the news?"

It took Troy a moment to remember Bood and Cassie's baby. "Yeah! It's great."

"I know. I'm stunned, honestly. But, man, he fucking deserves whatever's coming to him."

Okay. That was a weird way to show excitement for someone becoming a father. "I . . . guess."

Dykstra, who was sitting next to Wyatt, said, "I hope he never plays again."

What the—

"Why do you hope that?" Troy asked, beyond confused.

Wyatt's brow furrowed. "I assumed you'd feel the same way."

"Are we talking about the same thing? Bood, right?"

"What?" Dykstra asked. "No—why wouldn't we want Bood to play hockey again?"

"I don't know!" Troy said, exasperated.

"We're talking about Kent," Wyatt said.

Troy's heart stopped. "What about Kent?"

Wyatt and Dykstra grinned at each other. "You didn't hear?" Wyatt said. "He got charged. Five women came together and pressed charges. He was arrested right before this meeting."

"What?" Troy couldn't believe it. Was Dallas actually going to get punished? He knew that being charged didn't mean he'd be convicted, but still. This was huge.

"Amazing, right?" Dykstra said. "Those women are brave as hell."

"Yeah." Troy reached into his pocket for his phone, then realized he'd forgotten it at home in his rush to get to the meeting. Harris must have sent him a million texts about this already.

"Is there video footage of Dallas being arrested?" Troy asked, because he wasn't entirely a nice guy. Not yet.

"Hell yes there is," Wyatt said, and held out his phone so Troy could watch the short clip. There was Dallas Kent, head down, expression dark. He looked more annoyed than anything, like he expected this to all be over soon. Troy desperately hoped it wouldn't be.

And, holy shit, this meant Dallas wouldn't be playing in the Pride Night game. It was a selfish reason to be excited, but damn. What a fucking load off.

"This is the best movie I've ever seen," Troy said, as it played for the second time.

"Yeah, well," Dykstra said as he stood and patted Troy's shoulder. "Let's hope it has a happy ending."

As soon as Wyatt and Dykstra left, Coach Wiebe walked over to Troy. "It's something else, huh?"

"Yeah. It's, um. I can't believe it, really."

"I think this should keep Crowell off your back. I'm sure he blames you for this in his twisted way, but what can he do? It's a legal matter now."

Troy wasn't sure Crowell would back off, but at least this would make it harder for the league to defend Kent.

"Are you okay?" Coach asked, and Troy was surprised to see concern in his eyes.

"Why wouldn't I be?"

"Kent was your friend," Wiebe said simply. "I wouldn't blame you if you felt conflicted about this."

"I don't," Troy said quickly. Then he acknowledged the knot in his stomach. Dallas wasn't a good person, but he'd been Troy's first friend in the NHL. Most of Troy's good memories with him were tainted now, but they'd spent many hours in hotel rooms and on planes talking and making each other laugh. "Maybe a bit. I don't know. I shouldn't feel bad for him. It's just weird, I guess. We were tight for a long time."

"Sometimes it's hard to stop caring about someone, no matter how much you know you should." The way Wiebe said it made Troy think he was probably speaking from experience, but he didn't ask.

Instead he just said, "I've got better people to care about now."

"Wow," Troy said. "This is really . . . professional."

Harris chewed his lip, unsure if Troy liked the video or not. It was the morning of the Pride Night game, and Harris had barely slept because he'd been working hard on the video, obsessively tinkering with it to make it perfect. Now they were standing beside each other, hunched over Harris's computer monitor in his office. "If it's not how you pictured it, I can change it."

"No," Troy said quickly. "No, I like it. I'm just kinda blown away. Like . . . you *made* this."

"*We* made it."

Troy shook his head. "You filmed it, edited it, and basically wrote the words I'm saying. You made it."

"I didn't write what you're saying. I just helped you tweak it a bit." Harris's heart sank. "I didn't steamroll you, did I? This is so personal and I don't want it to feel like—"

Troy stopped his babbling by putting his hand on top of Harris's. "I love it. It's just a little surreal, watching it. Watching *me* say those words."

The video had featured Troy talking over some footage of him playing hockey, and doing some of the off-ice community stuff. Harris had included video footage from the team's hospital visit, Troy and Ilya's Christmas photo shoot, Troy playing with Chiron, and from team practices, as well as some game highlights. He'd cut it with video he'd shot of Troy sitting in the same chair he'd sat in when he'd done the Q and A video. His voice was steady and strong as he told the world that he was gay, and then explained why he was choosing to come out now.

It was a good video. Harris knew he had done a good job, and he was proud of Troy for deciding to make it. It had been a really tough season for Troy already, and this would no doubt complicate things even more. But Harris was confident that Troy's decision would ultimately make his life better.

"So, um," Troy said, standing back from the desk. "When should I post it?"

"It's up to you. You could post it now, or this afternoon. Or right before the game."

Troy stared into the middle distance as his jaw worked.

"Or," Harris added, "you don't have to post it at all."

Troy's gaze snapped to Harris. "You worked hard on it, though. You were up all night."

"Not *all* night."

"I woke up a million times last night, and every time you weren't in bed."

"Okay, fine. I could use a nap, sure. But you don't have to post it. Really. If you're not ready—"

"I'm ready." Troy sounded so sure, and Harris felt an intense swell of affection rush through him.

"Okay. Well, maybe you could post it just before—"

There was a knock on the door, and both men turned to face it. One of the security guards, Remy, was poking his head in. "Hey, guys. I was told Troy was in here, and I've got a guy named Curtis who says he's your father. Said you weren't expecting him."

Harris looked at Troy, whose face had gone ashen.

"Oh," Troy said. "He's . . . here?"

"Yeah. You want to see him, or . . ."

For a moment, Troy didn't say anything. Then he blinked and said, "Okay."

"I'll come with you," Harris said.

"No." Troy's voice was sharp, with a hint of panic. "Don't."

Harris wanted to argue, but Troy's expression told him he shouldn't. "All right. I'll wait here for you."

Troy nodded, eyes wide and terrified, and left.

"Dad, what are you doing here?"

Curtis narrowed his eyes at him, and Troy glanced down at his own T-shirt. It had the official Ottawa Centaurs Pride logo on it. Every member of the team was wearing the same shirt today, but Troy still felt like he'd been outed.

"Why do you think I'm here? I thought it would be fun to see you play against Toronto." He smiled, but it wasn't kind.

"It's a good rivalry," Troy said quietly. God, he sounded as scared as he felt.

"Thought I'd see Kent play, but then all that bullshit happened. Poor kid."

Anger flared up in Troy. What a fucking douchebag this guy was. "It's not bullshit."

"And," Dad continued, ignoring him, "I didn't know *this* was happening tonight." He waved a hand at Troy's T-shirt.

Troy swallowed hard. What could he say? A few minutes ago, he'd been ready to come out to the world. Possibly minutes away from posting that incredible video Harris—his *boyfriend*—had made. He'd been excited about tonight. Nervous, yes, but ready.

Now he felt like he'd been hurled back in time to the not-so-distant past where he would rather die than have anyone find out his sexuality. What if everyone looked at him the way his father was looking at his T-shirt right now?

"Troy?"

The voice came from behind him, and he turned to see Harris standing a few meters away. Troy had asked him not to follow, but he was grateful he'd disobeyed. He needed the reminder, right now, of what was important.

He liked who he was with his new teammates. He almost loved who he was with Harris. He couldn't stand that Dad was here to tarnish all of that.

"Harris. This is, um. This is—"

Of course, Harris walked confidently up to Curtis and held out his hand. "Nice to meet you, sir. I'm Harris Drover, the social media manager for the Centaurs."

Curtis seemed to have a hard time deciding what to snarl at hardest: Harris's own Centaurs Pride T-shirt, the array of Pride-themed pins on his denim jacket, or at the outstretched hand. Troy knew there was no way Dad was going to shake it.

"Social media, huh?" Dad said. "So they let you hang out with the team?"

"Every day," Harris said. His voice was cheerful, but Troy could hear the underlying irritation in it.

Curtis glanced at Troy. "In the *locker room*?"

A jolt of fury rocketed through Troy so forcefully that he almost lunged at his father. Instead, he curled his hands into fists at his sides and said, "I think you should leave."

Curtis looked baffled. "Why?"

"Because I don't want you here. You're a bigot and a shitty father."

"Troy, what the hell are you—"

"Leave before I get security," he said between gritted teeth.

Curtis looked at Harris, as if *he* was going to help him, then back at Troy. "Are you serious? You wouldn't *be* in the NHL if it weren't for me. I paid for all your hockey growing up, all those elite teams and camps. Taught you everything I knew. You'd be nothing without me."

"I'm *happy* without you," Troy said steadily. "You never cared about me or Mom. You only care about yourself."

Curtis huffed. "Your mother. Figured this had something to do with *her*. What ideas has she put in your head?"

Troy raised his chin. "That I can be myself, and she'll still love me."

"The fuck is that supposed to mean?"

Troy could say nothing. He could get Remy and have Curtis escorted out of the arena right now. This could be over. But instead, he reached for Harris's hand.

Harris gave him a questioning look, and when Troy nodded, he took his hand, tangling their fingers together and squeezing.

The color drained from Curtis's face.

"Harris is my boyfriend, Dad. I'm gay."

Troy took comfort from Harris's warm hand as he braced himself for Dad's response to that bombshell.

Curtis just gaped a moment, then said in the quietest voice Troy had ever heard him use, "What?"

"I'm gay," Troy repeated, refusing to cower. He held his father's gaze with his shoulders back and his head high.

"You—" Dad said. Then he shook his head, clenched his jaw, and turned away.

He didn't look back, and Troy felt a chill run through him as he watched him exit the arena. An adrenaline drop, probably.

"Come on," Harris said quietly, and gently tugged on Troy's hand. "Back to my office."

Troy had no memory of how he got from the security desk to Harris's office, but suddenly he was safely behind a closed door, alone with his boyfriend.

And then he collapsed to the floor, curled up with his head on his bent knees. He was crying, but he didn't even know why. It was over. He'd never have to be afraid of his father again.

Harris was beside him instantly with an arm over Troy's shoulders. "I'm so sorry, Troy. That was awful."

Troy couldn't speak. He just nodded against his knees.

"But I'm proud of you. God that was brave."

He let Troy cry for a few minutes, rubbing his back and murmuring reassuring things. By the time Troy got himself under control and raised his head, he was sure his face was a mess.

"I'm relieved, mostly," he said in a small, battered voice. "I think I'm just letting some pent-up emotion go." He sniffed. "This is good."

Harris grabbed a box of tissues off his desk and handed them to him. "I think so too."

Troy used the tissues to get himself cleaned up a bit. He felt calm now, like he'd released a million burdens at once. He'd let so much bullshit, so many toxic people, guide him in the past. He'd made so many terrible decisions, and valued all the wrong things.

But somehow it had all led to this moment, sitting on the floor of a drab office while his wonderful boyfriend handed him tissues.

"I love you," Troy said.

It was terrible timing; he had red eyes, a snotty nose, a hoarse voice, and they were both at *work*, but he couldn't help it. He loved Harris, and he needed him to know.

Harris's eyes were suddenly a little wet too. "Troy . . ." he whispered.

Troy started laughing, his body shaking with as much force as when he'd been crying. "I'm sorry," he squeaked out.

But then Harris's arms were around him, fierce and tight. Harris kissed his temple. "I love you, too. God, Troy. Of course I do."

Troy's heart felt like it would burst out of him. Everything bad was a distant memory. "I could have picked a better time to tell you," he said, his laughter subsiding.

"It's okay," Harris said. "We'll get it right eventually. I plan on saying it a lot."

Troy pulled back so he could see Harris's smile. It didn't disappoint.

They kissed, even though Troy was a mess. Harris didn't seem to mind at all, climbing into Troy's lap and devouring him.

By the time they stopped kissing, Troy was sprawled out on the floor, Harris on top of him.

"Well," Harris said. "This is unprofessional."

"I should probably let you work."

"Yeah," Harris sighed. "I do have a ton of stuff to do, honestly."

He pushed himself up off Troy, and offered Troy his hand to pull him up. They both looked like they'd been making out in a hurricane.

"I'm going to post the video now," Troy said.

"Yeah?"

Troy spotted his phone where he'd left it earlier on Harris's desk. He opened Instagram, then frowned. "Wait. How do I post it?"

Harris laughed, and held out his hand for the phone. "I'll do it."

Troy watched as Harris did whatever needed to be done, then handed the phone to Troy to write the caption underneath. Troy kept it simple: *This is me.*

He added emojis of a rainbow flag, a heart, and a hockey stick. Then he posted it.

Holy shit. He fucking *posted it.*

Harris wrapped his arms around him from behind and kissed his shoulder. "I'm proud of you."

Troy covered one of his hands with his own, holding it tight over his own heart. "Thank you. I couldn't have done any of this without you." He turned so he could face Harris. "I love you."

Harris beamed at him. "Better already. I love you, too. And you can thank me by kicking Toronto's ass tonight. Don't make me have to post about losing after all this!"

Troy grinned. "They don't stand a chance."

CHAPTER TWENTY-SIX

Troy didn't look at Instagram for the rest of the day after he posted the video. He told Harris not to tell him what the reaction was, and not to read him any of the comments. He needed to play this game with as clear a head as he could manage.

Now he was in the dressing room, getting ready for the warm-ups. Everyone on the team was wearing their Pride jerseys that featured rainbow Centaurs logos on the chest, and had their sticks wrapped with rainbow tape. They wouldn't wear the jerseys during the game—they would be sold online to raise money for local LGBTQ charities, and the sticks would be swapped for ones wrapped in black or white tape; most hockey players were particular about their tape colors during games. Troy had already decided he would use rainbow tape on his stick for the entire game, even if it was a bit flashy. He figured he may as well go all in.

The room was as lively as ever before a game. Music was playing and there was lots of yelling and laughter. Troy was quiet, but it wasn't because he was miserable. He was simply trying to absorb this moment.

No turning back.

When it was time to head to the ice to warm up, Troy spotted

Harris in the hallway outside the locker room. He was taking video with his phone of the guys leaving the room. When he saw Troy, he nearly blinded him with his smile. Troy tried to keep his expression neutral for the camera, but it probably wasn't working. Especially not when he noticed the tears in Harris's eyes.

"Don't start," Troy warned. "You'll get *me* going."

Harris stopped filming. "Can't help it. Wait'll you see the replies to your—"

"Nope. Shut it. Later, okay?"

"Okay." He pressed his lips together, as if that was the only way he could stop himself.

Bood nudged Troy playfully in the back as he walked by, causing Troy to stumble into Harris. "Kiss him for luck, Barrett."

Harris smiled at him. "It might work."

So Troy kissed his boyfriend, a little awkwardly because he was wearing full hockey gear and his skates made him a couple of inches taller than usual. Harris didn't seem to mind. He went up on his toes and kissed Troy like he was made of cookie dough ice cream.

"Wow," Troy said when they broke apart. "You really went for it."

"Hockey gear. You know what it does to me."

"I can't believe they let you work here, pervert."

Harris kissed his cheek. "I'm proud of you. Now get out there and win."

"It's just warm-ups."

"Then stretch better than anyone has ever stretched before."

Troy laughed, and turned to face the entrance to the ice. Then, after a deep breath, he stepped on the ice for the first time as an openly gay man.

He kept his head down for the first lap around the Centaurs' end of the ice. He could admit to himself that he was scared to look up.

Ilya fell into stride beside him. "Is nice, right?"

Troy finally raised his head, and then slowed to a stop.

The first thing he saw was a giant hand-painted banner hanging from the second level of seating. It said *We love you, Troy* in rainbow letters with big hearts on either end. As he turned to look all around him, he saw rainbow flags and fan-made signs with his name on them everywhere.

"Holy shit," he murmured.

Ilya draped an arm over his shoulders. "Not bad. Must be how it feels to be Scott Hunter."

A weird sputter of laughter burst out of Troy. Dammit, now his eyes were damp. "This is for you, too, you know. Even if they don't know it."

"Yes. And maybe they *will* know, soon."

"Oh yeah?"

"I hope so." Ilya removed his arm. "We are all using the rainbow tape sticks tonight. For the game, not just warm-up. To show support." Then he grinned and skated away.

Troy had to put his head back down to hide the raw emotion on his face.

Harris was impressed with himself for not falling apart completely during the presentation before the game. The team had invited two local LGBTQ activists to drop the puck for the ceremonial face-off, and instead of Ilya meeting the Toronto team captain to do it, Troy was chosen to represent the Centaurs.

When Troy's name was announced, the crowd gave him a standing ovation. Harris could see, on the big screens, that he was struggling to keep his emotions under control. He waved at the crowd a few times, lips pressed tight together. He nodded stoically and seemed a little embarrassed, but the ovation just kept going. Eventually, Troy had to cover his face with one of his big hockey-gloved hands.

Harris fell apart a *tiny bit*.

The Toronto captain seemed uncomfortable with the whole thing, but who cared about that guy? This wasn't about him. After the puck drop, the two activists each shook the Toronto captain's hand, and then gave Troy a hug. With a final wave at the crowd, Troy skated back to stand on the blue line. Harris noticed Ilya nudging him when he got back. He also noticed that Ilya's eyes didn't look entirely dry.

This was a huge night. Not just for Troy, but for hockey. For *Harris*. He'd grown up loving hockey, and knowing it would have been a rough place for him if he'd played. There would be queer kids watching tonight that this presentation would give hope to.

It was also a very busy night for Harris, but he'd never enjoyed his job so much. He would do the best job he could documenting the game, and hopefully Troy would want to look at it all someday.

And if not, well, Harris was going to be watching the video footage of Troy's standing ovation roughly one billion times.

His phone lit up with a text from Anna. That was so beautiful what the hell. Are you ok?

Harris grinned. His whole family was at the game, all wearing Troy Barrett T-shirts and waving rainbow flags. Troy had seemed touched and surprised when Harris had told him they were going, and maybe a bit sad. Harris understood, and he wished Troy's mom could be here. He wished his dad weren't a worthless prick.

He replied to Anna: I'm not a total puddle yet.

ANNA:

I am!

Harris laughed, and yes, it was a little wet sounding.

* * *

Troy almost regretted being named the first star of the game. He had earned it, certainly, by scoring two of Ottawa's four goals. They had won the game, and Troy knew he would never forget this incredible night.

But when he skated out to salute the crowd after being named first star, there was another standing ovation that went on far longer than usual. He felt fragile after his emotional roller coaster of a day, as well as the hard-fought game, and this was too much.

There were so many signs. A lot that said *We Love You, Troy* and *Proud of Troy Barrett* and similar things. Troy couldn't really process it.

He gave a final wave and left the ice, eyes burning. He didn't have enough fluid left in him to cry right now.

The game had been tough because Toronto was a good team, even without Dallas Kent, but they had been unusually quiet. Troy hadn't gotten the insults and slurs he'd been expecting, and maybe that was because of the fans' massive show of support, or maybe it was because his teammates made it clear that they had Troy's back. Maybe losing Kent had taken some of the wind out of the Guardians' sails. Whatever it was, Troy was grateful. He hadn't wanted to have to punch someone in a building that was so full of love for him.

The energy in the locker room was sky-high. When Troy walked in, everyone cheered.

"Enough," Troy said, though he couldn't stop smiling. "Please."

Ilya wrapped him in a hug. He was bare-chested, so Troy's face was mashed against his ugly grizzly bear tattoo. "Amazing," Ilya said. "Like a Disney movie."

"The one where the prince gets hugged by a sweaty oaf at the end?"

Ilya released him. "I hope you are ready to talk to the press for hours."

Troy groaned. The night had been awesome, but he really wanted to go somewhere private with Harris and maybe alternate rounds of sex with bouts of happy crying.

The press did come, and they did want to talk to Troy forever. He answered their questions as best he could, but mostly he was trying to peer through the scrum for Harris. Finally, the cluster of reporters broke apart, and there he was, smiling at Troy and holding a bouquet of flowers.

Troy stood and went to him. "These for me?"

"Nope. But you can have them."

Troy laughed and shook his head, then kissed his boyfriend. There were catcalls. It also occurred to him that the press were still in the room, and were definitely taking pictures.

"You okay with them photographing us?" Troy asked.

"I am if you are."

Troy kissed him again. He wouldn't mind having a professional photo of this moment.

When they broke apart, Troy was surprised to see Remy, the security guard, standing nearby. "Troy," Remy said, "there's someone here for you."

All good feelings evaporated instantly. Troy looked at Harris, who shrugged.

"Fuck. He wasn't supposed to come to the game," Troy said. "Why would he?"

"It's a woman, actually," Remy said. "Julia Frasier. She says she's your mom. Your family's not real big on calling ahead, huh?"

"What?" Troy whispered. He thrust the bouquet back at Harris and took several strides toward the door before he realized how rude that was.

"Sorry," he called back to Harris. "I love the flowers!"

But Harris was smiling. "Forget about the flowers. Go!"

Troy ran out of the locker room as fast as he could in the slide sandals he'd put on after removing his skates. He was still wearing half of his gear, and was drenched in sweat, but if his mom was really here, he was going to hug her and she was going to have to deal with it.

He rounded a corner and spotted her near the security desk, almost exactly where his dad had been standing that morning. Charlie was standing beside her, but stepped back when he saw Troy coming.

"Mom!" Troy cried out. And then she was in his gross, sweaty arms, her head tucked under his chin. He was probably holding her too tight, and parts of his gear were likely digging into her, but he couldn't let go.

For a long moment, neither of them said anything. Then they broke apart and Troy said, "How are you here? When did you get here? Why didn't you tell me?"

She laughed. "We wanted to surprise you. When you told me you were planning to come out before this game, I decided I had to be here. So we flew home, and then here."

"Why didn't you tell me, though? I could have gotten you tickets, I could have—"

"We got our own tickets, and we saw the whole game. I knew you had a lot going on before the game and I didn't want to add to it."

Troy hugged her again. "I'm so glad you're here. Oh my god, I've missed you."

"Me too." When he released her this time, she said, "I think we're done traveling. We might hang out in Ottawa for a while."

"Really? That's awesome! I'll get you tickets for every game, if you want. Playoffs too. We're going to the playoffs!"

"I know!" She craned her neck and peered over Troy's shoulder. "Is that your man back there?"

Troy turned and saw Harris, waving sheepishly at them. Troy waved him over. "Harris, this is my mom, Julia, and her boyfriend, Charlie. Good to see you again, Charlie, by the way."

"You too," Charlie said, stepping forward and shaking Troy's hand. "It was a great game and a really nice ceremony before."

Harris greeted everyone and shook their hands. Or tried to—Mom wrapped him in a hug, which Harris didn't seem to mind at all.

"I am so happy to meet you, Harris," Mom said. "Thank you for making my son smile again."

"Mom," Troy protested, but it was weakened by the fact that he was, in fact, smiling.

"My pleasure," Harris said. "I like his smile."

"They're staying in Ottawa for a while," Troy said.

"That's great. Are you staying with Troy?" Harris asked. "I can leave you three alone tonight so you can catch up."

"No way," Mom said. "We're not here to intrude. We've got a hotel for now."

As thrilled as Troy was to see his mom, he was relieved to hear her say that. He really needed to be with Harris tonight.

"I need to shower and stuff," Troy said. "And then, honestly, I'm probably going to need to crash. But let's meet up tomorrow morning for breakfast."

There was another round of hugs and handshakes, and then Mom and Charlie left.

"Today really was like a Disney movie," Troy said as he watched them walk away.

Harris took his hand. "It was amazing. And I have a great idea for an ending."

"That sounds like a different kind of movie."

"There isn't a Disney movie where the prince's boyfriend rims him until he begs to be fucked?"

Troy huffed. "I don't know. I don't watch Disney movies."

Harris snapped his fingers. "*101 Dalmatians*. That's the one I'm thinking of."

"You are so fucking weird." Troy began walking back to the dressing room.

"Can I read you some of the replies on your video?"

"No."

"Can I tell you that Scott Hunter replied?"

"No. Wait. He did?"

"He's very proud of you."

Troy's belly squirmed. "That's nice."

"Tons of other players wrote stuff in the replies too. And liked the video."

"This is dangerously close to you reading me the replies, you know."

"Sorry. I love you."

Troy smiled and stopped walking. "Give me your phone."

Harris handed it to him. "Are you going to read them?"

"No." Troy put his head next to Harris's and held the camera an arm's length away. "Smile."

Instead, Harris kissed his cheek, and Troy snapped a few pictures.

"Hey, what are you doing?" Harris asked when Troy didn't give his phone back.

"Logging into my Instagram. Just a sec."

"Are you posting that right now?"

"Shh."

Troy picked his favorite of the photos, uploaded it without a filter, and quickly typed: I am so happy right now. Thank you, Ottawa, for an amazing night, and for being the place where I met my wonderful boyfriend. I love you, Harris. He posted it without a second thought, then handed the phone back to Harris.

"You'll have to log yourself back in," he mumbled.

Harris read the post, and then he pressed his fingers to his lips as his eyes welled up.

"Oh no. Don't cry. I can't take any more emotion tonight."

Harris shook his head. "We look so hot together," he said in a wobbly voice.

"I was thinking," Troy said cautiously, "maybe you could help me look for a house. Maybe something in the country?"

Harris covered his mouth with his hand. "Stop it."

Troy smiled. "Maybe something big enough for Chiron."

"Can I visit sometimes?"

"If you bring pie."

Harris sniffed, but his eyes were bright with happiness. "So you like Ottawa now?"

Troy placed a hand on Harris's cheek and said, honestly, "There's nowhere else I'd rather be."

Don't miss The Long Game, *the next book in Rachel Reid's Game Changers series, available wherever books are sold.*

HOW WELL DO YOU KNOW YOUR FRIEND?

Grab a feral friend and guess their answer before they input their own to see if you're forever destined for the same TBR.

PLAYER 1		PLAYER 2
GUESS PLAYER 2'S ANSWERS	**MARK X IF MATCHED**	**CIRCLE YOUR ANSWERS**
Salmon | Mom's apple fritters		Salmon | Mom's apple fritters
Eggnog latte | Black coffee		Eggnog latte | Black coffee
Troy's brooding mystery | Harris's sunny optimism		Troy's brooding mystery | Harris's sunny optimism
The Kingfisher | Monk's		The Kingfisher | Monk's
Redemption arc | Slow burn		Redemption arc | Slow burn
Speaking out | Secret supporting		Speaking out | Secret supporting
Hotel room | Family farmhouse		Hotel room | Family farmhouse
Opening up about the past | dreaming about the future		Opening up about the past | dreaming about the future
Mario | Yoshi		Mario | Yoshi
Troy's protectiveness | Harris's playfulness		Troy's protectiveness | Harris's playfulness
Portage Brewery | Drover Cider		Portage Brewery | Drover Cider
Watching hockey | Cooking together		Watching hockey | Cooking together
Standing up for yourself | Learning to listen		Standing up for yourself | Learning to listen
Chiron | Lila		Chiron | Lila
Car makeout | Hotel room hookup		Car makeout | Hotel room hookup

TOTAL MATCHED

1-5: Have you even met?

6-11: Fine friends.

12-15: Just hook up already.

ACKNOWLEDGMENTS

This book, like all of my books, would only be a fraction as good without my amazing editor, Mackenzie Walton. I'd also like to thank my wonderful agent, Deidre Knight, for story notes, hockey gossip, and general cheerleading. Huge thanks as well to my friends, fellow authors, reviewers, and readers who encourage me and have shown my fictional hockey boys so much love. And special thanks to Jenn Burke for her Ottawa expertise (although any Ottawa-based mistakes are definitely my own).

This book was written entirely in 2020 during the pandemic and I am enormously grateful to my husband and kids for giving me time and space to write even when we were all trapped together. Also to my parents and in-laws for taking the kids off our hands from time to time, which made it easier to write sex scenes.